NAVIGATORS OF
DUNE

OTHER BOOKS

NAVIGATORS OF
DUNE

Brian Herbert

and

Kevin J. Anderson

TOR

A TOM DOHERTY ASSOCIATES BOOK

NEW YORK

This is a work of fiction. All of the characters, organizations, and events portrayed in this novel are either products of the authors' imaginations or are used fictitiously.

NAVIGATORS OF DUNE

A Tor Book
Published by Tom Doherty Associates, LLC
175 Fifth Avenue
New York, NY 10010

www.tor-forge.com

The Library of Congress Cataloging-in-Publication Data
is available upon request.

ISBN 978-0-7653-8125-5 (hardcover)
ISBN 978-1-4668-7880-8 (e-book)

Our books may be purchased in bulk for promotional, educational, or business use. Please contact your local bookseller or the Macmillan Corporate and Premium Sales Department at 1-800-221-7945, extension 5442, or by e-mail at MacmillanSpecialMarkets@macmillan.com.

Printed in the United States of America

0 9 8 7 6 5 4 3 2

After writing fourteen books and numerous short stories in the fantastic Dune universe, a labor that has spanned nearly two decades of our lives, we cannot forget the key people who made this great journey possible.

We want to dedicate this book to our wives, Jan and Rebecca, for their unfailing support and love throughout the process.
And to Beverly Herbert, the devoted wife, companion, and creative adviser to Frank Herbert for almost forty years.

To our publisher, Tom Doherty of Tor Books, our editor, Pat LoBrutto, and our agent, John Silbersack, who had faith in our abilities and our stories over the course of the series.

And, most of all, to the imaginative genius Frank Herbert, who created this grand literary universe more than half a century ago and gave us so many wondrous places and ideas to explore.

ACKNOWLEDGMENTS

Our names are on the cover, but we didn't write *Navigators of Dune* alone. We would like to thank the able assistance of the production and publicity staff at Tor Books, as well as the foreign rights department of Trident Media Group, and also a special thank-you to Kim Herbert and Byron Merritt of Herbert Properties LLC for tirelessly helping to keep Frank Herbert's legacy alive; and Kevin's typist, Karen Haag, who valiantly kept up with the work, chapter by chapter.

NAVIGATORS OF
DUNE

All things begin, and all things end—there are no exceptions.
Or, is this a myth?
—Debating topic, the Mentat School

The Emperor's ceremonial barge orbited high above Salusa Secundus, in the midst of huge, ominous warships. Its interior glittered with gold and precious gems; its flashy hull was sculpted with curves and adornments that served no purpose. By far the most ostentatious vessel in the fleet, the barge was a stunning sight to those who were easily swayed by such things. Salvador had adored it.

Even though Roderick Corrino, the new Emperor, found it much too gaudy for his tastes, he understood the necessity of ceremony, especially so soon after assuming the throne following the death—no, the *murder*—of his brother.

Another Imperial necessity was for him to bring justice to Directeur Josef Venport, the man who had engineered Salvador's assassination. His warships were gathering.

Roderick had thick blond hair and chiseled features, and stood tall in the scarlet-and-gold robe of his noble house. Feeling regal as well as powerful, he faced a wide viewing window in the barge's multilevel command center. Gathered in orbit, his assembled strike force—hundreds of battleships—prepared for a surprise attack against the Venport stronghold.

Roderick was eager to see them launch, but this had to be done with absolute precision. The Imperial Armed Forces would have only one chance to overwhelm Venport by catching him unawares.

The Emperor watched his warships glide into holding arrays within an immense foldspace carrier that orbited ahead of the barge. The carrier's Holtzman engines could traverse great distances in the blink of an eye, although the carrier pilot was effectively flying blind without the guidance of an advanced Navigator.

Only Venport Holdings knew how to create Navigators, advanced beings who could foresee safe pathways through the vast reaches of space, and Josef Venport had withdrawn them all from Imperial service when his crime was exposed. As soon as the outlaw Venport was defeated and his assets seized, though, the entire Imperium would have Navigators. That was merely one more benefit—and an important one—of crushing the Directeur. Roderick clenched his fist.

General Vinson Roon, commander of the strike force to Kolhar, stood at crisp attention beside him. He held his red-and-gold officer's cap in his hands.

"I anticipate a swift and glorious victory, Sire." Roon acted indignant on the Emperor's behalf. The noble-born General was in his late forties, Roderick's age, though he was shorter and more muscular. Roon had dark skin, jet-black hair, and an intense manner. The two men had a tumultuous personal history, which Roderick did his best to ignore right now.

"Yes, swift and glorious would be my preference, Vinson." He used the General's first name intentionally. He and Roon had been boyhood friends until an unfortunate falling out—over a woman, of course. Since then, they had spoken only during formal military meetings with other officers and high-level advisers, but it was time to put all that nonsense behind them. The Imperium was at stake.

Roderick knew he could count on this man, whose loyalty and dedication to the Imperium had never been in doubt. Without turning from the viewing window, the Emperor said, "Venport Holdings must be struck down before they have time to entrench themselves further. We need to move soon."

Roon nodded.

This strike force had been assembled hastily in secret, and would launch within the next few days. The Emperor was gambling a significant portion of his military defenses that were normally stationed around Salusa Secundus, but a successful crackdown on VenHold would greatly increase security all across the Imperium, making it worth the risk. Roderick intended it to be a swift decapitation mission to kill or capture Directeur Venport, seize his operations on Kolhar, and cripple his widespread business operations.

Then Roderick would be in firm control of the Imperium.

Two months ago, just when his guilt was revealed, Venport had escaped with the aid of Norma Cenva. Since then, the Directeur had abruptly withdrawn all VenHold commercial ships, cut off trade, and left many planets in dire need of provisions. The repercussions were only beginning to be felt, and they would grow much worse. Private fleets scrambled to pick up the slack, but no other interstellar transport company was as reliable as the VenHold Spacing Fleet—because no one else had Navigators.

Venport also held part of the Imperial military hostage, thanks to a disastrous circumstance. One entire battle group of the Imperial Armed Forces— seventy warships—had been traveling routinely aboard a VenHold carrier when the whole crisis began. The Imperial ships were powerful, but did not have Holtzman engines, so they needed to be delivered to their destination via space-folders. For years, VenHold carriers had transported the Emperor's battleships as part of their service to the Imperium, but now a key portion of those powerful vessels were being held by the enemy, locked away and taken off the board like pieces in a galactic chess game.

Roderick muttered, "He means to hamstring us, and force us to bow to his demands."

"Do we even know what his demands are, Sire?" asked the General, still watching the ships move aboard the gigantic carrier. "He has been silent since he withdrew to Kolhar. I thought he was on the run and hiding from justice."

"His demands are obvious to me. Venport wants to do whatever he likes. After killing an Emperor with impunity, he wants me to be a figurehead ruler while the tentacles of his commercial empire extend everywhere. He also wants me to eradicate the Butlerian fanatics." His thoughts whirled. *Something that Salvador could never do.*

Roon gave a distasteful snort and lowered his voice. "After all the destruction Manford Torondo has caused, would that be such a terrible thing, Sire?"

As he thought of all the damage the antitechnology mobs had caused, even killing his beautiful little daughter, Roderick let out a low sigh. "Not as such, no . . . but if it means we must cooperate with the man who assassinated Salvador, then I cannot agree. I will *never* agree to that, Vinson." He shook his head. "I would not be surprised if Venport had something to do with Anna's disappearance, too."

Roon blinked in disbelief. "But your sister vanished from Lampadas, Sire— during the Butlerian siege of the Mentat School. I would suspect Manford Toronado, but how could you think Venport is responsible for that?"

"You're right." He shook his head. "I seem to find ways to blame that man for everything . . . when he is really only responsible for half of my problems."

The General scowled, obviously disgusted. "When I think of all the Directeur's dealings—a monopoly on safe foldspace travel, his secret Navigators, the spice industry on Arrakis, his banking operations across the Imperium . . . no one man should control so much power, and—"

Roderick cut him off. "Not true, Vinson—*I* should hold that much power, and no one else."

Roon straightened. "Our fleet will take care of him, Sire. You can count on me."

"I know I can, Vinson." Roderick allowed a hint of warmth into his voice. With this man about to lead a vital assault that would change the course of history, it was good to remind him of a friendship they once had.

The anticipation was palpable as the two men watched more battleships moving into position aboard the giant carrier. Roon cleared his throat. "There's something I must say to you, Sire. Thank you for not letting our personal differences stand in the way of my recent promotion. And thank you for your faith in me to lead this mission. A lesser man would have behaved differently."

Roderick gave him a reassuring nod. "Those differences were a long time ago, and I need to rise above them for the good of the Imperium." He gave a small smile. "Haditha would not have tolerated anything else. She asked me to pass along her regards and her best wishes for your success."

Roon responded with a bittersweet smile. "You did win her heart, after all. I had to accept that defeat long ago. You're a better man than I am, Sire—always have been."

Roon's promotion was well deserved due to his proven skill and reliability, and he had risen even more swiftly in the ranks because Roderick's overhaul of the Imperial military had swept away so many incompetent upper-level officers. Vinson Roon had been the logical person to replace the ousted Commanding General Odmo Saxby, and this retaliatory strike would be his first real chance to prove himself.

The Imperial Armed Forces had been in terrible shape after years of neglect under Salvador, bloated with undeserved ranks, teeming with corruption, graft, and outright ineptitude. Upon taking the throne, Roderick had conducted an extensive audit and purge of the military.

He extended his hand. "Perhaps when you return victorious from Kolhar, we might spend more time together."

"I would like nothing more, Sire. We were great friends once, weren't we?"

"Yes, we were."

Roon grinned, as they shook. "I'll buy the brandy."

"I look forward to it."

Despite every precaution being taken to keep the preparation of the strike force a secret, Josef Venport doubtless had spies on Salusa. If the foldspace carrier launched swiftly enough, though, General Roon's warships should reach Kolhar faster than any spy vessel could sound a warning. Time was of the essence.

Nevertheless, with or without spies, Venport was no fool. He would surely anticipate some kind of response from Salusa, and Kolhar was not without its own formidable defenses. . . .

Roderick was impatient to break the stranglehold of Venport Holdings and restore his own legitimate power. The fledgling Imperium had existed for less than a century since the end of the oppressive thinking machines, and Roderick had to assert his authority for the good of the human race and, just as importantly, to avenge his brother.

The General donned his cap and saluted as he turned to go. "Please excuse me, Sire—I have many details to supervise before we launch the strike force. Speed is our best guarantor of secrecy."

Roderick's voice sharpened. "Take care of him for me, Vinson. I'll await your triumphant return."

"You have my promise, Sire. I will move the stars and planets to prove myself to you."

"You may have to do just that."

There are those who see influence and power as a reward rather than a responsibility. Such men do not make good leaders.
—DIRECTEUR JOSEF VENPORT, internal Venport Holdings memo

K olhar was a fortress, but Josef Venport did not let himself feel complacent as he waited for the Emperor to make his move. He knew that the brunt of Imperial military forces would be poised to annihilate him the moment they saw a chance.

To increase his planetary security, he'd had to withdraw numerous well-armed ships from the VenHold Spacing Fleet and station them in Kolhar orbit, pulling them from lucrative commercial routes. Josef also intensified the planetary shields and increased the number of picket ships and scouts around the star system.

Now that his defenses were in place, he might find a way out of this mess. If only he and Emperor Roderick could just sit down and negotiate like rational men!

Josef had never wanted any part of this debacle. While it had been necessary to remove that buffoon Salvador and place his more competent brother on the throne, he had never thought his role in the assassination would be discovered. Rather, Josef planned to be partners with the new Emperor, to their mutual benefit. The Imperium was poised to thrive—if Roderick would just see reason.

This was a time of existential crisis for human civilization, a historical moment requiring hard decisions: Humanity was still recovering from the long nightmare of enslavement to the thinking machines, followed by the chaos and violence that spawned the reactionary Butlerian movement, rabid fanatics who wanted to purge all vestiges of "evil" technology. By installing a competent man on the throne, Josef had meant to help the human race; instead, he had pre-cipitated an unforeseen disaster.

Now the Emperor would stop at nothing to crush Venport Holdings, to arrest Josef and quite probably execute him. Why couldn't Roderick Corrino see how much damage his dogged insistence on revenge would cause? VenHold should just be levied a substantial blood fine—which Josef would pay in spice or money, whichever the Emperor preferred—after which interplanetary commerce and government could get back to normal. He stroked his thick reddish mustache, pondering deeply. There had to be a way out of this!

Sick of the interminable waiting, he left his multitower skyscraper headquarters and stepped out under the overcast sky. He needed to feel the cool air on his skin and see the reassuring activity around him. He liked to remind himself that he was still one of the most powerful men in the Imperium.

His wife, Cioba, met him just outside the headquarters tower. She was a tall, elegant brunette whose bloodline came from the telepathically powerful Sorceresses of Rossak. Her long hair fell to her waist; her regal bearing and calm demeanor came from years of Sisterhood training.

Silent but supportive, Cioba walked with him across a paved landing field that should have been crowded with commercial ships and spice haulers. Now, though, the spaceport resembled a military operations field. Rumbling tankers moved back and forth, fueling defensive ships and shuttlecraft. Scout patrols launched into orbit. When Josef sucked in a deep breath, the air held the sharp tang of exhaust fumes and the brisk brittleness of winter.

Cioba paused, as if she had run calculations in her mind. "Kolhar is as impregnable as we can make it, my husband. While we dare not lower our guard, we should not be paralyzed by needless fear. We are strong and secure."

Josef had told himself the same thing many times, but he refused to relax. "Overconfidence is a greater weakness than fear and worry. We need to stay vigilant until we ride out this crisis."

"I know we will. We have advanced weapons and defenses that the rest of the Imperium can't even imagine." Her lips quirked in a smile. "Defenses that are sure to give nightmares to Manford Torondo and his Butlerians."

Josef responded with a smile of his own. Together, they watched three mechanical figures patrolling the spaceport perimeter—spiderlike cymek walkers taller than many of the buildings, fresh deliveries from his secret weapons laboratory on Denali.

Cymeks had once been the scourge of humanity—disembodied human brains mounted inside armored machine bodies. The original cymeks had been destroyed at the end of Serena Butler's jihad, but Josef's brilliant scientists had redesigned and re-created them. Rather than being guided by fallible, power-hungry minds, these new cymeks were controlled by the evolved brains of Navigator candidates. Now the mechanical guardians patrolled the area around the Kolhar headquarters, their pistons pumping and sensors alert for any threat.

When Josef commandeered a groundcar, Cioba did not need to ask where they were going. Visiting the tanks of evolving Navigator candidates had become a daily ritual for him, especially as tensions increased.

As he drove, Josef shook his head in dismay. "Instead of being at each other's throats, Roderick and I should be working together to fight the real enemy! The Butlerian fanatics pose as great a threat to civilization as the thinking machines did. And the half-Manford has warships of his own."

Cioba lifted her chin. "Those antique ships aren't enough to defeat you, Josef. One hundred forty old spacefolders dating back to the Army of the Jihad. Think of your ships, of your monopoly on Navigators, and your intensely loyal employees. More than half the planets in the Imperium depend on VenHold for commerce, and they still trade with you, even though the Emperor branded you an outlaw. What does that say?" She turned her classically beautiful face toward him, raised her eyebrows. "You have more ships, more power, more influence than *anyone*, even the Corrinos. If people were forced to decide, would they choose some figure on a throne on far-off Salusa Secundus, or would they rather have regular shipments of food and spice?"

He knew she was right. Josef guided the groundcar over a rise and then down into a broad, bowl-shaped valley filled with hundreds of tanks, each containing one of his Navigator candidates. Cioba leaned over and kissed his cheek as he halted the vehicle amid the sealed tanks.

They walked among the thick-walled chambers full of concentrated spice gas. Through the murky plaz windowports and swirling fumes inside, Josef could see mutated figures undergoing constant mental convolutions to expand their minds. No unmodified brain could grasp foldspace calculations and the prescience necessary to guide a ship through the void, but the spice-enriched transformation made it possible.

Josef marveled at these freakish but oddly impressive Navigators. Even if the Emperor's ships came for Kolhar, his military spacefolders would be clumsy and blind because they had no Navigators. While antique FTL ships were relatively safe in their passage through space, they were unconscionably sluggish, taking weeks or months to travel between star systems. VenHold ships, on the other hand, were fast and safe.

He and Cioba paused before a large central tank on a marble platform, like a shrine. Josef was pleased to see that Norma Cenva, his great-grandmother, was present in the chamber, surrounded by her personal spice-dreams and the infinite possibilities that stretched far into the universe.

More than a century ago, Norma had become the first Navigator. Although she was more than a mere human, she still maintained contact with Josef, and remained aware of Imperial politics for her own purposes.

"The human race is at stake, and I feel a tremendous obligation," Josef said to Cioba, although he suspected that Norma would be eavesdropping. "I am the one with the rational thinking and the wherewithal to save us. I must stay alive, and I must *win*. Roderick will not break through our defenses, and with all my commercial ties across the Imperium, I can pull strings and force decisions that are beyond his capabilities."

Though Norma helped to make Venport Holdings strong, Josef knew that her driving goal was to promote the creation of more Navigators. Unlike her protégés, Norma had the ability to fold space simply with her mind and travel at will, while all other Navigators needed to use great ships powered by Holtzman engines to travel. Sometimes her enclosed tank would vanish for days on obscure business of her own, but for now she remained here, where she meditated and observed.

Needing to know answers, Josef stepped up to the tank and asked without further preamble, "What do you think, Grandmother? If I am more powerful than Emperor Roderick, should I hide here and build my defenses, or should I think in grander terms?"

Norma spoke in a warbling voice through the tank's speakerpatch. "You have the power and ability to seize the throne—if that is what you wish."

He was surprised to hear her say this. Some men fantasized about becoming great rulers, but Josef had always considered himself a businessman, a consummate commercial leader, but not one who was interested in political aggrandizement.

"You know that isn't what I wish. I want *Roderick* to be the Emperor—a sensible one. I placed him on that throne, damn it. I want him to be strong and wise . . . and to ask for my counsel! I have my own business empire. My planetary banks are brimming with money that depositors entrusted to me. I have tremendous spice operations on Arrakis, even though the fool Salvador tried to take them away. For me, politics is a tool to accomplish my business interests, nothing more."

He let out a sigh. "But I've been backed into a corner. We're at a turning point of civilization, and if Emperor Roderick won't do what is required of him, then am I the one to replace him?" He pondered, but still saw no clear answer. "I would much rather go back to how it was a year ago, when I could focus my energies on annihilating Manford's barbarians."

"And our spice operations—for my Navigators," Norma said. "We need to go to Arrakis, rather than stay here. You and I should go."

"We'll do it soon, Grandmother." He had already planned a long-delayed inspection trip, but first he needed to attend to a last few details here.

"Soon," Norma insisted, "I will take us there."

Frustration welled up in him. While the Emperor wasted time and resources trying to retaliate against him, the fanatical Butlerians were running rampant, erasing the progress that Josef had achieved at such a dear cost.

Well, Josef had already taken action. Even as he built his defenses here on Kolhar, he had dispatched an important commando force to Lampadas, the headquarters of the Butlerian movement. Maybe after his invincible cymek forces slaughtered that vile little cripple, then Josef could be truly satisfied.

"You have already made your decision," Norma said in her distorted voice.

"I came here to seek your advice, Grandmother."

"You have already made your decision," Norma repeated, and she would not answer further.

I will choose my allies as best they suit me, but God has chosen my enemy—the enemy of all humankind. God Himself is my staunchest defender. Why do I need you?

—MANFORD TORONDO to Emperor Salvador Corrino

D raigo Roget, Josef Venport's leading Mentat, arrived in a fast VenHold warship covered with stealth armor so it would remain unnoticed by Butlerian orbital patrols. With its integrated weaponry, this small vessel was capable of destroying a dozen of the old-model Jihad warships that the fanatics used.

But Draigo had not come to Lampadas to battle a planet full of barbarians, not at the moment. This time he was merely a pilot on a proof-of-concept mission that might well eliminate this threat to civilization. He would demonstrate the power of their new cymeks.

Lampadas . . . He had been trained in the Mentat School here, and here he had learned to loathe Manford Torondo and his followers, extremists who had corrupted and then torn down the great school. The Butlerians had arrested and beheaded his mentor and headmaster of the institution, Gilbertus Albans. Draigo would never forgive them for that.

Unable to rescue Gilbertus, Draigo had managed to escape with the damaged Anna Corrino and the memory core of Erasmus, the infamous robot responsible for so much cruelty and havoc during Serena Butler's Jihad. Now, Anna was a vital bargaining chip, and Erasmus was a key resource for the Denali scientists; together, they would ensure Directeur Venport's victory, the triumph of reason over fanaticism, of civilization over barbarism.

That was, after all, what the ongoing conflict was about. Every one of Venport's people understood that.

Tonight, Draigo's cymeks would fill the enemy with terror and possibly even kill Manford Torondo, which would neutralize the fanatics once and for all. If nothing else, the cymeks would prove their horrific destructive potential; many of Directeur Venport's scientists would be eager to see the results.

Of the three cymeks in the hold of Draigo's ship, two were guided by enhanced Navigator brains, while the third was controlled by Ptolemy, the first *voluntary* new cymek, a genius driven by his hatred of Manford Torondo. Ptolemy had opted to discard his frail human form, exchanging it for any mechanical body he liked. A powerful, destructive body.

Manford had certainly generated a lot of enemies.

Secure in orbit above the quiet planet, confident that the stealth systems would keep him hidden from the primitive Butlerian warships, Draigo prepared for the mission. Ptolemy's brain canister was installed in his warrior form, while the two Navigator-driven cymeks moved their walkers into armored drop-pods. The Navigator brains were silent and brooding, as always, but they followed instructions. After checking the thoughtrode connections, Draigo pronounced all three machines ready for launch.

Ptolemy raised one multiclawed hand and clacked the long, sharp pincers together. His words came through the speakerpatch. "That sadistic monster burned my friend alive and forced me to watch. Manford Torondo must die."

"He also tries to kill human intellect and progress. That man has sowed many seeds of hatred, and we all wish to take part in the harvest." Draigo smiled at the brain suspended in pale blue electrafluid before closing the last section of the pod. They were ready for launch. "This is your chance."

⸛

CARRYING THE RESPONSIBILITY of humanity was a burden Manford Torondo did not gladly bear, but he did it nonetheless. What choice did he have?

The current crisis in the Imperium was more than a struggle for resources or territory; it was a war for the human soul. After centuries of enslavement to thinking machines, mankind was free at last, cut loose from the stranglehold of technology. Reborn, they could return to a new Eden—but only if they chose to do so. Unless their own weaknesses destroyed them.

Twisted men like Josef Venport wanted to enslave mankind once more, making the exultant human spirit beholden to machines again! After the end of the Jihad, Rayna Butler—Manford's beloved mentor and teacher—had guided people along the true path, but such a way was not without violence and resistance, not without those who threw bombs in crowded rallies. . . .

Swallowing hard as he sat propped up in a cushioned chair late at night, Manford looked down at where his body ended below his hips. The reality of his disfigurement was sometimes shocking to him, even now, years after the explosion that had nearly killed him, leaving him just half a man. "But twice the leader!" as his loyal followers shouted during their rallies.

The future was so uncertain, the weight so heavy on his heart. How Manford wished that wise Rayna were still here to lead the movement! Oh, he had loved her so! He felt warm tears trickle down his cheeks.

Anari Idaho, his fiercely loyal Swordmaster, noticed the tears and stepped closer, concerned. She would have thrown herself in front of any enemy for Manford, would have given her life to save his. Now she seemed just as willing to defend him against his own emotions.

Anari was a large-framed woman trained among the Swordmasters of Ginaz; for years she had tended him in his simple fieldstone cottage on Lampadas. The interior walls had been fitted with bars and handholds, so Manford could move himself around with his strong upper body. Whenever he wished to present an imposing figure to large cheering crowds, or to his enemies, he would ride in a harness on Anari's shoulders. From that perch, Manford did not feel less than a man; instead he seemed the most powerful person in the Imperium.

His Truthsayer, Sister Woodra, came to speak to him, but she blurted out her business concerns without noticing his heavy mood. "Emperor Roderick still thinks we are responsible for the disappearance of his sister after we overran the Mentat School." Her voice had an annoying edge. "You should convince him otherwise, Leader Torondo. Anna Corrino must have escaped somehow."

"We had nothing to do with her disappearance, whether or not the Emperor believes it." Manford suspected the flighty girl had been devoured by a swamp dragon as she tried to flee the siege. "Fortunately, the Emperor's anger has turned toward Josef Venport. I'm not worried." Manford could not help but think it was a miracle in disguise.

"Perhaps," Anari said, "but he will never forget his daughter was killed by a Butlerian mob. He will have enough anger for us."

"That was an accident, nothing more," Woodra said dismissively, as if she thought the matter was ended. "We cannot be blamed for that."

"And yet, he will blame us regardless," Anari said.

"Alliances can shift again," Manford said. "Roderick Corrino must be made to see his true destiny as our ally—preferably through reasonable appeals, but by coercion if necessary."

Sister Woodra brought out logbooks and lists that she wished to discuss in detail, but Manford did not have the energy for it at this hour. Sensing her master's weariness, Anari shot Woodra a scolding glance. "That is enough business for now. Manford needs to rest and contemplate. Otherwise, how can we expect him to lead us?"

The brusque Truthsayer sniffed at the implied dismissal. "The success of our movement depends upon details as well as strong leadership. And we must make time for the details."

Woodra had been trained among the Sisterhood before the terrible schism that tore the school apart. He knew Woodra was as vehemently against technology as any of his followers, and she had also proved to be a useful asset, not only as a Truthsayer, but as an adviser. She was blunt, however, and lacked finesse; sometimes Manford found her exhausting. Right now, he was too preoccupied, no matter how much she insisted. "Anari is correct. I'm weary. Take me to my bedchamber."

The Swordmaster picked him up as if he were a pet and plodded toward his private rooms, where she placed him in an austere, narrow bed. She opened the window to let in the fresh night air.

Outside, Empok, the capital city of Lampadas, sparkled with warm orange lights in the countless simple buildings. Insects made quiet songs, and the planet seemed deceptively peaceful as Manford composed himself for a contemplative sleep. Until a thundering roar shattered the darkness.

Heavy objects screamed down through the atmosphere, wreathed in the flames of deceleration. Three projectiles struck the ground outside of Empok.

Anari shouted in alarm and burst into the bedchamber to protect him.

People streamed out of their homes to investigate the disturbance, then howled in alarm. The three impact sites simmered ominously, lit by afterglows of white and orange and highlighted by angular shadows. Shielded pods split open like the jagged petals of armored flowers, then mechanical forms emerged. Heavy piston-driven legs lifted weapon-studded body cores, each containing a disembodied human brain. Three towering cymeks began to march on the city.

As Anari swept Manford out of the bed, he saw the distant movement through the window, and knew his enemies were coming for him.

Seizing him, the Swordmaster said, "I will save you."

Humans claim that deep personal tragedy can cause severe changes in mindset. I have experimented with these effects in my studies of laboratory subjects, inflicting damage to people and testing their reactions. Yet I was never able to verify the hypothesis through direct experience—until the death of Gilbertus Albans.

—ERASMUS, Secret Laboratory Notebooks

Inside the Denali laboratory domes, Directeur Venport's researchers worked on vital projects, hidden in the poisonous atmosphere of the isolated planet. The scientists had been recruited based on their intellect as well as their hatred of the Butlerians.

Now the research teams regarded the Erasmus memory core with fascination, calling him a priceless trove of historical experiences—which pleased the independent robot. At long last, Erasmus found himself among like-minded persons, and he reveled in the attention.

Draigo Roget had rescued his memory core when the fanatics overthrew the Mentat School. Erasmus appreciated the man's efforts in saving his life, just as Gilbertus had saved him decades earlier. Erasmus had owed much to his human ward Gilbertus. The robot had raised a feral child from the slave pens and shaped him into a nearly perfect human being. And those irrational barbarians killed him! Defeated, Gilbertus had simply bowed to the thuggish Swordmaster Anari Idaho, who then hacked off his head with her sword.

Erasmus had simulated emotions in his programming, but this personal experience, this sense of terrible loss, had been far greater than anything he had previously recorded.

Now, in a well-lit research chamber against the poisonous gloom outside, his gelsphere core rested on a stand, connected to an imperfect sensory apparatus. Lovely young Anna Corrino, sister of the Emperor, hovered beside the memory sphere, while curious Denali scientists gathered close, hanging on the robot's words, waiting for him to continue.

Erasmus realized that with his thoughts about Gilbertus, he had lapsed into silent anger. Yes . . . the *human* emotion of anger. He reviewed the unique experience in the same way he gathered all interesting data, particularly psychological data in his constant attempt to comprehend the complex human mind.

"I have much information to convey to you," he said to Anna. "Highly useful information. If I can help you destroy the enemies of reason, I will do so."

The violent, unnecessary, and confusing death of Gilbertus had changed mental paths in his gelcircuitry. Normally, he would have delighted in receiving new revelations, but the loss of his friend had not pleased him. Not in any way.

"Tell them about the Mentat School," suggested Anna, smiling in her eagerness. The young woman's small blue eyes and her quirky personality reminded Erasmus of stained glass, disjointed colors and distorted images. After her brain had been damaged by psychotropic poison at the Sisterhood school, Anna had become skittish, intense, and unpredictable. Her mind had never been the same afterward, and her concerned brothers had sent her to the Mentat School for treatment. There, Erasmus had found her, and made her into his most interesting human subject. He had guided the damaged young woman, manipulated her mind, helped her . . . but although he had tried to make her fit a perfect mathematical model, his work had not been a complete success.

"I spent many decades hidden at the Mentat School," Erasmus said, "as Gilbertus Albans taught his students how to organize their thoughts." His erudite voice was piped through speakers mounted around the room. He remembered what his original voice had been like in his flowmetal body. How glorious he had been back in the heady days of the Synchronized Empire, before the rampant humans wrecked everything . . . as they had done later at the Mentat School. One could not depend on humans to behave in an organized, rational fashion.

But Erasmus had the capacity to think in the long-term, and he was finally among allies now—those with the potential to cause retaliatory damage. They were all united in their desire to eradicate the Butlerian disease.

"Gilbertus hid my memory core for my own protection. He knew that if I were ever discovered, I would surely be destroyed. Unlike you like-minded people of Denali, others in the Imperium would never accept the benefits of my knowledge. They destroy what they don't understand."

Anna fidgeted as she moved about the chamber. Her voice sounded husky, as if overwhelmed with misplaced emotion. "If Erasmus had been destroyed, then billions of people would never learn how brilliant he is! How admirable he is."

Erasmus had made her believe all those things when her mind was soft and malleable, but now it had solidified from opinion to dogma.

The scientists tolerated her interruptions, because Anna was such a valuable hostage, but they paid little attention to anything she said. Sweet, oblivious Anna didn't understand her own worth, and Erasmus wanted to ensure that his hold on her delicate mind did not loosen. He appreciated the young woman's rapt attention to him, even if her devotion verged on obsession. He tolerated it, though. Over the centuries, he had certainly endured enough hatred from humans; he could accept misplaced adoration now.

He continued to address the attentive researchers. "At the Mentat School my sensors and spy-eyes allowed me to continue my observations of humanity, make projections, and test hypotheses. I was hampered by the lack of a physical body, but Gilbertus repeatedly promised he would obtain a vessel to hold my memory core. Somehow, he never managed that." Erasmus paused. "It was the only way he ever failed me. . . ."

The Denali scientists took notes on their Tlulaxa datapads. For days now, the cooperative robot had discussed his thoughts and conclusions almost nonstop. He had so much knowledge to dispense, so many discoveries, so much data, that simply *organizing* everything was a task that stretched their abilities to the limit.

"My experiences are pivotal," he continued. "I intend to help you find ways not just to defend Venport Holdings, but to annihilate the Butlerians." He realized that his words might sound boastful, but a thinking machine had no pride. "If only we had more time. It is difficult to distill centuries of experiences into such a compressed time span."

While he waited for the scientists to catch up with their notes, he accessed the last surveillance images of Gilbertus being led from his imprisonment, forced to kneel down and wait for the swing of the Swordmaster's blade. . . .

Near the laboratory table, a preservation tank held the disembodied brain of Administrator Noffe, the first of the new cymeks. Now his detached tank sent signals through the flickering electrafluid, which were converted to words by the speakerpatch. "The facilities of Denali are at your disposal, Erasmus. Our mission is to provide Directeur Venport with the weapons to fight ignorance and strengthen human civilization. Share with us weapons designs from the Synchronized Empire. Help us eradicate the savages."

"They killed Headmaster Albans," Anna said, her brow furrowing with concern. "They tried to destroy Erasmus—and me! I don't know why my brother hasn't just killed them all."

"Of course, I will assist you in destroying the Butlerians," Erasmus said, primarily to soothe Anna, because she could become fixated on a single thought. He had little confidence that Emperor Roderick Corrino could stand up to the fanatics or even to Josef Venport. But the robot intended to assist, because he had his own score to settle, and his own price to demand, when the time was right.

"My greatest desire is to watch the Butlerian leader die, and the more painfully the better. I wish to experience the satisfaction of revenge." This, too, would be a new sensation, another key detail in his grand quest—and that in itself was exciting.

One of the scientists, a quiet Tlulaxa biological researcher named Danebh, had taken copious notes. He sat back. "I would appreciate data on your biological research, Erasmus. You conducted many dissections back on Corrin, but you also organized intensive genetic data. I understand you even grew a clone of Serena Butler herself?"

"I did, and though the new Serena seemed perfect in every way, she wasn't nearly as fascinating as the original woman, merely a poor copy. Identical biology does not produce an identical set of experiences and personality."

As he spoke, his memory core linked into all the facility's data systems and accessed Dr. Danebh's background. The Tlulaxa man had conducted innovative work, which the Butlerians branded "unclean," forcing him to flee his home planet and seek sanctuary with Venport Holdings.

"I can provide all the data you need," Erasmus said, "as long as the knowledge is used against the Butlerians."

Administrator Noffe spoke from his preservation canister. "It will be. We all have sufficient reasons to hate those people."

"Then you can also provide me with guidance," Erasmus said. "I have never been able to understand the emotion of *hatred*, and I wish to study it more."

Anna Corrino looked at him with a suddenly ruthless smile, which he found unsettling.

The universe is full of intriguing probabilities that can be calculated.
A Mentat must learn to ignore the vast majority of such temptations,
however, or he will surely go insane.

—The late HEADMASTER GILBERTUS ALBANS,
addressing one of his first-year classes

Still new to her role as Mother Superior, Valya Harkonnen ignored the biting cold from the wind that whipped across the Wallach IX landing field. A passenger ship set down, carrying a group of Sisters of questionable loyalty, whom she had recalled from the Imperial Court. Valya strode out to face them.

The weak sun overhead provided so little warmth in the early afternoon that she wore a heavy ornamented robe, but she could endure the chill. Her home world of Lankiveil was even colder, and besides, for her, easing discomfort was largely a matter of readjusting her metabolism.

Valya had short black hair that framed an oval face; her hazel eyes absorbed everything around her. She turned to watch the women emerge from the vessel, but did not offer them a smile. Now that the Sisterhood's schism was ended and she had emerged victorious, Valya had summoned these disloyal women to face their new Mother Superior.

Mother Superior . . . Though still young in physical years, Valya was a Reverend Mother and thus carried the memories of millennia in her mind. She had held her important position for only a few months, since the death of Raquella Berto-Anirul. She was still testing her responsibilities, duties, and power . . . and had to make sure that other Sisters did not challenge her. These Sisters from the Imperial Court were suspect, but Valya had options.

It was a matter of survival for her to notice tiny details that others might miss. Although Valya was not trained as a Truthsayer, she had always possessed an instinct for discerning truth and loyalty. At first glance she could detect no buried violence in these new arrivals, no immediate threat from them, but if any of these women launched a physical attack on her, Valya would be a formidable opponent, and she was sharpening her control of the new Voice technique that could compel others to do as she wished.

She had to decide whether these Sisters from the former rival faction could be trusted, or if they would have to be discarded.

In addition to protecting herself against enemies, the Mother Superior also had to reaffirm and strengthen her closest allies in the Sisterhood. At one time, she had even suspected Fielle—the loyal Mentat Sister standing beside her now—of being overly ambitious, yet Fielle had become one of her closest advisers. Fielle was a large-boned, detail-oriented woman with a fleshy face; after finishing her training on Lampadas, the Mentat and Truthsayer had become one of old Raquella's favorites, and now Valya viewed her as a powerful tool.

Black-robed Sisters marched out of the ship and lined themselves up as if in a funeral procession. Valya identified many of the Orthodox Sisters, including her fervent rivals Ninke and Esther-Cano, but not all of the women were known to her. Not yet. Valya intended to obtain reports on each of them, from which she would decide their fates. These women had broken their loyalty oath to Mother Superior Raquella, and even though the Sisterhood was unified again—in accordance with the old woman's dying wish—Valya knew she could not trust them without significant reassurances. They had wounded the organization.

A promise broken once can be broken twice.

Sister Olivia took charge of assembling the newcomers so that the Mother Superior could address them. Although faithful and dependable, the blonde had a tendency to get excited, and Valya detected a nervous edge in Olivia's voice. Nevertheless, she was attentive and conscientious, and Valya counted on her as another ally.

When Olivia had arranged the women, Valya stepped forward and raised her voice. Her tone was artificially bright. "Today you have an opportunity for advancement, rather than punishment. But you must discard the harmful ways that Dorotea taught you. The consolidated Sisterhood is strong again, after the damage caused by her rebellion against the Mother Superior."

Valya's gaze wandered over these women, probing their expressions and postures for signs of resistance. Some were anxious, cowed, or meek, while others were nearly unreadable. On the surface, she saw apparent submission, but only time would tell. "You will be interviewed carefully, and it is my fervent hope that we can welcome all of you back into the Sisterhood."

Despite their suddenly uneasy expressions, Valya dismissed them, and Sister Olivia led the group toward a groundbus. Valya's personal guard would take the new arrivals to an isolated section of the secure dormitory where they would be closely monitored. These Sisters would only be released after they had affirmed their allegiance to Valya and submitted to rigorous reeducation. Or they would die. Valya didn't care if she happened to lose a few along the way. The Sisterhood would once again have one voice and one mind, and it would belong to her, instead of Raquella.

As the women were led away, Valya made eye contact with one of her steely guard escorts—her young sister Tula Harkonnen, who was among the best fighters in the Sisterhood, thanks to the rigorous training Valya had imposed. Beneath Tula's soft, sweet beauty and curly blonde locks lurked the danger of razors. When the young woman glanced at Valya now, a look of uneasiness flashed in her eyes before she escorted the group of Sisters into the bus.

That brief moment disturbed Valya, and she tried to assess what it revealed. Tula had asked for permission to go back home to their family on Lankiveil, at least for a brief sabbatical, and she had certainly earned it . . . but Valya wanted to understand why Tula would make such a request. She had shed Atreides blood—as ordered—and proved her loyalty . . . as a Harkonnen, if nothing else.

Tula had implemented the perfect revenge by marrying young Orry Atreides and killing him on their wedding night. Such a delightful, wicked touch! The murder had sent Vorian Atreides into hiding along with Orry's brother, Willem. The two had vanished from Caladan, and even with the Sisterhood's connections Valya could not determine where they had gone.

But Tula had not shared her sister's joy. Afterward, she had expressed remorse and guilt for killing Orry, as if convinced that she held true feelings for the victim. Tula had even expressed regret that the situation couldn't be different between the two families. *Different?* Valya could not even conceive of that possibility, not after generations of blood feud.

The girl obviously needed time to contemplate her priorities, and it would be good for her to go back to Harkonnen holdings to be reminded of her family connections. Valya had arranged to send her to Lankiveil, until she was needed for another mission. Even so, Tula would have to be watched; this strangely reticent behavior concerned Valya. . . .

Fielle stepped up to report, interrupting her superior's thoughts. "I am ready to depart for Salusa, Mother Superior. My companions and I are prepared to fill the new vacancies in the Imperial Court, as you commanded. If the Emperor will have me, I will be his new Truthsayer."

"He will have you. He needs a Truthsayer, now that Dorotea is dead." Valya smiled at the loyal woman. "And I will be glad to have you there. We need to make sure Emperor Roderick gets the proper advice." Valya gazed at the shuttle, while male workers moved about, testing and refueling. "As soon as the shuttle is cleared to go, you and the other Sisters may board." The EsconTran foldspace carrier would take them back to the capital planet.

"I will gain the Emperor's trust by providing him with the information about Josef Venport that we discussed," Fielle said. "He is naturally concerned, as are we, about how Venport has killed so many people to maintain his spice monopoly. He presents a danger not only to Imperial operations that remain on Arrakis, but to the entire Imperium."

"It is a fine line we walk," Valya said. "When Venport learns what you have revealed, he will see it as a betrayal on our part. He helped the Sisterhood in its time of need, arranging for us to move to Wallach IX and saving our new school here."

"And his wife helped us retrieve the"—Fielle looked around, to make sure no one was listening, because what she was about to say was known to only a limited number of Sisters—"computers from the jungles of Rossak. Without them, we would have lost all our breeding records."

"Yes, Venport served our purposes." Valya nodded. "His wife, Cioba, is one of us, and a Sorceress as well. Her personal loyalty to us is above reproach, but in marital and business matters, one can never be entirely certain. We did what we had to do. But that is in the past, and we would be better served by siding with the Emperor."

Fielle sounded sad. "Mother Superior Raquella was always grateful to Venport for helping us."

"I am not Raquella," Valya said. "She did not consider the implications of obligating the Sisterhood to one commercial magnate, and he thinks he can pull our puppet strings. I would rather send Venport a monetary reward for past services and be done with him than be beholden to him, as he undoubtedly believes we are now. He does favors, expecting to be repaid with high interest, like a warlord." She pondered with a deepening frown. "In his own way, Directeur Venport is as difficult as Manford Torondo. Two troubled, troublesome personalities." She nodded somberly. "We don't want either of those men as enemies."

"I understand the importance of remaining neutral," Fielle said with a respectful bow. "I will be careful when I speak privately with the Emperor."

As the Mentat Sister prepared to depart for Salusa Secundus, Valya felt reasonably content that the moving parts were falling neatly into place. At the back of her mind, she heard the excited chatter of women in Other Memory, those long-dead Sisters who surfaced periodically in her consciousness. They were ancient and unpredictable, but they provided her with valuable, yet often contradictory, advice. She heard one voice after another.

"Reverend Mother Valya! You focus too much on your vengeance against the Atreides," one voice said.

"It is your legacy to be greater than Vorian Atreides, the most famous hero of the Butlerian Jihad," said another.

"The Sisterhood is more important than the enmity of your two families. Rise above it."

Another wise-sounding voice added, "How better to be victorious than to overshadow that man's legacy? Greatness is your destiny, Valya Harkonnen, not pettiness. Think of the Sisterhood—not mere revenge!"

The voices faded into the background noise of other ghost memories, but Valya was not convinced. *Why can't I advance the interests of the Sisterhood and my Great House at the same time?*

She frowned as she walked away, preoccupied. The messages from Other Memory were always important, but she didn't know whether to heed their advice. Her life and destiny were on a different course, and those long-dead women knew it. Attaining her revenge was not just a personal matter; it affected all of House Harkonnen. She had vowed to see that her family was reinstated to the prominence that had been stolen from it.

I will stay on course, she thought, *no matter what the inner voices say.*

It would be difficult, if not impossible, to write a comprehensive biography of Vorian Atreides. He has lived so long and experienced so much in so many places. He is like the wind, passing through and moving on for centuries.

—HARUK ARI, historian of the Jihad

K epler might have seemed to be a dull world, but Vor had cherished his quiet, sheltered home here for many years. It was exactly the kind of calm, uneventful life he had once sought. He'd been happy, a different man who had retired from his past. He had married a woman he loved and raised a large family—it was as much as anyone could want.

Now, he feared that all these people were threatened because his own past had ricocheted outward. The Harkonnens might be coming for them.

When he and young Willem Atreides arrived in the main Kepler village, Vor recalled those happy times, but he didn't want to be remembered, or noticed. He had left this place behind, had sworn a promise that he would never return. Now, no one on Kepler could know who he was, but he would send discreet warnings about Tula Harkonnen, alerting them to keep watch for her. What if Tula came here, hoping to seduce and murder another young Atreides man, just as she had done to Orry? If they knew ahead of time, they could stop her.

Nineteen-year-old Willem, tall and black-haired like Vor, looked to be his son but was actually a distant descendant, many generations removed. For their purposes, Willem called himself Vor's nephew. The two of them were disguised as bearded, down-on-their-luck laborers, looking for work . . . the better to keep their eyes open for threats to the extended Atreides family on Kepler. Neither of them would ever forget what Tula looked like.

Even though this was the first time he had ever left Caladan, Willem was dead serious about their mission to verify that Vor's other family was safe from the Harkonnens, that Tula had not come here. For now, the two men would lie low and keep watch for any danger.

On the transport from the landing field to the village, they asked about finding work, playing their role. Vor recognized one of the local storekeepers, but the man didn't give Vor a second glance. "Work?" The grizzled storekeeper shrugged and gestured vaguely out of town. "Check at any orchard. Pickers are always needed at this time of year to bring in the buriak crop."

Buriak trees bore large, juicy fruit that was good to eat raw, and a smile came to Vor's face as he remembered the taste. He and his beloved Mariella had managed a small orchard early in their marriage. "The Tulind family orchard is a few miles out of town. I hear they need a lot of laborers."

A woman brought a jacket up to the counter for purchase, and she joined in the conversation. "The Tulinds need pickers because they run that orchard like a police state, and there was a mass defection of workers last week."

"Doesn't sound like a place we want to work," Willem said.

"Let their damned fruit rot on the trees." The woman laid the jacket on the counter, brought out her money, and counted it. "There are plenty of better operators. Good people. The Urions are fine, except for the fact that they'll try to convert you to their obscure religion."

"They're Shohkers," the shopkeeper said. "Refused to accept the Orange Catholic Bible that Emperor Jules imposed on the Imperium."

"Or, you might try the Atreides orchard," the woman suggested. "They're solid, honest people, and they feed their pickers well. Worker housing is basic, but adequate. It's walking distance, less than an hour north of town on the main road. The owners are Geoff and Nobinia Atreides."

"I've heard of them," Vor said guardedly. "Thanks, I think we'll try there first."

Vor had heard what he needed to know. Geoff was one of his great-grandsons, though they had barely met. If Vor and Willem could get hired there, it would be less risky than getting close to Vor's actual sons, who might recognize him . . . which could put them in danger.

Before leaving, Vor displayed an image of Tula Harkonnen, blonde and beautiful, like an angel, taken on the day of her wedding. The image did not show the blood on her hands or the poison in her heart. "Have you seen this woman? A stranger coming through? She would have arrived recently."

The shopkeeper raised his eyebrows and smiled. "No, I would have remembered her!"

"She's a wanted murderer," Willem said coldly. "Ruthless and dangerous. Watch out for her. We have reason to believe she might be coming to Kepler."

Leaving the store, the two men set off on the main road. They had departed from Caladan after the horrific murder of Willem's brother Orry. Even though Vor doubted the Harkonnens knew about this branch of his family, or that Tula would come here so soon to continue her deadly plans, he needed to make sure. Once he had satisfied himself that she wasn't here, then he and Willem could go hunting for her.

They headed up the road in the sunny autumn day, and Vor remembered how comfortably warm it usually was at this time of year. Buriak orchards on either side of the road were heavy with fruit—red, yellow, and pink varieties. His heart ached with memories, and he longed to just stay here and disappear. But that was not possible.

Vor led the way down the long dirt driveway of the Atreides orchards, while Willem looked around at the strange sights. "This land used to be owned by my wife's brother," Vor said, reminding the young man of his other family. "Let's see if we can fit in."

He saw half a dozen pickers working the trees, with portable lifts that elevated flat boxes for the fruit. An old farmhouse and several outbuildings sat at the end of the long driveway. Vor bent to pick up a bright pink buriak that had fallen to the ground. He took a knife from his belt, cut off the bruised part, and pared off a slice, which he passed to Willem before cutting another for himself. Vor savored the half-forgotten sweetness. "This is how life should be, simple, pleasurable, without hatred and warfare. It's not an easy thing to attain."

Willem's voice cracked as he spoke. "Orry and I had that on Caladan. The fishing, the rescue jobs. Life was normal there—until *she* came." He plucked another fruit for himself and took out his own knife, but in his tense anger he seemed to be attacking the fruit more than peeling it.

"And now Tula might be coming here, to hunt down more of my family." Vor sectioned the rest of the fruit and ate it, then tossed the core away before cleaning his knife with a handkerchief. "You and I won't see much of that sort of life for some time. Enjoy it while we can—but always stay alert." He led his "nephew" toward the farmhouse. . . .

The two visitors were hired with very few questions asked, and the foreman accepted their false names without any hesitation. He and Willem said they were from Alarkand, a far-off minor planet that none of these people had ever heard of. Vor had once fought a space battle near Alarkand during the Jihad, crushing a machine fleet that had concealed themselves in the asteroid field.

Geoff and Nobinia Atreides lived in a large estate house with their children, some of whom were in their late teens. Vor could see from Geoff's rough hands and ruddy, sun-weathered complexion that he worked in the orchards himself. Vor remained alert for news about his other descendants, who were scattered farther from the main town. Everyone seemed safe, normal, and content.

As part of the picking crew, Vor and Willem each received a bed in the bunkhouse, and they began working on the next afternoon shift. All of the orchard workers were invited to dinner that evening in the estate house, where a long table was set up for everyone, including ten young children who were too small to work.

"We send our boys and girls into the orchards when they turn eight." Geoff Atreides chuckled. He had rough creases on his face. "And the more children we have, the better, since it's hard to get enough pickers during the harvest season." He glanced across the table at his daughter Kauree, who was several months pregnant. "Her husband Jacque is the orchard supervisor, and he's busy outside now. He'll eat later."

"I like large families," Vor said. "Wish I had one myself."

While Willem looked sidelong at him, Vor ate in silence, suddenly nostalgic to think of the large family that he really had, here on this very world—and another one on Caladan so long ago. But he couldn't allow himself to be part of either of them. Too many people would be in danger.

Not long ago, his wife, Mariella, had been murdered by a pair of assassins who were searching for Vor. Those two had eventually tracked Vor down on Arrakis and killed his friend Griffin Harkonnen—after which the Harkonnens blamed Vor for the death, inflaming the blood feud that had already gone on for generations. Those assassins were gone, but other hunters had taken their place. It saddened him that there would always be hunters tracking him down.

Soon he would turn the tables, and he and Willem would track Tula down to make her face justice. . . .

As days passed quietly on Kepler, Vor and Willem worked in the orchards. While Vor remained at the farm most evenings, wanting to watch over his family, Willem would walk the short distance into town to visit various businesses, including an entertainment hall. He reported back to Vor that no one had seen any young woman answering to Tula's description, but he had spread her image around so that all the people here would be on guard. Tula would not be able to slip in unnoticed.

Vor was also interested in keeping up with his family here. In his cautious research, he learned that his son Clar owned a successful restaurant and roadhouse outside of town; his other son, Oren, managed a skytruck company with offices in several cities on Kepler. Some of the children of Clar or Oren came to the orchard on occasion, including Clar's teenage daughter, Raiga.

She had a pretty brunette friend named Opalla, and Willem flirted with her, took her out to dinner and dancing several times. Vor remembered when he had been young and aloof, with a girl in every port as he flew from planet to planet for the Army of the Jihad. Willem wasn't serious about Opalla, and Vor knew the young man would forget her soon enough as they moved on in their hunt for Tula Harkonnen.

They decided to stay for two more weeks, until the next spacefolder arrived. Now that VenHold had suddenly withdrawn ships from commercial trade routes in a dispute with the new Emperor, there were far fewer transport options available, which greatly affected backwater planets such as Kepler. The secondary carriers were said to be less safe, but a non-VenHold ship was the only option they had. Vor wanted to see who disembarked, in case Tula Harkonnen happened to be one of the passengers, but if she wasn't among the new arrivals, then they could go.

Staying on Kepler was a pleasant thought, but if Tula truly didn't know about the Atreides here, then his family was safe. And that meant Vor and Willem had to search elsewhere for the treacherous, violent Harkonnen.

One should not enjoy revenge, even when it is justifiable and deserved.
—PTOLEMY, personal records, post–cymek surgery

After surrendering his biological body, Ptolemy grew accustomed to his new existence as a cymek. He had volunteered for this fate and did not regret the cost, not for a moment. For too much of his life he had felt weak and insignificant. But not anymore.

After the drop-pods landed in the darkness outside the capital city on Lampadas, Ptolemy activated his mechanical legs. The precision thoughtrodes that he himself had developed were efficient and accurate. The sensations were different, but his bodily control was precise and so much more versatile, and the integral weapons he controlled were like extensions of himself. For weeks, he had practiced for this moment out in Denali's poisonous atmosphere, and now it was time.

Joined by his Navigator cymeks Adem Garl and Rikon Po, Ptolemy stepped away from the open drop-pod, and the three behemoths marched together toward the nearby dwellings and commercial buildings. Each step was a loud thump that shook the landscape and buildings. Though launched at night, this was not a stealth operation—far from it—but one meant to cause the maximum terror and mayhem.

Ptolemy's enhanced optics discerned locals emerging from their dwellings, staring in horror and despair, and he intended to increase their suffering. It was what these misguided people deserved.

Manford Torondo was the true evil behind the movement, but his mindless followers also had blood on their hands. Butlerian mobs destroyed advancements that would help others, denied medical technology to the sick and injured, and simply burned anything they did not like.

He flinched at the memory of his friend Dr. Elchan's dying screams, and in doing so he involuntarily ignited one of his fire cannons. The belching spear of flame set one of the nearby dwellings ablaze. Seeing the results of that accident, he opened fire with great gusto, and leveled the home. They were just beginning their mayhem.

He and his fellow cymeks marched forward. The other two walkers launched projectiles, wrecking storehouses, smashing primitive vehicles, and mowing down people as they fled. The attacking force had to cause as much damage as possible in a limited time, before they were recalled to Draigo's stealth-shielded ship.

Ptolemy used his internal systems to scan the landscape and orient himself. The drop-point had been imprecise, but the cymeks knew exactly where Leader Toronto lived. His cottage was undefended. Ptolemy adjusted course, and the two other Nav-cymeks charged alongside him, blasting indiscriminately. They made their way to Manford's residence.

His audio amplifiers picked up frightened shouts as Butlerians tried to escape; others stood their ground, holding up laughable and ineffective implements— clubs, spears, old-style projectile weapons—but even sophisticated armaments could not have damaged the shielded bodies of the new war machines.

The three cymeks stomped on victims as if they were insects and kept moving forward. According to Directeur Venport, their goal was not planetary conquest, but a demonstration attack with the objective of causing as much mayhem and destruction as possible. Ptolemy's personal goal was to find and kill the Butlerian leader. If not tonight, then they would return with a much larger force when it was time for the full assault.

Ptolemy believed they could accomplish the entire objective with only three cymeks, though. In fact, he would consider it a matter of pride if he could do so.

Others might look on him as a monster, might see this action as the slaughter of countless innocents . . . but to him, none of these victims were innocent. He knew what they had done, or what they had allowed to happen, in the name of their fanaticism.

As his mechanical body approached Manford's cottage, his conscious mind drifted back to his wonderful laboratory on Zenith. He and Elchan had worked on developing innovative cybernetic technology, meaning to help those who had lost limbs—people like Manford Toronto. They had created replacement arms and legs that an invalid could use just like natural limbs. But when he and Elchan had offered a new set of legs to the crippled Butlerian leader—simply because they wanted to help—the madman had destroyed the offering and sent his fanatical mob to ransack the Zenith laboratory and burn Elchan alive.

Manford had claimed he was teaching Ptolemy a lesson. Even though those fires had long since burned out, Ptolemy remembered his friend's dying screams. And his hatred remained as bright as ever. . . .

When the three cymeks reached Manford's home, Butlerian followers rushed forward to stand as useless guards and shields. They were defiant, determined, and ridiculously impotent.

The Navigator cymeks paused to assess the situation, but Ptolemy activated his flame cannon and roasted the would-be defenders alive, reducing them to insignificance, just like Elchan . . . though their deaths were much swifter.

Then the three cymeks fell upon Manford's home.

⤲

AS SOON AS she saw and heard the demon cymeks approaching, Anari Idaho knew they had come for Manford. Even her intimidating sword would not be effective against the titanic machines. Her priority was to save Manford.

Without a word of warning or cry for help, she grabbed him in his room, raced to the open window, and lowered him to the ground outside. After she dove through, she snatched him up and bounded away into the darkness. Holding him in her muscular arms, she practically leaped across the landscape.

Behind them, the cymeks were getting closer, their path obvious from the explosions, the fires, the screams.

"Where are you taking me?" Manford protested. "Those are my people being massacred!"

"They are giving their lives so you can escape. If we're cornered, I will defend you as long as I can."

She glared back at the towering machines, remembering when she had slain combat meks as a game during her Swordmaster training on Ginaz. In that controlled exercise, it had taken a team of well-trained warriors to bring down even the smallest war machine.

She was alone now, and there were three of the things.

Gasping for breath, Anari ran across the surrounding grain fields. It was late in the harvest season and many fields had only a stubble of stems and straw. No place to hide. Ahead, she spotted five shadowy heaps of hay piled up for livestock. The hay would have its own internal heat, maybe enough to mask Manford's thermal signature. Maybe. She couldn't run far enough, and no normal hiding place would be proof against the cymeks. That was her best chance right now.

She reached the nearest haystack. "In here, Manford."

He flailed. "How can I hide? I'll be found too easily."

"You'll be unseen. The natural heat inside should mask you." She moved loose hay aside and stuffed his legless body into the pile. "Stay here and don't move. Wait for me to come back for you."

He nodded, obeying Anari because he believed in her. He must realize they had little chance otherwise.

After securing him, Anari watched the cymeks use a flame weapon to incinerate a group of brave defenders near Manford's cottage. Raising her sword, Anari ran toward them, intending to fight to the death; she also hoped to draw their attention away from Manford's hiding place. She longed to stand in front of those machines and give up her life for the sacred fight, but she could not leave Manford unprotected. She had to survive.

As she ran, Anari watched the cymeks fall upon the cottage, tearing down the fieldstone walls and ripping off the roof as if they were peeling a boiled egg. Articulated metal arms reached in and grasped a black-robed woman, who screamed and flailed. Sister Woodra. One of the cymeks held her up in the air, lifted a second clawed metal arm, and ripped her in two, like tearing apart a doll. Satisfied, the machine demon tossed the two parts of her ragged, bloody corpse in different directions.

The monsters leveled Manford's home, but failed to find him there. Impatient and furious, they marched across the landscape, launching more explosions, causing more destruction.

Screaming in rage, Anari ran after them, brandishing her sword, but the cymeks moved in the other direction, wrecking clusters of homes, setting more buildings on fire. Though outraged and weeping, she took solace in the fact that they were going away from Manford's hiding place.

An hour later, leaving a swath of destruction behind them, the cymeks returned to their drop-pods and launched themselves into the sky, like fiery meteors in reverse.

In the aftermath, Anari stood helpless, holding her sword. She couldn't guess how many hundreds—thousands?—had been slain this night, and she grieved for them. Nevertheless, she felt a steely joy in knowing that she had saved Manford. At least he was still alive!

She ran back to retrieve him from his concealment, already considering their retaliation against the vile Josef Venport.

Though loyalty is an admirable quality, it is often misplaced.
—DIRECTEUR JOSEF VENPORT,
private consultation with Draigo Roget

Preoccupied with building up Kolhar's defenses, Josef had allowed his grasp on Arrakis spice production to slip. Norma was agitated and needed him to accompany her to the desert planet, where he could crack down on the chaos and restore the melange-harvesting operations.

Before he could head off to Arrakis, though, Josef needed to take care of one more item of business. He shuttled up to the large foldspace carrier in orbit, which served as a detention vessel holding the Imperial battle group he had taken hostage.

Roderick's military had many well-armed ships dispersed around the Imperium as peacekeepers, but few of those were equipped with Holtzman engines. Thus, the Imperial military had to be carried aboard other large ships, and the Venport Holdings Spacing Fleet had provided transportation services for years, delivering military ships wherever they were deployed. At the time when the Emperor declared Josef an outlaw, this VenHold carrier had been hauling seventy Imperial military vessels to quell Butlerian unrest on outlying worlds. In retaliation for the arrest order, Josef had simply captured all those battleships, refusing to let them rejoin the Imperial Armed Forces. Instead, he took them to Kolhar and held them in orbit; the carrier had become their prison ship. For the time being, Admiral Umberto Harte and all his subcommanders just had to remain on the sidelines.

Of course, the victory owed more to fortuitous circumstances than to tactical genius, but Josef wouldn't complain. He had taken those strategic pieces off the game board, and he had no intention of letting the Emperor have his assets back until he and Josef resolved their differences. This could be settled so easily, if only the Emperor would see reason!

As his shuttle cruised over the sweeping curve of the city-sized foldspace carrier, Josef was pleased to think of the neat, bloodless victory here. The carrier's cavernous cargo vault held those Imperial warships locked into place like prisoners manacled to the walls of a dungeon. He hadn't even needed to send his people aboard; there had been no fighting, not a single casualty. He wished all coups could be so swift and simple.

Right now, he would have the same discussion with Admiral Harte as he'd had before, but he expected no different result. Still, it had to be done before he traveled with Norma to take care of their business on Arrakis.

Once aboard the carrier, he spoke briskly to one of his VenHold employees. "Summon the Admiral—he will try to stall, as a form of passive aggression. But don't let him be late. It's a matter of courtesy to me."

He made his way to the piloting deck, where the carrier's Navigator rested in a spice-filled chamber surrounded by sweeping starry views. Inside the tank drifted a distorted figure with atrophied arms and legs, a swollen head, and oversized eyes. If Josef recalled correctly, this one's name was Dobrec, although Navigators rarely used names, considering such labels beneath them. Without even acknowledging the Directeur's presence, Dobrec drifted in his tank while staring into the infinity of his mind, pondering foldspace calculations or other incomprehensible thoughts.

Josef had long since stopped viewing the mutant creatures with revulsion; with their advanced minds they accomplished things no mere human ever could. And although not all Navigator candidates were volunteers, strictly speaking, and many didn't survive the physical transformation, he did not regret what he did to them. He saw it as a tremendous opportunity, even if the candidates themselves did not always agree.

While waiting for Admiral Harte, he peered through a lens-window in the bulkhead wall to view the captive Imperial warships stacked in their holding array inside the carrier's huge hold. Each vessel bore the Corrino crest.

The hostage battleships made him feel sad as well as triumphant. He and the Emperor should be on the same side, fighting against the Butlerian nonsense. But Roderick refused to set aside his personal vendetta, his need to make Josef face justice for the death of Salvador. That was the Emperor's primary mistake. It would have been far better for the Imperium if he would just move on.

In the meantime, Josef could not let Roderick have these troops back. Although Harte's crew considered themselves prisoners of war, the soldiers were still a viable, angry fighting force, which made them dangerously unpredictable. Their weapons-command systems were neutralized, but Josef wanted to come to terms with the Admiral, to make the best of an unpleasant situation.

Before the Imperial commander arrived, Josef smelled a pungent burst of ozone and saw a pale blue shimmer in the air, just as Norma Cenva's sturdy, ornate vault appeared on the deck next to Dobrec's tank.

Josef gave her a wry smile. "So, you decided to join us, Grandmother."

Norma stared through the curved windowport. "I am concerned for my Navigators . . . for the continuing flow of spice from the planet Arrakis." She paused, then added, "I am anxious for this distraction to be over."

"We will go there soon, Grandmother. Spice production continues, even though our operations are more limited than before. Even though the Imperial guardian ships can still harass our work, they are not very effective. The flow of melange will continue—don't be concerned."

"Spice is always a matter of great concern. Prescience shows me turbulence in the future. How can you ensure a sufficient supply?"

He smiled. "I have tasked my Mentat administrators in Combined Mercantiles to establish an enormous stockpile, a spice bank. We'll hide it in the deep desert, a guarded reserve that should see us through any difficulties."

She drifted, as if trying to grasp what he was saying. "How will you hide it and guard it?"

"Combined Mercantiles just purchased an entire sietch in the desert, bought out the tribe of people who are living there and forced them to move. I will show you as soon as we reach Arrakis. Soon, we will fill those caves with spice so you and your Navigators will always have what you need. We can ride out any political turmoil in the Imperium."

"It would be wise to enlarge our existing reserves on Kolhar and Denali as well," she said. "We don't want to put all of our eggs in one basket."

"Of course, but those will be smaller stockpiles. Arrakis is the best place to hold the big reserve."

"All right. Now finish your meeting so that we can go."

He turned as the straight-backed Umberto Harte was escorted onto the piloting deck. Harte's every step was like a parade presentation. He was handsome and middle-aged, with crow's feet just beginning to appear around his eyes. His trim brown hair was perfectly in place, and his medal-bedecked uniform was spotless and freshly pressed. Despite his cool professionalism, his gaze smoldered.

"Thank you for joining me, Admiral," Josef said. "As before, I'm here to verify the health and disposition of your troops, who are my guests."

"Prisoners, you mean."

"Your crew is being held so they cannot harm either my interests or themselves. It is necessary until this unfortunate situation is resolved."

"We are loyal to the Emperor. That will not change."

Josef raised his eyebrows. "Do you mean Emperor Salvador, who dispatched you on patrol? I prefer not to speak ill of the dead, but let's not delude ourselves. You know that man was bringing the human race to ruin."

Harte sniffed. "Roderick Corrino is Emperor now. Our loyalty transferred to him as soon as he accepted the crown."

Josef made a dismissive gesture. "Roderick has not yet shown himself worthy of your loyalty—or mine." He stroked his bushy mustache. "Though I did have such high hopes."

"Directeur Venport, it is the duty of my soldiers to fight against all threats—including your uprising. We are loyal to the Imperium."

"The *Imperium* . . . a weak and shaky construct that has existed for less than a century. We are talking about the future of civilization itself! Who is most qualified to lead the human race, to guide us where we wish to go? The insane Butlerians, who want us to hurl ourselves over a cliff into a new dark age? Believe me, Admiral, I would much rather work with Roderick . . . but if he doesn't have humanity's best interests at heart, then I will be forced to make a political shift."

He leaned closer to the indignant commander, noted tiny beads of perspiration on the man's brow. "I do not question your loyalty or your military skill, sir. I believe your captured fighters are good men and women, but they are operating under a misguided sense of their own best interests. That's why I'm forced to hold your ships until this misunderstanding is over. It should not take too long, I hope."

Harte's response was cold. "You are a traitor. Do you intend to seize the throne for yourself?"

Josef laughed. "I'd rather not be Emperor unless it is absolutely necessary. I am only interested in a stable future for humankind so I can conduct important interplanetary business." He realized that this discussion was going nowhere, and Norma was anxious to be off to Arrakis. "You are dismissed, Admiral. My representatives will see that you are well cared for. Do your soldiers have any special needs at the moment?"

"Yes, our freedom."

"I'll take that under consideration. Thank you for your time."

Josef felt disappointed. Under different circumstances, Umberto Harte might have been a very worthwhile asset, but Josef had to let cooler heads prevail. Eventually, Roderick should come to understand the best solution. A man blinded by revenge was not a fit negotiator.

Norma was still there waiting, drifting in spice gas, and he turned to her tank. "Let me say goodbye to Cioba, and then you and I will head off to Arrakis."

I'm going to rule all of that someday.
—SALVADOR CORRINO at age ten, to his father,
Emperor Jules, while gazing up at the stars

I don't understand the politics of the Sisterhood at all," said Haditha. "They insist they aren't religious, yet they follow rituals and practices suggesting exactly the opposite." She lowered her voice. "Frankly, I don't trust them."

"My love, there are a great many people whom I don't trust—Josef Venport and Manford Toronodo foremost among them," Roderick said. "Yet the Imperium must function, and I need a new Truthsayer."

His auburn-haired wife wore a white dress with gold brocade on the collar and sleeves, and a beret to match. They stood together in one of the palace gardens, awaiting the arrival of the Truthsayer who would take Dorotea's place. With the new Mother Superior, most of the Sisters were being replaced at the Imperial Court. Something to do with internal politics, his advisers had informed him. A changing of the guard.

While waiting in the quiet greenhouse gardens, Roderick used the time to kneel on a pad and plant the cutting of an ornamental rose, taken from rootstock that had been in the Corrino/Butler family since before the Battle of Corrin. Emperor Faykan, Roderick's grandfather, had started the tradition of planting roses as a sign of good luck for the reign, and Roderick intended to carry it forward. Salvador had not done so, complaining that it was unseemly for an Emperor to get his hands dirty with gardening work. Roderick did not place stock in superstitions, but his brother's reign had not gone particularly well. . . .

Now that he was Emperor, Roderick had decided to establish another tradition. He would rule the people of the Imperium with a just and honorable hand, and would raise his twelve-year-old son, Javicco, to behave in the same manner. Roderick supposed all Emperors began their reigns with silent vows, of one sort or another.

"I still think you should consider negotiating with Directeur Venport," Haditha said. "At least make the attempt."

"If General Roon is successful, I won't need to negotiate." The large strike force had just departed for Kolhar, with all the ships finally loaded aboard the military carrier.

"The Imperium still needs Venport's ships, his Navigators, his technology. Isn't a resolution better than a conquest?"

He frowned at her. His wife always tried to be the voice of wisdom and reason. "He murdered my brother. I must make him feel profound pain before I can consider his debt paid."

Haditha knelt near him, closely examining an exotic flower, one that bloomed all year, no matter the weather. Then she looked at him. "Is that what's best for the Imperium, or is it just your own personal vendetta?"

"The Emperor and the Imperium are one," he said, with a deep sigh. "Let us wait and hear the report from General Roon. If Kolhar is defeated, it will put our negotiations on a much different footing. We both want this conflict over, but we have very different ideas of how to accomplish that."

He finished tamping down the new soil around the rose planting, and then straightened with her as an escort of Imperial guards led several black-robed women into the greenhouse garden. At the front of the group, a large-framed woman presented herself with a formal bow. "Sire, I am Reverend Mother Fielle. I have been assigned as your new Truthsayer."

Roderick wiped his hands on a cloth, looked at the entourage. "And these other Sisters?"

"To fill the roles of those who were recalled to Wallach IX at the request of Mother Superior Valya." They all bowed. "Sire, we exist to serve."

Roderick caught his wife's suspicious frown and admitted his own uneasiness. "But whom do you serve? Your Emperor? Or your order . . . or perhaps the highest bidder among the noble houses?"

Fielle's fleshy face showed no reaction. "Who could possibly bid higher than the Emperor himself? We serve the Sisterhood as well, but that is a school where female candidates seek to achieve the greatest human potential. We develop a special set of skills, such as my ability to discern truth from lies. The Mother Superior deemed me worthy of filling that role for you, and I am pleased to be here."

"Then I accept your services," he said. "Provisionally." He did not know the new Mother Superior Valya any more than he knew Fielle. "We shall let you prove your worth."

Fielle bowed slightly. "Sire, to begin my service with a goodwill gesture, I am prepared to offer secret information about your rival Directeur Venport. You may find it valuable, or at least interesting. And it will begin to prove my value to you."

Roderick was intrigued. "Information about Venport could indeed be of use to me."

The Sisters conferred in whispers, and then Fielle reported, "Venport Holdings is desperate to control the spice operations on Arrakis for reasons that go beyond mere profits. I'm sure you realize that the Imperial military force your brother left there is not capable of maintaining control over the planet. Combined Mercantiles, a puppet corporation for Venport Holdings, continues harvesting spice, producing far more than the independent Imperial contractors. Sooner or later Venport will no longer tolerate the Imperial presence, and their incentive will be to drive out your ships. Combined Mercantiles has more spice-gathering crews on the desert planet than you do, and greater military might to defend them. The resources that Directeur Venport is willing to expend to control Arrakis exceeds what you can spare, especially with Admiral Harte's battle group held hostage."

Roderick scowled. "I do not have any spare ships that I can use to impose my authority on Arrakis." *But if Roon is successful at Kolhar, I will win control over all the VenHold operations anyway.*

Roderick ground his teeth together. That infernal planet had caused so much trouble, and his brother's inept handling of an attempted takeover had led to the current crisis—as well as his own death. Frowning, he said, "That confirms information I already have, Truthsayer. You have told me nothing new."

"You cannot extract your mining crews and troops from Arrakis. They are struggling to defend their spice operations, but they have no feasible way to deliver the spice they produce, other than by using black-market runners, who steal as much as they sell. Your citizens are addicted and demanding melange, and they are growing restless. They need to see the flow of spice restored."

Roderick admitted, "We didn't station enough firepower there to hold spice operations under Imperial control, and I don't have the forces to recapture it. Venport's profits must be immense if he continues to expend so much to maintain his operations there."

"Spice means more than just profits to Directeur Venport. You must understand this, Sire." Fielle gazed at him. "He *needs* to provide a constant supply of spice for his Navigators. Without spice, his Navigators cannot envision safe paths through the universe. Without spice, he cannot create more Navigators. Without spice, Venport Holdings cannot function. That is why Arrakis is so vital to him."

"And how did you come by this information?" Haditha interjected, looking suspicious.

"I cannot reveal our internal source, but Mother Superior Valya requested that I share this knowledge with you."

Frowning, Roderick said, "I will consider it thoroughly." Then he spoke to the honor guard. "Take these women to the quarters vacated by the previous Sisters. Reverend Mother Dorotea served me well—so when I have need of a Truthsayer, I hope I can trust you as I did her."

As if choreographed, Fielle and the women bowed in unison, then turned to follow their escort, leaving Roderick and Haditha next to the new rosebush. He spoke quietly, relying on his wife as a sounding board, as he always did.

"I am far more worried about Venport and his control of Arrakis than I am about the schemes of those women. But General Roon and his strike force should reach Kolhar soon. If he breaks Venport Holdings, then we will have all the time we need to reassert control over Arrakis." He drew a deep breath. "The Imperium will be stable again."

A plan is only that—a plan. It is not the actual doing of a thing.
—SUPREME COMMANDER VORIAN ATREIDES,
Annals of the Jihad

After the pilot checked and rechecked his manual calculations, the giant foldspace carrier plunged into the labyrinth between space, carrying the Imperial strike force toward the Kolhar system. The carrier would arrive close to the VenHold stronghold, depending on the variance and navigational errors.

As soon as the Imperial carrier emerged above the planet, the attack ships would be dispatched in an overwhelming surprise assault. Without any time to respond, Venport Holdings would fall. Anticipation built among the troops.

General Roon stood on the bridge, hands clasped behind his back, waiting. He looked forward to the spectacle, since it gave him the opportunity to prove himself. A defeat of Directeur Venport would dispel any lingering personal issues between himself and Roderick Corrino. At last.

Roon had served on the staff of Commanding General Odmo Saxby, where he'd seen firsthand what a fool Saxby was, but he had never reported his superior (although perhaps he should have). Finally, Saxby's incompetence came to the attention of the new Emperor, and Roderick had ordered sweeping changes. Now, it was Roon's turn to lead. He had earned this opportunity.

The surprise strike force was a significant portion of the Imperial space military, in order to guarantee victory and take down the man who had assassinated Salvador Corrino. But the logistics of gathering, preparing, and loading so many ships aboard the gigantic carrier had delayed the launch for more than a day. Mechanical issues, checklist irregularities, personnel reassignments. But it all had to be done properly. General Roon would have only one chance, and he wouldn't let Roderick down.

As the carrier moved out of Salusan orbit, his technicians had gone over the Holtzman diagnostics, studying the space-navigation panels. Since they did not have the use of a Navigator, the course to the Kolhar system had been calculated and recalculated. Just to be safe.

When Roon finally gave the order, reality folded around the carrier, and they plunged into a shortcut through dimensionally uncharted space.

Every Imperial warship in the hold was loaded with advanced weapons, crewed with highly trained soldiers, the best in the fleet. Pilots of space fighter-craft had climbed into cockpits; large destroyers were prepared to drop out of the carrier's hold immediately upon arrival. This strike force would smash through any defenses Venport had managed to mount.

One chance. Roon tightened his fist.

The foldspace passage did not take long, but seemed to take forever. He transmitted to all ships, all soldiers. "Prepare for arrival. This will be quite a surprise."

The engine pitch changed, while lines and streaks of color around the spacefolder slowed in their fantastic flow.

Roon stared ahead through the wide windowport as the carrier snapped back into normal space again. He expected to see the planet below, a defensive ring of VenHold ships taken off guard, scrambling to prepare their defense.

Instead, the bridge deck was filled with blazing light, raging ionized gases, stellar fire. "Navigation error!" someone yelled.

The carrier's course was only fractionally off, a tiny mistake on a cosmic scale—but enough to drop the warship into the broiling fringes of Kolhar's sun.

The First Nav Officer shouted, but Vinson Roon could see nothing at all because the searing light had rendered him blind, along with everyone else on the flight deck. There was no time for further screaming or whimpering.

Coronal loops swirled up and around; fiery convection cells churned plasma below. The foldspace carrier vaporized instantly, taking with it a hundred grand battleships.

❦

ONE OF THE VenHold picket ships patrolling the Kolhar system detected a flash in the extended sensor net. Long-distance imagers caught what appeared to be a large foldspace carrier emerging in the fringes of the star, but coronal activity and the glare of radiation obscured details.

Directeur Venport had already departed for Arrakis, leaving Cioba as manager in his absence, and she reviewed the inconclusive images. She dispatched several picket ships to patrol closer to the sun, searching for any sign of an Imperial attack force that might be hiding within the stellar glare.

But they found nothing—no foldspace carrier, no ships, no wreckage. Nevertheless, they continued patrols and remained vigilant.

Many primary forces influence events in the universe: physical constants, gravitational forces, the laws of thermodynamics, elemental interactions, quantum mechanics. But I have learned that there are also less quantifiable forces that are unpredictable and destructive. These forces include human emotions.

—ERASMUS, Laboratory Journals

Flying back to Denali from the Lampadas proof-of-concept raid, Draigo Roget scanned the domes concealed beneath the dark, poisonous atmosphere. So much brainpower down there, so many innovations, so much destructive weaponry being assembled under Directeur Venport's patronage.

Draigo would feel more satisfied if the cymeks had found and killed Manford Toronto. Although that had not been the full objective of the mission, it would have been a welcome accomplishment. Even so, the three monstrous walkers had caused a breathtaking amount of destruction in a limited time and then departed before any Butlerian warships could find Draigo's shielded ship. In that regard, success was complete.

The two cymek walkers were stored in the cargo hold, with their brain canisters detached. Two of the Navigator brains hung in silent contemplation, possibly dreaming of pathways among the stars, places they might have flown if they had become real Navigators.

Meanwhile, Ptolemy's brain conversed with him, providing insightful conversation. Draigo and the obsessed scientist had a great deal in common. Both wanted to defeat the Butlerian threat, although Ptolemy's need to kill Manford Toronto and his followers was so bright and focused it was like a star that would burn out too soon.

As their ship dropped through Denali's swirling green-gray clouds into darkness, Ptolemy mused, "We should have stayed longer, and continued the hunt for Toronto. He is an evil man."

"We showed the Butlerians that they are helpless against even three of our new cymeks—and we are building a hundred more. When we launch our full attack, Lampadas is doomed."

"But Manford still lives." Ptolemy sounded bitter.

"And he will be terrified of us now."

The disembodied scientist seemed to take heart from that. Draigo did not mention, though, that he had run extensive Mentat projections; he was concerned that instead of making them cower in fear, this attack would undoubtedly cause Manford to take more personal security precautions, and might provoke the barbarians into even more rampant violence. The forces of sanity and reason had to be ready for it.

Draigo landed the ship, stabilized it, and powered off the engines. Nearby, the bright blisters of habitation domes glowed in the hazy gloom. As he completed the shutdown procedures in the cockpit, automated arms lifted Ptolemy's preservation canister and installed him in the stored cymek walker body, which was lowered through the bottom hatch. Before long, the other Navigator cymeks joined Ptolemy, and the three walkers strode across the landing field.

Draigo extended the cumbersome connecting tube so that he could pass from the ship into the habitation domes. Through sealed windows, he watched a dozen armored walkers approach from across the landscape to meet the arrivals. Soon enough, he knew, there would be more than a hundred such warrior machines to unleash upon the Butlerian stronghold.

Draigo entered the laboratory dome, prepared to deliver his report. All the Denali scientists shared the goal of saving humanity from the dark age that the fanatics desired. In the briefing room, Administrator Noffe's brain canister rested on a stand, connected to observation apparatus. The Erasmus memory core waited inside a small display case outfitted with external sensors so that he could see and hear. Lovely Anna Corrino, anxious to be part of any decision or debate that involved Erasmus, remained close to the gelsphere, as if to guard it with her life. Two Tlulaxa biological researchers were already present. Immediately behind Draigo, a whirring cart rolled in, carrying Ptolemy's brain canister, now disengaged from his cymek body outside the dome.

Draigo shook his head slightly as he looked at the group: a robot memory core, a pair of cymek brain canisters, exiled biological researchers, and a mentally damaged woman. What a bizarre and unorthodox audience this was! But they were all fighting against the same enemy that threatened the future of civilization.

Draigo proudly presented his report, playing images of the Lampadas strike and the havoc recorded by the three cymek marauders. "Our attack was quite effective. The Butlerians will remember this night for some time to come."

"Total assessment of damage?" asked Administrator Noffe from his tank.

"Seventy-eight dwellings and nine commercial buildings destroyed, with another thirty-seven homes burning at the time the cymeks withdrew. Eight hundred sixty-two confirmed fatalities—primarily bystanders, collateral damage."

"Not collateral damage!" Ptolemy protested. "They were all targets."

"And Manford Torondo?" asked Erasmus. "Is he dead? Finally?"

"Manford is an evil man," said Anna Corrino.

Draigo delivered the disappointing news. "We destroyed his cottage, but were unable to locate him. He escaped, and in that technological wasteland we had no means of tracking his whereabouts."

"You couldn't find a legless man?" asked Noffe.

Ptolemy added defensively, "We should return to Lampadas immediately with a larger force. Primitive Butlerian weapons are no match for our cymek bodies—we just proved that, so the people there pose no threat. We can scour the entire planet and make sure he is killed."

Erasmus spoke in a coolly reserved voice, "That is not likely the most efficient means of destroying the Butlerian leader."

Ptolemy seemed agitated. "Manford Torondo has caused all of us too much pain. We have more than a dozen cymeks ready to go and countless more in the final stages. Why wait?"

Draigo narrowed his gaze, calculating. "We all know why you hate Manford so much, Ptolemy. I hate him as well. He executed my Headmaster, and I saw firsthand what he did to the Mentat School. I will never forgive him for that."

The Erasmus core throbbed with pale blue light. "I have been analyzing my experiences and . . . my feelings about the execution of Gilbertus ever since we escaped from Lampadas. I believe I now understand what a human parent feels upon the loss of a child, because Gilbertus Albans was in effect my son. I am also beginning to understand revenge and hatred as more than just theoretical concepts. It has been a most disturbing, but enlightening experience." Anna hovered over the gelsphere, adjusted his sensors. The robot core continued, "I can help you design new weapons. I will ensure we have the means to eradicate that man we all despise."

Anna moved about the chamber, fidgeting with her hands. Her gaze flicked back and forth in agitation, as if she wanted to hide. "So much hatred!"

"Yes," Draigo said with a firm nod. "And we shall put it to good use."

An injury to a man's pride may inflict more pain than a wound to his body.

—HEADMASTER GILBERTUS ALBANS, Mentat axiom

Though badly shaken by the cymek attack that had nearly killed him, Manford Torondo took advantage of the aftermath. He had never seen such an infusion of energy as when his outraged followers howled for revenge. *Human* energy. And he could use that.

In a blood-red dawn following the attack, the stunned Butlerians worked together with shovels and bucket brigades to extinguish the spreading fires. Manford's faithful rescued the injured and gathered the bodies of the slain. One crew recovered the mangled remains of Sister Woodra and gave her a proper burial, which Manford supervised.

As more reports streamed in, Manford struggled with disbelief. This was his *home* on Lampadas, his stronghold and sanctuary! He hadn't felt so vulnerable since an assassin in Arrakis City had shot one of his body doubles. God had protected him then—as He had done again during this cymek assault. Manford's current body double, a legless man with features similar to his own, waited to perform the same duty, if called upon. But there had been no time during the cymek attack.

In his office in the heart of the city, Manford was trembling as he listened to the damage and casualty summaries delivered by his deputy, Deacon Harian. The bald deacon was a perfect follower, willing to do anything for the Butlerian movement without remorse or hesitation. Incensed by the cymek attack, Harian had been like a cocked, spring-fired weapon waiting to be released.

Even before the fires were extinguished, Harian shouted, "We must retaliate,

Leader Torondo! Let me take our ships to Kolhar immediately to hit Venport. We will attack the heart of his stronghold, just as he struck us."

Manford considered this, then refused. "That is exactly how our enemy will expect us to respond: Last night's attack may have been meant to provoke us. The Directeur will have defenses we cannot break through. Even the Emperor is afraid to strike him on Kolhar."

"Our holy army is stronger and more dedicated than the Imperial forces," Harian insisted. "Our followers are willing to die for you. Give us the order, beloved Leader. We will destroy that monster, whatever the cost."

"You will all die in the attempt," Manford said.

Harian lifted his chin. "Then we will all become martyrs."

Manford knew the value of martyrs, but he still shook his head as he sat propped up behind his desk. "That would be a reckless waste of lives." How he longed to unleash these people, to throw them at the enemy by the hundreds of thousands, by the millions—but Directeur Venport also had fighters, as well as advanced weapons and warships, and Manford didn't wish to squander his people that way. "We will strike at a time of *my* choosing—when we are fully assured of victory. We will not be drawn into a trap."

As word of the cowardly cymek attack spread across Lampadas, more Butlerians came to Empok. Deacon Harian dispatched messages across the Imperium to other Butlerian-held planets, spreading and exaggerating the news, which would arouse countless more followers—and, in so doing, would strengthen the Butlerian movement.

Josef Venport had made a grave mistake by attacking here.

Manford kept his public reaction hard and cold, not allowing even Anari Idaho to see how much the disaster affected him. Not only had Venport struck him here—*here* on Lampadas!—the man had used cymek nightmares from the past. Venport no longer even bothered to hide his alliance with the thinking machines. The collusion was right there for all to see. Manford had hated Josef Venport for a long time, but this appalled him.

Overly protective now, Anari refused to let him out of her sight. The Swordmaster had not slept in two days. Her face looked haggard, her eyes shadowed; she carried her sword, ready to face an army of cymeks single-handedly. She had always vowed to lay down her life for his, but the giant walkers proved that even she wasn't equipped to defend him.

"This is a blessing. We have been shown that we are not sufficiently prepared," she said. Her stony façade did not completely cover her fear, and Manford knew her well enough to see it. "We survived, and now we can reassess our defenses on Lampadas. Our people are not strong enough to fight those machine monsters—and Venport will send more of them against us. This time it was three; next time it could be thirty, or three hundred."

Manford clung to what he knew was true. "Don't underestimate us, either, Anari. Our followers have a weapon that Venport cannot comprehend." He gestured for her to strap on the harness so he could ride on her shoulders. "Come outside. Let me show you." She did as he instructed.

He had called a rally to reassure his followers, and throngs filled the city, countless people swarming into the open spaces in Empok. Now, as Anari carried him out of the office building and down the street to the raised speaking platform, he drank in the vast, astonishing, and intimidating sea of faces. Riding tall on her shoulders, he felt strength and confidence swell within her.

When the Butlerians spotted him, the roar sounded loud enough to crack the sky. Anari had to anchor herself against the outcry—jubilation that Manford had survived, mixed with outrage at what their enemy had dared. Manford allowed himself a smile, knowing he could channel the people's energy with a single word, a slight gesture. At his slightest whim, the Butlerians could become a devastating army, and he just needed to aim them properly.

As he and Anari stood on the platform at the center of the storm of cheers, Manford no longer felt weak; he felt invincible. When the waves of applause went on and on, he leaned down, placed his lips close to Anari's ear. "*This* is what Venport doesn't understand—what he and his machine lovers will never have. The love these people have for me is real; it is not artificial."

He raised his hands to call for silence, and the noise faded away like a rumbling, diminishing thunderstorm. Manford had not planned this speech ahead of time, but the words came anyway. He knew what his people needed to hear, and inspiration did not fail him now.

Proud, determined, and fully in control of the Sisterhood, Valya gazed across the women she had summoned to the central grounds of the school complex. Reverend Mothers, Sisters, and young Acolytes all waited to hear her in the chill morning air, standing at attention on an expanse of brittle, blue-green grass. Clouds gathered overhead, threatening snow rather than rain, and the women struggled not to shiver.

Valya stood on a mound, waiting for a male technician to finish adjusting the voice-amplification equipment. Though the Sisterhood trained only women, the school complex hired offworld men to work on construction, maintenance, and low-skill technical duties.

The exercise field was encircled by prefabricated buildings with pitched metal roofs, structures provided by Josef Venport when he had transported the women here after their exile from Rossak. Lately, workmen had been upgrading the prefab buildings. With added insulation and reinforced walls, the buildings were acceptable, though sterile and utilitarian. Valya wanted to keep them as a reminder of the Sisterhood's hard times, when they were in the depths of despair and barely hanging on. Those times were in the past, now that she was Mother Superior. The Sisterhood no longer needed to rely on a generous benefactor.

On the opposite side of the field, a pair of three-story buildings with sturdy stone walls and red tile roofs were under construction—imposing, permanent structures, because Valya intended her Sisterhood to last for millennia. The school was one of many projects in her long-term plan, one that included not only the expansion of the order, but the redemption of her own family. For Valya, the two were not mutually exclusive. She fully intended to achieve both.

When the worker finished adjusting the voice amplifier, Valya dismissed him and focused her attention on the gathered women. Some were already her elite, others would become that in time, while some might not make it at all. But they were all her followers, her *Sisters,* and she felt a certain affection for them, although she knew that love itself was a dangerous weakness. She would have to be careful.

The speaker system carried her words across the silent throng. Some of the audience shivered in the cold, while others were more adept at controlling their metabolisms. "We stand at a critically important time for the Sisterhood. It was Mother Superior Raquella's dying wish that our factions be reunited, the rift healed, and I intend to lead my new Sisterhood united through a bright time of growth and strengthening."

As she spoke, snowflakes fluttered through the air, a few at first, and then a thickening mass. Valya glanced up at the clouds. Perfect. The weather predictions had been accurate.

"We must place more Truthsayers and Sister Mentats in the noble houses of the Landsraad League—make ourselves indispensible to the Imperium. Not only will this generate revenue for us, it will also make us vital to very influential people." She allowed a smile on her face. "But that is only a stepping-stone. We have much greater plans in store."

Snowflakes settled on the attentive Sisters. The Reverend Mothers and Sorceresses could ignore the cold and the wet, but some of the Acolytes struggled against their increasing discomfort. Valya had no sympathy for them; they would have to learn, or die.

"Your training will not be entirely mental and philosophical. I have developed new fighting techniques, which I've taught to many Sisters already. They will now train *you.* You will all be expected to master those skills." *We will never be weak again,* she silently vowed, *not individually nor collectively.* Filled with determination, she remembered how they had been scattered from Rossak by Emperor Salvador and the antitechnology fanatics.

Sister Ullora, one of the Reverend Mothers recently recalled from the Imperial Court, brushed snow from her hood. "Considering the weather, Mother Superior, perhaps this is a day better spent inside with other forms of instruction? Politics? Economics? Memorizing the Azhar Book?" She frowned at the blowing snow. "Some of the Acolytes are suffering."

Valya did not conceal her annoyance. Ullora had been far too loyal to Dorotea and had publicly disparaged Raquella and her "ragtag women" at the new school. Valya's reply was withering. "Combat is neither a courtly dance nor a pleasant, springtime conversation." She added just a hint of her new Voice control. *"You will fight when I command it."*

Ullora flinched, paled, and seemed to shrivel physically. She looked down in shame. The rest of the women showed their faith in Valya. Yes, she had them well in hand. As Mother Superior, she had to be firm with them. "Training may be harsh, but the rewards are worth the effort. We in the Sisterhood are the elite of all women, together as one, closer than any other friendship or loyalty. As individuals, many of you are already deadly warriors. Side by side, we are even stronger."

Several Sisters began to applaud, but Valya dismissed the distraction, wanting no empty cheers. An icy wind cut across the grassy area, and she saw Acolytes securing their robes tightly around their bodies, while others stood still and endured. Snow fell harder now.

"Our Sisters may be assigned to noble houses, but they remain loyal to us and gather intimate information which we can use. The greatest power is the unseen and unexpected power." She heard a murmur of concurrence in the assemblage, saw heads nodding.

"Our focus shall also include powerful business interests, traders, philosophers. Our influence must spread to backwater planets, where we can use indoctrination and conversion methods. Passive or uneducated populations will be swayed most easily."

Cold wind whistled through the voice-amplification system. From control decks, the huddled male technicians adjusted the electronics, so that her words remained powerful and clear.

"We will dispatch specialized Sisters as missionaries to such planets to plant seeds of superstition that can protect the future of the Sisterhood. Because beliefs among such people are often more powerful than knowledge, we will observe their fears and folktales and thus guide them so that they—unknowingly—begin to think *and believe* along lines that are useful to us."

By now, with the heavy snow collecting on the ground, even the Reverend Mothers struggled not to shiver. It was a useful observation. In addition to the many regimes of intellectual and psychological study, each Sister should know how to control every nuance of her body, including her core temperature. Cold such as this should be no more than an inconvenience. Valya noted which ones seemed most able to endure the discomfort and decided to choose them as the women best suited for the challenging work on primitive worlds. They would be the first such missionaries.

All the pieces would fit together, wheels within wheels within wheels. Yes, the Sisters would become so much more than Raquella had ever imagined! The Sisterhood had been whipped too often, had served others too often. The new

Mother Superior would insist that they be *active*, not passive. To outsiders, they would continue to look subservient and useful, but internally they would have their own powerful agenda. Valya's agenda.

We will be invisible, but still strong. We will have the power, not the glory.

She would create a harsher, edgier Sisterhood of women willing to use any tool or weapon they possessed—mental skills, ruthless combat methods, even seduction and manipulation. And the Sisterhood would become an extension of her personal goals for House Harkonnen. As the order advanced, so too would her Great House . . . and the historical injustices committed against her family would be reversed.

She only wished Tula would be part of it, but her sister had gone home, at least temporarily. Tula seemed unsettled, and Valya hoped the young woman would come to her senses quickly, leave her self-imposed exile on Lankiveil, and become a strong member of the Sisterhood again. Tula might need firm encouragement . . . but Valya's patience with her had not run out. Not yet.

In any event, she had discreet operatives who were subtly keeping watch on the girl, just to make sure Tula did nothing foolish. It was best not to take chances.

The wind howled as the storm became a blizzard, but she knew that a far more powerful storm was coming. Valya shouted, "Now strip down to your fighting clothes, all of you. It is time for combat training."

When immersed in the vivid memories of actions I have taken, I can
revel in them or regret them, but I cannot undo them.

            —TULA HARKONNEN, lament written on Chusuk

Though Lankiveil was her home, Tula felt that any sanctuary was only an illusion. She had trouble grasping who she really was anymore, and didn't know how she could find her own purpose in life. Was she her own person, or the Sisterhood's pawn . . . *her sister's* pawn?

Valya had transformed her into a weapon of vengeance, but that weapon had already been fired, and it was time to either reload or discard it.

Tula sat near a warm fire in the Harkonnen great house. Outside, the skies were overcast, and a chill spring wind ruffled the water in the fjord. Her father and his crew had gone out on a three-day fur-whale hunt, but Tula remained home with her mother and brother, Danvis. They were glad to have her home, and Tula felt calmer in their company, although she pretended to be much more content than she actually was. She constantly jumped at shadows, always watching for someone dangerous and unexpected out of the corner of her eye—possibly Vorian or Willem Atreides. She knew they would never let her rest after the bloody scene she had left behind on Caladan.

Tula spun the flywheel of her baliset and toyed with the strings, strumming familiar childhood songs, but the music did little to soothe her heart. Danvis sat down next to her with an uncertain smile. "I remember that one! I forgot that you could play the baliset so well."

"It's been a long time . . . a long time since I've had a reason to play music."

Her brother was sixteen now, with black hair and dark blue eyes. The two of them were as close as brother and sister could be, maybe even as close as Valya and Griffin had been before Vorian Atreides killed him. Now, as Tula's thoughts began to ricochet down that dark hallway, she tried to focus instead on the music, and then on Danvis, who made her realize how sweet and innocent she herself had been before Valya reshaped her into a deadly tool.

Her family had no idea what that training had entailed, how Tula had been taught to use her every manipulative and sexual skill in order to ensnare one particular young man on Caladan: Orry Atreides.

After killing Orry as instructed, Tula had returned to Wallach IX, where she received Valya's deep appreciation, but she'd been disturbed and unhappy instead. Valya clearly didn't understand her mood, nor why Tula wanted to go home to Lankiveil to recuperate. Even here, her family was full of questions about what had happened, where she had been, and what she had done. Tula remained tight-lipped.

"Is Valya coming home soon too?" her mother pressed, cheerful and thinking small.

"Valya is never coming home. She is the Sisterhood's Mother Superior now. She has larger concerns than our welfare."

No matter how she tried, Tula could not hide from her own guilt. She spent a lot of time now with Danvis, who was still her best friend, and he could sense that she was troubled. He wasn't shy about asking questions, even after she told him she didn't want to answer, and he kept pressing. Once, when her agitation made her drop her guard, she let slip, "I got married," then clamped her mouth shut again.

After that, Danvis peppered her with more questions, but she refused to reveal Orry's name or speak about his gentle personality, his foolish-looking smile—and all that blood. Killing the Atreides had been her mission, and Tula had not dared to disappoint her sister. Under other circumstances, though, Tula might actually have grown fond of the young man.

Danvis watched her play the baliset for a long time and then blurted out, "I'm applying for a position in the Imperial Court." The interruption made her falter on the strings of the instrument. He continued in a rush, "Valya used to tell me that she hoped I might do this someday, and I don't want to let her down. I don't want to let House Harkonnen down. It's a great opportunity! Emperor Roderick is filling his staff with members of the Landsraad, and now that our family is stronger, we can regain the political ground we lost."

Since their disgrace at the end of the Jihad, House Harkonnen had suffered hardship on top of hardship—which Valya blamed squarely on Vorian Atreides, although their standing had also fallen because of unwise commercial decisions their father had made. Thanks to a recent infusion of wealth from an unknown benefactor, their family was on solid financial footing again, but Valya had not forgotten her grudge against the Atreides—and she made sure her sister would never forget either.

"I've never been to the Imperial Court," Tula responded to Danvis.

His eyes sparkled. "Won't you tell me where you went instead?"

She concentrated on the baliset, generating a soft melody. "What does it matter? I'm here now, but I can't stay on Lankiveil for long."

Danvis looked disappointed. "Will you go back to the Sisterhood school?"

"No!" she answered, too quickly. Hadn't she done enough? What was she to do now? If she returned to the Sisterhood, Valya would undoubtedly give her another murderous mission. . . . "Please don't ask me any more questions. There are things I can't share, not even with you."

"You're my sister. You shouldn't need to hide anything from me."

"You're right, I shouldn't. But I still have to."

Tula didn't dare tell her brother what she had done, what Valya had *forced* her to do. She had been ruthless in her mission—Valya was proud of her—but ever since fleeing Caladan, Tula had discovered a surprising thing inside: her own conscience. During these days on Lankiveil, she was trying to remove the blindfold of Sisterhood programming.

She retuned to the baliset and began to play a song that the musicians on Caladan had performed for her wedding ceremony. She remembered gazing with well-masked hatred upon Vorian Atreides, who had not recognized her. And young Willem, who looked so proud to see his brother getting married. And Orry beside her . . . handsome, gullible Orry, intoxicated with love and stunned by his apparent good fortune. He had so looked forward to their wedding night—as had Tula, but for different reasons. Such a pity that he had to be an Atreides.

She recalled Orry talking about his dreams, his plans for their long life together. Tula had limited any discussion of their future, because she knew that the future held only death for Orry. She remembered the sweetness of his kisses, the beautiful time they had shared on their wedding night—before she'd stabbed him and slashed his throat, then bounded out through the night streets to hunt down Vorian Atreides as well. She had barely escaped Caladan with her life.

Now she was back in the shelter of her family, but she could not stay here. Vorian and Willem Atreides would surely track her down. Or Valya would. She didn't know which of the two possibilities bothered her more.

Her mother emerged from the kitchen, wiping her hands on a towel. "I made honeyflower pastries for dessert. Those were always your favorite." Her mother smiled, but questions burdened her eyes.

Tula felt a wave of nostalgia. If only she could remain here and act like a child again, without a care in the world. "Thank you, Mother. That's very kind."

Since coming home, Tula had been curt with her mother, volatile enough that Sonia Harkonnen knew something was wrong. But Tula couldn't explain anything to her, either.

Danvis jarred her from her thoughts. "You stopped playing."

"What would you like to hear?"

He thought for a moment. "'The Lost Whaler's Song.'"

"That's a sad one."

When her brother shrugged, Tula realized that he was less familiar with sadness than she was. She envied Danvis for his comparative innocence. She had once felt satisfaction in knowing she had a purpose. But everything had changed.

She tried to remain calm, setting the baliset aside. She had been working on a decision in her mind. "I can't stay here. I have to leave again and go far away."

He lowered his voice to a conspiratorial whisper. "Are we in danger? Our family?"

She looked at him long and hard, surprised that he had sensed something. "Possibly. But far less than I am. Demons are chasing me, and I can't get away from them if I stay here. They'll find me." She swallowed hard. "And Valya scares me too."

Danvis looked disturbed, but she couldn't reveal any details that would make it better for him. If she confessed what she had done in the name of House Harkonnen, her brother would be appalled; their parents would be horrified and ashamed of her. Better that she kept it all inside herself.

"Lankiveil isn't where I need to be. I realize that now. I have to find a place without memories for me . . . entirely without memories." She glanced down at the baliset. "I think I'll go to Chusuk. I have heard good things about that world . . ." Her voice trailed off.

Danvis stared, obviously yearning to understand what was wrong with her. He laced his fingers together.

She thought again of how handsome Orry had looked. Tula had awakened in the quietest hour, as planned, and gazed at his peaceful face as he slept, so satisfied and content. So unknowing. She had given him that happiness at least, before completing her mission. His expression had changed terribly as soon as she stabbed him in the chest—

She drove that image from her thoughts, choosing to focus instead on his handsome face, even though Valya insisted the blood was the part she *should* remember, in the name of House Harkonnen.

In Tula's mind, there was no way to make vengeance a pretty picture.

Before long Emperor Roderick will come to his senses and beg me to restore the use of VenHold ships. Without my Navigators, the Imperium will lose too many carriers and people in foldspace; too many missions will fail. It is only a matter of time.

—JOSEF VENPORT, conversation with his wife, Cioba

Now that Vorian had arranged passage on the next outbound spacefolder, they would be leaving Kepler soon. From all indications, this unobtrusive branch of his family was safe; Harkonnen operatives had made no outside inquiries or threats. No one had seen any newcomer matching Tula's description.

He was relieved, but not surprised. His life on this isolated planet had been quiet, unremarkable, and invisible. He had meant to hide from history here for all those years. How would the Harkonnens ever learn of his family's existence here? How would Tula know enough to come here to strike at other members of his family?

It had all seemed far-fetched. And yet Vor needed to see for himself. Ignoring the possible threat to these innocent people was not a mistake he wanted on his conscience. Now, at least, he felt reasonably sure.

He had dispatched anonymous warnings to Atreides households, including an image of the young Harkonnen murderer. Vor couldn't reveal too many details without exposing his or Willem's identities, but at least his extended Kepler family now knew to watch out for her. Tula would never be able to come here and do what she had done to Orry, and Vor was satisfied with that. He and Willem had succeeded.

Now they could go on the offensive.

He felt a warm wistfulness just having seen his family again, remembering happy days here. If circumstances had been different, he could have stayed here without a care for the rest of the Imperium, could have forgotten his past and vanished into obscurity. But it was time to take a more active role beyond just waiting and watching. Willem was right in wanting to hurry things up: They should be tracking down Tula, rather than merely hovering in the shadows on Kepler. Justice needed to be served.

If Tula wasn't actively trying to eliminate Vor's extended family, she might have fled back to the Sisterhood school and the protection of her sister Valya— in which case, he and Willem had little chance of breaching the Wallach IX defenses. Or perhaps she had returned home to the Harkonnen holdings on Lankiveil—Vor felt that was their best chance. He decided that was the next place to go.

He had spent time on Lankiveil, so he knew where to look. In a noble but clumsy attempt to salve his conscience, he had secretly saved the embittered family from financial disaster. Vor had spent time with Vergyl Harkonnen, tried hard to make amends for the setbacks that Abulurd's disgrace had caused them . . . not that he would expect any thanks from the Harkonnens even if they knew the truth. He had wanted the feud to end. He had just wanted peace.

But now Orry's blood, splashed all over the honeymoon bed, made peace impossible, at least until Tula paid for her crime. To that end, Vor and Willem would go to Lankiveil and search, and if they did not find her there, they would continue to hunt wherever the clues took them.

Willem's dark eyes flashed with anger. "Even if she isn't there, we can hurt her family. Make Tula feel the pain she inflicted on me. None of the Harkonnens are innocent."

Vor placed a firm hand on the young man's shoulder and shook his head. "Tula is the one who killed your brother, not the others. We Atreides have honor."

"Even if the Harkonnens do not?"

Vor narrowed his eyes, leaned closer. "Even if the Harkonnens do not. Tula needs to face justice, but we won't harm the rest of her family for what she did. I refuse to stoke the flames of this feud. It needs to end."

Willem scowled. "Orry paid with his life because of something *you* did a long time ago."

"I know. And I won't perpetuate that kind of injustice."

Willem was not happy with the decision. He still wanted to harm the Harkonnens, maybe burn down their warehouses or sink a fleet of fur-whale boats, but Vor held firm. "No, I remember Vergyl Harkonnen—Tula's father, *Griffin's* father—and I won't destroy an innocent man because of his unfortunate bloodline. I don't want to commit the same crime Tula did." He lowered his voice. "There's been too much collateral damage already. We won't sink to their level."

During the brief time the two men had spent working the buriak orchards,

Vor had either observed or learned about his grown children from a distance, surprised to discover how much had changed. Had he really been gone only two years? He longed to see their expressions and hear their voices; he wanted to tell them the stories of what he had done since Emperor Salvador forced him into exile, but that would put them in danger. It pained him to keep himself hidden from them, but it was better to stay away. They would never know he had watched over them.

For decades—a full life span—he had lived here on Kepler, no longer a hero, just a family man, yet now that life seemed no more than a dream, and this branch of his family had moved on, thriving without him. He wasn't surprised. They all led normal lives, untroubled by Imperial politics or dark schemes of revenge.

Vor was content to let them stay that way. He could go now, confident they were safe. If he and Willem found Tula on Lankiveil, he hoped they would take care of the matter with efficient violence and ensure his family's future safety.

The day before the scheduled arrival of the commercial spacefolder, Vor made a decision that he hoped wouldn't cause trouble. His wistful "nephew" had planned a last date with his local girlfriend, and Vor invited himself along, because he had learned that his sons Clar and Oren would be in town with their children for Clar's fifty-first birthday celebration.

After changing clothes at the end of their shift in the orchards, the two men walked into town. On the way, Willem asked in an irritated tone, "You're not really going to act as my chaperone, are you? This is my last night with Opalla. We'll never see each other again."

"I remember your reputation with the ladies on Caladan." Vor gave him a serious nudge. "Just be careful. In my early days fighting in the Jihad, I myself left many women behind—and probably a fair number of children I never knew about. That's not fair to any of them."

Willem sniffed. "We're not serious. Opalla knew that from the start." Then his expression darkened. "I don't have time for romance until we hunt down Tula. This is just to say goodbye."

⁓❦⁓

THE LARGEST ENTERTAINMENT hall in town had a crowded bar adjacent to an elegant restaurant, from which patrons could watch the gaming floor through large plaz windows. Vor took a seat where he had a view of people arriving, while Willem went off in a dark mood to join his date.

Vor positioned himself where he could watch the entrances, and perked up when his estranged family arrived, his two sons and their spouses, his grand-children. All of them were strangers to him. He made no move to reveal himself and join them, just sat in wistful, longing isolation, hoping distance and his beard would conceal who he was.

He sipped a glass of local white wine, watched them laughing and talking, celebrating Clar's birthday. He tried to read their lips, imagine their conversations. Not that much time had passed since he'd last seen Clar, who was tall and had the hawklike Atreides nose, while Oren looked more like their mother, Mariella. Vor let out a silent sigh.

No one took notice of the quiet stranger at the bar, absorbed in his drink. Vor noted several small children he hadn't seen before—including a pair of baby girls. He wanted to swing them around in the air and make them laugh, wanted to hug his grown children . . . wanted life to be normal again, even ordinary.

After a long moment, he looked away and wiped his eyes. Out on the gaming floor, he saw Willem and the pretty brunette playing a battle game with chips and dice, with two armies lined up against each other on a large table. The young man and his date were laughing, but Vor could tell that he remained wary and vigilant, glancing around every few seconds.

Vor watched his family for another half hour before slipping out a side door and walking back to the ranch alone, letting Willem have the time he wanted.

Tomorrow, they would be off to avenge Orry.

For centuries, the Venports have seen and seized opportunities. We built large spacecraft—first for military purposes, then for commercial transport. We developed shields and foldspace engines. We commercialized the spice industry.

After all we have accomplished and all the adversity we've overcome, I have no interest in hearing your complaints about the inconveniences of this desert environment.

—DIRECTEUR JOSEF VENPORT, letter of reprimand to Combined Mercantiles staff in Arrakis City

K olhar might have been a fortress, but while Josef was preoccupied with defending his headquarters, Arrakis had degenerated into a lawless, dangerous world where various parties fought to control spice production and distribution. The turmoil was causing him to lose business here daily, and that angered him.

He would have to direct more battle-ready ships to Arrakis to ensure that the spice operations did not slip out of VenHold control. The Venport family had spent a great deal of time, money, and blood here, turning the desert world into a highly lucrative holding. Melange came from this world . . . spice . . . and only from here. He did not intend to let Imperial interlopers and black-market parasites take it from him.

Norma Cenva navigated the vessel through foldspace to Arrakis and arrived flawlessly in close orbit around the planet. A disarray of unmarked trading ships cluttered the orbital lanes: blockade runners and smugglers who seized loads of melange, fled on uncharted paths, and then delivered the contraband spice to hungry customer planets because VenHold's own operations had been disrupted.

Emperor Salvador had also placed Imperial troops here in an inept and unsuccessful attempt to take over the planet; a substantial force remained on Arrakis, establishing their own contract spice operations, but those ships, soldiers, and workers were outnumbered, more of a nuisance than a threat. They had the Emperor's authorization, but not the might to back it up.

The new Emperor had kept his troops in place on Arrakis, but he had neither the additional fleet nor reliable foldspace carriers to impose real control.

A handful of Imperial guardian ships remained behind to maintain order as best they could, but the small force could not govern an entire unruly planet. If Josef hadn't diverted so much of his fleet to defend Kolhar, he could have wiped them out entirely.

Nevertheless, Josef's Combined Mercantiles operations on Arrakis were more than enough to thwart the Imperial troops stationed there, and his people were holding their own. There had been skirmishes in the desert against Imperial patrols, flash point struggles that had not erupted into outright war, because neither side dared allow that to happen.

Eventually, Josef would have to expend the effort to oust them, or else consolidate their resources under his own VenHold operations. That would likely provoke Roderick even more, but Josef couldn't ignore what was happening here.

He scowled as he saw the surprising number of ships in orbit. With Venport Holdings declared an outlaw company, these parasites were stealing spice—*his* spice! How much influence and profit was he losing for each day that this nonsense continued?

Although his own small spacefolder had formidable VenHold weapons, it was still only one ship, and he could not single-handedly chase off all these interlopers, much less the Imperial forces. Not today.

"I can at least make a point, though," he muttered.

When he noticed two small smuggler ships racing away, Josef activated his weapons systems and opened fire without warning. One vessel exploded on the first blast, and the second took evasive action, but Josef shot it out of space as well, leaving a cloud of debris. Satisfied, he nodded to Norma in her tank. "Let the rest of them see that." Already some of the other small traders in orbit were scattering, but he had no doubt they would sneak back before long.

Emerging from the other side of the desert planet, two Imperial warships approached, attracted by the weapons fire. Although Josef guessed that he outgunned those large ships as well, he suspected it would be a close fight. *Not today.* Instead, he told Norma to evade them, and they raced over to the night side of Arrakis, where his personal shuttle could drop out of the hold. He had business to do at the headquarters of Combined Mercantiles. Norma would eventually join him, but she could transport herself by folding space with her mind.

As his initial move, Josef intended to create a large spice stockpile, which would provide stability in the melange markets, and then he could devote his efforts to mopping up these operations and chasing away the Imperial interlopers. Maybe that would be the leverage he needed to reach some sort of peace with Roderick Corrino. Restored spice trade would be best for the Imperium, by far.

But if the new Emperor proved to be intractable, Josef might have to take the throne himself, however reluctantly. That was by far the least desirable solution, though. If he seized the Imperial rulership, that would, no doubt, cause countless headaches and bring him very few genuine rewards. Still, "Emperor Josef Venport" had a nice ring to it. . . .

Flying his shuttle down to Arrakis City, he had to remain alert for local traffic that flew in unregulated patterns. No one gave him guidance for landing in the spaceport, so he chose his own spot and set down without incident. When he disembarked, his first breath of the bitterly arid air scoured his throat and lungs.

Because water was so extraordinarily expensive on this planet, locals fitted themselves with desert survival suits and moisture-reclamation units, but Josef hated those things and refused to wear one. He was not flaunting his wealth and power—he just disliked the inconvenience.

As he made his way to the Combined Mercantiles headquarters he studied the city with its insulated shops, moisture-sealed doors, window coverings to shade from the raging sun. Ragged, dust-covered people moved through the streets with their heads down. Arrakis City had degenerated substantially since his last time here. That would have to change. So many things to take care of once he secured his operations. . . .

He arrived at the headquarters of Combined Mercantiles and saw that a veritable army of guards was stationed outside. Mercenary troops huddled in sealed pillbox turrets, alert for bandits or, more likely, a move by Imperial forces.

He was glad to see the security. He chose only his most trusted administrators to run the spice operations. Before the crisis had forced him to reassign his Mentat to more pressing matters, Draigo Roget had been in charge here, a model of efficiency. Josef felt another flash of anger over how dramatically the situation had changed. If only Salvador had left well enough alone and focused his efforts against the Butlerians!

After passing through all the layers of security, Josef was wryly amused to watch Norma Cenva's tank simply appear in the meeting chamber with a rush of displaced air.

The two Mentat administrators, Rogin and Tomkir, had begun their training under Gilbertus Albans and then transitioned to final instruction under Draigo Roget. The two men were around the same age, though Tomkir's skin was much darker, and Rogin's complexion had been ravaged by the pockmarks of disease. They had already assembled summary data for him to peruse.

The third man in the meeting room looked furtive and out of place. He was thin and dirty, as if he had been left in the sun to dry out from a storm, and he regarded Norma's tank with superstitious horror.

Josef knew about the desert people on Arrakis, tribes that haughtily called themselves the "Freemen," although their freedom on this dry, bleak world seemed more miserable than the civilized slavery from which they had escaped more than a century ago. Yet he knew the desert wanderers had been useful before, and he expected that Rogin and Tomkir had enlisted this man for the important new stockpile project.

Tomkir indicated the desert man. "Modoc here was about to depart after delivering his report, Directeur, but we prevented him from doing so. We thought you would like to meet him."

Rogin interjected, "Thanks to Modoc's tribe, we will have an established, secure location that we can repurpose for the facility you requested."

The desert man shrank away from Norma's mutated, naked body drifting in the spice gases. "You captured a demon?" He looked up with his unnaturally blue eyes, caused by a lifetime of spice ingestion. "Are we safe from it?"

"She is my great-grandmother," Josef said. "Her mind can encompass the entire universe in ways that your desert gods could never comprehend."

Modoc took a tentative step forward, fascinated. "I always laughed at my brother Taref for imagining so many fantastical things. I didn't believe him."

Josef raised his eyebrows. "You are from Taref's tribe?" He remembered the desert operative he had trained, and trusted—for a time. Until the man had simply abandoned his responsibilities and walked away.

Modoc lifted his chin, gazed at him with irritation. "I am the Naib of my sietch, and yes, Taref was cast out. He was worthless, of no more use to my people."

"He was of no use to me, either," Josef muttered. He remembered that the man's guilt and silly superstitions had driven him mad, and he had wandered off into the desert. "Taref told us you had no interest in civilization or spice production, and that it was futile to negotiate with you."

With a shake of his head, Modoc said, "That was when my father served as Naib, but thanks to his recent and fortuitous death, I am the leader now. And your representatives here"—he nodded toward the two Mentat administrators—"offered our tribe an extraordinary amount of your foreign money . . . money that allows us to obtain certain things."

Rogin said, "We bought their sietch outright, Directeur—an entire cave city in the deep desert. They have kept it hidden and secure for generations. It will make a perfect protected location." The Mentats were careful not to explain what exactly Josef intended to do with this place.

"That doesn't sound like a bargain the Freemen would make. Abandoning their sietch for any amount of money?" He looked at the desert man. "Where will you go?"

Modoc merely shrugged. "The desert has countless hiding places, and we know where to find them. Our scouts discovered another network of caves even farther out in the Tanzerouft, so we will move there. We can build a new sietch, outfit the caves, install moisture seals. Our tribe will live as before, but now we will also have great wealth." He spread his callused hands on the clean metal table and smiled. "As Naib, I made the most pragmatic decision."

From inside her tank, Norma said, "Prepare Modoc's sietch quickly. Fill it with spice for my Navigators. A large stockpile is necessary for our security." Her inhuman voice startled them.

Josef flashed a surprised look at Norma. He had not intended to reveal to this desert man that the facility would be a spice bank. "We have not yet determined what we will put inside the storehouse."

"Spice for my Navigators," Norma said. "Enough to last for years."

The Freeman faced her, strangely delighted to hear the mutated woman speak from the tank. "My tribe is already preparing to move out, and we will leave our old caves for you. I will guide your representatives there. You'll be satisfied, I promise. You can store all the spice you like."

Josef hardened his voice. "I did not say what the sietch will be used for."

Modoc narrowed his eyes in a cagy expression. "Come now, Directeur. Such a secure facility would only be used to store something of great value. On Arrakis, that means either spice or water, and since I know you offworlders do not place the proper value on water, then I assume you would fill my sietch with spice, just like the many spice silos and guarded vaults you already have." He grinned, looking flippant. "But my people can go out into the desert and glean whatever spice we need for ourselves, and with your money, we can purchase all the water we desire."

Josef grumbled, wondering what it would take to buy this man's silence. He even considered killing him.

Yet if Josef drove out the Imperial guardians that Roderick had left here, and placed enough VenHold security around the planet, as well as around the spice bank, no one would be able to threaten it. He wasn't worried about a few bandits and black marketeers.

Modoc continued, annoyingly persistent. "So much melange! My sietch is large and spacious, Directeur. How will you ever get all that spice?"

Tomkir said, "We are running feasibility studies. The amount of spice the facility would hold is indeed beyond our present production capabilities."

Josef announced, "Then we acquire spice in other ways. Increase our raids on Imperial ships and spice silos, seize any available melange in Arrakis City and in desert outposts. Divert part of our exports to the stockpile and blame the shorter supply on the present turmoil in the Imperium, which will also drive up prices. Our spice bank will be complete in no time." Grinning, he turned back to the tank. "Grandmother, we will then be safe against any crisis that cuts off our supply."

Modoc looked perplexed and amused. "Like my brother Taref, I do not understand offworlder foolishness. What is the point of hoarding spice in an empty sietch, when one can simply go out into the desert and gather more? There will always be spice."

Josef's respect for the desert man diminished. "I have encountered enough obstacles that I no longer believe in the concept of infinite resources."

He does not suffer from a lack of ambition; rather, his ambition is con-
trolled and rational.

—From "Prince Roderick Corrino," a biographical sketch

I n his fur-lined ceremonial cloak, Roderick felt too warm on the blocky
throne. Carved from an immense green crystal, it had been fashioned into
this impressive seat for Emperor Faykan Corrino after the Battle of Corrin; the
throne was intended to awe and impress the frayed survivors of humanity as they
rebuilt their civilization.

The Imperial Audience Chamber was also ostentatious with gilded mold-
ings, frescoes, glaxene chandeliers, and a marblene floor, but—as with the Imperial barge with which he had launched General Roon's strike force—Roderick
understood that such trappings represented authority and the perception of
stability.

A line of carefully screened supplicants moved toward the elevated throne,
escorted by uniformed guards. His new Truthsayer Fielle stood on one side, an
imposing woman in her black robe. The scowl on her fleshy face and the intensity of her gaze seemed designed to intimidate anyone who might utter a lie in
the Emperor's presence.

Roderick knew he needed to quash Josef Venport's defiance before it was
widely seen as a rebellion, but he had heard nothing yet from Vinson Roon . . .
which added another knot of tension. By now the surprise strike force had surely
attacked Kolhar. Perhaps the mop-up operations were taking longer than expected, but the General should have sent a courier back immediately. Directeur
Venport had made no outraged announcements, nor were there any reports of
a great space battle, nor had Venport sent gloating messages of victory, and the
silence filled Roderick's head with imagined disasters.

If all went as planned, the force should have been more than sufficient to deal with VenHold defenses. *If all went as planned.*

If Roon's battle group had been defeated or captured, however, the damage to the Imperial Armed Forces would be severe. Those ships comprised a significant portion of Roderick's home defenses, and he had gambled them in a surprise attack. It was as if the strike force had tumbled into a void in space.

Roderick hated to feel helpless. As Emperor, he should be the most powerful man on countless worlds, but he was being pulled in opposite directions by Manford Torondo and Josef Venport, caught between the two dangerous extremes.

How he had suffered because of those two men! Venport's insatiable commercial ambitions had led to the murder of Roderick's brother, while out-of-control Butlerian mobs had trampled his beautiful daughter to death. His sister had gone missing when Butlerians overthrew the Mentat School on Lampadas, and Manford Torondo was likely to blame, although the Butlerian leader flatly denied any knowledge of Anna's fate. A lie? Probably, but there was no proof.

Neither of those monstrous leaders accepted responsibility for the tragedies they had caused. In order to secure his rightful power and influence, Roderick needed to cancel out both extremes. How perfect it would be if Manford Torondo and Josef Venport could simply be induced to eliminate each other. . . .

This scheduled court appearance was a distraction, but he knew that holding the fabric of government together required finesse as well as power, and the various nobles and businessmen needed access to their Emperor in order to keep peace in the highest ranks of society.

Roderick leaned back on his throne and faced his visitors. This morning the supplicants were a colorful assortment from many planets. Some carried documents—petitions for him to review, or proposed changes in laws on their worlds. He noticed that Fielle listened carefully to each visitor, filing away her thoughts, which she would dispense in a later report to him. As his new Truthsayer, she seemed determined to be thorough.

Roderick also listened to complaints, issuing his counsel, opinions, and judgments. He always tried to be fair-minded and respectful, graciously accepting the gifts they brought from distant worlds.

Next in line came four rough-looking people, and something about them caught Roderick's attention. The leader was tall and broad, a singularly unattractive woman with a rough face and curly black hair that was thin in patches. In contrast with her more ragtag companions, she wore a wondrous cape that had the form and movement of fabric, but shimmered like an alloy of metal and crystal. The cape captured distorted reflections of the chamber as it flowed, as if alive. Behind her, the woman's companions carried a gilded chest, which had been thoroughly inspected by his guards.

The bearers set the chest on the first step of the dais, and the leader bowed. "Sire, I am Korla of Corrin." She smiled. "Yes, *Corrin*, where the thinking machines made their last stand against humanity. My people settled among the ruins to reclaim those once-glorious cities. Some call me the Queen of Trash, but my people have salvaged many unique and valuable materials." She tugged on the marvelous, swirling cloak so that it created a hypnotic dance of colors. "This fine flowmetal cape is but one example."

Her companions opened the chest to reveal another cape inside. Korla removed it, held up the shimmering metallic garment, and Roderick leaned forward to see facets within facets, prisms within prisms, and an incredible array of shifting colors. The nearest courtiers gasped as they watched the spellbinding play of light and color, and Roderick smiled, knowing that Salvador would have been overjoyed.

Pleased by the reaction, Korla took a step closer. "Sire, this cape is an item of salvaged flowmetal. It is my gift to you. Would you like to try it on?"

The guards closed in, suspicious, but Roderick glanced at the Truthsayer, who was intent on Korla's words, tone, and demeanor. "I sense no outright danger, Sire. She sincerely intends to honor you with this gift."

Roderick reached out to touch the cloak, feeling the slick, tingly metallic fabric. The Queen of Trash lowered her husky voice. "I have reason to believe this garment may once have been worn by the robot Erasmus himself."

The Emperor flinched at the name of one of the most monstrous villains in history and pulled back his hand. Then he remembered, and said, "I have seen historical images that show him wearing something similar."

Korla backed down to the main floor, and her companions began removing more objects from the open chest—metallic shapes, some smooth and bulky, others warped by the tremendous heat of a nuclear attack. "Even damaged, these are valuable artifacts, trophies from a vanquished enemy. As humanity's leader, you should have them." Korla draped the marvelous cape on top of the open chest.

Many in the crowded audience chamber muttered, nervous to see relics of the abhorrent thinking machines. Roderick knew that when Manford Torondo learned about them, he would demand that the Emperor discard all the relics as unclean. His followers would insist that he purge them from the palace, and that Roderick himself undergo some kind of ritual cleansing.

The thoughts brought a wave of anger to him. *I am the Emperor. A group of fanatics cannot dictate my decisions.* He smiled at the Queen of Trash. "You have indeed brought me fine gifts, Korla—reminders that we defeated the thinking machines, not the other way around."

Roderick dismissed her. Korla and her fellow scavengers backed away from the throne. Guards folded the flowmetal cape, handling it cautiously, and tucked it back inside the chest, which they carried away. . . .

Hours later, when the visitors and courtiers had left, Roderick sat alone on the great throne, letting his thoughts wander out into the vastness of the Imperium. Fielle moved so subtly and silently that he was not aware that she had stepped closer. He saw great concern in her dark eyes. "You performed admirably today, Sire, but I noticed signs that you are troubled. I surmise that you are grappling with the intractable Butlerians? Or is it Venport's rebellion?"

Roderick scowled. "I can deal with the fanatics as soon as Venport is neutralized . . . but I fear something terrible has happened to General Roon's strike force." He slammed a fist down on the arm of the throne. "I had expected this to be over by now."

Fielle responded with an odd, knowing smile. "There may be another way to damage Directeur Venport, without a large military investment." He looked at her, waiting for her to speak. "As I mentioned earlier, *spice* is his real vulnerability, Sire. He needs it not only for his commercial enterprises, but for the creation and sustenance of his Navigators. He continues his operations on Arrakis with impunity, even though you have an Imperial force there."

"That force is too small to be effective, and I am not in a position to prosecute a full-scale war on Arrakis." *Especially if Roon's strike force is gone.* "I'd like to know what's really happening there, though. If Venport is expending all his resources to defend Kolhar, then does he have any vulnerabilities on Arrakis?" He feared, though, that the opposite was more likely the case—that Venport could divert his own military might and overthrow the Imperial forces. Spice, and that damned desert planet, had been at the root of this whole mess.

"Arrakis has as many opportunities as vulnerabilities, Sire. I may have suggestions that could be useful." Fielle gave him another peculiar, mysterious smile. "With your permission, let me look into the matter before giving you a firm recommendation. Never underestimate the eyes of the Sisterhood." The woman bowed and left the throne room.

The mind of a Mentat is no trivial thing.
It can become a deadly weapon.
—GILBERTUS ALBANS, late Headmaster of the Mentat School

Erasmus noted a metallic ring to his voice as it emanated from the speakers on a custom tray attached to his memory core. "Be careful not to jostle me." The system obviously needed adjusting.

Dutifully, Anna carried his gelsphere through the large cymek assembly hangar. His memory core also had a new sensory module developed by Dr. Danebh and inspired by the work of Ptolemy, which could supposedly simulate all five human senses, though it was a poor substitute, and not at all the same as having his own body. Erasmus had been detached, inefficient, and *helpless* for too long.

At first, Danebh's new sensory module had worked passably well, but the distortions and exaggerated responses had grown progressively worse over the past several days. Now, each jarring move sent a resonating feedback of signals into his core.

Anna sounded guilty. "I am so sorry. I don't mean to hurt you."

"Of course you don't," he replied, then added, "I appreciate your efforts." The words had a soothing effect on her. He had become adept at intercepting potential emotional crises.

"What else can I do, Erasmus? I want to help."

He had studied this young woman enough to know that she *needed* to help him, needed to be with him. Their relationship had come to define her existence. At first the idea had been interesting and gratifying, exactly as he had programmed her to be, but now it had become more of a challenge. He had made Anna this way, out of the wreckage of her mind, but he now realized he would have found an independent personality to be far more interesting. "Just locate

Administrator Noffe so I can discuss my needs with him. Then we will go to my own laboratory, where conditions are better."

Danebh had designed the sensory module to keep Erasmus satisfied so that he would continue to provide the Denali researchers with exhaustive information. The robot had intended to do so in any case, to help destroy the Butlerian fanatics who had killed Gilbertus, but he did not mind bargaining for something he wanted.

"This new module is inferior to anything that was available to me on Corrin. In particular, the simulated olfactory senses are extreme and distracting." What he really wanted was a mobile and efficient new body. Perhaps even a biological one. And now it was time to ask.

Anna wrinkled her nose. "I don't like the smells on Denali either. This building is not as well sealed as others. Stink leaks in from the outside air."

She was so easily distractible. He reminded her of her current task. "Have you found Administrator Noffe yet, Anna? It is important to me."

She turned around, searching among the busy scientists working on the machine walkers that were being readied for the major Lampadas strike. In the high bay, a matrix of elevated walkways granted workers access to the towering machines. Finally, she pointed to where technicians were accessing the connections inside an open armored fighting body.

A smaller, dronelike walker carried Administrator Noffe's brain canister so that he could observe the operations. The Tlulaxa Dr. Danebh worked with him, tinkering with a walker's thoughtrode connections.

"Take me up there," Erasmus said. "The administrator can make the decision, and Danebh can advise."

Carrying the memory core on a special detachable tray, Anna boarded a lift platform that raised her to the secondary catwalk, where Danebh and Noffe were discussing adjustments to the thoughtrode linkages. Danebh looked up, and Noffe's cymek form swiveled to focus on them.

Erasmus said without preamble, "My sensory module suffers from flares, distortions, and feedback. The distractions make it difficult for me to ponder weapons concepts from the Synchronized Empire."

Noffe said, "Your information has already been valuable. We have sent your designs back to Kolhar for large-scale manufacturing."

"And I intend to provide even better information. I have many centuries of memories to impart, but my present form is no longer viable for optimal functionality. My memory core has been vulnerable for far too long. Therefore, I require something more appropriate from you—to benefit all of us."

Danebh looked at the exposed gelsphere and the array of enhanced sensors. "I can make some adjustments and build an armored case around your core."

"No need for that, Erasmus," Anna interjected. "I'll protect you."

"That is not good enough! I have been a vulnerable gelsphere for eight decades, listening to one excuse after another. If I am to continue my work, I require a physical form. Surely with all the technology available on Denali, you can provide me with a useful body."

"I would like Erasmus to have a body," Anna added with building excitement. "I would like that very much."

Erasmus ignored her, as did Noffe and Danebh. The cymek administrator answered in his artificial voice, "I know the simulated sensations you have are far from adequate. Perhaps we could find a standard robot body, a combat mek or worker mek to accommodate your memory core. In that form, you would be more independent and able to conduct research much more efficiently."

"That would be an improvement, but still unsatisfactory." Erasmus remembered when Gilbertus had given him a cumbersome old fighting robot to test, and Erasmus had been so ecstatic about the sensations that he'd ruined the machine body in the Lampadas swamps. "I prefer something more sophisticated than a robot body. I am entitled to it." He directed his words to Dr. Danebh. "My primary body on Corrin was a marvelous flowmetal construction capable of expressions, full movement, sensitive responses to external stimuli. It would be too great a challenge to re-create something similar here. However, I have observed Tlulaxa cloning abilities. Considering the limitations, a biological tank-grown body would be my preference—a human form at long last."

Anna's surprise was so uncontrolled that she jostled his tray, but the sphere remained secure. She exclaimed: "That would be wonderful!"

Erasmus wanted to feel human, truly *human*. For so many centuries, studying the species had been his obsession, and that journey of understanding had also been frustrating. He only had an inkling of what it meant to be a mortal person. He could not quite grasp all the nuances, and the gaps in his understanding were maddening, yet he kept his voice calm. "I would find it appropriate and useful."

Danebh's eyes narrowed as he considered the question. "My own specialty is the interface between man and machine, thoughtrodes connecting a human mind to artificial components. It is all based on Dr. Ptolemy's work. A machine memory core with a biological body . . . Combining the two would be quite a challenge, but Ptolemy could offer his assistance."

Administrator Noffe moved his little mechanical cart. "My brain was removed from my damaged body, and my situation is much improved now. I can connect to any mechanical form I like. Is it possible to link a robot mind to a human body? All the nerves, the tissues, the muscle control . . ."

Smiling, Anna pressed her face closer to his gelsphere. She sounded warm and sincere. "I enjoy talking with your memory core, but I would rather have *you*. In the flesh."

As he pondered the question, Danebh began talking quickly. "It will not be simple, but the principle is sound. The gelsphere contains an extremely sophisticated mind. When a clone body is grown in a tank, it is a blank slate, an empty cellular structure. I see no fundamental reason why a pristine brain can't be replaced by the gelsphere." He smiled. "Yes, it might be done. Let me consider how we might implement such a procedure."

Erasmus felt satisfied with the discussion, thus far. "I look forward to it."

Next, he had to choose the proper body to be grown for him, something that he would be proud to wear as his physical form. The Tlulaxa scientists could grow a body from any cells, living or dead. Erasmus had analyzed human bodies for centuries, studying them, dissecting them, even vivisecting them. He knew the differences, strengths, and weaknesses. He did not wish to be in a small-statured Tlulaxa form, but there were many other workers and scientists here at Denali. Many cells to choose from.

After studying the research dome databases, however, he discovered that Draigo Roget had managed to preserve a few last cells from Gilbertus Albans—hair follicles found on his garments from when he had tried to rescue the Headmaster from his Butlerian captors.

Erasmus knew exactly which body he wanted the Tlulaxa to grow for him. It would be perfect.

Since Manford's cottage had been destroyed by cymeks, Anari found him an adequate and defensible replacement home, with rooms designed for Manford's mobility whenever he walked on his hands. When she commandeered it, the owners were only too happy to surrender the dwelling to the Butlerian leader.

After night fell, Anari checked the perimeter of the house and then left Manford to rest and meditate. He remained alone in his new quarters with the few possessions that had been salvaged from the rubble of his destroyed residence. One of those rescued items was the small icon painting of Rayna Butler, chipped and scratched but still beautiful. He knew that the saintly woman's spirit was watching over him. Rayna had given a young Manford his mission in life, had led him and trained him, and now he stared at her beautiful visage, her soul-filled eyes. After a moment of indecision, he turned the icon facedown. He could not let holy Rayna Butler see what he was about to do.

After listening to silence for a few moments, gathering his courage, Manford took out his most frightening possession, the laboratory journals of the evil robot Erasmus, which had been found on devastated Corrin eight decades ago.

Anari was afraid of the books and would have liked to burn them, but she didn't dare defy Manford's orders; he insisted on keeping them, studying them. Even if his loyal Swordmaster didn't understand why, *Manford* needed to read the terrifying yet insightful writings for himself.

He was horrified, yet fascinated by the thoughts of the sadistic thinking machine and the descriptions of what he did in his documented experiments on human beings. As Manford read, he felt like a rodent caught in the hypnotic gaze of a serpent. Tortures, experiments, analysis—some appallingly wrong, yet many conclusions seemed frightening and apt.

In the quiet night after most of the residents of Empok had bedded down, Manford read the robot's strange musings. Erasmus had coldly dissected and vivisected countless human beings without remorse. He considered every experiment to be necessary scientific research for his own understanding of mankind. For the independent robot, it had been an obsessive pursuit, with the ends justifying the means to attain them—though he had never fully succeeded. His target, his prey, was elusive and constantly outdistancing him.

Manford had already read these journals several times, and was sickened by them, but he was also convinced the difficult task was necessary so that he could understand the enemy's twisted thought processes. It made Manford feel superior, even smug, to know that despite all of the robot's research and all the pain he'd inflicted, Erasmus had never acquired even the most basic comprehension of the human soul. . . .

Wealth and power are measured by whether one can take an important thing away from those who desire it.

—DIRECTEUR JOSEF VENPORT, financial
briefing memo, Venport Holdings

After Josef had purchased the isolated sietch outright, Modoc's people packed up and prepared to depart. They would find another home out in the deep Tanzerouft, and the new VenHold spice bank would be hidden and secure out in the most barren wilderness on Arrakis.

Although Josef was impatient to see the sietch, his inspection expedition was delayed when the satellites predicted inhospitable weather. "An impending Coriolis storm, Directeur," said the Mentat Rogin. "It would not be safe to take fliers out there. Even the black marketeers have hunkered down until it passes."

Josef narrowed his gaze, looked out on the sands, saw dust clouds in the distance. "Have the spice crews been withdrawn?"

"Many of them," said Tomkir, "but some are risking it on the fringe of the projected storm path. They work on commission."

"But the Freemen are going away unprotected?"

"The desert people are often irrational. And yet they survive."

Josef frowned. "What about the spice crews working under Imperial contract?"

"Three Imperial operations are still working, despite the weather. It's possible they are very brave and willing to take such great risk. More likely, they simply don't have access to our weather satellites, and are unaware of the danger they're in."

Josef stroked his mustache. "So they are vulnerable—I can't pass up such an opportunity. We have a significant mercenary fighting force, and it's time to use them. Launch a raid immediately to strike those Imperial operations, seize whatever spice they've harvested, and destroy the equipment and crew." He shrugged. "Easily explainable as storm damage."

As his Mentats scrambled to implement the orders, Josef glanced at Norma's sealed Navigator tank while she spoke. "We will use the additional spice to fill the vaults in our new stockpile."

The storms whipped through the desert, exactly as predicted. Josef's mercenary commandos slipped in to attack the Imperial crews without mercy. They jammed communications so the contract workers could not transmit an alarm, although static from the wind-borne sand was sufficient to block most signals anyway. The Imperial guardian ships in orbit were unaware of the disaster that had wiped out their ground crews.

Josef considered it excellent progress.

With a series of rapid strikes as the storm worsened, VenHold commandos destroyed the harvesters and seized a significant haul of melange. Once he consolidated his military forces, he would engage in overt strikes against the rest of the Imperial operations, but he wasn't ready to do that yet. In this particular case, the storms gave him plausible deniability, and Emperor Roderick could not retaliate. It was a risk Josef considered worth taking.

⤜⧽

WHEN THE STORMS finally passed and the confiscated spice had been cached in various hidden holding vaults, Josef insisted on going out to inspect his new spice bank. By now, the Freemen had abandoned the caves, and Modoc would be waiting there to turn over the site, and to receive his final payment.

Under cover of night, when there was less chance they would be seen by the few remaining Imperial patrols, an expedition cruised low above the desert and flew for hours out into the great emptiness. Josef transmitted ahead for the Naib to meet them, but when the desert-rigged fliers landed in a sheltered basin surrounded by high, moonlit rocks, they saw no sign of life. The stronghold looked desolate and empty. When they received no response, Josef began to grow uneasy. What if Modoc had betrayed him, taken the payoff, and given him false coordinates?

Before he could formulate a retaliation, two of his guards spotted movement up in the rocks, and several figures in camouflaged desert cloaks crawled out of cracks where they had hidden. The shadowy figures approached in the moonlight, and he was relieved to see that one of them was Modoc. "You have come to inspect your new desert fortress, Directeur?" He looked around warily. "You didn't bring the demon in her tank this time?"

"She travels where and when she wishes."

The desert man chuckled. "Even more mysterious! I told my comrades that I had seen her appear out of thin air, and they did not believe me. But when they saw the wealth I brought to our tribe, they no longer questioned my claims."

Modoc gestured to his companions, who flitted among the rocks. Josef's private guards emerged from their fliers and took positions to protect the Directeur.

The Naib gestured, showing off his sietch. "The sheltered walls keep us safe from sandworms. Shai-Hulud knows of this place, but He cannot enter. You have seen a sandworm before?"

"Yes, I watched my cymek machines destroy one of them."

Modoc grinned, and his comrades chuckled. "Ho! Now you say things that even I cannot believe."

"I don't care whether you believe it." Josef strode forward. "Show me my spice bank."

Modoc clapped his hands and yelled at the desert people. "The Directeur is waiting!"

Josef's guards kept their weapons at hand, but the desert people seemed unconcerned about any threat from these outsiders. Together, they climbed a rugged thread of trail that was clearly visible in the light of First Moon; they picked their way among the rocks, slipping through cracks so narrow that Josef was forced to turn sideways and inch his way along. These places would have to be widened with explosives so that his people could move materials in and out efficiently. He felt tense and vulnerable—if this was an ambush, his party was doomed.

The group passed through a narrow defile where rugged rock walls towered on either side of them, their way illuminated now by glowglobes. Finally they emerged into an open warren of caves where hundreds of shadowy people moved about in the dim light, packing up belongings, emptying out chambers, draining every last drop of hoarded water from reservoirs.

"I thought you said the place was ready," Josef said.

"Most are gone, but a few still linger, clinging to the past." Modoc sniffed. "This was our home for many generations. Naib Rurik, my father, never wanted any change. He would have buried himself in the sand rather than accept any comforts from outside."

Some Freemen grumbled as they departed. Sensing their displeasure, Josef frowned. "You said your people agreed with this decision to give over these caves to me."

Modoc seemed proud. "I am their Naib. They do as I say."

As Josef looked around, he was satisfied with the secure location. This sietch had never been detected by his company's overflights or census scans; therefore, he was confident it would stay hidden as his fortress stockpile. Combined Mercantiles could fill it with enough melange to ride out any shortage or political turmoil. Arrakis was his most fortified planet, and this stockpile would be the most fortified place on the surface.

Emperor Roderick understood the value of spice production—even the fool Salvador wasn't blind to the outrageous profits—but the Imperial Armed Forces were inferior to the advanced warships that Venport Holdings could bring to bear, and Josef had just dealt a crippling blow to the Imperial forces.

For the time being, though, Roderick would likely target Kolhar, assuming it to be the heart of Josef's operations, but Arrakis was so much more important. Always spice . . .

Once commerce got back to normal, after this problem with the vengeful Emperor was resolved one way or another, Josef would build additional secure stockpiles on other planets, and distribute the supplies as well as the risk. For now, they would keep loading melange here in the abandoned sietch, far from prying eyes.

Many of the caves were natural chambers and tunnels, while others had been carved by hand out of the desert stone. All of them would be mapped, catalogued, and filled with concentrated spice. His Combined Mercantiles operations already had seventeen dispersed stockpiles from their prior operations, and now they would consolidate all that spice here, where it could be more easily protected.

The Naib led him through the dusty chambers, showing off the honeycomb of passages. Although the Freemen had felt safe here, Josef intended to add several more layers of security, including scantronics. Impatient, he looked around at the people still moving about. "When will they all be gone so I can begin my operations?"

"Three days, Directeur. Possibly sooner. We had to hunker down during the storms." The Naib lifted his chin in pride. "But our ancestors were the Zensunni wanderers, and we have not forgotten how to move swiftly and silently. The sietch will be ready for you, as promised."

These desert people had already moved most of their belongings, their children, and their elderly across the desert. Such a journey could kill even a healthy, resourceful man, but somehow the tribe members didn't appear to be overly concerned. Josef would be glad to have them gone.

Maybe Modoc's people would all die out in the sands, devoured by the enormous worms, or they might simply collapse from exposure. That would be fine with him, because then no one would learn about the spice bank. It was a system ancient pharaohs had utilized, putting builders and architects to death after the construction of a pyramid.

But Josef didn't want to kill people who had helped him. As a general rule, that was bad business.

⤳

THE IMPERIAL TROOPS that had been stranded on Arrakis didn't know what hit them. After more than a month of uneasy coexistence, with neither side ready to ignite a shooting war, the Imperials had lowered their guard. Josef's mercenaries had already seized most of their spice operations during the recent storms, and now he struck even harder. He made the calculations, and Norma encouraged him to finish what he had already begun. He would not disagree with the prescient Navigator woman.

The flow of spice had to remain uninterrupted, and under Combined Mercantiles control. Norma needed to care for her Navigators—she'd made that abundantly clear—and VenHold required continuing supplies of melange to feed the clamoring market that this feud had already disrupted. Thus, he needed to eliminate interests that were in opposition to his own.

Since the Imperial warships were cut off and had no hope of imminent reinforcements, they could not withstand a concerted attack. Norma summoned her Navigators and brought in a dozen more VenHold warships. Soon enough, Josef's forces overwhelmed the remaining Imperial ships without firing a shot, taking the enemy commanders into "temporary detention" until Emperor Roderick could arrange for their release and return to Salusa Secundus.

Now, Josef could push his spice operations without further complications, and within a week he had made significant progress in filling his spice bank. Modoc's Freemen had evacuated, per the agreement, and the teams now working inside the sietch were all trusted VenHold employees.

The Mentats Rogin and Tomkir organized the inventory stored inside the numerous cave chambers and passageways. Engineering crews installed armored doors and moisture-sealed vaults to preserve the melange.

Among the workers were three silent and eerie men who walked with a swaying gait, as if their spines had been irreparably curved. From their large heads and smooth skin, Josef knew that these were Navigator candidates who had nearly drowned in the spice gas before their transformation was terminated. They had been rescued, but were forever altered; now, they volunteered to work in the VenHold spice bank, and Norma had a special connection to them. The three moved in complete silence, as if they could communicate through thoughts and expressions.

From her tank, Norma approved of the large, protected stockpile. Her sealed chamber appeared just inside the narrow defile and the open area that led to the cave warrens. When Josef explained the continuing plans, she listened in silence, absorbing the data.

In order to gain ready access to the modified sietch, his engineers had blasted open a cave roof and torn down several rock walls. Right now, two cargo fliers cruised through the dusty air carrying large loads of packaged melange, some of it stolen from black marketeers. Other supplies had been moved into the sietch from other VenHold stockpiles.

The cargo fliers hovered over the open area while spice-laden pallets dropped out of their belly compartments. Suspensor packs lowered the deliveries to the ground, stirring up a burst of sand. Josef no longer had to worry about Imperial patrols, and although someone might notice all this activity, the only possible prying eyes now belonged to desert nomads or poachers, and Josef would install enough security to be proof against that.

"This is excellent progress. So much spice for my Navigators," Norma said in her otherworldly, wistful voice. "Enough to create hundreds more."

"With this stockpile, we'll have enough to last for years—for my purposes, *and* yours."

"The universe is ours," Norma agreed.

VenHold now had so much spice it would take weeks to load everything into the secure chambers, but he could see that the situation was well in hand here. It was time to go back to Kolhar, to make sure the defenses would stand against any Imperial attack. By overthrowing the Emperor's spice operations here, he might have provoked Roderick into making a hasty move. "We need to go home, Grandmother. Our place is back on our homeworld until the end of this dispute."

Her voice took on a strange, alarming tone. "Yes. We must hurry."

Her comment gave him an uneasy feeling. He wondered if Norma had seen something through her spice-enriched prescience, something she had not told him yet. . . .

The human mind is more difficult to reprogram than a thinking machine. There is a limit to how much effort we should expend in trying to retrain the Orthodox Sisters. Our patience is not infinite. We may have to kill them.

—MOTHER SUPERIOR VALYA, in a session with her inner circle

Mother Superior Valya meant to build the Sisterhood into something far more powerful than it had been in the past, but first she needed to be absolutely confident she could rely on her people. At Valya's feet, an unconscious woman lay on the floor of the windowless cell, bleeding from her ears.

For weeks, Sister Esther-Cano had undergone rigorous reeducation, but had resisted every step. Valya and her subordinates had isolated the defiant Sister with barely enough food and water to stay alive. Esther-Cano had been commanded repeatedly to admit that Dorotea's misguided Orthodox beliefs had caused the devastating schism in the Sisterhood, and to admit that there had never been any hidden computers. Though Valya knew the last part wasn't true, since she herself had stored them in ultra-secure underground chambers, she wanted to force Sister Esther-Cano to utter the words.

Yet the beaten woman remained pathologically stubborn.

Valya had interrogated Esther-Cano for two hours that afternoon, improvising original methods when the traditional ones had failed. There would be no crude and clumsy torture implements such as the Scalpel interrogators used. No, this prisoner was an accomplished Truthsayer and a Reverend Mother, but Esther-Cano had no defense against the manipulative power of Voice that Valya had mastered.

Testing her abilities, Valya showed that she could overcome Esther-Cano with mere words. Sharpening her verbal weapons, the Mother Superior attacked her subject with vocal jabs that subdued her and turned her into a bleeding wreck on the floor. Valya had not laid a finger on the other woman, but her soft hypnotic Voice had convinced Esther-Cano that the sound was tremendously loud, rather than the whisper that it really was, and the mere suggestion of noise had actually destroyed the inside of her ears. Amazing and unexpected! When Esther-Cano returned to consciousness she would realize that she was completely deaf.

After the rough session, Sister Olivia would come in to help handle the unconscious prisoner, although even faithful Olivia was not allowed to learn about the use of Voice. Not yet. Valya had used the technique on Olivia, too, making her forget that she had ever received the eerie, irresistible command. Now Olivia returned, looking confused as to why she had gone. "Would you like me to take over now, Mother Superior?" She knelt beside the unconscious woman. "Oh, she's bleeding! What happened to her ears?"

"Perhaps they could not stand to hear any more of her own lies."

Olivia rose to her feet. "Shall I summon the medics?"

"Not just yet."

Valya was learning her own abilities, experimenting with the effects. She wondered just how much physical damage a person could psychosomatically inflict on her own body. Could the victim's mind cause subconscious constrictions to stop her own heart, burst her liver? Maybe the intractable traitor Esther-Cano could be useful to the Sisterhood as an experimental object.

On the cold floor, the woman began to stir, clutching at her ears and whimpering in pain. Seeing the blood smeared on her hands, she struggled to a sitting position, glared at the Mother Superior. "What have you done to me? I can't hear my own voice!"

Valya leaned over and spoke softly, knowing the woman could not hear her. "I was trying to toughen you. I must teach you the proper way of thinking, of seeing the world."

Esther-Cano seemed to be having trouble even sitting up, perhaps from dizziness. She shouted her reply. "I don't understand what you're saying or doing to me, but your actions are corrupting the Sisterhood. Mother Superior Raquella would never have condoned this! I can't believe Dorotea ever agreed to rejoin your faction of heretics."

Valya smiled and continued to whisper, "Dorotea did what she was told." Then she rose to her feet and turned her face away from the victim, addressing Olivia, "Kill her."

Olivia recoiled. "But why? She needs to be retrained, rehabilitated—"

"No, I will spend more time training *you*, developing your expertise. And killing is a skill we need in our repertoire now. This woman—she is no longer worthy even to be called a Sister—is too tainted to be useful, except in one way.

She can serve the Sisterhood as a lesson to you—one that you will pass on to others."

"What do you mean?"

Valya's voice became throaty, otherworldly. *"Kill her."*

Olivia obeyed reflexively. She delivered a kick to Esther-Cano's larynx that snapped her neck, followed by a quick finishing blow to the center of her face, crushing her skull. Olivia blinked in astonishment at what she had done.

Satisfied, Valya returned to her living quarters, where she would enjoy dinner alone in celebration. She had just made another step in the progress of the new Sisterhood. *Her* new Sisterhood.

It seems as if we are going in a circle: we are chasing the Harkonnens, and they are chasing us.

—WILLEM ATREIDES, comments recorded by Vorian Atreides

ankiveil was cold and cloudy, its air laced with frigid mist. After Abulurd Harkonnen's exile here, Vorian had come to admire the Harkonnens for their fortitude in this windswept, backwater place. Recently, they had even begun to thrive.

Vor had not asked to become their enemy, but Abulurd's descendants had painted him into that role. He and Willem were taking a grave risk by coming here, but Tula had slain Orry, and if she was on Lankiveil, they would hunt her down—for justice, and to keep the rest of his family safe.

Arriving in the main town in the sheltered fjord, both men wore warm clothing of the local style so they would not look out of place. As the pair tromped along a wooden boardwalk into the heart of the village, however, the effort to look unobtrusive was in vain; the locals spotted outsiders at first glance.

Vor could tell that Willem was growing angrier by the moment, staring at the townspeople as if he considered all of them to be murderers. He placed a hand on the young man's shoulder to steady him, but he could feel the thrumming tension inside him. "Careful," he said.

"Careful, yes," Willem said, "but I won't forget."

The wooden buildings were weather-beaten, their metal roofs corroded. Not long ago Vor had stayed here for a month in disguise, after Griffin's tragic death on Arrakis. Vor had considered the young Harkonnen man a friend, and had wanted to see how the family was faring. Under an assumed name, Vor had worked alongside Vergyl Harkonnen on a whale-fur boat. He had performed grueling chores without complaint, and afterward, knowing the family's dire financial situation, he paid off Harkonnen debts anonymously. In his mind, Vor had done a good thing, and had felt better for it.

Then Tula had seduced and murdered Willem's brother.

As the two bearded men continued through town, the large, weathered Harkonnen house was prominent along the shore of the fjord, at the far end of the docks and the cluster of shops and inns. Willem stared ahead as if he had seen the lair of a beast. "Is that it? Is that where Tula lives?"

Vor looked at the shingled house with its pointed, sloping gables in the distinctive architecture of Lankiveil. He knew there would be a cozy fire inside; Sonia Harkonnen and her servants would fill the house with the smells of cooking and baking. If Vergyl wasn't out on his whaling boat, he would be in his study attending to the family accounts. "That's where her family lives," Vor said. "We don't know whether or not Tula's there herself."

"Then we need to find out. Before she can get away."

Vor looked up to see the sky darkening with an oncoming aurora storm; beyond the fjord cliffs, he could see flashes of color. He knew the weather would rapidly get worse. "Later. We'd better find shelter for now."

On the fjord, the Harkonnen great house loomed tall. Several lights burned in the windows in the afternoon gloom as the aurora storm worsened.

Willem's expression darkened. "We've been spotted in town already, and someone might ask questions. We can't wait. We'll have to go to the Harkonnen house and see if Tula is there, before she can bolt."

Vor took his arm and led him toward an inn only two blocks away from the house. "If she's there now, she will stay inside during the storm—as we should be doing." They walked up the creaking wooden steps of the inn's entrance. "We've come all this way. Wait until the weather clears, ask more questions, find out exactly where we stand . . . and find out if Tula's here at all." He opened the inn's door, stepped inside.

Willem seemed reluctant. "But think about it—if we take our vengeance sooner, the storm will give us cover to help us get away. If they resist, we may have to kill the rest of her family, and good riddance!"

"No," Vor said. "Only the guilty ones—only Tula, unless we find proof that more of them took part." The sky crackled overhead, and the wind picked up. He wasn't sure how many additional Harkonnens, if any, were involved. Tula had the most obvious blood on her hands.

The innkeeper came into the foyer, rubbing his hands, as Vor entered. The man had a forced grin, but looked harried. "One room left, if you want to keep warm and safe from the storm. The staff and I are sealing the windows and preparing the generators, so we should be fine."

Vor nodded. "Yes, my nephew and I would like a room. Probably just for one night."

The innkeeper's face showed sudden alarm, and he shouted past Vor. "You don't want to go out there! And close the door!"

Vor spun to find the door wide open and the wind blowing into the foyer. Willem had ducked back out of the inn and set off up the street. With an angry sigh, Vor headed after him, calling Willem's name, but his voice was lost in the increasing wind and commotion. Though it was only afternoon, the sky had turned dark, and more lights had come on in the houses and shops.

Willem had rushed ahead, determined, running up the reinforced stairs to the front porch of the Harkonnen great house. He pounded on the door, shouting, as Vor finally caught up to him.

The door, emblazoned with the familiar Harkonnen griffin crest, swung open to reveal a middle-aged woman in a fur-lined housecoat. She looked surprised to see Willem, his hair windblown and his face flushed. "What are you doing out there? You shouldn't be—" Then Sonia Harkonnen recognized Vor, and called him by the false name he had given during his last visit. "Jeron! Come in out of the weather." She gestured them inside. "Who is your young friend?"

Willem stalked into the parlor, and Vor followed, grabbing his arm. "Wait!"

Willem looked around, glared at the older woman. "We're here for Tula."

"Tula isn't here." Sonia appeared confused. Her eyes widened as she seemed to notice the young man's dark expression. "She left for Chusuk days ago. I'm afraid you missed her. But come in, come in!" She called down the hall as she took them into the parlor. "Vergyl! Jeron has come back!"

Feeling trapped, Vor tried to intercept the young man who was coiled for violence. "This is Willem. He's my nephew."

"Willem *Atreides!*" The young man threw it out like a challenge just as Vergyl Harkonnen emerged from the study.

The older man had a welcoming smile that changed as soon as he heard Willem's outburst. "Atreides?" Vergyl looked from the flushed young man to Vor. "Jeron, what is he talking about?"

Sonia's expression visibly altered: revulsion and fear covered by shock. "He is an *Atreides?* And he's your nephew, truly?"

Vor paused, his thoughts racing, and then he reached a conclusion. He added in a strong voice, "Yes. My real name isn't Jeron Egan. It's Vorian Atreides."

Vergyl Harkonnen stumbled, resting a hand against the wall for support. He looked stricken. "*Vorian Atreides*—the man who murdered our poor Griffin!"

Now that Vor had his chance, he tried to explain. "I didn't kill your son. I tried to protect him. We were actually friends."

Sonia gave Vor a fierce scowl. "Why did you come here? Why did you use a false name? To spy on us?"

"At first I came to check on you, to make sure you were surviving. I saw to it that Griffin's body was returned home for a proper burial. I wish I could have saved him from the violent people who were after me. I have done everything possible to atone."

Vergyl snorted. "Atone?"

Impatient and angry, Willem pulled himself free of Vor's grip. "Your daughter Tula married my brother on Caladan. She seduced him, tricked him—and then murdered him on their wedding night. She is a killer, and she escaped justice."

Sonia and Vergyl were both shaking visibly. "Tula on Caladan? Married? And you accuse her of murder? What in the nine hells are you talking about? Our sweet daughter would never harm anyone!"

Willem reached inside his pocket and grabbed printed images, which he scattered on the floor in front of Vergyl and Sonia. Beautiful wedding portraits showing Tula and Orry, the happy couple. And gory images showing how young Orry lay slaughtered in his bed. "She told my brother she loved him, then she slashed his throat as he lay sleeping."

"You're lying!" Sonia cried.

"She was acting so strange . . . ," Vergyl said in a small, lost voice.

"Tula has to pay the blood price," Willem said. "The Harkonnens have to pay." He reached for the long Caladan knife he kept at his waist.

Vor seized his arm. "Not these people. They did not kill Orry."

As Sonia and Vergyl stared in shock and horror at the images, trying to deny what they saw, Vor took the knife away from Willem and dragged him back to the door. "We need to leave now."

"No!" Willem struggled, but he was no match for Vor. "Someone has to pay for Orry!"

Vor leaned close and hissed in the young man's ear. "We know where she is now! Chusuk. These people are not responsible for her crimes."

Old Vergyl picked up one of the horrific images, staring at it. "No, no, no!"

As Vor pushed Willem out the door into the rising storm, behind them in the Harkonnen house another young man emerged, drawn by the shouts. Danvis—a pale teenager who looked alarmed and unsteady. "What's happening?"

Willem struggled, but Vor was firm, pushing him out into the streets and fury of the weather. "Not here. This isn't our target!"

Vor felt the crushing shadows all around him, and he needed to leave. He and Willem had just shattered the lives of these good people—and if Tula was long gone, it would do no good for them to stay any longer.

"We have to get off this planet—and make our way to Chusuk."

Outside, the aurora storm had arrived in full force, reflecting colorful shimmers that dropped along with the clouds in the sky. The clatter and hiss of hail struck the roofs and the paved street, while signs were torn away by the wind. Yet Vor felt that the storm itself was preferable to staying inside with the devastated Harkonnens.

Norma Cenva resided inside her tank of swirling orange spice gas, but she lived primarily within her mind. Her physical body was merely an appendage, of secondary importance. She required her biological machinery to survive, but she immersed herself so deeply in esoteric matters that she rarely thought about her body at all.

Her chamber rested on a dais overlooking the other Navigator tanks on Kolhar, on the outskirts of the capital city. Since returning from Arrakis, she had felt restless and disturbed within the ripples of fate, and even with her expansive thoughts, she could not understand the reasons for her discomfort. The large and fortified spice stockpile would help stabilize their supply, and now that Josef had tightened his control on the desert planet, melange harvesting and distribution should grow.

With the supply of melange, the future for her precious Navigators should be stable and bright . . . but she still felt grave concern for them, and for mankind.

Gazing toward the VenHold headquarters towers in the distance, she transmitted her wishes to her handlers—failed Navigator candidates with varying degrees of physical abnormalities—and they responded immediately, without questioning why.

The handlers arranged a heavy suspensor hauler to carry her tank across the gray sky, delivering it to the roof of the VenHold headquarters tower. They deposited the ornate chamber on the high rooftop, secured it, and then left her alone, as she requested. Unlike any other Navigator, Norma could have transported herself with her own abilities, but that would have disrupted her complex train of thought.

She felt she was on the verge of a revelation, an epiphany . . . possibly a specific warning.

Ever since she had rescued Josef from the Imperial Palace on Salusa Secundus after his role in the assassination was exposed, she had monitored the ongoing crisis in the Imperium, assessing second- and third-order consequences. But even with spice prescience, she experienced troubling blind spots that prevented her from seeing certain events and choices. Even prescience held imperfections, too much uncertainty, and for the sake of her Navigators, she needed to *know*.

This perch on the giant tower gave her a new perspective, from a cosmic standpoint. She gazed outward, and her mind extended beyond the limitations of human vision into the deepest tapestry of space-time. It was like a much larger version of the gas inside her tank and in an infinite variety of colors, with swirling nebulae and galaxies, so beautiful but challenging to her as well, for the difficulties they presented to her prescience.

She strained to envision all the way to the other side of the universe, and from there she peered back at herself with a powerful sense of reflective vision. From that infinite perspective, she gazed down upon Kolhar and her field of developing Navigators. Their tanks sparkled in the bright morning sun. Hundreds of Navigators, tank after tank, stretched across a wide, grassy field.

The universe is ours.

As her concerns knotted into questions that tangled into paradoxes, she needed this different vantage to help her find new solutions to serious problems.

Even though Josef had secured a stronger grip on Arrakis and had created the strategic spice bank, Norma was troubled by his recent rash of increasingly aggressive actions, which could well have unpleasant reactionary consequences. He had swept through the Imperial guard forces left behind on Arrakis, destroying Imperially sanctioned contract operations and seizing the profits for himself.

Norma agreed with the result of such actions . . . but not the provocative nature of the actions themselves. Roderick's retaliations would cause more problems. Surely, Josef could see the danger. It did not require prescience to predict the Emperor's response.

Josef considered himself invincible, but Norma could foresee possible disastrous consequences—and how they would affect her Navigators. Through a sudden spark of clarity, she recognized that they were all in the gravest danger!

But she couldn't see the source of it. Was it the Emperor? Uncertain. She would have to monitor very closely. . . .

Money is the root of all control.
—HADITHA CORRINO, advice to her husband

As dawn light cast its soft glow over the city of Zimia, Emperor Roderick sat in his palace office, rubbing his eyes from lack of sleep. It had been a long night, but he needed the quiet time to attend to countless matters of state. His predecessor, Salvador, had delegated many of the decisions and details, often to his brother, but Emperor Roderick planned to keep a firm grasp on his government. *The machinery of an empire has an infinite number of tiny gears.*

And one of those large gears was going to crush Josef Venport. Roderick read a confirmation of action and exhaled a long, satisfied sigh. Even without the results of General Roon's strike force, whatever had happened to it and all of the soldiers, Roderick had just secured a clear victory against his enemy, a different kind of attack that would bring VenHold to its knees. When he reread the document, he could already feel the Imperial treasury swelling with new wealth. And the Directeur could do nothing about it.

In an unprecedented move, Roderick had used his authority to seize control of all VenHold banks operating on Imperial planets. This one executive order would deprive the tycoon of significant assets, freezing much of his wealth. Venport's commercial empire would suddenly find itself without cash to continue operations, to buy fuel or commodities, to hire traders, to pay the salaries of pilots and crew. The man undoubtedly had other sources of wealth and hidden funds in illicit accounts, but this would hurt him, and hurt him badly.

Far too much time had passed since the departure of the Kolhar strike force, and by now Roderick feared that General Roon had been defeated or otherwise lost—a crippling blow to the Imperial Armed Forces. But this seizure of assets was an even greater wound to the man who had murdered Salvador.

Roderick knew it wasn't good enough, though. Directeur Venport's fleet of fast spacefolders traveled throughout the Imperium with impunity; he still held Admiral Harte's entire Imperial battle group hostage over Kolhar; and in a bold move Venport had just reasserted control over the lucrative spice operations on Arrakis, neutralizing the Imperial guardian ships and seizing the contract melange harvesting teams.

But now the lion's share of Venport's operating capital had been pulled into the Imperial treasury. Yes, it had been a very productive night.

Hoping to catch at least a little rest, Roderick tidied his papers and message cylinders. Although dawn's light already streamed through the crystal windows, he wanted to slip back to his suite before Haditha awoke, so he could spend just a little time beside her in bed; he wouldn't sleep, but he always felt rejuvenated next to her.

When he opened the office door, though, he was surprised to see his Truthsayer standing like a statue under the glowing lights, as if she had known exactly when he would emerge. "I must speak with you, Sire. I have news. Another solution for the Venport problem. I think you will be pleased."

Roderick noticed a second figure next to Fielle, a wild-eyed man trying to hide in the large woman's shadow. The stranger had a lean, tanned face and unkempt black hair. He wore the exotic desert clothing of a worker from offworld.

Roderick was ready to shout for the guards. "What is this? How did he get into the secure section of the Palace?"

Fielle gestured the stranger forward. "I slipped him in here, Sire. He only just arrived by a black-market transport from Arrakis. We paid handsomely for his passage, but it will be worth every solari." She stood between the stranger and Roderick, and the Emperor sensed that Fielle would instantly kill the man if he made an inappropriate move.

"Speak," he said coldly.

"As you authorized, Sire, I made overtures to my contacts on Arrakis. Even though Combined Mercantiles controls most of the melange operations, and your Imperial ships have been rendered impotent—there are other ways to sabotage Directeur Venport."

Roderick controlled a smile. Perhaps this night would be even more productive. "How?"

"Our spies located several willing desert men, who found other cooperative desert men, who asked further questions, that led us to this man." She glanced at the stranger. "His name is Modoc. He and his companions are willing to offer their services to you. That is why I brought him here in this fashion, so he would not be seen."

Roderick eyed the strange, anxious offworlder. "And what can he provide for me? How can he hurt my enemy?"

"Modoc knows of a vulnerability that Directeur Venport doesn't even realize he has. I have already interrogated him in my special way, and I believe he is sincere."

The Freeman bowed awkwardly, then looked up with a peculiar air of confidence. He spoke with a thick accent. "I don't understand the vastness of your Imperium, Sire. I once had a younger brother who spoke of offworld wonders, and we considered him strange. I may have been hasty in dismissing his dreams."

Still wary, Roderick pressed, "And what information do you bring?"

The desert man seemed to be calculating, considering how to say something, but Fielle spoke sharply to him. "Tell the Emperor what you told me."

Modoc said, "I know the precise location of an enormous hidden spice bank that Josef Venport built. He evicted my tribe so that he could fill the chambers with his stockpiles of spice, including all the spice he confiscated from your operations. These are all of his reserves."

Roderick frowned. "Even knowing where it is, I could not send enough of a military fleet to breach Venport's defenses."

Modoc narrowed his blue-within-blue eyes. "Ah, Venport thinks he is untouchable, but my people know exactly how to do it."

The Truthsayer had more to offer. "With your authorization and tactical support, Sire, Modoc and his people will destroy the stockpile for you—for a fee."

Roderick struggled to keep his expression neutral. He had just crippled VenHold finances by seizing the bank assets, and if he could also eliminate such a large stockpile, then Venport would receive a second immense setback. Surely, it would be a mortal wound. "It could bankrupt him," he said in a low voice.

Roderick could not afford to redirect what remained of his main Imperial fleet from defending Salusa, but if these desert bandits could deal a blow to Venport through an efficient commando operation, he had nothing to lose.

With a nod he said to Fielle, "Make the arrangements and give Modoc what he needs. Destroy the stockpile, and that might very well destroy Venport."

Modoc bowed. "Consider it done, Sire."

Roderick dismissed them and stepped away from his office. Dawn was brightening, and he was eager to get back to his room, though he no longer felt the need for sleep.

Within days of Josef's return from Arrakis, Draigo Roget finally arrived from Denali to deliver a personal report of the cymek test run on Lampadas. In Kolhar headquarters, the Mentat presented the images taken by Ptolemy.

As Josef watched the mayhem caused by the warrior forms, he could tell that Draigo was proud of what the new cymeks had accomplished, even if they had failed to find and kill the half-Manford.

When the images were finished, Draigo straightened. "I am pleased to announce the clear proof of concept, Directeur. So much destruction was accomplished by a mere three cymeks. And soon we will have many more. Within a month, we will have a full hundred ready to go."

Josef smiled. "The savages had no viable defenses against a sophisticated technological attack, and the complete cymek force will eradicate them down to the last simpering man and woman."

"There will be collateral damage, innocents killed," Cioba said, raising a note of caution.

"The blame lies entirely on the shoulders of the Butlerians," Josef said. "Civilization is at stake."

Draigo nodded. "I believe you are correct in your assessment, Directeur."

"How many cymeks are ready to be placed into service right now?" Cioba asked, tucking her long hair over her shoulder as she sat beside her husband. "Do we have to wait a month?"

"Thirty-one at present. The other walker forms are being modified and tested, and many more are nearing completion, but the new Navigator brains must prove their adeptness on simulated battlefields."

Josef fidgeted and paced around his desk, walking to the window of his office, high in the headquarters tower. "Every day that this barbaric stupidity remains unchallenged is another day that weakens civilization. I am anxious to end this war against ignorance." He stared out at the bustling landing field below and smiled. "And once I eliminate the Emperor's Butlerian problem, he is bound to soften his stance against me."

He nodded to himself. He could use the Imperial forces he had recently captured on Arrakis as a bargaining chip, and could offer to return Admiral Harte's ships that were being held aboard the foldspace carrier in Kolhar orbit. He would be happy to pay the price, provided Roderick withdrew the punitive decree against him. Then the Imperium could get back to normal.

He took satisfaction that at least his spice-harvesting operations were under way again, without so many roadblocks, and addicted citizens would be happy to have their melange available to them. His large stockpile would help him guarantee distribution through any future political turmoil. Josef felt stronger and more optimistic than he had in a long time.

Cioba leaned closer to the Mentat. "And the Erasmus memory core? I am curious—has his knowledge proved as advantageous as we hoped?"

Draigo's smile was a surprise on his normally aloof face. "Erasmus has been exceptionally cooperative, even enthusiastic to be among so many dedicated scientists. Many of his insights on old-style machine invasion tactics and traditional weapons have been invaluable to our planning, and he says he has other resources to offer, which he has not yet revealed. As a reward, per his insistence, the Tlulaxa scientists are growing a biological body for him so that he can be a more effective asset."

"Never trust a thinking machine," Cioba warned.

"We don't need to trust him to use him," Josef pointed out. "But is it wise to give him his own body?"

"The robot made it a condition of his continued cooperation," Draigo said, "and I projected that it would be a harmless concession, with minimal risk. Should it prove problematic, the new biological body can easily be restrained or destroyed."

"It does seem a small thing," Cioba said. "Why would an evil robot cooperate with us so fully? He must have some scheme of his own."

The Mentat said, "I believe Erasmus wants to be important and relevant again, but he also has a different incentive—if we can believe him. He truly feels hatred and revulsion toward Manford Torondo."

Josef laughed. "Don't we all?"

"I would be reluctant to assign human emotions to a thinking machine, Directeur, but the Butlerians executed his ward and friend, Gilbertus Albans. After conversing with the robot at great length, I believe his hatred may be genuine, even if he himself doesn't understand it."

"We have a strange ally . . . ," Cioba mused.

"I will take every bit of help we can get in these dark times." Josef allowed himself to relax, feeling more confident now. "Very well—as soon as the rest of the Denali cymeks are trained and ready, we will launch a total attack on Lampadas and leave that planet a smoking ruin—and this dismal and distracting year will be over. The Imperium and the human race will be ready to move forward under wise leadership."

"That all depends on whether Emperor Roderick will see reason," Cioba said.

Josef looked at the Mentat and cocked his head. "After we purge Lampadas, maybe I'll even let you establish a new Mentat School there, Draigo. Would you like that?"

"Very much, Directeur. It will preserve the great work of my mentor."

SOON JOSEF'S OPTIMISM was shattered when two VenHold commercial spacefolders delivered the same disturbing report. The first agitated captain hurried from the landing field to the headquarters tower with his urgent news. At the same time, the second spacefolder arrived, broadcasting wild alarms.

Josef's anger flared even before he had all the details.

The first captain barged into the office. "I just came from Subiak, Directeur! I tried to deliver a full load of spice, large farming equipment from Ix, and expensive musical instruments from Chusuk. That was when we discovered that all VenHold financial assets have been impounded, the planetary bank seized!" The captain blinked. "Directeur, all your wealth on Subiak has been frozen, by order of Emperor Roderick Corrino."

Josef's hackles rose. "But that bank is secure, like my others. All financial assets are held not just in the name of Combined Mercantiles, but in the names of countless other depositors. It's a separate entity! Roderick has no right!"

"He *is* the Emperor, after all." The captain sounded defeated. "He simply changed the law as he saw fit. Any trade with VenHold is forbidden."

Josef slammed his fist down on the desktop.

Draigo narrowed his gaze, appeared to be running Mentat calculations. "You have been declared an outlaw, Directeur, and therefore your assets are subject to forfeiture. Roderick has taken them away from you."

The second spacefolder captain entered the headquarters offices, looking just as alarmed. He confirmed the news, saying he'd heard of banks on three other worlds that had also been impacted, their operations cut off and assets confiscated.

Josef felt deeply betrayed. "My company cannot function without that cash flow! The wealth stored in any one of those planetary banks is enough to buy an entire world." He lowered his voice to a growl. "The Emperor knows he can't fight me militarily, so he's resorted to this childish ploy. Trying to flex his muscle."

"Childish, perhaps, but effective," Cioba said. "If all of our banks have been stripped from us, Venport Holdings cannot operate. All across the Imperium our ships are loaded with cargo that needs to be delivered, otherwise we have very little operating capital. He's cutting us off, painting us into a corner."

Josef dismissed the two captains, leaving only Draigo and Cioba with him in his office. "We have other assets that even the Emperor doesn't know about. I will liquidate them to buy more time." His voice became a low, dangerous growl. "He just moved this conflict onto an entirely different level. It is no longer a dispute, but an outright war."

Draigo straightened. "Directeur, perhaps it is time for me to go to Salusa Secundus as our ambassador. I will open negotiations with the Imperial Court. I can facilitate a compromise solution that restores Venport Holdings to the Emperor's good graces."

But now Josef was enraged. "No, we're a long way past that point. Roderick thinks he can force me into submission, but I will not bargain from a position of weakness! Emperor or not, he cannot treat me this way. I put that man on the throne, and now I find out he's not fit to rule the Imperium."

Angry thoughts clicked like the beads of an abacus in his mind as he tried to measure the assets Roderick had just seized, but the number seemed incalculable. Josef inhaled several long breaths. "I never wanted to be Emperor—I've said it countless times—but he has just forced my hand. I cannot ignore this. I *will not* ignore this."

"He seized your assets, and in retaliation you seize the Imperial throne?" Draigo said.

"I will at least threaten to do so, until he surrenders. After which, he can make an appropriate act of contrition, and I will generously restore him to the Imperial Palace—with a far better understanding of his place." His voice held a sad weariness. "I had high hopes for that man. Why couldn't Roderick just operate like a sensible businessman? Now I have to save the human race from their own Emperor as well as the barbarians?"

"How will you accomplish that?" Cioba asked.

"VenHold military forces exceed anything that the Emperor commands. I have Admiral Harte's expeditionary force held hostage here, and I've seized his guardian fleet at Arrakis. I certainly have enough military might to move against Salusa." His eyes brightened as a thought occurred to him. "Draigo, you said there are now thirty-one battle cymeks ready on Denali?"

"Yes, Directeur, although we were expecting to use them against the Butlerians when—"

"We'll use them against our *enemies,* wherever they are, and we'll force Emperor Roderick to behave responsibly—for the benefit of our collective future. In addition to an overwhelming fleet of VenHold warships, all those cymeks will make the citizens quiver with fear." He smiled. "I'm going to assemble our most effective military force with all of the top commanders, and contact Norma to have her rally the Navigators as well." He crossed his arms over his chest. "I am left with no choice except to conquer Salusa Secundus."

The human form is admirable, both as a work of art and as a sophisti-
cated biological machine, but it was designed by the gradual process of
evolution. As a result, the human body possesses numerous flaws and
weaknesses that thinking machines do not suffer.

In my cultural studies, however, I have learned that imperfections
themselves can make a work of art valuable. Viewed in the light of its
imperfections, the human body is a masterpiece, and I have studied it
intently, person after person, piece after piece.

—ERASMUS, Secret Laboratory Notebooks

As she watched the male body growing inside the Tlulaxa biological tank, Anna Corrino felt as if she were coming alive along with it. Grown from cells of the late Gilbertus Albans, it made her feel sorry that the poor Headmaster had gotten his head chopped off. But seeing the body also made her happy.

The physical form drifting in the nutrient fluids reminded her of marble statues around the palace square in Zimia, but Anna could only think of it as Erasmus now. *Erasmus!* Her secret friend, her savior, her most steadfast companion, the one who had saved her from the dark and confusing mental labyrinth where she had been lost. . . .

She glanced at the pulsing gelsphere resting on the table, connected to its sensory apparatus. "That will be *you* as soon as it's finished." She divided her attention between the growing body in the tank and the robot's detached memory core, uniting them in her mind.

"I have been without an appropriate body since the Battle of Corrin," Erasmus said. "I miss my original flowmetal form, but removing my memory core from it was the only way for Gilbertus to save me from the mobs overrunning our city. Now I am eager to have the ability to move around as I please, to see and touch and experiment at will. The added biological component will be fascinating, I am certain."

Erasmus had been a comforting presence at the Mentat School whenever she drifted off to sleep, a wise and friendly voice that spoke through a secret conduit in her ear, advising her, testing her, helping her through the turmoil in her shattered mind. She would have been lost without him.

"I can always help you, even before your body is ready." Anna bent close to the gelsphere as if whispering in his ear.

She knew her mind had been damaged from the poison she had taken at the Sisterhood school, but did not consider herself to be foolish or overly gullible. She knew all the stories, had read the history of what the independent robot had done to his human captives, but she was also pleased that he found her fascinating. He had helped Anna in so many ways. How could she not forgive him?

The robot continued, "Dr. Danebh says the body will be ready in nine days for the implantation of my memory core. The waiting is difficult. I am tempted to power down my processor clock, stop my own subjective time, and wake up when the body is ready. I want to see with my new eyes, walk with my new legs, and feel temperatures, textures, pleasure, and pain with my new hands."

Anna said quickly, "Please don't shut down in the meantime. I can keep you company. Won't it be interesting for us to discuss what you can do with a biological body? I have so many ideas, so many suggestions."

She regarded the biological tank and the human body suspended there. She tapped the smooth, transparent walls, but the naked male form drifted away, bent in a partial fetal position, its arms and legs curled up. "I wonder what it'll be like to touch it, to feel skin—and know it is you." Her breath fogged the curved plaz.

"I wonder if it will make me feel more human to be in a human body," Erasmus mused. "Theoretically, it should."

She brightened. "You know it will! You'll sense with nerve endings, feel what real people feel. It won't just be data. At last you'll be a real person yourself."

"I conducted tens of thousands of experiments and collated so many experimental results in my attempts to understand humans, but still something has always been missing. Some key factor keeps eluding me . . . a parameter that cannot be measured by even the most advanced laboratory apparatus."

"You'll feel the difference," Anna said.

"I anticipate sharing many results with you."

"And I'll assist in every way possible." She let out a long sigh.

Erasmus spoke as a disembodied voice. "When I see that body growing in the tank, I see only Gilbertus Albans, and it makes me feel . . . heavy." He paused, as if troubled or confused. "I am experiencing an indefinable set of reactions that I suspect would be broadly categorized as sadness."

Anna's expression fell. "I'm so sorry, Erasmus." His sensors shifted, and she knew he was reading her face and identifying the genuine sympathy there. "Gilbertus was a good Headmaster," she said. Her gaze flicked back and forth. "He wanted to help me, wanted to make me a Mentat."

ERASMUS HAD BEEN analyzing and manipulating humans for centuries, all for the purpose of fully understanding them. Such an intriguing species! The evermind Omnius, who held dominion over the machine empire, had let him conduct thousands of experiments so the thinking machines could defend against the capricious human enemy. But Erasmus had always yearned for more.

Since the collapse of the Synchronized Empire, his overall purpose hadn't changed, but because he was the last independent robot, his need to understand humanity had taken on a personal urgency.

After centuries of research with the vast resources available in the machine capital of Corrin, Erasmus once thought he had conducted every possible test. But after the barbaric execution of Gilbertus, he had finally experienced a true breakthrough.

With his perfect memory, he could replay the images of Anari Idaho's brutal sword strike, how the blade sliced smoothly into Gilbertus's bowed neck and decapitated him. The robot struggled each time he reviewed the images, and most of all he couldn't comprehend the strange look of calmness on Gilbertus's face in the final seconds, the beatific acceptance that his life would end.

What had he seen in those final moments? What had he known?

That mystery posed an even more compelling question, making Erasmus desperate to experience what was missing inside him . . . a level of nobility and perception that all humans possessed even without trying. Perhaps with a perfect biological body he would experience the secret by feeling his nerves, his heart, all his senses. As a sentient biological organism—or as close as he could get to becoming one—he would know what it was like for warm tears to stream down his fleshy cheeks. He would absorb existence . . . the mysteries of life . . . in the same way that even strange, confused Anna did.

And once he assessed his new sensations, he wondered if he would be able to detect something so esoteric as the soul. It seemed possible to him, and he intended to look for it with all due diligence.

The supply shipment to the Sisterhood school brought an unexpected message from Lankiveil, a panicked recording from Danvis. Valya was consumed with planning the long-term growth of the order, yet a part of her mind always remained focused on restoring her Great House to glory . . . and completing her revenge against Vorian Atreides.

But now the Atreides had come to her own family home! They'd gone there hunting for Tula, and threatened her parents, as well as Danvis! Shock and anger burned bright inside Valya.

Her sister had stayed on Lankiveil for a brief time before slipping away to Chusuk, as if running away from something. Maybe she had known Vorian Atreides would come after her. The Mother Superior's operatives had discreetly followed Tula, continued to watch her, and they had secretly arrived on Chusuk as well. Valya was confident that the young woman would come to her senses eventually.

But now Vorian Atreides was after her! He and Orry's brother Willem had shown bloody images of the revenge Tula had achieved for her family honor. Valya understood the implied threat—what would stop Vorian Atreides from murdering her family for revenge? Fortunately, Tula was long gone before they arrived, but the Atreides men had been in her family home!

In his message, Danvis sounded angry and frightened, but he clearly didn't comprehend the magnitude of the threat Vorian posed. Her sister was unaware of the grave danger she was in on Chusuk, and Valya needed to help her. The

Harkonnens had to protect their own. The Sisterhood had to protect its own. She would send more watchers to guard Tula.

As Valya felt a knot of tension tightening inside her, she needed physical exertion to burn off her restlessness. She hiked away from the main school complex and climbed the rugged escarpment of Laojin Cliff, from which old Raquella had threatened to leap if the feuding Sisters did not resolve their differences. Valya had an entirely different kind of resolution in mind now.

Her mind swirling, she made her way up the steep path to the rough training ground at the rocky summit. She could sense danger in the air as the dedicated women took risks.

On the summit a group of advanced Sisters in white robes—all elite daughters of Rossak who carried ancient Sorceress blood—sparred and tested themselves. Most of the Sorceresses had been killed in the long Jihad against the thinking machines, and more had died afterward when Emperor Salvador attacked the old Rossak School. The few remaining Sorceresses in front of her were special assets with strong mental powers, and they trained in ways more rigorous than other Sisters would dare attempt.

They practiced edgy, over-the-top fighting techniques developed long ago in the Rossak jungles, and Mother Superior Valya encouraged them to continue their training so they could instruct other women. In her vision for the Sisterhood, Valya wanted to synthesize many different combat methods into a new way of fighting that no one else could practice. Someday, Valya might find herself pitted against Vorian Atreides. Her lips curved into a grim, hard smile. She intended to be ready.

On the rugged ridge, she also saw three white-robed trainees stationed on ledges below the lip of the cliff. Sister Deborah, a lean and angular Sorceress, stood watching them. "Mother Superior, welcome. Have you come to participate in the exercises?"

"Not today. I just want to observe." She was still preoccupied with Danvis's report and hoped the sparring would settle her. Valya stepped close to the precipice to see the Sorceress trainees conducting their hazardous routines near the sheer drop-off. The three Sisters seemed to be showing off for her, engaging in dramatic leaps and practice attacks, landing on narrow ledges. They used nudges of telekinesis to balance themselves on the tiniest spaces.

"Impressive," Valya said to Deborah, "but these feats are impractical for Acolytes who do not have the Sorceress bloodline or abilities."

The white-robed woman smiled. "We have a less demanding practice ground on the other side of the slope. Follow me."

Deborah led her along the crest trail to where a line of Acolytes waited at the verge, ready to tumble down a steep slope. Though it was not a sheer cliff, the practice slope still looked treacherous; this was not just a test of physical ability but agility, balance, and swift reflexes. Valya had undergone this herself, and expected nothing less from her initiates. If a young woman used her training, conditioning, and intelligence during the fall, she would reach the bottom with little or no injury. If not, she would be broken. . . .

The first two Acolytes had already plunged over the edge, rolling and springing back to balance on the ledges, dodging boulders, and continuing to the bottom as swiftly as they could. Somehow, both trainees managed to survive and even show grace, ultimately landing on their feet at the base of the sheer rock wall.

The third Acolyte, however, experienced trouble shortly after she tumbled over the verge. She made it neatly to the first ledge on the course, then lost her footing when a loose rock broke away. As the trainee tumbled out of control, a Sorceress observer sprang into the air and used telekinesis to cushion and guide her plunge. With her white robe and long, flowing hair, the Sorceress plucked the Acolyte off the slope just as she was about to smash into a jagged rock outcropping. Together, they reached the bottom, where the shaken and bruised Acolyte stood on unsteady feet.

Valya turned to observe the rest of the young women who were lined up for their tests. When she saw the next Acolyte hesitate before throwing herself over the edge, she snapped, "What are you worried about? Your enemy is fear, not the fall. I have ensured that someone will rescue you if you lose control."

A flush suffused the young woman's cheeks, and a quick flash of anger lit her dark eyes. "With due respect, Mother Superior, it is the opposite. I cannot experience—and conquer—my fear if I know a Sorceress will swoop in and save me should I fail. I want to face the full risk, so that I can develop as quickly as possible." She lifted her chin. "Tell them *not* to help me."

Valya smiled with surprise. "Mother Superior Raquella said something similar to me once. What is your name?"

"Sister Gabi, Mother Superior."

Gabi reminded Valya of herself not so long ago—young, brash, and anxious to advance. She raised her voice for all to hear. "This Acolyte is completely on her own for the exercise. No Sorceress is to assist her in the fall—no matter what happens."

Deborah leaned close to ask in a low tone, "Is this wise? If she is killed, it might demoralize the others."

"This must be a real proving ground, and a memorable event will make it even more so." Each Sister was taught to focus on the attainment of perfect bodily control, mastering their reflexes, their movements, one muscle at a time. Anyone who knew the techniques could easily survive such a fall with grace.

As Gabi stood on the edge, mentally preparing herself, the Sorceress spotters withdrew along the slope. The young Acolyte shot an appreciative glance in Valya's direction, and without further hesitation, hurled herself down the precipitous slope. She rolled and dodged, controlling her plunge so well that she seemed to flow over the ground. She avoided the sharp rocks, landed briefly on tiny ledges, rebounding and continuing down, until she reached the bottom and landed on her feet, breathless and triumphant.

Energized by the success, more Acolytes followed Gabi over the edge, demanding no rescues, and many did not fare as well. At the end of the exercise, two had suffered broken bones, several with lacerations, and one experienced a concussion. But none of them died.

"One should never expect to be rescued," Valya said to Deborah as they watched the end of the exercise.

A wave of sadness overtook her. No one had saved her brother Griffin from the evil Vorian Atreides. . . .

For hours, Valya had let her mind work through her own treacherous obstacle course, with dangerous consequences for failure. The Atreides knew that Tula had assassinated Orry, and now they were hunting for the young woman.

Even so, she realized that Vorian could have attacked and killed her family on Lankiveil, but had refrained from doing so. He was a difficult man to understand.

Valya wouldn't make the assumption that they were safe now. She would send Sisters to Lankiveil to watch over her family, in case the Atreides returned. She couldn't leave her family vulnerable, although she doubted if Vorian would come back to do them harm, now that he had forfeited his chance.

House Harkonnen must not remain in the shadows forever: eight decades of disgrace was long enough. At the same time, Valya needed to protect her family—every one of them.

Memory may be a safety net, but forgetfulness is a blessing.
—TULA HARKONNEN, songs from Chusuk

Chusuk's scars from the Jihad had been nearly erased. The planet had been a smoldering wreck after the brutal thinking machines were driven out, but with songs of victory and freedom in their hearts, the survivors had reclaimed their world, rebuilt their cities. The people focused on universities, festivals, cultural expressions, and craft guilds that built the finest musical instruments in the Imperium. Chusuk had become a planet of art and poetry, as if the nightmarish subjugation of the thinking machines had altered the psyche of the population, inspiring them and providing emotional depths for them to draw upon.

Tula Harkonnen could try to forget her own dark past here, vanish into everyday life, and exist as a normal young woman with a quiet demeanor and shy disposition. No one on Chusuk knew who she really was . . . any more than the people of Caladan had known when Valya sent her there to seduce and murder Orry Atreides.

Now, she dressed in plain clothes and bound her long blonde hair back. Tula was too beautiful to be invisible, but she tried not to draw attention to herself. When she played her family baliset, she was proficient enough that people stopped and listened, while some skilled practitioners offered her some advice.

No one could see the blackness that surrounded her heart. The young woman had been so fierce a fighter, so focused on reclaiming Harkonnen honor against the vile Atreides that she believed everything Valya told her—and did as she was commanded.

But each night now as she went to sleep in her lonely bed on Chusuk,

Tula thought of her traumatic wedding night, of how handsome Orry had looked dozing beside her, languid and fully vulnerable after their lovemaking . . . unprepared for the sharp, swift edge of her knife.

Initially she had not questioned the mission, but once it was complete and she returned to Wallach IX, she had begun to wonder about what she'd done. Following orders like a soldier, Tula had killed a young man whose only crime was that he had Atreides blood in his veins. But young Orry had been isolated on Caladan all his life, generations removed from the harm that Vorian Atreides had committed against their great-grandfather. Orry had known nothing about how Griffin had died on Arrakis.

Valya had been vehement, though: "Only the death of an Atreides innocent can begin to repay the crimes that Vorian committed against our family."

Tula wasn't foolish enough to think that the price had been paid in full. Every day that she recovered here on Chusuk, she expected Valya to dispatch Sisters to find her. Ostensibly, they would claim they were coming to "protect" her and bring her back to Wallach IX so she could continue her training and go after the Atreides again, in another way. But now Tula was afraid of that training. She was also sure that Vorian and Willem Atreides would try to track her down to kill her. An unending cycle of violence.

Tula's emotions swung like a pendulum. She just wanted to be left alone and forget she was a Harkonnen, forget she was anyone at all. But she doubted that was an option. If Vorian ever found her, he would make her pay the ultimate price . . . and if Valya found her, she would make Tula pay in a different way.

Tula liked to bring her baliset into the market, where she would find a place under the colorful awnings. She played songs—not to attract an audience, but simply to create music near other poets and musicians who did the same. She chose favorite tunes of the fur-whalers on Lankiveil, songs no one on Chusuk had ever heard. She also created her own melodies, exploring the music with her fingers and imagination.

Each day a young man, nearly her age, set up a workbench nearby, where he could listen to her. He was surrounded by the fumes of lacquer and turpentine as he built handcrafted balisets, which he also played to test them. He flashed Tula a smile whenever she turned her attention toward him.

She didn't want to encourage him, didn't want to use the Sisterhood's psychological manipulation and seduction techniques she'd mastered in order to make herself irresistible—regrettably—to Orry Atreides. Tula could easily have enticed the young baliset maker into her bed, but the very thought formed a knot in her stomach. She concentrated on her own music instead.

The young man finally identified himself as Liem Valjean. "Your instrument is in tune, but if you adjust the flywheel, the tone will be richer. I think you have a slightly defective one." He asked if he could see her baliset, and checked the pegs securing the strings, repaired and balanced the flywheel, and then began to play the instrument.

He was highly skilled, and the music he evoked was far superior to her own. When he offered to instruct her, she hesitated for only a moment. Liem was not her mission; she didn't need to spy on him, seduce, or slay him. On the other hand, aside from Danvis, she could not think of anyone she even considered a friend. And a friend was what she desperately needed.

She played her baliset as he watched and listened. At first she picked out a sad song, and then she decided to play something livelier and more cheerful, one that Liem seemed to like better, as did she.

Allies can have different priorities. Some may be focused on personal gain, while others seek revenge. As for me, I am driven by my own destiny. That is my priority.

—DIRECTEUR JOSEF VENPORT, speech
before dispatching the Venport Holdings fleet

A s Josef strode across the field of Navigators, his thoughts were awhirl with his decision. He could no longer just sit back, gather his defenses, and wait for the Emperor to come to his senses; Roderick Corrino had forced him to go on the offensive.

Overhead, Kolhar's midday sun was a bright spot trying to burn through the clouds. Josef stewed as he walked among the sealed tanks, smelling the sharp odor of vented spice. The candidates inside squirmed with their horrific transformation, but he was preoccupied with his own problems.

Josef had never considered himself a revolutionary, nor had he harbored any aspirations to overthrow the Imperial throne, but the Emperor had changed the rules. Damn the man! Rather than focusing on their mutual enemy, the dangerous Butlerians, Roderick's pointless vendetta made collaboration impossible. By proving that he intended to destroy Venport Holdings at any cost, by showing that he wanted to ruin Josef and erase his legacy, Roderick demonstrated that he would never compromise or negotiate of his own free will.

So, Josef would *make* him negotiate—or he would crush the Emperor entirely. He needed to assume a position of overwhelming strength and finish the matter on his own terms. Roderick Corrino would either be reasonable, or else he would be replaced.

Josef peered through the murky plaz of a nearby tank to see a figure adrift inside, its eyes closed, as if at peace with the universe. But he drew no insight there, and moved on up the slope to the midst of the tanks.

Understanding the crisis in her own esoteric way, Norma Cenva had contacted her Navigators, who brought their scattered ships from across the Imperium, one by one, and waited to launch for Salusa Secundus. Cioba and Draigo oversaw the preparations while Josef came out here to contemplate. His ships would overwhelm the Imperial capital soon enough.

As a matter of tactics, the foldspace carrier holding Admiral Harte's hostage Imperial battle group would remain here as leverage. Josef liked to have plenty of options. A third of his VenHold ships would also stay behind to protect Kolhar, just in case the Emperor's bank seizure was a ploy to provoke him into leaving his headquarters vulnerable.

"You have to prepare for that possibility, my husband," Cioba had advised him. "Emperor Roderick may have plans within plans."

"I agree with your caution," Josef had said, "but I am skeptical that he has the military resources for a full-scale, two-pronged attack. In fact, all the ships in his Imperial Armed Forces can't defend Salusa Secundus against us."

He was counting on that. His forces would lay siege to Salusa, and when the Emperor was put in his place, Josef would graciously give him everything back, provided concessions were achieved. Business as usual in the Imperium, efficient and profitable—that was all Josef wanted, but he could not let Roderick's foolish political or personal decisions cause further disruption.

Draigo Roget had completed another rushed trip to Denali, returning with a foldspace carrier that held the thirty-one new cymeks, their warrior forms tucked away in the hold, ready to be dropped on Salusa Secundus—a terrifying threat from the past that should result in Zimia's immediate surrender.

Standing among the Navigator tanks, Josef turned to look back toward his main base of operations, where he could see two of the towering warrior forms marching in the distance—Noffe and Ptolemy. The rest of the Navigator brains remained in orbit, ready to be deployed once they arrived at Salusa, but these two seemed very restless.

Norma's dais was empty, because his great-grandmother had already transported herself to the Navigator deck of the VenHold flagship. She was ready to go to Salusa, ready to end the chaos that disturbed her Navigators. The hidden spice stockpile on Arrakis ensured stability, but the political unrest imperiled their continued prosperity.

The two cymeks marched toward him, covering a great distance with their long strides. Noffe's simulated voice came through his comm as they approached, "Directeur Venport, Ptolemy and I wish to speak with you."

"I am here," he said as the huge machines picked their way across the field. "Take care not to damage the Navigator tanks."

"We are quite agile in our walker forms," Ptolemy said as the machines stepped gracefully among the transformation chambers. Since Norma's tank was gone, the top of the rise was clear, providing room for them to meet. Josef was not intimidated by the mechanical warriors. He could see the preservation canister connected to each body core, with thoughtrode linkages that allowed the brains to direct the complex mechanisms. Optical sensors swiveled to focus down on him as he looked up at the two cymeks, hands on his hips.

Noffe's simulated voice said, "We have devoted our minds and skills to making you strong, Directeur Venport. That is the reason for Denali's existence. You brought us together because we all have the same incentive. We all hate Manford Torondo."

"We need to see the Butlerians defeated," said Ptolemy. "Noffe and I are concerned about using our completed cymeks to attack the Imperial capital. That is not why we were designed, and the Emperor is not our principal enemy. It is a distraction. We are not interested in political squabbles or dynastic challenges. We are anxious to attack *Lampadas* in full force. Not Salusa."

Josef faced them, annoyed. He had far more serious complications than coddling his cymeks and research scientists. But even though he wanted to tell them to fall back and do as they were told, because *he* made all the important decisions, he suppressed a harsh comment.

Instead, he said, "Lampadas will be our next target, I promise you—but the Emperor has provoked this immediate action. My company has to survive, or there will be no further attacks on the barbarians. Unless we can regain access to our financial assets, we won't be able to finish building our cymek army." He smiled. "In the meantime, once they see how easily our new cymeks overthrow Salusa Secundus, how can the Butlerians not shiver in terror, knowing they will be next?"

The two warrior forms raised themselves higher. Body turrets swiveled, then turned the optical sensors back toward him. "Very well, Directeur," said Noffe. "We will help you take over the Imperial capital."

Ptolemy added, "And then we attack Lampadas."

The walkers marched back to the landing field, where Josef's military preparations continued.

The most blessed gift I can give is to correct the error of a person's ways and guide him onto the proper path.

—MANFORD TORONDO, private consultation with Anari Idaho

After the overthrow, the Mentat School had been cleansed and restructured to Manford's liking, and the Butlerian leader was proud of the accomplishment. Zendur, the school's deputy administrator who had served under the traitorous Headmaster Albans, was weak, terrified, and easily manipulated. Therefore, Manford considered him the perfect person to fill the position.

Even before the overthrow of the institution, many Mentat students had been Butlerian followers, and the rest were being properly reeducated now. In the aftermath of the siege, the school complex had been rebuilt and fortified along the shore of the marsh lake. The buildings were connected by wooden platforms, atop pilings driven deep into the soft soil. The ornate roof arches and walkways linking one structure to the next gave the complex the appearance of serenity, an elite academy dedicated to human contemplation. From now on, that contemplation would consist only of orthodox ideas.

As Anari Idaho brought him to inspect the new facility, Manford saw that Headmaster Zendur was a broken, nervous man. Despite being a Mentat, the administrator seemed unable to extrapolate his own situation and put it in the proper context. Zendur had been trained by Headmaster Albans and was therefore suspect, but for now, at least, he would serve as interim manager over a carefully prepared curriculum, with students rigorously selected on the basis of their philosophical beliefs, rather than mental acuity.

For Manford loyalty was primary; everything else was secondary.

When Zendur came out to meet them, he pressed his hands together and bowed deeply. Manford had no doubt that this school would be exactly as expected, and this inspection visit was merely a pro forma exercise. The replacement Headmaster and the remaining Mentat students had learned their lesson. They understood that their role was to calculate and advise, not to lead some kind of thought-revolution.

Carrying Manford in her shoulder harness, Anari strode along the wooden walkways. Beside them, Zendur babbled about the new classes, the progress of the students, and even the survival-training sessions out in the swamps. Their footwear made noises on the wood.

"Has there been any sign of Anna Corrino yet?" Manford interrupted. "Any hint as to how she escaped? Any remnant of her body?"

"No to all that, Leader Torondo," said Zendur, "but she never was a strong girl. If she fled into the swamps, there is no chance she survived."

"You understand probabilities, Mentat, so you know there is always a chance, however infinitesimal it might be. Emperor Roderick fears that I had something to do with her disappearance. If I can return Anna Corrino to him, then I will secure his gratitude and cooperation, which is something I need."

Anari made a dissonant noise. "We didn't need Emperor Salvador as our ally. We simply made him do as we asked."

"Roderick is different from his brother," Manford said, but because Zendur was listening, he didn't add his own concerns about how difficult it would be to manipulate or bully the new Emperor. Roderick saw through Butlerian strategies in ways that Salvador never had.

In a clear snub, the new Emperor had pointedly not invited Manford to his coronation. With Anna gone missing during the Butlerian siege of the Mentat School, as well as Roderick's young daughter killed by an out-of-control mob during a rampage festival, the Emperor had sufficient cause to turn against their movement . . . or worse, join forces with Directeur Venport to eradicate him and his followers. Manford had been very concerned.

But then a miracle had happened when Venport was revealed to be the man behind Salvador's assassination! The vile business mogul had become an outlaw, hated by Roderick, and this political shift gave Manford and his Butlerians a chance to regain ground.

From his perch on Anari's shoulders, he asked the new Headmaster, "How many of your Mentats are trained well enough to be put into service? I need at least two to accompany us to Salusa Secundus."

Zendur stammered, calculated, and nodded. "I have what you require."

"Good. We will take them to the Imperial Palace as a gift to the Emperor. My followers on Salusa will help me cement a new position for our movement. We can provide Roderick Corrino with whatever he needs, and with a sufficient show of force, we will keep him on the straight and narrow path."

Those without a true sense of history fail to see how volatile and tran-sient human leadership is, even on the scale of empires. When viewed from the perspective of a mere lifetime, we tend to see our governmental structures as permanent and unchangeable. This is entirely false.

—FAYKAN CORRINO I, first Emperor after the Butlerian Jihad

Inside her tank on the Navigator deck of the VenHold flagship, Norma waved a webbed hand. "We are ready to depart. My Navigators will guide us to Salusa Secundus." She drifted. "I am anxious to restore stability to the Imperium."

Josef paced on the bridge beside her. He stared out at his orbiting spacefolders—more than three hundred of them. "I have no doubt our fleet will arrive flawlessly, thanks to you, Grandmother, and we will quickly overwhelm the Imperial defenses. Soon this will all be over. Does your prescience foresee an easy victory? We certainly have the military advantage."

Norma floated away from the plaz wall of her tank. "My prescience sees many possibilities around Salusa Secundus. I cannot say which one will become real."

Without giving further details, she used her own control to activate the Holtzman engines, and Josef could feel the hull pulsing as the energy built up. The Navigators aboard the other ships coordinated their moves, and Josef quickly held on, bracing himself. All three hundred vessels vanished simultaneously into foldspace.

Disoriented during the passage, he clenched his fist, sucked in his breath. He wished Cioba could be at his side, but needed her to guard Kolhar as well as manage the commercial activities of Venport Holdings in his absence. Business went on. Despite the bank seizure, hundreds of his trading ships continued to travel throughout the Imperium illicitly delivering vital supplies—especially melange.

With their financial assets frozen, VenHold was crippled in conducting regular operations, but he would resolve the situation quickly and aggressively. Once the Emperor saw the enormous force arrayed against Salusa, he would have only one rational solution available to him, and Josef counted on him being a rational man: that was the gamble he had made all along, although Roderick had certainly disappointed him so far.

Guided by Norma and her Navigators, Josef's well-armed ships reappeared in a tight cluster high above the capital planet. Knowing the amount of space traffic around Salusa, Norma had intentionally brought them to the upper fringe of the primary orbital lanes, where the VenHold ships need not worry about colliding with the bustle of governmental and commercial vessels. Nevertheless, it was a show of force that could not be denied.

At their stations, the VenHold crewmembers on the Navigator deck breathed a sigh of relief. "We are in a safe position for battle, Directeur. All VenHold vessels present and accounted for. Weapons ready."

"They've seen us, sir!"

On the wide screen Josef saw the orbiting Salusan ships suddenly move erratically, like fish stirred in a bowl. He smiled. "Of course they have. That is our intent." He would let them see and absorb the sheer military might he had brought with him—the biggest stick in the Imperium.

"Will you be addressing the people, Directeur?" asked the comm officer.

Josef placed his hands behind his back and walked slowly away from Norma's tank. "Not yet. I want to give them time to think about the power we have brought to bear on them. Let them feel the crisis in their *bones* before I deliver my ultimatum to Roderick Corrino."

From the bridge of one of the adjacent spacefolders, Draigo Roget reported. "The Emperor's defensive fleet appears to be even smaller than anticipated, Directeur—no more than a hundred warships—and none of them a match for ours. What happened to all the rest? Our earlier intelligence suggested another full strike force here, but those ships are not in sight."

Josef was concerned. "Are they otherwise deployed?"

"I cannot make that projection, sir," the Mentat said.

Josef looked at the flurry of orbital activity, the trading and diplomatic vessels trying to escape while the greatly outnumbered Imperial military ships scrambled to form a defensive line. "Send no transmissions just yet. The Emperor will demand to know why I have come, and then he'll ask for my terms." He had decided that Roderick should bare his throat in some way, to prove that he understood where the true power lay. "And then he will surrender, but it'll just be a formality. Afterward, we can put all this behind us."

Anyone could see that the VenHold fighting force could overwhelm the

Salusan defenses, should they choose to do so—and the Emperor would not dare let this turn into an all-out, bloody space battle. But Roderick had demonstrated a recent penchant for stubbornness and irrationality. . . .

Josef was ready to fight—decisively—if necessary. And take the capital. "Launch our cymeks," he said.

Landing pods fell out of the lower hold of the Denali spacefolder, dropping into the atmosphere like precisely guided meteors. Josef watched them streak down, knowing the fear that such immense and powerful machines would evoke.

"General Agamemnon and his cymek Titans attacked Salusa repeatedly during the war against the thinking machines," Norma said from her Navigator tank. "Now we are the invaders sending in cymeks."

He could not tell if her voice contained irony. "I regret the necessity, Grandmother, but it is the swiftest solution. Such a threat will make them tremble—and concede."

From the bridge, he watched the bright downward trails arrowing toward the palace district on the west side of Zimia. Down there, Emperor Roderick and his advisers must be staring aghast at what was coming their way.

Josef addressed his ships. "Tighten the noose. Activate weapons and shields, and be ready to fire on my command."

From his ship, Draigo said, "The Imperial ships cannot outgun us, sir, but if we let them form tight ranks, they might force us to cause more destruction than would be wise. I would prefer not to massacre them."

"Agreed. Move out. Disperse and neutralize those fighting ships."

From inside her tank, Norma spoke, "I do not believe Roderick will concede so easily."

"I do not need prescience to agree with you, Grandmother, but we can hope for the sake of the Imperium that he does." He realized he was being optimistic, perhaps even naïve. Roderick Corrino's pride would not let him surrender to the man who had killed his brother. What would it take to get him to abandon that useless vendetta? Josef would have made concessions, within reason.

The Salusan communication channels were in an uproar, and the orbiting Imperial warships scrambled to form a barricade against all the ominous VenHold ships. But Josef's well-coordinated fleet plunged in, ignoring all the commercial and diplomatic vessels that escaped into interplanetary space; rather, they targeted only the Imperial military ships and scattered them in tactical confusion. Josef had warned each of his captains to exercise restraint, to fire only for defensive purposes, and then just enough to paralyze specific threats.

The VenHold ships succeeded with very little weapons fire. Some of the Imperial defenders blasted at them, but their weapons could not penetrate VenHold shields. Two Imperial vessels engaged in suicide runs, opening fire and trying to ram one of Josef's ships, but the Navigator aboard easily dodged out of range of the blasts.

In her tank, Norma flinched.

"Hold positions," Josef transmitted to his fleet. "Roderick must already see he has been defeated."

Telemetry recorded when Ptolemy, Noffe, and the Navigator cymeks landed on the outskirts of Zimia. Moments later, images broadcast from the emerging walkers showed multiple views of the streets. The enormous warrior forms towered above the ornate governmental buildings.

From his bridge, Josef stared at the planet below, the sea of clouds, the oceans, continents, and sprawling cities. Zimia was the Imperial capital city, and Salusa Secundus had been the heart of the League of Nobles during the centuries of the Jihad. He had been here many times on business. Now he needed to take care of a different sort of business.

Josef had to ensure he could hold his victory here long enough to restore order across the Imperium, to get commerce back to normal. He wanted to put an end to this nonsense, but first Roderick had to back down. With a single word and a gesture, the Emperor could lift Josef's banishment, restore the VenHold banks, and return everything to normal.

It was time for him to do so.

Josef faced the screen and activated the comm, then spoke his thunderous words like a conquering general. "Roderick Corrino," he said, intentionally choosing not to include the title of Emperor, "I am a loyal citizen of the Imperium, focused on the future of human civilization. I only wish to conduct my business under a mutually beneficial arrangement with you, but your actions have made that impossible. When you stole my financial assets, you destroyed the peace and prosperity of the Imperium.

"Your brother Salvador caused incalculable harm to us all, and it was my hope that you would be a better leader. I gave you every chance to work with me, to prove yourself, but my optimism has been dashed. Today, I come to end this. I will present my terms for your surrender."

An Emperor rules through wealth, military might, alliances, and influ-
ence. But he keeps his rule through the wisdom of his decisions, the re-
spect of his subjects, and the momentum of history. Should he lose any
one of those factors, his position is greatly weakened.

—EMPEROR JULES CORRINO, seventh address to the
Landsraad League

When Venport's Navigator-guided ships crowded space over Salusa Secundus, Roderick rushed to the Palace's satellite command center. The gall of the man!

The Emperor had already stationed the bulk of his fleet around the planet, but his once-titanic military was tissue thin now that he was missing General Roon's strike force as well as Admiral Harte's battle group, which Venport held hostage at Kolhar, not to mention the peacekeeping force he had recently lost at Arrakis.

Even so, he had never expected Josef Venport to make such a bold and irrevocable move. To attack the Emperor directly! Venport was a manipulator, not a conqueror—did he actually want the throne for himself? It did not seem conceivable, but such an enormous, threatening force was not merely for show.

Roderick's military advisers and Salusan Defense Council officers filled the command center, scanning and collating data to assess the unexpected threat. The Emperor didn't need to hear their reports, though; when he saw their stricken expressions, he realized how bad the situation was.

"The attackers are perfectly coordinated, Sire," said Shaad Aliki, his home defense commander. "Those VenHold ships appeared exactly on target, in high orbit, dropping down to wreak havoc among our commercial, diplomatic, and military ships. With such precision, they operate like a force of thinking-machine vessels."

"Not thinking machines." Roderick watched the enemy vessels position themselves among his orbiting guardian ships and render them impotent.

"Venport's Navigators guide his ships with a level of accuracy and safety we cannot match." As he watched the invaders' vise-grip tighten, he was sickened. "He has declared war on the Imperium! He's got to know he can't win against the allied noble houses. The Landsraad League will all turn against him and stand by me."

Or would they?

A chill went through him. Roderick's feud with Venport had disrupted commerce throughout the Imperium, and the bottleneck had also cut off regular supplies of spice, now that Arrakis was in turmoil. Many of his nobles were addicted to melange . . . and he suspected they would rather do without their Emperor than without spice.

Roderick had held the throne for only the past two months, and Salvador's reign had been an embarrassment of corruption and incompetence. Why would anyone be loyal to the Corrinos? Since the end of the Jihad and the formation of the Imperium, there had been only two Emperors before them—Jules and Faykan—and the Corrino dynasty was barely a paragraph in human history. Yes, it could be overthrown. Governments and dynasties did not exist forever.

Roderick's throat went dry. It was indeed possible that Josef Venport could usurp the throne and form a new Venport line of rulers. With the great force he had brought to bear, the Directeur had the power to do exactly that . . . if it was what he wanted.

As if reading his mind, Haditha rushed into the command center and said, "Directeur Venport has many connections in the Landsraad League, he has a military force that is clearly superior to ours, and he's the one who can guarantee trade across the Imperium. That is what the people want above all else." She lowered her voice. "I fear that he can break you, my love."

"He's a coward," Roderick muttered. "He murdered my brother and fled justice. I have to keep standing up to him. Such a man can't be allowed to do business as if nothing happened."

"He won't take the throne from you, Sire. That will never happen!" Shaad Aliki cried. "God is on our side."

"Maybe so," Roderick said, "but right now I would rather have more warships on our side." He studied the numerous images being transmitted by his outnumbered orbiting defenders. The VenHold fleet was enormous.

"You know why he took such extreme action," Haditha said. "It all stems from your brother. Salvador provoked Venport's original overreaction when he grabbed control of the spice operations on Arrakis."

"Possibly his most unwise decision," Roderick grumbled under his breath. *Among many.*

Haditha continued, "And now we have pushed Venport into another corner by seizing his assets. His response is predictable. We escalated the crisis and forced him to take extreme action."

"But is this just a threatening growl? I am the Emperor—does he really mean to destroy political stability throughout the Imperium?"

Inside the command center, tacticians displayed images from orbit, as Roderick's embattled captains inundated the Palace with panicked requests for instructions and reinforcements. "VenHold ships outnumber ours three to one, Sire, and their weapons are superior."

"As is their coordination," said Aliki, wearing a deep frown.

Roderick felt helpless anger and dismay. "We *have* to resist them, fight in every way possible. We are in the right!" His heart felt cold, and he was unable to find a way that his defiance would be anything more than empty words. Would the people fight for him, or would they pledge their allegiance to a new Emperor Venport?

When the VenHold invaders launched orbital drop-pods, several Imperial warships tried to intercept them, but the siege vessels opened fire and neutralized the Imperial fighters, targeting engines only and removing those ships from play so that the drop-pods could continue their descent.

"The VenHold ships do not seem intent on destroying our fleet or killing our soldiers." Aliki sounded puzzled. "They have exercised obvious restraint. They are just preventing us from interfering with whatever they're doing."

Roderick drew little hope from that observation. As the drop-pods streaked down through the atmosphere, evacuation alarms sounded across Zimia. One of the Imperial guards stepped up, his face grim. "Sire, we have to move you to a safe place—the emergency command center. Our shielded underground chambers should be proof against any attack."

Roderick straightened as the drop-pods continued to hurtle down. Big pods. "Take Haditha and our children first. I shall remain at my post. I can lead better from here."

Commander Aliki put a firm hand on his arm. "You can't lead if you're vaporized, Sire. They could have brought atomics, and we don't have the planetary shields in place to withstand such a bombardment."

Haditha sounded more outraged than afraid. "Atomics are forbidden!"

"Treason against the Emperor is also forbidden," Roderick pointed out to her. "I wouldn't look to Venport to follow every rule."

Once the drop-pods crashed around the outskirts of the Imperial capital, they disgorged armored walkers taller than most buildings. Cymeks! Roderick felt nauseated.

With utmost urgency, guards escorted him and Haditha to the secure underground chambers, where Roderick stared in dismay at displayed images of the enormous articulated machines.

Cymeks had not struck Zimia in more than a century. Back during the Jihad they had been deflected by powerful high-energy shields in the Salusan atmosphere, but after the annihilation of the thinking machines and the rebuilding of civilization, the enormous expense of maintaining the shields against cymeks had been deemed unnecessary. Machines posed no further threat to the human race.

But now more than thirty giant warrior forms emerged from the drop-pods and advanced toward the capital city. Ground troops mobilized, along with artillery to defend against the cymeks, but the machines easily brushed off the attack. They looked capable of leveling Zimia if they wished.

For now, however, the cymeks stopped outside the city and simply loomed there, threatening.

Then Josef Venport finally transmitted his ultimatum.

Honor is the backbone of the Freemen of the desert, and our tribes are bound by unbreakable trust and respect. The honor we show to off-worlders, however, is entirely different.

—MODOC, Naib of his sietch

The caves of his tribe's new sietch were spacious and secure. Modoc was surprised that no other Freemen had discovered them, and they were made habitable in short order. His people resented being forced to move from their ancestral home, where generations had lived in harmony with the desert, but he thought they took offense too easily. The new sietch they had constructed was basically the same as the old one, in Modoc's opinion, and the huge fees they collected from Josef Venport would grant his people many more luxuries.

His father, Naib Rurik, had been a bitter and unimaginative man, shunning improvements to his tribe's standard of living. He had spurned outside offers of food, medicine, and equipment. Modoc had laughed when his weakling brother Taref talked about the wonders of the Imperium, but that had been primarily to curry favor with their father. At the time, the Naib's own horizons had extended no farther than the walls of the caves and the surrounding desert, and he was not impressed by his son's talk.

Taref had been cast out after allying with Josef Venport, but maybe there was something worthwhile in what his brother had babbled about after all. Yes, the desert people could claw out a rough existence by hoarding every last drop of moisture and extracting melange dust from the sands, but did life need to be so harsh and primitive? If offworlders offered modern luxuries, what sort of leader would force his people to keep suffering simply out of his own stubbornness? When water was offered, would a thirsty man rather drink pride?

So, although his people had been inconvenienced by having to abandon their sietch and build another one, their cisterns were now full of water purchased from the garden tanks in Arrakis City; their larders were stocked with packaged honey, preserved food, offworld meats, dried fruits, delicacies they had never before tasted—all because of the generous payment Venport had given them.

And now, Emperor Roderick was paying them even more to bring about Venport's downfall! Modoc had accepted that mission as well. He saw no problem with his duplicity. This obscure offworlder conflict was not his war, nor was it any of his concern. He would profit from it and laugh at both sides.

Now, as his tribe members made their move on the spice bank, they were well armed with new weapons—purchased, ironically, with Venport's own money. And they had enough explosives to complete their plan.

To be sure, their old sietch would not be an easy target, and the Directeur placed an extraordinarily high value on his stockpile. With the spice harvested by his crews, as well as what Venport's raiders took from Imperial holding warehouses and black-market traders, Modoc estimated that more than a year's worth of spice production was already stored in his tribe's old caves.

But VenHold's mercenary defense forces and advanced technology only made the place *seem* impregnable. The Directeur had obtained the best security systems and weaponry available in the Imperium. But in order to load the new spice bank swiftly, his foolish engineers had widened mountain passageways and defiles that had originally restricted access so that only a few Freemen could pass through at a time. Now, the ways into the sietch were broad thoroughfares.

Obvious vulnerabilities.

Modoc doubted if his raiders would have any trouble completing the mission. They were skilled warriors, and the Naib had inflamed their anger toward Venport by exaggerating any slight the business tycoon had committed against them. His people would fight for an enormous payoff, which they had already received from the Emperor, but also to punish the man who had taken over their sietch and driven them from their ancestral home. . . .

At midmorning, Modoc led his hundreds of handpicked commandos out onto the sands, knowing how long it would take them to cross the desert. He planned to arrive at dusk.

Secure in their stillsuits against heat and moisture loss, his spotters took up positions while experienced worm callers arranged themselves on the high dunes before pounding resonant spikes into the sands, hammering out a rhythmic, irresistible beat to summon the great sandworms.

All of his people had ridden the behemoths before, and each warrior was adept at mounting and guiding each manifestation of Shai-Hulud. The Freemen believed Shai-Hulud watched over their tribes and cared nothing for the invaders who now infested Arrakis like dune lice.

Their beliefs were reaffirmed when sandworms responded to the thumping call. Ripples across the open dunes indicated where the monsters traveled beneath. Spotters on the highest dune crests shaded their eyes in the midmorning sun and pointed at the approaching wormsign. The drummers continued pounding on the spikes, causing more worms to come.

Shai-Hulud was on their side.

When the first worm surfaced in an explosive spray of sand and spice, the Freemen had already surrounded the area. As Naib, Modoc was allowing the more ambitious warriors to do the difficult work. After all, he had created this opportunity that offered such great rewards.

When the first sandworm arose, desert fighters scrambled up its side with maker hooks, and inserted spreading wedges between the ring segments to separate them and expose sensitive flesh beneath. In this way they kept the worm from plunging back into the sands. As the giant creature rolled to avoid pain to its sensitive areas, the warriors added ropes and kept scaling the hard-crusted body, imposing their will on the much larger creature. When twenty fighters had climbed to its crest, they shifted their maker hooks down the curvature of the sandworm's body, forcing it to turn in the direction they wanted. The worm opened its enormous mouth to show a cave filled with sharp crystalline teeth. They drove the creature out onto the sands, heading toward their old sietch.

When the second worm came, Modoc mounted with the next group of fighters.

In all, seven of the beasts surged along, coiled for violence but kept under control by their Freemen riders. The normally territorial creatures did not like being in close proximity to other worms, but Modoc could use their instinctive anger in a different way. The worms would lash out against any target the desert warriors designated—and Modoc planned to give them that target.

The sandworms arrived at the old sietch at sunset, when the shadows were long and Venport's spice bank was preparing to lock down for the night. Though the sunlight was low and blinding near the horizon, the enormous worms could not be hidden as they stormed out across the desert. This would be an open attack, a full onslaught.

Modoc prepared his fighters as the worms reached the line of rocks. They guided the first creature toward a once-narrow defile that VenHold engineers had widened for access. As the worm approached, four demolition experts leaped off its back, carrying explosive packs. They landed on the sand and rolled, then rushed to the safety of rock, where they implanted the powerful canisters.

Inside the former sietch, VenHold security forces sounded emergency alarms and brought their weapons to bear on the intruders, but the desert commandos planted their bombs and slipped away into openings in the rugged rock formation. The nearly simultaneous blasts sent columns of fire and smoke into the sky, triggering a sustained rumble of avalanches as the cliff walls fell—widening the gateway to the desert.

Modoc drove his worm forward into the breach, and the other six followed. He knew how much spice wealth was contained inside the vaults, and though he had struggled with possibilities for more profit, he could not find a way that he and his people could seize it all for themselves and sell it back to the Imperium.

Emperor Roderick had ordered him to destroy Venport's stockpile. He remembered a Zensunni proverb, "What is stolen once can be stolen again, but what is destroyed is gone forever." They would take what they could, carrying it in packs on their backs as they fled, but they had to move swiftly through the desert.

As the behemoths plunged through the enlarged passageway into the sheltered basin, Modoc and his fighters were ready to let the collective Shai-Hulud do the destruction for them. These worms were a weapon against which Venport's mercenary fighters could not defend.

The sandworms surged into the enclosed rocky arena fronting a curvature of cliffs that held the protected spice bank. Choosing their time carefully, the desert people slid down the crusty worm segments, dismounted, and raced toward the most protected rocks.

Venport's mercenary force opened fire, cutting down some of the Freemen. Modoc saw ten of his fighters fall, but that was unavoidable. They were all heroes.

As the worms smashed into anything within reach, the Freemen dropped additional explosive packs along the bases of the cliffs, bigger ones this time, with activated timers.

Venport's defenders didn't have a chance.

Knowing what was to come, Modoc and his fighters jogged away and took shelter just before the additional explosions went off. A thunderous series of blasts shook the rocks and weakened the cliff faces. Trapped within the enclosed rock walls, the worms became thrashing, violent battering rams.

Modoc and his commandos backed off to watch the destruction, letting the sandworms do most of the work for them. The behemoths hammered themselves against the cliffs, breaking down the caves and crushing anything that moved. The Freemen would wait until the fury had run its course, with the sietch devastated, and then they would set new explosives to release the trapped sandworms from their enclosure, hoping all of them survived. He convinced himself that they would; it would take a lot more than rock walls to destroy Shai-Hulud.

After letting the worms out, the Freemen would slip in to kill any surviving defenders that hid in the deep tunnels. They would take all the water and blood they liked, and their treasure in spice would be far more than they could carry.

When Modoc took his people back to the new sietch, he wouldn't even have to embellish the story of what had happened to make this day one of the most legendary in the history of his tribe.

To negotiate, both parties must want something that is tangible and compatible. If one party wishes only the destruction of the other, no solution can exist.

—Landsraad League records, Salusan proceedings

The Emperor, besieged in Zimia, remained at a frozen standoff with the VenHold ships in orbit. The threatening cymeks loomed at the edge of the city, and the invaders held Roderick's military ships at gunpoint. The Emperor had failed to respond to Josef Venport's demand for surrender, but he would have to answer the ultimatum soon.

Roderick knew the Directeur could crush them and take over Zimia whenever he pleased. Venport had superior shields, newer and more powerful weapons . . . and three times as many ships. Roderick could see that he had lost; all that remained was to minimize the number of casualties.

But he would not just relinquish the Imperial throne!

Although the Directeur seemed to be in no hurry, his patience could be wearing thin. His next transmission was more gruff than the previous one. "I still await your response, Roderick Corrino. We have wasted enough time on the inevitable, and the Imperium needs to be set back on course. I require your immediate surrender. My terms will be reasonable—if you are reasonable."

Inside the armored underground command center, Roderick clenched his fists, but did not transmit. "How can I negotiate with that man?"

His wife and children had been brought into the deep bunker. If he surrendered, would Venport kill his whole family anyway? Just to clean the slate?

Roderick had to find some way to drive back the cymek monstrosities and orbiting warships, but the invaders were more powerful than any forces he could rally. Should he order them to fight anyway? A suicide mission, for honor and glory if not victory? But if he incited an outright shooting war, his own people and his military would be cut to ribbons. And then what would the cymeks do to Zimia?

Would the people even fight and die for him?

Did he have any alternative but the surrender Venport demanded?

"The Director has shown unexpected restraint," Haditha pointed out, without reminding him that she had advised Roderick to negotiate sooner, before they reached such an impasse. Too late for that now. "That means he wants something other than just to kill you. He knows, and we all know, he could smash into the palace and seize your throne."

Roderick narrowed his eyes. "Is that what he really wishes? That man repeatedly claimed that he has no desire to be Emperor. So what does he want?" He realized the irony that *he* had never wanted to be Emperor either, but the Directeur, through his own machinations, had placed Roderick on the throne.

Haditha continued to sound calm beside him. "As a businessman, Directeur Venport's overriding goal is to restore stability so he can build his commercial empire. He could devastate Salusa Secundus, but that would harm him as well. It would be a poor business decision, unpopular with the nobles. That is his weak spot and your advantage. Find some alternative that he will tolerate, a concession you can give. He will insist that you make some kind of gesture just to prove that he's won. Maybe that will be enough."

"What alternative could satisfy him without destroying me or the Imperium? Will it be enough for me to surrender publicly, and then he will withdraw? But if I surrender to him, even as just a formality, my ability to rule will be forever broken. The Landsraad nobles would see me as weak and defeated, and they will tear me to pieces. I could no longer serve as Emperor, and it would render the throne impotent for generations." Roderick stared down at his hands, then looked into the concerned eyes of his beautiful wife.

There had to be some way to save face, to salvage the desperate situation. Roderick paced the shielded bunker. Without question, Salvador had been maddening and foolish, making so many bad decisions that Roderick spent much of his time mitigating them. Countless other advisers had whispered about the need to remove Salvador from the throne. *But he was my brother.*

His three children were wide eyed and frightened. He turned to his son. The twelve-year-old Crown Prince Javicco had been raised to fill his role as the next Emperor, although he was still too young to fully grasp what that meant.

Then Roderick realized that it wasn't so much the Imperium at stake, but his rule. *He* was the one whom Venport needed to defeat, not the Landsraad League, not the throne itself. It was personal . . . because Roderick had made it that way.

Maybe only a personal solution would be acceptable.

He kept his voice low. "I can transfer the throne to Javicco to preserve the Corrino dynasty—set him up with a stable rule and let me take the fall. I may even have to sacrifice my life."

"No!" Haditha cried out.

"Maybe I don't have to die. In any event, I don't mind being the scapegoat, as long as the Directeur raises no impediments to Javicco's reign, and so long as the Landsraad League fully supports our son." He stared hard at Haditha. "I can offer that as an alternative to Venport. He will see that it would be a far easier transition than asking the Imperium to accept a usurper. Unless he wants years of civil war in the Landsraad, he will see that it's a viable option. A good business decision. He'll have gotten rid of me, and that's what he wants."

On the comm, Directeur Venport was transmitting again, demanding the Emperor's response. Roderick focused on his own decision, ignoring what he was hearing.

Javicco stared, confused and overwhelmed by the suggestion, but Roderick knew he had to do this. Before Haditha could argue, he raised his hand. "Commander Aliki, open a comm channel and tell Directeur Venport that I will present myself to him to discuss the matter."

Aliki was appalled. "Don't do that, Sire! He will kill you, just as he assassinated your brother."

"He had Salvador killed for entirely different reasons. I have to hope that he is more interested in stability than in revenge." Roderick squeezed his son's shoulder. "For my family's sake."

Haditha did not like the option. "If Javicco takes the throne, Venport will insist on appointing his own regent to oversee him. Our son will be no more than a puppet."

"But a Corrino would still hold the throne. He'd be alive—and you and I might be as well." He hardened his voice. "We still have many allies in the Landsraad. A throne that is overthrown once can be overthrown again. It can be retaken."

As Aliki grudgingly followed orders, Roderick drew a breath, as if this could inject clarity into his decision. He composed himself and reached forward to activate the comm response. No sense in delaying longer.

Before he could speak, though, his sensor technicians shouted, peering closer at their screens. The staff generals rushed forward to inspect the broader view of the Salusan system. Screens suddenly displayed a flurry of new blips arriving in space.

Aliki couldn't believe what he was seeing. "Sire, more than a hundred large warships just appeared out of foldspace! They seem to be old-model spacefolders, but they are fully equipped battleships."

Roderick felt as if his breath had been snatched away. "Venport's reinforcements? Does he wish to grind his boot-heel down even harder?"

A transmission came across all channels, bold and loud. "Emperor Roderick, it appears you need assistance."

The face of Manford Torondo, a man as reviled as Josef Venport, appeared on the screen. "I brought my loyal Butlerian forces to join you in an alliance for humanity's future. 'The mind of man is holy.' I pledge all these ships against the demon Venport and his machine-loving army." He smiled. "We are ready to fight beside you."

Enemies and allies are like planets whirling in a complex solar system.
Sometimes they align, sometimes their orbits intersect . . . and some-
times they collide, with devastating consequences.

—NORMA CENVA, recorded conversations,
subcategory: Spacing Guild

O n the Navigator deck of his flagship, Josef felt the tension build as the standoff continued. Why did Roderick refuse to respond? What was he waiting for? The Imperial defenders over Salusa were afraid to open fire, because they knew they would be destroyed by retaliatory strikes. The giant cymeks under Josef's control stood on the outskirts of Zimia, ready to be unleashed. It was only a matter of time.

He didn't want to devastate the capital city: the people would hate him, and there would be disastrous financial consequences, as well as historical ignominy for Josef. But the Emperor was taking his damned time even acknowledging his defeat! If Roderick backed down, restored VenHold finances, and erased the charges against Josef, this could all be over.

Josef transmitted with an edge to his voice, "There's no need for us to be on opposing sides, Roderick Corrino. If you are the man I believe you are, then you'll want to do what's best for all of humanity. We must discuss terms."

Before the cowering Emperor could answer, though, alarms blared on the Navigator deck as another fleet appeared out of nowhere. Josef's subcommanders responded with confusion, and he ran to the nearest screen to see a group of spacefolder warships—nearly 140. He blinked, unable to process all the signal blips on the tactical projections. "Where did they come from? Who are they?"

"Antique models, Directeur," Draigo transmitted after only an instant of assessment. "They date back to the Army of the Jihad."

When magnification displayed the enhanced images, Josef felt a chill, followed by a hot surge of anger. The garish and ominous symbol of the Butlerian movement was painted on the hulls: a black human fist clenched around a red machine gear.

The loathsome Manford Torondo suddenly appeared on the comm channels, broadcasting to all of Salusa Secundus, as if he were some sort of a holy savior. He offered his assistance to the besieged Emperor.

Now the reason became clear—Roderick had been waiting for this, playing for time!

Josef was outraged. This unexpected force of Butlerian warships changed the balance of the conflict. Even with their inferior weapons and shields, the extra 140 warships joined with the Imperial defense fleet made the odds more even. And the reckless fanatics were willing to fight in suicidal fashion, which made them far more dangerous.

No wonder Roderick had dithered and remained incommunicado! This must have been a trick. Josef felt another twist of betrayal. Had the Emperor's demonstrably weak Salusan force merely been bait to lure Josef's ships here and trap them? So that VenHold would think they had an assured victory?

"Roderick couldn't possibly have known about our siege," Josef said. "And the savages could never have responded from Lampadas in time."

"Manford does not have Navigators," said Norma, sounding distracted inside her tank. She did not even acknowledge the arrival of the Butlerians. "But I sense another emergency elsewhere. . . ." She placed her splayed hands against the window-port. Her distorted face was filled with alarm. "An emergency I cannot ignore—"

Even before the half-Manford had finished speaking, Josef shouted to his command crew. "Prepare for immediate attack."

He knew Roderick also hated Manford, blaming the fanatical leader for the murder of his daughter and the disappearance of his sister. A rational man would never ally himself with such a monster as Manford Torondo.

"The spice!" Norma cried in an eerie voice. "It is in danger!"

But Josef was focused on the immediate space battle threatening them. "I will see that your Navigators get spice, Grandmother. We have more important matters right now." He turned to his tactical officer for an answer.

"We still outnumber them, Directeur. And our warships are superior in every way."

Manford Torondo, though, didn't seem to care. The Butlerian forces raced pell-mell into the already crowded Salusan orbit. What could one expect from a pack of wild humans? Watching their clumsy and frantic maneuvers, Josef flashed a harsh grin. If he decimated the Butlerians right here, that would take care of another one of his problems.

"Then let's demonstrate our superiority. Cut them to pieces!"

ON THE BRIDGE of the main Butlerian ship, Anari Idaho stood beside Manford's custom chair. She gripped her sword, which was of no use in a space battle, but she held it like a talisman. She also possessed a great deal of tactical and strategic expertise, thanks to her training on Ginaz. Manford relied on her.

Propped upright in his specially modified chair, he stared at the screens. He had never expected to find Venport here, but this was an extraordinary opportunity, although the battle would cost him a great many ships. A worthwhile sacrifice, however. A satisfied smile crossed his face. "This is a miracle. Once we save Emperor Roderick, he will be beholden to us."

"We can defeat the machine lovers." Anari was utterly confident. "They may have better ships, but we have superior souls. Destiny is on our side."

Manford's antiquated warships soared forward, opening fire often before the gunners had acquired locks on their targets. The front ranks were merely cannon fodder, a vanguard filled with those who had already volunteered to be martyr soldiers.

With immense pride, Manford watched his ships move forward, saw how the VenHold vessels had entwined themselves like a cancer around the far-outnumbered Imperial Armed Forces. He had flown here from Lampadas on a mission of his own, so he had no idea how long the demon Venport had besieged Salusa, but Manford would smash that siege now—even if it cost him most of his fleet and many dead.

It would be worth the price. He could always find more converts. In fact, seeing the bravery of his Butlerian fighters, many witnesses on Salusa would join the movement, and his ranks would swell more than enough to make up for the losses.

Assuming that Manford survived—and he had no doubt he would, by God's graces—he would insist that the grateful Emperor provide him with more warships so the Butlerians could continue the fight until Venport and his machine-loving comrades were eradicated and humanity's soul was pure again.

"'The mind of man is holy,'" he whispered.

"'The mind of man is holy,'" Anari intoned. On the bridge, the rest of his followers responded in kind.

The Butlerian ships drove forward to what would surely be a titanic clash. Manford narrowed his gaze and watched as the expendable vessels reached orbit and opened fire in eerie silence. When the VenHold battleships retaliated, Manford could see that his followers were in for a bloodbath.

EMBOLDENED, THE IMPERIAL defense forces also opened fire as Josef's fleet engaged the oncoming Butlerians. One of the orbiting Imperial ships shot at a nearby VenHold vessel. The defensive shields held and damage was minimal . . . but the equally brash VenHold captain responded without orders—and vaporized the Imperial ship.

Josef yelled across the comm, "I said crippling shots only!" He knew this was problematic. "But feel free to destroy as many of the barbarians as you can."

Now all the Butlerians charged into the fray, wildly opening fire. The Ven-Hold ships were forced to respond with all their weaponry. Silent explosions peppered space, and two of the fanatic ships were wiped out in the first salvo. But their crews didn't even seem to care. They kept coming, using their available weapons.

"Josef, our spice!" Norma cried from inside her tank. "We have to protect it!"

"Yes, Grandmother!" He didn't know what she wanted him to do. "We'll take care of the spice."

In the heat of the battle, he tried once again to appeal to reason, transmitting to the Emperor in his sheltered bunker. "Roderick Corrino, you know the Butlerians are our mutual enemy! They are the savages who bullied your brother into bad decisions. They are the monsters who killed your daughter. You know Manford Torondo is an evil man. We should be fighting him together. I implore you, Sire, let us make peace between us."

Norma spoke more loudly through the speakerpatch. "Josef, we will go. Now."

Incensed, the Butlerians swept on toward the VenHold ships, and Josef's fleet continued to bombard them. Another Butlerian vessel exploded, but one of the smaller VenHold ships also erupted in a bright flare as their shields failed and reactors detonated.

Josef was on edge, but excited. He didn't want to be overconfident. He knew the half-Manford's barbarians were mad and chaotic, accepting no rules of engagement, giving no thought to their own survival. "Choose your targets and open fire. We have to save ourselves"—he lifted his chin and added something he truly believed—"and the Imperium."

Norma took him completely by surprise. "We go *now*, Josef." As weapons fire built up and the VenHold ships closed in, ready to slaughter the barbarians, she spoke with a strange, determined tone. "My Navigators are required elsewhere. This battle is no longer relevant."

At first, Josef didn't comprehend what she said. Then he felt the foldspace engines power up in a rushed preparation for departure. Across the board he watched the same thing occur on the rest of his vessels, even in the thick of battle against Manford's forces. "What the hell is happening?"

Agitated, Norma thrashed her webbed hands. "Draigo's ship will remain here to retrieve the cymek Navigator brains. I have already dispatched orders. All other VenHold vessels will depart now."

Victory was only moments away, but Josef watched the first three ships of his fleet fold space and vanish from the combat zone.

Josef's jaw dropped. "No, Grandmother! We're in the middle of a critical battle—we can't leave!"

"My crisis supersedes political squabbles. It may already be too late."

Josef rushed over to Norma's tank. "What is it? We can't—"

She cut him off. "Our spice bank on Arrakis is being destroyed. It is under attack!" His flagship twisted, jumped, and vanished into folded space.

❦

NORMA'S MIND WAS the universe, wrapped in the fabric of folded space. When necessary, she could tighten her thoughts, focus and simplify concepts in order to converse with mere humans, such as Josef. But her Navigators were her children, her companions . . . a new enhanced species. They were the only ones who could truly understand and share with her.

The universe is ours. That had become her motto, and all Navigators shared that hope with her. She had to create more of them.

With the resources of Venport Holdings, Josef had been supporting her aspirations in the same way that she'd been assisting in his political ambitions whenever she could. Yet Norma's priorities were her own. Her murky window of prescience showed a much larger picture, a future that he might not entirely endorse. No matter.

Right now, Norma's choice was clear. Josef could return to Salusa Secundus and butt heads with Emperor Roderick later, but she refused to ignore the urgent, sundering alarm that yanked at her strings of prescience, a dissonant clamor from the minds of the failed-Navigator assistants who were stationed on Arrakis at the secret spice bank. That stockpile was in great danger!

She whisked all the VenHold spacefolders to Arrakis.

❦

FROM HIS FLAGSHIP Manford was astounded to see the VenHold fleet move about in confusion briefly until, in rapid succession, all of their warships vanished—folding space and retreating! Josef Venport transmitted no defiant words, issued no challenges, made no vows that he would return to finish the battle.

The entire VenHold fleet simply and inexplicably fled into space!

Manford's bridge crew cheered and stomped their feet. Anari just stared. "We defeated them in a matter of minutes! They ran like dogs with their tails between their legs!"

Before long, heavily armored pods containing the cymek walkers rose from the Salusan surface and docked with the lone remaining VenHold ship. Then even that vessel spun away and folded space, as well.

"God has granted us a perfect victory," Manford whispered, awed at what he had just seen.

Unable to contain his delight, he shouted for his communications officer to open a channel to the surface. He wanted to address Emperor Roderick, along with all the people he had just saved. Manford intended to take credit for this astonishing victory, even if he didn't understand it himself.

Terrible things in the past should remain there, locked away and never spoken of.

—MOTHER SUPERIOR BERTO-ANIRUL, following her
own Spice Agony

Sitting in her austere chambers, Mother Superior Valya reviewed plans in her mind, going over the way she had been constructing the perfect Sisterhood she envisioned, training a growing number of elite, highly capable women with little reliance on males.

Young and healthy, Valya had the biological urgings of any person. She had taken a few casual lovers over the years, four on Lankiveil in her youth and perhaps a dozen more since beginning her training with the Sisterhood, men who had worked for the Rossak School or in the facilities on Wallach IX. Some had been inept and clumsy in their attempts to pleasure her, while others were quite skilled.

Back on Lankiveil, one starstruck, fumbling young man had accused her of being too intense, asserting that Valya was overly preoccupied with thoughts and concerns that she refused to share with him. The observation was valid but pointless, and she had not bothered to see him again.

She recalled the naïve young man's boyish features illuminated in memory, his sea-blue eyes and sheepish grin: Benaro Zimbal, son of a whale-boat captain. She'd liked him a little, she supposed, but even in her teens she had concentrated on the future of House Harkonnen. As a lover, Benaro was adequate, but she had not been able to picture him as a husband; he could never have advanced the position and wealth of her family beyond Lankiveil, and thus Valya could never allow herself any sort of permanent relationship with him.

Her brother Griffin had been more of a romantic, and had dreamed of true love and a lasting marriage, which she thought was a waste of time. They had to rebuild a dynasty, recapture the Harkonnen place in the Landsraad League . . . and eliminate the Atreides.

Valya was a powerful woman now, with great influence and unlimited potential. Considering the political, psychological, and physical training that all of her Sisters underwent, they could accomplish most anything she requested. Gradually, she would turn them loose in much greater numbers, placing Sisters throughout the Imperium, insinuating them into important positions in which they could observe and guide.

Many of the most beautiful and adept Sisters could use sex for another purpose—the primary biological purpose of reproduction, used for the further-ance of the Sisterhood and its breeding program.

"Not for the Sisterhood, for your own selfish purposes," said a voice in her mind, a resounding condemnation that rose up from the low, often impercep-tible hum of Other Memory. In that mysterious realm, an endless procession of long-dead memories was carried forward in the genetics of living Sisters, but only those who had survived the agonizing transformation into Reverend Mothers could tap into such wisdom, and never at will—only when the collec-tive memories chose to surface in her consciousness. Within those memories crowded inside her DNA were countless experiences that saturated Valya, hun-dreds upon hundreds of generations going far back into ancient times. She might be physically young, but she carried the weight of millennia in her mind.

Sometimes the voices advised, sometimes they quarreled, and Valya could not control them. "My purposes *are* the Sisterhood's purposes," she said now, pushing back against the voices. "A well-coordinated breeding program can build our own goals in the long term, and the proper use of seduction can establish obligations and manipulate behavior in the short term."

The advisers in Other Memory were unpredictable and sometimes more both-ersome than helpful. Valya—*Mother Superior* Valya as well as Valya *Harkonnen*—could build her own future, using the resources she had available.

The wealthiest and most powerful Landsraad nobles were primarily male, and Valya did not entirely dismiss them in the political framework of the Imperium. She even admired and respected some for their leadership abilities or specific skills and talents. But she did not need to rely on them. Her Sisters in the order had an entirely different skill set.

More voices pestered her. "You should be building the Sisterhood to become strong, make our members valued. We can be the bright pathway to improving humankind, creating the pinnacle of civilization." The voices overlapped, sound-ing wistful, as if all those past lives wanted to exist vicariously in an age far more perfect than any previous generation had been born into.

"Precisely what I am doing." Valya waved a hand in front of her face, as if the presences in Other Memory were a cloud of irritating gnats to be shooed away. "The breeding index in the hidden computers shows all the best permutations of human genetics. By training the appropriate Sisters to breed, we can obtain whatever bloodlines we need. The future is in our control."

"You are obsessed with the breeding program, wasting the time and energy of yourself, and of your Sisters. There are other matters of great importance as well, especially the spread of our influence in all the noble houses of the Landsraad, where Sisters can advise the powerful, subtly guiding political and financial decisions."

"I'm doing all those things for the Sisterhood, so your criticisms are not valid. Besides, I am the Mother Superior now, and the future of the order is mine to decide."

"The Sisterhood is the Sisterhood, and it belongs to no one person."

In her mind, Valya unfolded her far-reaching plans for the growth of the all-female organization, how she would not only place Sisters in the noble houses, but would also dispatch missionaries throughout the Imperium, to infiltrate their representatives and beliefs in harsh, primitive societies. In those remote, backward places Sisters would create and enhance superstitions like seeds, to bear fruit millennia in the future. And through it all, with her breeding volunteers the order would navigate the largely uncharted sea of human genetics to create and preserve the bloodlines that Valya wished to emphasize—such as House Harkonnen.

With the churning past lives in Other Memory cowed by the breadth of her plans, Valya said, "While I value your wisdom, you represent the past, and I must look to the future. I will listen, but I may override. I am the one to guide the Sisterhood. I will decide."

The arguments swirled around, but they were merely a background hum of muttering, until one said, "You are Harkonnen before you are a Sister. You should leave all things Harkonnen outside, and not bring them with you here."

"I am both the Mother Superior and a proud Harkonnen. One does not preclude the other."

"You leave bodies in your wake."

"Only those who deserve it. Sister Ingrid and Reverend Mother Dorotea threatened to upset Mother Superior Raquella's breeding program by attacking the use of computers. Both needed to die; both were a danger to the best interests of the order."

"You've turned Tula into a murderess, too. Is that the future you envision for House Harkonnen, and for the Sisterhood—advancement through murder? The combat exercises you have Sisters performing are really preparations for murder—assassination squads."

"That is not the purpose of the exercises, even if killings are sometimes necessary. All strong leaders in history understand that it is necessary to take lives. It is an unfortunate historical truth, a necessity. I do not shrink from it, nor from any of my responsibilities. Like Ingrid and Dorotea, the killing of Orry Atreides had to be done—although admittedly he had to be eliminated for the benefit of House Harkonnen. I feel no shame for ordering his death. I am a Harkonnen by blood, and I will not abandon my own Great House and history."

"We can stop you," one of the voices said.

"We can, and we will," said another.

Valya heard a murmuring of concurrence from within.

"We won't sit idly by," said a shrill voice, "not with so much at stake. Not with the entire Sisterhood at stake."

"We can drive you insane," said another voice, lower and more ominous than the others. "We can keep talking, endlessly, not allowing you to sleep or think." This one had the most to say. "We can make you jump off a cliff, or kill yourself in some other way. You are good at killing people, aren't you? Well, that expertise should prove very useful when you determine how best to do away with yourself."

"You can't make me do anything," Valya said, though this assault took her by surprise, and she wasn't sure if they could follow through on their threat. "I am my own person. I'm not your puppet. I won't do your bidding each time your voices emerge from your deep sleep, each time you are displeased with one thing or another."

The voices grew louder and more unpleasant, a mounting roar in her mind. If they defeated her, Valya was uncertain what would become of her, and of her hopes and dreams. As the voices grew more maddening, she wanted the cacophony to end.

Ways to kill herself flashed across her mind. Death might be a relief.

She stared at a sharp knife on a table, looked at the ornate carved handle, the sharp, gleaming blade that would cut so smoothly through her skin, into her internal organs.

Were the dead Sisters in Other Memory reading her thoughts? Manipulating them? Valya assumed they were. They continued to grow louder and more clamorous in her brain.

She considered reaching for the dagger and plunging it into her heart . . . or was that a suggestion they planted in her mind? Like she had driven Dorotea to kill herself?

Out of her deepest despair and uncertainty, Valya felt her courage mounting, coming forth like her own army of voices, with a stronger will than this outspoken mental multitude, and she had a greater determination to win. Valya was stronger than they were, and she could overcome them.

She began to laugh, and went through several combat exercises by herself, striking out at the air, spinning around, doing flips and airborne kicks, as if she were attacking physical forms that went with the voices. In her mind she envisioned faces and forms to go with the specific voices she could recall. She even saw a large group of Sisters massed in opposition, making an outcry against her. But that was all they could do—they could only talk. They could not really harm her if she did not allow them to gain control of her body and physical powers, making her injure or kill herself.

She shouted over their clatter of noise. "You can't make me do what I don't want to do! At one time, House Harkonnen fell low, losing most of the influence and glory we once had—but so did the Sisterhood! When Emperor Salvador drove us away from Rossak and disbanded our order, we were nothing . . . just as my Great House was nothing after Vorian Atreides humiliated Abulurd Harkonnen. Now we will both rise from the ashes like the mythical phoenix, the Sisterhood and House Harkonnen side by side!" She allowed herself a hard, satisfied smile as she felt the Other Memory voices begin to recede in defeat. "And I am making it happen," Valya insisted. "I am not sending the Sisterhood to ruination—I am strengthening it!"

The voices grew quieter and quieter, until she heard nothing.

Pushing the annoying experience aside, Valya went to her bedchambers to retire. She felt strong and confident.

Though she was the Mother Superior, she occupied only Spartan quarters that had previously belonged to Raquella. Like her predecessor, she didn't need opulence or comforts, although she reminded herself that House Harkonnen was entitled to such things. Thanks to her relentless work behind the scenes, her family would have that wealth and influence again.

She got into her nightclothes. Then, intending to calm her thoughts before going to bed, she sat in a hard chair, to gaze through the open window at the nighttime sky. She heard a much quieter swirl of voices surrounding her, but this time she had the strength to push them back.

"I'm going to sleep in a little while," she announced in a firm, calm voice. "You won't bother me in my dreams, or disturb me anymore when I am awake—because if you do, I will destroy the Sisterhood. I will kill every last Reverend Mother, including myself, and when that is accomplished, all of you will vanish. You will have no outlets whatsoever for your displeasure, no human minds to occupy with your presence." She smiled to herself. "You say I am good at killing, and I don't deny that. All of you are physically dead, but you aren't completely dead, are you? With my expertise at killing, I can totally eliminate you."

The voices diminished, but only a little.

She spoke over them. "From this point forward, you are only to emerge if you have something to say that will help me advance the interests of the Sisterhood. I do have the interests of the Sisterhood at heart, and I alone have the strength to take it to the next level. I know this, and you know it. You also know now that it is dangerous to displease me."

The voices grew very quiet, with only a few outlying mutterings.

"Like living Sisters," Valya said, "you are under my command. All of you, whatever you are, whoever you are, and whatever experiences you have had in life, you will do as I say. Every one of you will cooperate with me . . . or you will die in a way that has never happened to you before. From this moment forward, you only exist at my pleasure."

The voices grew entirely quiet. She could not even hear a low background hum of hushed awe. They had seen what she accomplished, and what she *could* accomplish . . . and Valya felt certain they were impressed. And fearful of her.

She allowed herself a smile, then—feeling more satisfied than she had expected—she climbed into bed and fell into a deep and rejuvenating sleep.

Each life has numerous crossroads, paths taken and paths avoided.
After each such crux-point, one should examine the thought processes
that went into the significant decisions, the opportunities grasped, the
successes and failures. The same is true with personal relationships. All
important things in life can be distilled down to personal relationships.

—Old Earth philosopher (name unknown)

As they hunted for Tula Harkonnen on Chusuk, Vor knew they might face significant danger on this world, yet the potential reward—justice for Orry—outweighed any such concerns. But even if they were successful, would that be the end of the feud?

Wary and alert, he and Willem sat at a table in a crowded performance hall, surrounded by young dancers, hypnotic music, lights, and show-smoke. Occasionally eager partners tried to coax the two men out onto the dance floor. As part of his act, so as not to draw attention, handsome Willem let himself be swept away, even though he did not know the traditional dance steps.

He often behaved in an aloof manner with strangers, reminding Vor much of himself as a younger man, but Vor could also see that during the weeks the two had spent on Chusuk searching, Willem had grown close to a pretty brunette who found his helpless clumsiness endearing. Though Willem was coy toward her, even standoffish at times, Vor watched the attraction build between the two young people, as if a magnetic force were pulling them together—and seeing this made Vor sad rather than happy. It made him think of lost possibilities . . . Nevertheless, it was a night filled with bright music, laughter, and a haze of pheromones.

While Willem danced with the young woman he liked the most, Vor never dropped his guard, never stopped watching for their quarry.

After arriving on Chusuk, the two men had asked discreet questions, built around a story that instantly generated trust; they showed happy images of Tula from Orry's wedding day, and the tale of a runaway bride inspired sympathy, but

few useful answers. Some people claimed to have seen a young woman who resembled Tula in the square playing a baliset, but Vor and Willem had not been
able to find her; just recently, two helpful witnesses had even said she occasionally went to this performance hall. Could it be her?

Despite spending several evenings here, the two had seen no sign of her, but
they kept watching.

Willem blended right in—young, dashing, and fun-loving, although Vor
knew he had a hardened core beneath his friendly exterior. Now Vor let himself
be led out onto the floor by a laughing redhead, only half listening to her clever
conversation as he kept moving, scanning the crowd. Attractive, she appeared
to be in her late thirties, and would have no idea how old Vor really was—
more than two hundred years of age, from a strange procedure his cymek father,
Agamemnon, had administered to him in his youth.

Tula was somewhere on Chusuk—probably in this very city, and she might
have been seen in this place. He could not be sure if she guessed they were
hunting for her, but she did know what Vor and Willem looked like. They had
again disguised their features as best they could, but Tula Harkonnen had been
trained in the Sisterhood, and Vor would never underestimate her abilities.

They had to find her first, and get her before she got them.

The music rose and skirled. The local musicians used an assortment of unique
instruments, including a small harpsie that put out a grandiose sound, a trum-
petta played by three men at side-by-side mouthpieces, and a number of stringed
balisets, for which the master craftsmen of Chusuk were famed.

The band stage was flanked by warm pools of water, where shimmer-suited
couples cavorted in a splashing ritual of aquatic foreplay that usually led them
to rooms in the back. These lissome swimmers also provided entertainment for
the more lethargic audience members.

Here in the performance hall, few gave the two men a second glance, although
Vor did notice a pair of statuesque women eyeing them steadily. He supposed
that offworlders would naturally be seen as exotic. Those women, though, did
not flirt or ask either of the two to dance.

If Vor and Willem ever did find their quarry, they would certainly be remembered around here. Vor didn't think of himself as a cold-blooded killer, but after
living for more than two centuries and participating in a decades-long war, his
hands were by no means clean. He had made up his mind to deal with this himself, even though Willem wanted to kill Tula with his own hands. Instead, Vor
would do what was necessary—not for the pleasure, because he would feel none
of that. No, if they could not manage to get away, he would take the fall, instead
of Willem, who had most of his life ahead of him. Vor had nothing left to lose.

But first they needed to find her.

When the music paused again, the two men made their way back to the table, sweating from the dance. Willem stayed close to his date, a young woman named Harmona. She was thin and quite pretty, with a heart-shaped face and long black hair secured by a jeweled clasp on one side. Willem wore a dashing uniform for travel, altered from one of the air-rescue garments he'd worn on Caladan. Vor's redheaded dance partner left him to find a more attentive companion, and as soon as the music started again, Harmona pulled Willem back out to the floor.

Sitting at the table by himself, Vor froze, and his vision focused into a pinprick of searing light. Across the dance floor, Tula Harkonnen—it was unmistakably her!—slipped into a seat at a table with a young man. Vor knew the curly blonde hair, the classically beautiful face and generous lips . . . the hands that had killed Orry.

He'd been hunting, and now it was time to move in for the kill. He ignored the music, the lovers splashing in the pool, the dancers, the tables—all were just obstacles. He saw only his quarry. He would strike her before she could even take notice of him. Vor had fought her once before, in his lodgings on the night of Orry's murder, so he knew what a deadly fighter she could be.

As he moved, he signaled for Willem, who was deep in conversation with Harmona. When the young man finally noticed him, he became instantly alert, and surprise flared in his eyes when he also spotted Tula. He caught up with Vor, and moving together like predators, they slid through the crowded hall toward their target.

Tula's male friend looked up as they closed in. He gave Vor a casual glance, but did not otherwise react. With each step, Vor grew more certain that this really was the young woman who had married Orry and slit his throat as he slept.

Vor lunged forward for an initial attack—only to stagger when something struck him hard on the back of his head. He fell, trying to protect himself as he went down.

Out of the corner of his eye, he saw Willem rush forward to defend him, but an agile woman swept in from the crowd and struck him down, too. One of the statuesque women he had casually noticed now stood crouched in a well-practiced fighting stance, joined by her companion. The two women had moved so swiftly that they neutralized Vor and Willem, while drawing little attention from the crowd of bystanders.

The two men landed in defensive postures. At her table, Tula scrambled up, gaping in amazement at the surprise attack and her apparently unexpected protectors. Within Vor's hearing, one of the women snapped, "We detected the threat. He's the one you hate, isn't he? The older one? The Atreides." Two additional nondescript but powerful women also swept in from the crowd.

Though clearly surprised to see her guardians, Tula's eyes went wide when she recognized Vor and Willem. The color drained from her face. "They are both Atreides," Tula said.

As the women formed a barrier between the young Harkonnen and her two attackers, onlookers began to gather. Tula's male friend spluttered questions that went ignored.

With no further thought or restraint, but inflamed by memories of blood-spattered Orry, Vor launched himself toward Tula. Her female guardians might be skilled fighters, but so was he. He shoved one of them aside and threw himself upon his intended victim, connecting with a blow that should have sent her sprawling, but Tula countered with a hard, pinpoint blow to his temple.

Willem yelled, "Murderer!" but the young man had far less fighting skill than Vor or any of these women. A pair of female fighters pummeled him, broke his bones, and sent him crashing to the floor. They continued to beat him.

Trying to intervene, Vor struggled to reach Tula, throwing off one of the ruthless women who held him back, but a sharp blow struck him from one side. He felt and heard his ribs cracking, just before a hard kick to his midsection brought him down.

Trying to ignore the pain, Vor got back to his feet, caring nothing for the damage done to his body. He drove two of the women away with a volley of kicks and thrusts. His victim was just out of reach. . . .

Tula's expression showed more misery than fury. She seemed transfixed, was staring. Four more women melted out of the dance hall crowd. They grabbed Tula and whisked her away toward one of the exit doors.

Even though he was severely injured and on the floor bleeding, Willem managed to shove one of the guardian women back with sheer strength. He tried to get to his feet, but two more closed in on him from one side, and three from the other side. They hammered Vor with hard blows that sent him reeling. How many hidden allies did Tula have? It was a small army.

In dismay, Vor watched Willem fall again, but could do nothing to protect his young ward.

Burly guards now pushed through the crowd and crashed into the fray. A young woman shouted, "They're killing him!" Vor saw that Harmona was the one urging her noble guards forward. Soon they were all in a full-fledged brawl, and Tula's protectors were outnumbered.

Vor fought alongside his new allies, despite the bone-grinding and skull-cracking pain. Tula struggled as several women pulled her out the door, while her baffled male friend at the table watched in helpless confusion. One of the guardian women snapped to Tula, "We have orders to return you to Wallach IX. You will be safe there."

"No!" she cried, but they dragged her away.

The Sisterhood . . . Wallach IX. Vor realized that he and Willem would never be able to get to Tula there, if she was under the protection of her powerful order.

Then one of the remaining women struck Vor a blow to the head that drove him into unconsciousness. . . .

After Norma tore the VenHold fleet away from certain victory, Josef stood on the Navigator deck raging against her, demanding that she return to Salusa so his warships could get back to the space battle. "We were winning! We could have broken the Emperor's will and smashed the barbarians." He could barely keep his voice from becoming a roar. "The victory would have stood for all time."

But she simply contemplated in the murky spice gas of her tank, refusing to respond as she made the mental calculations and folded space to Arrakis. "Our spice bank is under attack."

"What do you mean?" Josef was startled by this remark, because he had left substantial forces in place at the desert planet, and he couldn't imagine any military force that could pose a meaningful threat to his spice stockpile.

Norma was powerful, capricious, incomprehensible, but Josef wanted her to be angry at the same enemies he was. How would he ever recover from this debacle now, after fleeing the battlefield? Emperor Roderick—and worse, the half-Manford—probably assumed the retreat indicated weakness or cowardice. The savages would crow that they had chased away his entire fleet just by puffing up their chests.

"My priority is Arrakis," Norma finally answered, her voice coming to him across the speakerpatch on the tank. She sounded distant, as if she were ahead of him in space and he had not yet caught up. "We must get there in time." As she spoke, they arrived, and the shimmers of folded space pulled away to reveal the normal universe again: a yellow sun and a cracked, waterless planet like a copper coin in space.

Josef stared down at Arrakis, and Norma peered out of her tank. "I fear our stockpile is already lost." Her voice was bleak.

As a captain of industry, Josef was able to hold the big picture in his mind, but he could also compartmentalize his thoughts and focus on one matter at a time. His guarded spice bank held years' worth of profits—so much melange that it could fund VenHold operations for a very long time. "That's not possible! We neutralized the Imperials on Arrakis, and we had the best security. Who is attacking us?"

Norma fell silent.

As the ships went into orbit, Josef called to his communications chief, "Give me a full planetary scan. I want to know if there are enemy battleships and troop carriers here. Any sign of an attack?" Norma had often admitted that her prescience was unreliable. He clenched his fists. If she had pulled his entire fleet from Salusa Secundus because of a hallucination . . .

The communications chief tried to establish contact with the hidden spice bank, but she finally shook her head. "No response from our facility, Directeur, but there are several sandstorms in the vicinity. They could be garbling transmissions. Can't tell if there is an enemy battle group here."

Josef spoke over the main comm across all the ships that the Navigators had moved. "My grandmother brought us here from Salusa for reasons she considered sufficient." He had to bite down hard on the words. "We expected to capture the Imperial capital—but now we're at Arrakis. The matter may be urgent. I want twenty armored landing vessels to accompany me down to the spice bank, and eighty more at the ready in case I call for reinforcements."

With knots of anger inside him, Josef left the piloting deck, not sure whether he wanted Norma to be right or wrong. He dreaded the answer either way.

FLANKED BY ARMORED landers as he approached the spice bank from the air, Josef could see a smoldering blot of destruction around what had once been a sheltered sietch. Though a passing storm swept dust and sand through the air, he saw lingering plumes of smoke, and felt sick.

Norma was right. Something terrible had indeed happened down there.

The troop transports descended like a flock of carrion birds. The pilots issued ominous reports as they approached the line of mountains, but Josef barely heard them. He looked through the windowport, thinking of the tall black

cliffs, the labyrinth of caves and tunnels . . . it was all gone. Thousands of Freemen had lived there unmolested for ages, but now, after only a month of active
operation, the VenHold spice bank had not only been raided, it had been
destroyed.

The armored landers had to circle in the increasing storm winds, but Josef
demanded they find a place to set down. He ordered all personnel to arm themselves, but he could already see that the battle was over. Norma had withdrawn
them from their victory at Salusa because of this, and now they had arrived too
late. The sand had been terribly churned up here, and he noticed a large break
in the rock formation, forming a wide path that led out into the desert.

This was just the aftermath, the scar. There would be no more fighting
to save the spice stockpile—just bloodstains and grief. The melange was gone.

He disembarked with his security troops, stomping across the sand. They
picked their way around boulders the size of houses. Soot stains, sand turned
into glass. The devastation was so great that the enclosed cliffs looked as if they
had been bombarded from space.

"What caused all this destruction?" he demanded. None of his security
troops offered an answer.

Inside the reeking, smoky sietch, he found smashed security walls, a number
of torn bodies sprawled on the churned sand, along with destroyed weapons and
ruptured crates of melange strewn about as if by a gleeful child.

A few fires were still burning, giving off the greasy smoke of oil and plastics.
On rock faces he saw the scars of projectile explosions, but not nearly enough for
this amount of damage. Such wild destruction had not been caused by traditional
weaponry or explosives. It seemed primal, wanton . . . and highly effective.

His main spice stockpile was gone, leaving only the much smaller reserves
on Kolhar and Denali.

Norma had transported herself down from the Navigator deck of the flagship and now her tank appeared there, resting on a pile of rubble. She drifted in
her rich bath of orange vapor, and ripples of tangible distress emanated from the
tank, an emotional reaction that Josef had never seen from her before. "So much
spice. Many Navigators will be damaged from lack of spice."

Josef looked around, his anger slashing like a machete as he analyzed the
signs, focused on the wide path leading out into the desert. "This was a ground
assault. Someone attacked us from the desert." Momentarily forgetting about
the abandoned victory on Salusa, his troops fanned out through the rubble,
searching for survivors, records, evidence, but everything was destroyed.

"Years of profits . . . gone." Josef made a vow for all to hear. "I will track
down the spice thieves. We'll find what they stole, take it back, and make
them pay."

"No," Norma said. "It was not stolen. These were not bandits. Our stockpile was obliterated. That was the message they meant to send."

Judging by the cinnamon-brown residue and all the smashed containers in evidence among the rubble, Josef realized she was probably right. "But this was enough wealth to buy a dozen planets. Who would just . . . wreck it? And why?"

"My prescience is unclear on this matter, but I know the spice is gone."

Josef's stomach knotted as the answer came to him. He could think of no one else who might even conceive of such a thing. It was a powerful, violent message, designed to cripple him. Josef looked around at the disaster site, smelled the smoke, and the rich, bloody scent of spilled melange.

"Roderick . . . Emperor Roderick did this."

Achieving vengeance and completing a quest are similar matters to an obsessive person.

—HEADMASTER GILBERTUS ALBANS, Mentat School teachings

After the rest of the VenHold fleet vanished inexplicably, Draigo's ship had remained in orbit just long enough to retrieve the cymek walkers that launched from their siege positions around Zimia. Retreating! But he had gotten the walkers away before they could be destroyed.

Draigo did not know what was happening, only that Norma Cenva had issued urgent instructions, just before the Directeur's battleships flew off in the middle of the space battle—leaving his ship alone and vulnerable.

When all thirty-one cymeks had returned to the carrier's hold, still intact, Draigo fought his way out of Salusan orbit as the unruly Butlerians swooped in, crowing over communications lines about their unexpected victory. In the aftermath, stunned Imperial ships took potshots at Draigo's ship even after the main invading fleet had gone.

His shields endured a tremendous pounding as he fought to escape, and his hull suffered some damage, but nothing structural, and the Holtzman engines remained intact. He directed his Navigator to fold space and escape.

But the Mentat remained baffled by what had happened.

When the Navigator-cymek brains were secure once more in their proper holding racks, the preservation canisters containing Ptolemy and Noffe trundled forward on carrier carts to the command bridge. They demanded answers, confused as to how their imminent victory had suddenly collapsed. Why?

Draigo was just as perplexed as the cymek scientists were. Even though he ran numerous Mentat projections, he could find no conclusions that logically fit the facts. Why would Directeur Venport have withdrawn all his ships without explanation, on the verge of a huge victory? A message from Norma Cenva instructed Draigo's lone ship to return the Navigator-brain cymeks to the safety of Denali. But why?

Draigo knew he would have to wait until he reconnected with Directeur Venport—where? On Kolhar? Impatient, he stepped up to face his ship's Navigator. "I need to be debriefed by Directeur Venport as soon as possible. Where has he gone?"

The Navigator would not look at him. "Directeur Venport and his ships went to Arrakis to protect the spice stockpile. Norma Cenva informed me that you would be of greater use on Denali, where you will continue to prepare against our enemies."

Draigo digested the information, which told him almost nothing. Beside him, the preservation tanks of Noffe and Ptolemy shimmered as electrafluid nutrients processed their agitated thoughts. "Denali has many weapons in prototype stage," said Noffe. "But our main thrust has been to complete the rest of our new cymeks for the conquest of Lampadas. The destruction of the Butlerians is our goal!"

Ptolemy pondered longer. "At first I questioned Directeur Venport's decision to turn our forces against the Emperor instead of the Butlerians, and yet we just saw that Roderick Corrino—supposedly a rational man—has entered into a dangerous alliance with Manford Torondo. Therefore, our work at Denali is more urgent than ever. We must have our full force of cymeks ready to attack Lampadas, and soon."

～⊱～

ONCE BACK INSIDE the laboratory domes, Draigo urged the scientific teams to work with renewed determination. While he waited for some kind of explanation from Directeur Venport, the Mentat assessed the various projects in progress, rating each concept's probability of success, as well as the destructive potential and how close each one was to completion.

Though Administrator Noffe's human body had been damaged in a horrific explosion, he still used his detail-oriented mind to monitor the projects. From his brain canister, Noffe presented feedback, while the robot Erasmus offered several thinking-machine weapons, but so far those designs were inferior to the other work the Denali scientists had produced. For the time being Erasmus seemed obsessed with his growing biological body. He promised more help, though.

Since the large cymek project showed the clearest probability of success against the barbarian enemy, most of the Denali workers devoted their time to that effort. The force of more than one hundred battle machines had to be ready.

Ptolemy was consumed with the idea of turning them loose on Manford Torondo. Draigo knew that back on Zenith, Ptolemy and Dr. Elchan had been naïve humanitarians, entirely unprepared when they inadvertently provoked the fanatics. Now Ptolemy was obsessed with destroying him. Ironically, Manford Torondo had created his own nemesis by inflicting such misery . . . and every researcher here on Denali had a tale similar to poor Ptolemy's. All these brilliant men and women were dedicated to the cause of destroying the Butlerians.

Unlike the Tlulaxa scientist Noffe, who had no choice but to abandon his ruined body, Ptolemy had *voluntarily* given up his physical form to become a cymek. For no reason other than that he wanted to be stronger, he had ordered Tlulaxa surgeons to convert him into a powerful weapon to be unleashed against the enemy.

Ptolemy's ruthless determination had pushed him to the edge of madness, which could have been a cause for concern, but Draigo wondered if madness, at least a form of it, might be the only effective way to stand against the insanity of Butlerian fervor. . . .

The day after they returned from Salusa Secundus, he went to inspect Ptolemy's work in the frantic push to complete the cymek army. Though Ptolemy's preservation canister could be installed in any number of walkers, he chose a smaller articulated mobile form with multiple limbs and attachments.

This mechanical body now worked inside one of the sealed hangars, tinkering with another cymek framework. Beside Ptolemy's artificial body, a team of human engineers also worked to strengthen the war-machine's components, installing a high-powered cannon.

Ptolemy swiveled his sensors to face Draigo. "This one is nearly complete. Later today, I'll present a detailed manifest of the walker forms, the weapons each one possesses, and which Navigator brains have trained on that unit. We will soon have our full force, Mentat."

"When will we be ready to launch the attack?" Draigo asked. "The Directeur will want to know. Especially after the rout at Salusa."

Ptolemy didn't hesitate. "We can go now with what we have, or tomorrow, or next week—whenever the Directeur unleashes us. And I hope it is soon."

"Soon enough. When we hear from him again."

With a whir of attached tools, Ptolemy's walker finished assembling a claw-like attachment and scuttled over to the Mentat. "With the data from our test mission to Lampadas, I have developed thorough plans for a complete cymek assault. I would like to submit my outline to Directeur Venport. I have the perfect plan."

"Is any plan really perfect?" As a Mentat, Draigo could always find ways for details to go awry.

"This one is." Ptolemy's simulated voice invited no argument. "With more than one hundred armed cymek walkers guided by Navigator brains, we will be invincible against the primitive barbarian defenses. We shall overthrow Manford Torondo and obliterate his mindless mobs. It must be done."

Draigo pondered. The arrival of the Butlerian warships at Salusa had altered the balance of that battle. At least that was the perception, although his Mentat projections suggested that Directeur Venport could still have won. But the Navigators had whisked all the VenHold ships away. He still didn't know why.

"I believe we will succeed," Draigo said. "But have you contemplated your next step after victory? What will happen after you get your revenge against Manford Torondo?"

The mechanical form remained motionless, while the electrafluid in the brain canister throbbed to show Ptolemy's furious thoughts. "After that, I don't care."

Every time he had been summoned to the foldspace carrier's Navigator
deck, Admiral Harte had memorized the route, the various decks and
access points, the security hatches and VenHold guard forces. He needed this
information in order to develop a plan. And now that they had their chance
to escape, he was ready.

Directeur Venport had claimed he didn't want outright war against the
Imperium, suggesting a negotiated settlement instead of conflict, but the idea offended Admiral Harte. His soldiers were infuriated at being held prisoner and
treated as pawns.

Yet Harte's fleet was not quite as neutralized as Venport thought they were.
His soldiers were ready to do something about their captivity, even at great risk.
They would follow their commander's lead.

But first Harte needed to find the right moment, the right opportunity.
Since being captured, he had kept looking for a chance to break free of their
orbiting prison and escape from Kolhar. That was the duty of any prisoner of
war, but so far he'd seen no opening.

Until now.

When Directeur Venport assembled a host of warships and set off for Salusa
Secundus, leaving his headquarters planet with only a skeleton crew of defenders, Harte knew he would have no better opportunity. Guessing what Venport
intended to do to the Imperial capital (and the rightful Emperor) forced Harte
to take action.

Umberto Harte had enjoyed a distinguished military career. He had been put to the test as a young officer under Emperor Jules during the religious uproar after the Council of Ecumenical Translators released the controversial Orange Catholic Bible. He had received a commendation for his meritorious service; Emperor Jules had personally pinned a gaudy medal on his chest. Harte served with equal distinction throughout Salvador's reign, but had never expected to find himself at war against Directeur Venport. . . .

His seventy Imperial warships were held inside the carrier's cavernous hold, but each remained separate and isolated, the crews given no opportunity to conspire or take concerted action. Per Venport's order, Harte and his individual captains could not meet in person, although they could hold virtual debriefing sessions through their communication links, which were closely monitored by VenHold. That made planning an intricate conspiracy and breakout very difficult.

But not impossible.

One of his engineers developed a simple communications limpet, a device that if attached to the hull of another ship could link up a narrow-beam comm network that could not be intercepted. Harte's flagship secretly dispatched several limpet-comms using compressed air, which left no energy signature. The drifting limpet-comms struck adjacent vessels, which neatly connected the Admiral in point-to-point transmissions with several other captains. After a number of excruciating days and failed attempts, they were all connected in a private network, and their VenHold captors could not eavesdrop on them. From there, Admiral Harte and his captains covertly planned their escape.

Once Directeur Venport and his assault fleet were gone, leaving Kolhar relatively unguarded, Harte signaled his ships, gave a shortened timetable for action, and when all the pieces were in place and his soldiers were ready, he sent the activation signal.

The breakout was on. They would have but one chance, one window of opportunity.

Everyone understood it was an all-or-nothing gambit, and that they would likely be executed if they failed. The soldiers also knew that Salusa Secundus would be under attack by their enemy, so there was more at stake than just their own welfare. They had all the incentive they needed. They *would* succeed.

But his hostage ships aboard the carrier did not have Holtzman engines, only standard faster-than-light drives, and even if they broke free of the prison ship, it would take weeks for them to reach Salusa.

Admiral Harte had a more ambitious plan than that. He intended to seize this entire foldspace carrier and fly them directly to Salusa, coercing the Navigator if necessary—but his people had never used Navigators before, so they could be resistant. One way or another, they would be home free. . . .

The plan went into activation. As Harte watched the seconds tick down, four of his widely spaced ships powered up their restored weapons. At the same instant, they opened fire with a long and powerful salvo inside the carrier's hold. Venport thought he had neutralized all the firing controls when he took the ships hostage, but Harte's engineers had rebuilt the systems from scratch.

Now their weapons fired at the opposite interior walls of the VenHold carrier, blasting through the exterior shell. The gunners had chosen their targets carefully so as not to harm the carrier's Holtzman engines, which Admiral Harte hoped to use, but the damage to the spacefolder's hull was dramatic and extensive.

The unexpected blasts caused an immediate uproar inside the VenHold carrier-ship, exactly as expected. Harte shouted over his comm-system. "Time to move!"

While the VenHold crew responded to the internal attack, the Admiral—whose flagship was directly connected to the access hatches into the main body of the carrier—stormed the connecting tunnel with his soldiers.

Two thousand loyal Imperial fighters, armed with hand weapons from the flagship's sealed armory, surged out while the VenHold crew was still reeling from the multiple blasts that had pierced the outer hull. Shaped explosive charges blew down the barricade door, giving Harte's team access to the main decks. They ran into the VenHold carrier.

The Admiral led them at a run to the carrier's command center and Navigator deck. This was no stealth mission; racing forward, they gunned down any VenHold employee who tried to stand in the way. They had to make it to the engine controls. Anyone in their way fell to a barrage of weapons fire.

Alarms shrieked throughout the carrier, and damage reports blared from speakerpatches in the walls. VenHold staff and crew streamed out of their work stations, as Harte's troops climbed to higher levels. Leaving bodies in their wake, they captured deck after deck, until they finally blasted through the last set of armored doors and charged onto the Navigator deck.

The carrier's piloting deck was surrounded by technological systems and broad viewing windows—and in the center, a large sealed tank held a mutated Navigator obscured by orange clouds of spice gas. The creature stared out at them with oversized, inhuman eyes, as if his prescience had told him that ruthless invaders would arrive at any moment.

Harte strode up to the tank. "We've taken control of your ship."

"You may believe so." The Navigator's voice seemed to come from a great distance.

"Yes, I do. In fact, I *know* so."

Imperial fighters swarmed onto the deck, yanking terrified VenHold employees from their seats, killing one woman who resisted; the rest surrendered. Three of Harte's technical officers rushed to the Navigator tank and disconnected the fittings to the nav-systems. Harte had specifically chosen fighters who were familiar with foldspace engines and piloting. They severed the linkages to the Navigator tank so that the mutated creature could no longer control the carrier.

"He's neutralized, Admiral," announced one of his tech officers. Unlike Norma Cenva, who could fold space with her mind, the other Navigators required a direct connection to the Holtzman engines.

The Navigator stared blankly at them, while other soldiers went to the control panels. Frantically, they studied the activation systems, ready to launch out of orbit and fold space.

"We don't have much time," Harte called. "Kolhar will soon respond and cut off this vessel. We have to fly this carrier out of here."

"Firing up the foldspace engines now, sir. Setting course for Salusa Secundus."

Harte stood before the Navigator tank. "What is your name?"

"Navigator."

"What was your human name?"

"It was . . ." The creature seemed to be searching deep into his past. "Dobrec . . . but *Navigator* is all that matters now."

The deck trembled as Harte's captive Imperial ships within the great hold blasted more holes through the outer hull, careful not to endanger the integrity of the main structural framework. Even with numerous holes in its outer shell, the giant carrier could carry them through folded space back to the Imperial capital.

"Tell all our hostage ships that we've taken control of the carrier, and we'll be home soon." Harte directed his pilots to activate the carrier's Holtzman drive. Thrumming increased throughout the decks as the foldspace engines gathered power.

The Navigator—Dobrec—blinked his large, soulless eyes. "You do not know how to navigate. There is danger in flying this ship without the prescience of my guidance."

The Admiral glared. "Then guide us—or risk dying with the rest of us. Your choice."

One of the tech officers cried out, "VenHold interceptors closing in fast, sir. If they damage our Holtzman engines, we'll never break orbit. We have to go."

"Activate those engines now," Harte snapped, then turned to the Navigator. "If you have any suggestions for course adjustments, tell us now."

He felt a smooth machine sensation as the engines went on.

Dobrec remained silent, as if accessing data. "I suggest a slight alteration to avoid colliding with a double star en route." He specified a variant set of coordinates.

"How do I know you're not going to fly us directly into a sun?"

"You must gamble as well. You must believe that I do not wish to die any more than you do. I still have too much of the universe to see and experience."

Harte stared at the mutated Navigator in the tank, but could read nothing on the strange, distorted features. He barked to his surrogate navigator at the controls. "Alter course as Dobrec says."

The soldier swallowed hard and made the change.

As VenHold ships rushed to close in around the embattled foldspace carrier, Admiral Harte drew a deep breath and nodded. His soldiers trusted him implicitly, and engaged the Holtzman engines.

The carrier folded space and vanished from Kolhar.

One man's demon is another man's angel.
—Ancient saying

E mperor Roderick Corrino I. Considering the recent siege by VenHold forces and how close he'd come to losing it all, he wondered if he could ever claim that lofty title again. He could not believe that Josef Venport had attacked him, attacked the Imperium—threatening the throne.

Manford Torondo and his Butlerians had rescued him, saved the Emperor— and now Roderick dreaded what that would cost him, what Manford would demand in return. The antitechnology fanatics might be even worse for the future of humanity.

As he stood at the high window of his office, gazing down at the activity in the sunlit central plaza of Zimia, he reminded himself that despite his human frailties and shortcomings, Roderick was responsible for leading civilization, to see that it became strong again. More than eight decades ago at the Battle of Corrin, brave and desperate fighters had finally overthrown the greatest enemy of the human race, the computer-mind enslaver of mankind.

Why are we so insistent on creating our own enemies?

The Butlerians had come to save Salusa, but not for altruistic reasons or out of loyalty to the Corrino throne. Manford undoubtedly intended to use his leverage to press other demands and make the Emperor his puppet. Although Salvador would have bowed to anything the fanatic leader asked, Roderick was not so easily cowed.

This meeting might be as dangerous as the VenHold siege.

With the Butlerian ships clustered in tight orbit around Salusa "for the Emperor's protection," although the sheer military might could easily have been interpreted as a threat, Manford had asked Roderick to prepare for the arrival celebration that he claimed was his due as liberator.

Even though the situation set Roderick's teeth on edge, he knew he couldn't just dismiss or insult the powerful man, who had moved into a key position. Those Butlerian warships, though old, outnumbered the Imperial forces, and had more combined firepower. He had to play this very carefully.

The Emperor dispatched a shuttle with an Imperial honor guard to Manford's orbiting flagship, and the shuttle would land shortly in the palace square. The shuttle would carry only the Butlerian leader and a small entourage; Manford had wanted to come down with dozens of his own ships, but Roderick refused to let him. Only the shuttle. He needed to keep some semblance of control over the dangerous situation, and Manford had agreed to the terms only after a long, tense moment when Roderick feared he would have to threaten to shoot down any "celebratory" Butlerian ships that flew into Zimia airspace.

Manford's followers were gathering in the square, raucous throngs that seemed to grow exponentially hour by hour. Many of Manford's people were landing far outside the restricted zone and simply walking for kilometers. Other followers were already in Zimia and they came to answer the holy call, rejoicing in their victory over Venport.

From his high window, Roderick watched the eager crowd gathered before the Palace. The Butlerians carried red-and-black banners that featured a human fist clenched around a machine gear. He knew that when Manford Torondo landed and emerged from the Imperial shuttle, he expected a cheering reception as the conquering hero who had saved Salusa Secundus. Although Roderick knew that the VenHold ships had truly run away in fear, he still didn't understand the reason for their unexpected retreat.

It was a delicate balance, because he knew that Manford could easily summon a murderous, rampaging mob if he felt slighted. Roderick was required to host him and treat him well—after all, they shared a common enemy.

Oddly, that was exactly the same argument the traitor Venport had used.

Roderick Corrino would express his gratitude for the Butlerian efforts, while also reminding Manford who was the ruler of the Imperium. The Emperor had imposed strict conditions on the upcoming audience, ensuring that this meeting would be a private conversation, without crowds, just two men discussing important matters. For the meeting, he allowed the Butlerian leader a retinue of no more than four people.

This man's mobs had caused the death of sweet Nantha, and they were almost certainly responsible for the disappearance of his sister at the Mentat School. Manford repeatedly denied any involvement since Anna had gone missing, but Roderick now had his Truthsayer, and he intended to get the real answers. Then he would see just how much gratitude Manford Toronto deserved. . . .

In preparation for the meeting, Roderick secured the sash of his ceremonial uniform and stepped out onto the open balcony in time to see the Imperial shuttle land in the middle of the palace square.

Attendants rushed in as the main hatch opened. The burly female Swordmaster emerged bearing Manford on her shoulders. The Butlerian leader wore a gaudy uniform with red-and-black piping and epaulets, and a high, old-fashioned military hat, crowned with long white plumes.

The Butlerian crowd cheered when they saw Manford, and he turned to face the golden-domed Palace. He raised a hand of greeting to Roderick on the high balcony, and the Emperor responded mechanically. The roar of the crowd grew louder, as if they imagined some great friendship between the two men, and an alliance.

Anari Idaho marched toward a ceremonial platform from which Manford could address the throng, but—as Roderick had ordered—the Imperial honor guard intercepted her and guided them directly toward the Palace entrance instead, before the charismatic leader could rile up the crowd any more than they already were.

Roderick and Haditha took their places in the Imperial Audience Chamber, waiting for Manford's arrival. She wore an expression of concern as she took her place on a throne beside his. Fielle stood two paces to his right, silent and imposing, and Chamberlain Bakim stood restlessly at the base of the dais with two advisers.

As Roderick settled onto his immense quartz throne, he tried to compose himself, tapping his fingers on the throne arm. Haditha whispered, "This is a difficult time, husband, but we are required to show the man some measure of respect. His ships did help turn the tide of battle. If they had not arrived when they did, Josef Venport would have forced you to abdicate. We know this."

"Yes, and I will go through the motions with him . . . but no more than necessary. Manford Toronto may have helped us in this particular instance, but much of the overall crisis is of his own making."

When the Butlerian leader arrived outside the closed chamber, Roderick gestured for guards to open the tall double doors. Anari Idaho strode in, carrying Manford in his harness. The legless man rode high on her sturdy shoulders, with the bald and intense Deacon Harian at his side. Contrary to Roderick's instructions, two dozen Butlerian followers surged around their beloved leader, forcing their way into the throne room. Several of them jostled the Swordmaster, but Anari held Manford secure. A contingent of Imperial guards rushed to the doorway to block more of them from getting in.

Roderick rose to his feet, in a stormy mood. "We agreed to only four in the entourage. All these others must leave."

Chamberlain Bakim shouted, red-faced, "There will be order before the Emperor! No unruly mobs."

Manford seemed to feign chagrin. "Excuse the enthusiasm of my supporters, Sire. They wish to join me everywhere."

"But not here. If you cannot follow my rules, then you will not be welcome in my Palace."

Looking offended, Manford said, "After the great service I just did for you, Sire, I expected a more respectful reception. I am the Protector of the Imperium, the vanquisher of our common enemies, the Savior of Salusa."

"And your mobs killed our daughter." Roderick words were like spears of ice, and the entire audience chamber fell quickly into a shocked silence. "I will not have chaos here. They will leave."

In the moments of pause, Imperial guards pushed the people back. Manford gave a quick nod to his followers, conceding the point. "Of course, Sire. We would not wish to cause unintentional pain from an old wound." He directed Deacon Harian and two other Butlerians in Mentat garments to stay in the small entourage. The Mentats were male and female respectively, both with close-cropped brown hair and slight builds, so they looked very much alike.

When the doors closed against the crowd outside, leaving the group standing before the throne, Manford said in a bright tone, "Sire, we should look forward to a glorious future. Venport and his terrible machines are our real enemy. My people have come to Zimia by the hundreds of thousands, and more are certainly on their way. You and I should celebrate our great victory—making the demon Venport flee in terror." His voice grew harder. "You would do well to be grateful for how we rescued you."

Roderick's tone was even sharper. "And you would do well to remember that I am your Emperor, and *any* loyal subject should have come to my defense, without requiring gestures of gratitude." He continued with cool patience. "I appreciate the unexpected service you provided, but I will not forget the harm your people caused in the past. The accounting is not yet finished."

He saw Manford hesitate. Without his howling supporters to shore him up, the mob leader seemed smaller than usual, even less than half a man. The feather on his ridiculous, gaudy cap jostled as he gestured to the two small-statured Mentats; he seemed eager to change the subject. "And as a loyal subject, I bring you a gift, Sire: two talented graduates from my Mentat School on Lampadas, both approved by the new Headmaster Zendur. Their highly developed minds can complete countless calculations and projections . . . whatever you want them to do. They are human computers, but are in no way corrupted by the machine apologists."

Roderick inspected the pair. Beside his throne, the Truthsayer glanced at them, then turned forward again without speaking. The Emperor said, "I agree about the usefulness of Mentats, Leader Torondo, but I already have one at my side. Sister Fielle is herself a graduate of the Mentat School."

Obviously flustered, Manford said, "If this woman was trained under Headmaster Albans, then her education and beliefs are suspect. There is proof that Albans collaborated with the robot Erasmus."

Roderick cut him off. "Proved to *your* satisfaction, perhaps, but I find the idea preposterous. In fact, I find many things preposterous about the reports of your takeover of the Mentat School." He leaned forward on the throne, staring hard at Manford, ignoring everyone else. "Sister Fielle has another skill that's just as valuable as her Mentat abilities."

The dark-robed woman glided down the dais steps so that she stood within arm's reach of the Swordmaster. Anari Idaho tensed.

Roderick continued, "She is also a Truthsayer with the ability to detect any nuance of diversion or evasion. She can tell if a person is lying. Therefore, I have one question to pose to you, Leader Torondo."

Swallowing visibly, Manford said, "And what might that be, Sire?" The tension increased in the room, like a palpable fog.

"Do you know what happened to my sister Anna on Lampadas?"

Manford froze, then smiled with relief. "No, Sire, I do not."

"Did you have anything to do with her disappearance? Anything whatsoever?"

Manford's smile broadened. "No, Sire. I did not. I honestly do not know what happened to her. Given the turmoil during the liberation of the school, she could have run off into the swamps and been devoured by predators." He spread his hands. "I cannot say, other than that I had nothing to do with it."

Fielle studied Manford for a long moment, before turning to face the throne. "He's telling the truth, Sire."

Sitting back, Roderick felt surprised and disappointed. "Very well, I accept your answer, and I accept the gift of these two Mentats. I am certain we can put them to good use, somehow."

With a bow from his harness on Anari's shoulders, Manford said, "It is my honor to serve you, Sire. I came to you as a dedicated defender in this war for the human soul, and I offer my loyal fighters to you. The Butlerian army will join your defenses, and together we can crush Venport in his stronghold. Countless throngs are already gathering here. Shall we go together to Kolhar, wipe him out once and for all?"

"It is not that simple." Roderick scowled. "Directeur Venport controls the largest and most powerful spacing fleet. Without his ships, we cannot restore commerce throughout the Imperium, which becomes more and more imperative each day. Even if we neutralize him by military means and punish him for his crimes, we need to keep his foldspace ships and Navigators. The Imperium requires them."

"I care nothing for his Navigator-guided fleet." Manford sniffed. "I travel from planet to planet using standard foldspace ships. We can make do."

"I don't want to 'make do.' I want the Imperium to thrive. Only Venport's Navigators can absolutely guarantee safe passage."

In an indignant tone Manford said, "Only *God* can guarantee safe passage!"

"Perhaps, but God guarantees safe passage more readily when VenHold Navigators are involved."

"We fight the same enemy," Manford said. "We must be prepared to lay down our lives to stop that man."

Roderick became more calculating. If nothing else, he could use the Butlerian fanatics as expendable shock troops in a frontal assault against the VenHold headquarters on Kolhar. More than anything, he wanted to get their warships away from Salusa, where they hung as an unspoken threat. It was a devil's bargain, but if the Butlerians threw themselves recklessly at Kolhar, the fanatics would suffer tremendous casualties. Not necessarily a bad thing . . .

The Emperor rose from the throne. Taking Haditha by the hand, he announced, "I shall consult with my advisers on how we might implement that. Your efforts would be most appreciated."

With the brief audience concluded, Imperial troops escorted Manford and his entourage back out into the great hall, where the Butlerian crowds cheered him. Though he had looked disturbed during the meeting, Manford seemed strengthened by the roar of the crowd. Thousands of them, with more and more coming every day. . . .

Watching him, Roderick felt uneasy, knowing how difficult it would be to make the fanatics leave Salusa—unless he managed to send them after another target.

⌘

THE NEXT DAY, no less than a miracle, a battered foldspace carrier arrived above Salusa. Despite its VenHold markings, the giant vessel carried Admiral Umberto Harte and the hostage Imperial fleet from Kolhar. Even though they bore no news of General Roon's strike force, which had vanished entirely, this restored seventy warships to the Imperial Armed Forces—enough to keep the Butlerians from making an unwise move.

Roderick was pleased to learn the even more astonishing news that Harte had captured one of Venport's mysterious Navigators. A specimen that they would study in great detail.

That indeed changed the state of affairs significantly.

Love does not make the world go around. Love is an obstruction in the gears of the universe.

—MOTHER SUPERIOR VALYA HARKONNEN

After the attack by Tula's protectors in the Chusuk performance hall, Vor and Willem were rushed to an emergency medical facility, a small building that consisted of two examination rooms and a lobby filled with portable beds. Seven doctors were crammed into that limited space, tending a battered Willem and Vor, along with a pair of bedraggled-looking women receiving treatment for injuries from a boating accident.

"This is a private facility, set aside for the use of nobles and visiting dignitaries," said the young doctor as she bandaged Vor's head. "The Princess authorized us to treat you—Vorian Atreides." She said his name with a slight smile. "I've never had a true war hero as a patient before."

Princess? Vor thought. A chill went down his back. "How do you know my name?"

The doctor raised her eyebrows, apparently amused. "Your young companion does not know how to keep a confidence."

Vor looked over at Willem, who remained unconscious. "No, I suppose he doesn't." Had he also inadvertently tipped off the disguised Sisters who had been watching over Tula? Even the murderous Harkonnen girl hadn't seemed to know she was being guarded.

Due to his life-extension treatment, Vor healed quickly, but Willem was much more seriously injured. He remained unconscious for hours and suffered from internal bleeding, along with several broken bones. Even after Vor felt recovered enough to leave, he stayed beside his companion. Vor slept restlessly on the portable bed, remaining on guard in case Tula sent anyone to finish the job.

He suspected, though, that she had escaped from the planet by now, fleeing justice.

In the morning Vor's injuries had dwindled to a lingering headache. His thoughts still spun from what had occurred in the dance hall. He knew he was a gifted fighter with exceptional reflexes, but those women watching Tula were experts in personal combat, trained by the Sisterhood. They were skilled enough that they could easily have killed both him and Willem. And they would have if the added force of guards hadn't arrived when they did.

Young Willem had suffered a concussion, broken ribs, and far more serious internal injuries, yet he had the good fortune of being aided by his friend Harmona. Who was she?

The pretty brunette and her retinue had come into the medical center before dawn and gathered at Willem's bedside as he awoke, groaning. When his eyes opened to see her there, he showed confusion, then smiled. He tried to sit up, but winced. He tried to take a deep breath and touched the tight bindings on his ribs, glanced at the medical apparatus connected to him. Harmona propped pillows behind his back and helped him to sit as comfortably as possible.

"Thanks for your help," Vor said to her. "I am Vorian Atreides . . . but I think you know that already." He wished his "nephew" weren't so forthcoming with details, but he chastised himself for not being more alert.

"I am Harmona Bach, a member of the ruling Landsraad family on Chusuk. You needed help—and it was about time my bodyguards did something. They're not usually needed here." She gave him a cursory smile, but her attention remained on Willem.

The young man spoke to Vor, sounding sheepish, "I didn't get a chance to introduce you. She's a princess."

Harmona showed embarrassment, but Vor could tell she was proud of her station. "It is mostly an honorary title. Chusuk is generous with such things."

Two of Harmona's large bodyguards stood outside the doorway, and Vor found their presence reassuring, even though—from what he had seen in the performance hall—the warrior Sisters could likely defeat them.

Harmona continued, "Willem told me the tragic story of his brother. I used some of my resources to help you find that woman, and I've been working with the authorities all night to try to intercept her. I fear that she managed to escape off-planet, though. Apparently, she had a lot of allies here."

He and Willem had come to Chusuk to hunt down the Harkonnen woman who killed Orry. It had been naïve to think she would be an easy mark, and that mistake could have gotten them killed. At the very least, they had lost her trail.

And now the Sisterhood was forewarned. They would shelter Tula.

"Good thing you had extra security," Vor said. "I certainly didn't expect her to be protected like that. If not for your bodyguards, the battle might have gone far worse."

With a grim expression, Harmona read Willem's medical chart. "This looks bad enough."

"He'll recover. He's strong," Vor said. "But we shouldn't stay here long. Either we have to go after Tula Harkonnen, or we need to move before they come after us."

Harmona placed her hand on Willem's shoulder, and the attending doctor came close, shaking her head. "That one isn't going anywhere soon, especially not off-planet. He'll need at least a few weeks to mend."

Barely conscious, Willem tried to argue, but his insistence made him swoon from the pain. Harmona eased him back down to the pillow. "You are staying here—under my care—until you are considered fit enough."

Unhappy, Willem said, "But we have to go. Tula's getting away—"

"I can go," Vor said. "Let me do some investigating."

"Orry was my brother!"

Vor shook his head. "And the entire Atreides-Harkonnen feud is my fault."

It had been eight decades since he'd fought in the Jihad, when he spent each day in a constant state of heightened alert. After retiring from service—and from public life—Vor concealed his identity and vanished into his own legend. For a long time he had tried to be a normal man, clinging to an ordinary life in hopes of putting the horror and bloodshed behind him. But it had been foolish to hope he could simply become a common man again. He could never escape the events in the Jihad, nor could he escape the enmity that generations of Harkonnens held toward him. He could never run away from the fact that he was Vorian Atreides.

He guessed that by now Tula Harkonnen had been whisked off to Wallach IX. Her sister Valya was there, someone who also hated him. And if Tula was enfolded in the arms of the Sisterhood, Vor and Willem would never reach her. He feared they had lost their chance.

Unless he could entice them out.

Vor said to the Princess, "Stay here and watch Willem. He may still be in danger, so guard him carefully and get him the best possible medical care. I can pay for anything he needs."

She shook her head. "Oh, he'll receive the best care, and we won't accept any money from you. I'm a member of the noble family here, so funds are not an issue."

He nodded gratefully. "Thank you. I need to leave today—I'll draw them out, find a way to get the Harkonnens focused on me instead of Willem."

"I will keep him safe," Harmona said. "He can heal on my estate, and no one will get through our security."

Vor nodded. "When the time is right, I'll send for him."

Willem again tried to argue, but he was fading, both from the pain and from a powerful sedative the doctor had given him. Harmona regarded Vor with a pragmatic look. "For years your face was on Imperial coins—Vorian Atreides, the greatest hero of Serena Butler's Jihad. My grandparents and great-grandparents spoke of you with admiration. It's terrible what happened to Willem's brother at the hands of that monstrous girl!"

"Someday this feud will be over," he said. "I want to end it—without putting Willem at even greater risk. This problem is of my own making, and I have to take care of it."

He had already begun planning his trap. Maybe he could lure Valya and Tula into coming after him. He knew they wanted him more than any other target. For his legacy and for House Atreides, he had to deflect the danger away from Willem.

Vor had spent a lot of time mentoring the young man, trying to envision him as the leader of the Atreides family. Yes, Vor could see it. In so many ways, Willem reminded him of himself, and he could still make something of his life. It was important for him to do so.

When Vor looked at Harmona, he knew he was leaving Willem in good hands. No regrets. "I am going to Corrin—a place where if the Harkonnens hunt me down, few innocent bystanders will get hurt. Maybe I can lure them to me, and turn the tables on them."

Vor considered the former machine capital a private place, *his* place. He had grown up there under the glare of its red giant sun more than two centuries ago, so he knew the world well. Yes, that was where it should end.

He would not ask Harmona to keep the destination a secret—in fact, he was seeding careful and subtle rumors himself about where he was going, so that the Harkonnens would know exactly where to find him. Remembering how the Sisterhood commandos had appeared last night, Vor suspected their spies were still on Chusuk, watching. With luck, they would take the bait.

"Please see that Willem is well taken care of. I'm going alone."

Hard measures are required in order to accomplish anything of true significance. When sculpting a statue, much of the stone is thrown away.

—MOTHER SUPERIOR VALYA HARKONNEN

E ven as Mother Superior, Valya continued to hone her skills and make herself more competent, more and more dangerous. The new combined combat techniques were intriguing and exciting, and she made sure her Sisters were proficient.

Under the small blue-white sun, she watched as Sister Deborah, dressed in her flowing white Sorceress robe, addressed the uneasy Orthodox Sisters who had been recalled from Salusa Secundus. They stood together, wary. None of them knew what had happened to Esther-Cano; they only knew that their colleague was no longer there. So far, none of them had dared to ask about her.

Valya wondered how many of these stubborn women would have to be removed . . . permanently, in the same fashion.

The dark-robed Sisters stood on a rocky promontory overlooking the fledgling Mother School complex. When the traitor Dorotea had pulled the rebellious faction together, she'd convinced her Orthodox followers to become schemers and spies, whisperers of clever and insidious disinformation, but she had not taught them to be aggressive fighters. Observing them closely, Valya saw that they possessed considerable potential. It would be a shame to kill them all.

Some of the Orthodox women proved to be more open-minded than Valya had anticipated, willing to learn new ways of thinking. Those who aligned themselves with the rest of the Sisterhood would not have to be discarded; provided they were sincere, she would welcome them fully into the order.

Others, though, were reluctant to give their allegiance to her, which she found disappointing, though not surprising. These last prodigal Sisters had to be retrained, or broken. Questionable loyalties created friction and vulnerabilities that Valya could not afford, especially now.

Her close ally Deborah, with her bony face and darting dark eyes, often reminded Valya of a bird. Her lean, angular frame did not carry an ounce of fat. She was a ruthless opponent in combat, skilled in virtually all of the techniques Valya had brought to the school.

As the training continued, Deborah called for a volunteer among the Orthodox Sisters. "I will demonstrate a new way of fighting to add to your repertoire. In extreme circumstances, you may need every weapon we can give you."

Valya gazed out upon the assembled women, their hair flowing in a cool breeze on the promontory. She spoke up. "Think of the slaughter on Rossak. We must never let ourselves be helpless again."

A slender woman stepped forward to volunteer, but a more muscular Sister pushed her aside. "No, I will do this." Though she was only in her mid-thirties, Sister Ninke's auburn hair was salted with gray. Ninke had once served with Valya as an assistant proctor under Mother Superior Raquella, before becoming one of Dorotea's traitorous followers.

Now Ninke faced the Sorceress instructor with a confident expression, and Deborah nodded somberly. "I have observed you in training sessions, Ninke. You are at the peak of your physical skills, but you lack something important . . . the ability to be wary. Confidence can lead to weakness, and overconfidence leads to mistakes. Where are you on that spectrum of danger?"

Ninke rolled her eyes in disdain. "Shall I just stand here, or would you like me to go into a fighting stance?" She was trying to provoke Deborah.

The Sorceress instructor remained cool. "You seem unaware of the fact that every word you utter, every move you make, is filled with weakness. My method will enlighten you. Yes, go into your best fighting stance, and I will demonstrate its flaws."

Ninke scowled at the verbal jab, but prepared for combat. Valya was quietly impressed with the way she held her body loose and poised, ready to leap in any direction. Ninke was fast—but not fast enough.

Deborah circled her practice foe, forcing Ninke to turn constantly to keep her instructor in sight. The Sorceress feinted to the right, which provoked a defensive move, and as Deborah drew back she did a smooth backward flip, followed by a quick forward flip, so that she stood a step closer to Ninke than before—all in a blur. Before Ninke could assess the new stance, the Sorceress repeated her movement, farther and faster this time, so that she landed behind Ninke and gave her a taunting slap on the shoulder.

Ninke whirled, but could not even glimpse her opponent. Deborah reached in and slapped the side of her head, moving so unexpectedly that Ninke could not follow her. Even observing, Valya could hardly keep track of the Sorceress. Deborah was so swift that she seemed to disappear entirely and then blur back into view.

Finally she stood behind Ninke again and said in a harsh voice, "Had we truly been fighting, I could have broken you with debilitating blows from any direction before you even knew where I was."

Ninke nodded with growing anger. "This is like witchcraft."

With a smile Deborah said, "Yes, our new fighting Way *is* witchcraft, and the most talented of you must master it—for the good of the Sisterhood. But our skills require tremendous concentration and force of will, along with abandoning the rules of motion that you previously thought you understood."

Ninke seemed unwilling to accept her obvious lack of skill in comparison with her instructor. In training the intractable Orthodox Sisters, Valya had decided that one of them must serve as a prominent example, for the benefit of the rest. The intractable Esther-Cano had already been killed, but in private. Perhaps Ninke would be the example these others needed.

"Let me show you a simple technique of our Way," Deborah said to the other trainees, and then she added to Ninke with a hint of scorn, "in slow motion this time, if that is what you require."

Ninke's nostrils flared at the affront, but the Sorceress ignored her. Deborah slumped to the ground, and as she got back to her feet she moved so smoothly she seemed to float on air. "Notice the liquid flow of muscles, just one constant motion. You must seek, and attain, utter relaxation, while your thoughts remain hyperalert. Your mind and musculature must be in complete synchronization. Try it yourself."

Ninke attempted to repeat the movement, but without the finesse. Deborah laughed at the attempt, and when the Orthodox Sister got back to her feet, she struggled to contain her emotions, but failed. She was red-faced and angry. Valya knew this was what Deborah had been trying to accomplish.

"Try it again!" The Sorceress demonstrated once more by dropping to the ground, and then floating back up. "See how my muscles flow. Pay attention this time!"

Rather than making the attempt, Ninke lashed out with a sharp kick at the Sorceress, lightning fast, but Deborah was not there for the kick to land. Coming in from one side, she slashed a hard retaliatory blow onto Ninke's forearm. All of the Sisters heard the sickening crack of bone. Rather than collapsing, Ninke struck out with her intact arm, but Deborah slammed into Ninke's stomach, driving her backward. Falling, Ninke hit her broken arm on the ground and cried out in pain.

As the woman tried to struggle to her feet, Valya stood over her. The goading had worked. "No truly trained Sister would ever let herself be provoked into such rash responses. For your own good, stay down! If you get back on your feet, I cannot prevent Deborah from killing you. It was not wise to challenge her as you did. She was merely trying to demonstrate your weaknesses—for your benefit."

Ninke glared up at Valya. "You intended for me to be injured. You arranged for it to happen—just as you found a way to eliminate Sister Esther-Cano. Will I be the next to die? Or do you think my wayward mind can be retrained?"

Valya was startled by the bold statement of facts. "I am your Mother Superior. Your fate is for me to decide."

Ignoring the pain of her broken arm, Ninke struggled to a sitting position. She looked at the other trainees watching them. "It does not escape our notice, *Mother Superior*, that Orthodox Sisters are assigned the worst jobs. Two of our number have been forced to become unwilling birth mothers—is that meant to humiliate, or is it an integral part of your rumored breeding program?" She narrowed her gaze. "Where are the computers you use to keep track of the genetic records?"

"Dorotea embarrassed herself by making such ludicrous accusations," Valya said, "and in doing so she nearly brought down the Sisterhood. Salvador's thugs found no evidence to support her absurd claims, but still they killed many of us and drove us from Rossak—all because of wild, unproven claims. Watch yourself."

"Just because they found nothing doesn't mean the computers weren't there. We never stopped believing they existed."

"Believing something and proving it are two different things. Report to the clinic, Sister Ninke, and get medical treatment for your arm."

Ninke backed away, favoring her injured arm but never taking her gaze away from the Sorceress, who stood poised and ready to kill at the Mother Superior's command. Deborah's blood was up, making her a dangerous weapon that needed to stand down and shut off.

As Ninke walked unsteadily toward the medical clinic, Valya called after her, "You will thank me one day for this, because it will make you stronger."

❧

LATE THAT AFTERNOON, Valya returned to the school complex to find Tula waiting for her at the private dining table. The watchers had delivered her safely from Chusuk, but Tula didn't look pleased about it.

The young woman rose to her feet and bowed, as if Valya were a complete stranger. She showed no warmth at seeing her older sister, but this did not cause

Valya to dampen her own enthusiasm. "I am delighted you've returned to us. Are you well? You look quite pale."

"Tired from the trip, and from the trouble on Chusuk." When Valya responded with a blank look, Tula added, "Two of the Atreides located me there, but they paid a price. You sent guards to watch over me, and they . . . took care of the threat." She sounded resentful.

Valya drew in a quick breath. "Are the Atreides dead?"

Tula shook her head. "Injured only. Vorian and Willem."

Valya caught her breath. "Vorian Atreides came after you himself? And you allowed him to live?"

"We were in a crowded place, with many witnesses, and security guards who got in our way. He and Willem were soundly defeated. That was enough." Her voice hitched. "Don't you think so too? Can't we put an end to the killing, or must it continue for the rest of time? Is that what you want?"

Scowling, Valya said, "I want the Harkonnens to be strong again, and that means the Atreides must be weak, or dead." She brightened. "Even so, I am glad you've returned to us, safe. And now that we know for certain Vorian Atreides is looking for you, I will send out my operatives. We will locate him again, and next time I'll use all the resources of the Sisterhood to finish him off."

Instead of the happy response Valya had hoped for, her sister merely ate the rest of her meal in silence.

What some men see as aspirations, others see as obligations. Either way, we find ourselves trapped.

—DIRECTEUR JOSEF VENPORT, private
conversation with his wife, Cioba

The loss of the huge spice bank on Arrakis was a disaster by any measure, and Josef had not even begun to calculate the second- and third-order costs to Venport Holdings. The initial investigation suggested that the raiders had used giant sandworms.

The stunning attack revealed a considerable vulnerability, of which he had been entirely unaware. Not only had the catastrophe cost him an incalculable fortune in spice to be sold throughout the Imperium, Norma's Navigators would now face short supplies. And because she had pulled all of his battleships away from the siege of Salusa in response to the raid, Josef had lost that gambit as well.

A cascade of setbacks.

Knowing how much his great-grandmother valued and protected her Navigators, he wasn't surprised she would rush off to save the spice bank—but, oh, the damage she had done in that moment of almost certain victory. It made the VenHold fleet look like skittish, impotent cowards, running away from Roderick Corrino and the half-Manford's capering savages. The timing could not have been worse.

Now it would require all of his capabilities to rebound. The victory he sought was not about achieving wealth and power, but to safeguard humanity's future. If he let the antitechnology fanatics win, the human race would certainly face an unprecedented dark age.

He left part of his fleet at Arrakis to make damned certain no one threatened his spice operations again. Josef and his remaining ships returned to Kolhar, where he could regroup and prepare his next move. He looked forward to seeing Cioba again. She would help him decide what to do.

But when the VenHold ships arrived at the headquarters planet, his wife had more bad news for him. While the bulk of the warships had been away, Admiral Umberto Harte had staged a daring overthrow of the foldspace carrier that had been holding his Imperial battle group hostage. They were gone.

Cioba showed him images as he stared in disbelief. "They nearly tore the hull apart, then made their way to the Navigator deck and took control." She turned her dark eyes downward. "I sent ships to intercept them, but the carrier folded space and vanished before we could block their way."

Josef reeled, feeling as if another giant boulder had crashed down on him from an unexpected direction. Norma Cenva, in her tank, listened and finally pronounced in a grave, eerie voice, "The Emperor has captured one of my Navigators."

Josef struggled to control his anger. He refused to let yet another disaster destroy him. He would find a way to snatch a victory out of even this collapse. He was Josef Venport, Directeur of Venport Holdings, and he refused to throw away a lifetime of work—*generations* of work.

Canceling all meetings, he locked himself in his high tower offices, asking to be alone. Brooding, he paced the room and looked out the plaz windows at the bustle of arriving and departing ships on the landing field. He worked out which part of the problem to tackle first.

Even with Harte's ships returned to the Imperial Armed Forces, it wasn't likely the Emperor would come to Kolhar, or Arrakis, in a direct attack. Emperor Roderick badly needed the reinforcements at Salusa, and although Admiral Harte's ships were not spacefolders, they did represent a significant military force. They could defend the planet, if Josef ever attempted his siege again. And who knew what the Butlerians might do with all those antique ships?

Worse, though, they had kidnapped one of his Navigators!

For years, rival foldspace shipping companies such as Celestial Transport and EsconTran had tried to learn how to create the superior mutated humans, but no one else had succeeded—even though it was obvious they were immersed in tanks of spice gas, that was only part of the secret.

Now, however, Roderick had a live specimen that he could poke and prod and interrogate and even dissect. Josef dreaded what the Imperial researchers would discover. It was just possible that his scientists might be able to derive the secret.

Navigators . . . Norma Cenva . . . spice . . . foldspace travel . . . the vast wealth in interplanetary banks . . . the tapestry of commercial interactions that held the Imperium together. It was all connected, with Navigators at the center. Josef would not let it all unravel.

Restless and agitated, he emerged from his office, surprised to find Cioba waiting for him there in the hall. With her Sorceress blood and Sisterhood training, she sometimes showed hints of prescience herself.

He reached out to stroke the side of her classically lovely face with its porcelain complexion, her long and silky brown hair. "Sometimes you surprise me, my love. How did you know?"

"Wherever you're going, I am pledged to accompany you."

The open field of Navigator tanks held hundreds of sealed chambers, each containing a candidate in metamorphosis. Some writhed and thrashed, inhaling melange gas; others drifted, curled in fetal positions. Thanks to modifications in the process, under Norma's careful guidance, two-thirds of the Navigator candidates survived the transformation, which was a vast improvement from earlier efforts.

He and Cioba passed workers using mobile pumping reservoirs to fill the spice tanks. The VenHold employees bowed in respect to the Directeur, but Josef was preoccupied with thoughts of how extraordinarily expensive melange was going to be until he managed to build up his stockpile again—a very difficult task if he had to worry about the security of his operations on Arrakis. The efforts of the Emperor and the barbarians had redoubled against him. . . .

Norma's platform was empty. She had vanished on one of her own voyages, as she sometimes did. "*The universe is ours,*" she often said. But the destruction of the melange stockpile as well as the loss of the Navigator Dobrec had affected her deeply.

Josef just stared at the empty space, feeling empty himself. He needed to speak with his great-grandmother, commiserate with her, even scold her for what had happened. Norma's mind was so distant from political realities, though, that he was not at all certain she understood the consequences of what she had done at Salusa, and the dire position Venport Holdings was now in. So much political damage to mitigate!

"Maybe it's best that she is not here," Cioba said. "Our needs and priorities frequently align with Norma's—but not always. She is focused on her Navigators, while we have to consider the entirety of Venport Holdings—and your own aspirations. What do you wish to achieve, my husband? If you could control every action and reaction, what would your preferred outcome be?"

Josef frowned. "My own aspirations? I thought they were clear, especially to you. I want to protect my company, conduct business across the Imperium, and ensure the steady growth of civilization. Without me, we would revert to a dark time of low technology and rampant superstition, of omens and signs and ignorance."

He saw one of the newer Navigator candidates spasming in the orange melange gas, her distorted face stretched in a rictus of pain, her eyes swollen shut behind reddened eyelids. Most of her hair had fallen out, and the remainder hung in odd tufts and wisps. The transformation process seemed like a horrific procedure, but in the end, successful Navigators did not regret it—or so they claimed.

"To achieve my goals, I need to have both Navigators and spice—and I need the barbarians defeated." He felt a knot in his chest. "Of utmost importance, I need the cooperation of Emperor Roderick, or some other Emperor sitting on the throne in his place . . . preferably not me."

Cioba stepped closer to the tank where the proto-Navigator twitched and turned to look at him. "After the fall of the thinking machines, humanity needed to achieve its potential," Cioba said. "Mankind became free to expand, explore, and evolve. Headmaster Albans founded his Mentat School to train minds that could think like the most advanced computers. Mother Superior Raquella founded the Sisterhood school to improve human abilities as well. Other schools also explore human potential."

She touched the smooth plaz of the tank, and the creature inside jerked away, as if that faintest of vibrations felt like a thunderclap. "And these Navigators—this is evolution too. Forced evolution. A supreme demonstration of what humans can achieve."

Josef drew close and peered into the tank, noting the awful physical changes that he himself had authorized. He didn't remember this particular candidate at all, was unaware of her name, didn't know where she had come from or whether she had openly volunteered or been forced into the tanks.

Looking around at all the tanks, he saw dozens of the creatures, many almost completely transformed, their heads and eyes enlarged, their bodies atrophied, their skin flaccid and discolored. Evolution . . . advancement of the species . . . but was this what humanity was destined to be?

He looked around and raised his voice, as if all of the Navigators were listening to their conversation. The VenHold employees with their pumping tanks and medical monitors studiously pretended not to hear. "I promise I have only the best of intentions for humanity. I don't need more power or wealth for myself—I have enough of both. I just want to do what is right for civilization."

Cioba's expression grew hard, and her voice carried a tone of warning. "I'm sure General Agamemnon and the Twenty Titans also had the best of intentions."

Josef was so surprised by her comment that he felt a chill go down his spine. He looked up to see movement inside all the Navigator tanks. The drifting, twisted forms, the successfully transformed candidates as well as the newer volunteers, all turned their faces in his direction, and Josef was certain that they were staring directly at him.

Achieving a goal can be a blessing or a disappointment. The reality is never exactly as one envisions it—for better or for worse.
            —Untitled philosophy book, the Erasmus library

With the optical sensors connected to his memory core, Erasmus inspected his new body drifting in amniotic fluid. When Dr. Danebh and his Tlulaxa technicians drained the biological vat and brought the pale, naked form into the open air, Erasmus felt oddly disturbed . . . and let down.

As Anna held his memory core in her hands, he could sense her trembling with excitement. She had rushed into the biological laboratory as soon as she received word that the body was fully grown and ready. The human form, alive but without a consciousness, lay face up on a medical table with supplementary nutrient tubes strung from the moist, soft flesh. The smooth chest rose and fell in rhythmic breathing, but the eyes were closed.

Erasmus had watched this body grow from week to week with accelerated development—a clone from the cells of Gilbertus Albans. With perfect recall he remembered how he, as an independent robot, had raised the real Gilbertus from a dirty, feral child more than two centuries ago. This cellular replica was a near-perfect copy of Gilbertus Albans, in physical form, but Erasmus knew that the sharp mind of his ward and protector was forever gone. Indelibly recorded in his memory sphere, Erasmus saw the last moments of the real Gilbertus, when the proud Headmaster had knelt before Anari Idaho's sword.

Now the robot noticed slight differences in the body, smooth skin that should have been scarred, a missing mole on the left shoulder. This mindless twin looked eerily similar, but was not the same. "Did you encounter any errors in the growth process?" Erasmus inquired. "Why are there any differences at all?"

"The DNA is the same, but even identical twins are not entirely the same. Biology is not perfect."

"Of course. I have realized that many times." He knew that this body was never meant to be a new Gilbertus Albans, but rather a new *Erasmus*.

"I think it's beautiful," Anna said. "And it will be even more beautiful once it becomes *you*, with your mind and storehouse of memories."

"The body is acceptable," Erasmus said. He could think of so much to do after he entered this body and controlled its movements, so much to experience! So much to see and touch and feel! "A far greater challenge will be to install and interface my memory core with the nervous system."

"We have experience with similar situations," Danebh said. "Our cymek work has paved the way."

In recent months, the Denali surgeons had become quite adept at connecting human minds to compatible, receptive machine components. Now they had to do the reverse: unite a thinking machine memory core with human systems.

Utilizing the sensory package connected to his gelsphere, he watched Anna study the newly decanted body. She reached out to touch the face, caressed the skin.

Soon, Erasmus would have his new body and would feel her touch—a biological form for the first time in his centuries of existence. His thoughts churned with anticipation. He said to Danebh, "I am anxious to begin."

⤛⤜

USING THEIR SOPHISTICATED cymek bodies and precision surgical apparatus, Ptolemy and Administrator Noffe performed the operation themselves, supervised and assisted by Danebh.

Once disconnected from the sensory package he'd been using thus far, Erasmus could not determine exactly what was happening around him. He was in limbo, with no stimuli except for his own thoughts and memories . . . all internal. So he immersed himself in replaying an accelerated recollection of his existence under the computer evermind Omnius—the days of humanity's enslavement and his own part in their eventual revolt, followed by the years of hiding.

Today, Erasmus would at last achieve a new stage, the greatest of his long list of experiments involving human beings! He had dissected countless specimens, pried apart innumerable human bodies and minds (sometimes when the subjects were still alive), all in an effort to understand them.

Now he could finally become one of them. . . .

When the lengthy installation procedure was done, Erasmus opened his eyes, and the bright lights of the laboratory dome flooded him with a new reality, revealing to him for the first time the way humans looked at things. Every sense in his body awakened at once with an accompanying avalanche of sights, sounds, colors, smells—so many sensations pouring in through the myriad nerves that were woven through the flesh.

It was as if all filters had been torn away and the sensory inputs had been turned to maximum levels. He could hardly stand it, and could scarcely get enough. He flexed his fingers, inhaled the air, smelled the laboratory and its blend of odors.

Anna reached out to touch his face with an expression that he interpreted as wonder. Her contact felt warm to him, and her expression was filled with adulation. And as she touched him, he felt the complexity of her fingertips.

When Erasmus spoke a moment later, he experienced the sounds coming from his lungs, his chest, his larynx, and his mouth all at once—unlike the bland speakerpatches he had used for his entire previous existence.

"I am awake. I am alive," he said, and his voice sounded wonderful to him. "Finally, I am human!"

Money and effort cannot always secure a desired goal. Some things are unattainable.

—Tlulaxa warning

To study the captive Navigator specimen Admiral Harte had delivered to Salusa, Roderick commanded the most advanced research laboratory that Imperial funds could construct on short notice. Desperate to understand how he could make such creatures for his own Imperial purposes, he staffed the facility with skilled and eager scientists, most of them drawn from the Suk Medical School. Roderick knew that time was short and the research itself was dangerous. He had no idea what Josef Venport would do next.

Not daring to inflame the Butlerians who still infested the capital city, the Emperor had ordered the construction of the underground laboratory in great secrecy, and stationed more than a thousand soldiers to guard it. If Manford Toronto ever learned that a captive Navigator was held somewhere in Zimia, he might summon a mob in an attempt to breach the facility, smash the large tank, and destroy the critically important work. Even worse, that might just be the beginning: Roderick recalled reports of what the violent, rampaging Butlerians had done to another Navigator they seized on Baridge.

He hoped the heavily armed soldiers he had stationed to guard the Navigator would prevent that, and he was also concerned about something else. When Roderick ordered the stationing of the troops, he'd said to the commander, "Just as we were about to arrest Josef Venport in the throne room, Norma Cenva appeared in her tank and whisked him away, vanishing into the folds of space. If her tank appears anywhere near our captive Navigator, you are to immediately open fire on the prisoner. We will not let her have him back. . . ."

Now, through a secure access, the Emperor and Haditha entered the underground facility, accompanied by a confident Umberto Harte. Roderick smelled the odor of melange, noted the jumpsuited scientists and assistants who surrounded the creature's tank. The Suk researchers monitored the thing's vital signs while trying to glean useful data from blood and cellular samples. Roderick had authorized all investigatory measures, including dissection, should the thing die in the course of research.

"It says its name is Dobrec," said Harte, looking at the tank.

"It also says it has no use for appellations, or for our concerns." Roderick had read the preliminary reports. "We need to find answers, so we can seize this advantage from Directeur Venport."

"Are you saying we need to create our own Navigators like this?" Haditha stopped beside the tank, looked deeply troubled. "What horrible things Directeur Venport must do to them—"

The Navigator swiveled toward her, pressing close to the speakerpatch. "Wondrous things. I am much more than I ever was before."

"I doubt we will convince him to switch his allegiance, Sire," said Harte. "But if we understand the process, we can recruit new Navigators—ones that are loyal to you."

Roderick frowned. "That is still a long way off, Admiral."

"You are incapable of understanding what to do," Dobrec said. "Only Norma Cenva knows how to guide and nurture us through the transformation." He enfolded himself in the dense gas.

"I hope you can find some use for him, Sire," Harte said.

Roderick was impressed with the Admiral. Umberto Harte was not an egotistical man, and accepted the need to hide the sensational news that he had captured a fully developed Navigator alive. For the time being, Harte's soldiers were sequestered, not allowed to communicate with their own families. A press announcement assured the cheering Zimia citizens that the survivors were just being debriefed about Directeur Venport's defenses at Kolhar. The entire force was confined at one of the largest Salusan military bases, many kilometers from the Imperial city. In order to keep the important secret, Roderick would likely dispatch them on another off-planet mission for the time being.

A small man in a scarlet-and-gold jumpsuit approached from the back of the laboratory—Demos Athens, the head of the facility, accompanied by a much taller man in a long black garment. Athens nodded toward his dour companion. "Sire, may I present Robér Cecilio, an adept of the Scalpel order of the Suk Medical School, one of our most skilled deep-interrogators. His talents will be useful in extracting information from the captive Navigator."

Cecilio bowed. "With your blessing, Sire, I am ready to help unravel the secrets this creature holds in its mind."

Roderick had some unpleasant experience with the infamous Scalpel torturers. His brother had used them often—far too often, and Roderick had seen them in action. "I have never approved of your cruel methods." He drew a breath, reminding himself that he was the Emperor now, not just a brother and a top adviser. "But I understand what may be necessary to obtain the information we desperately require."

Haditha looked concerned. "We need to understand the origin of the Navigators, but that creature is no longer human. Scalpel methods may not be effective in this case."

Roderick knew what she was thinking, and agreed. "I do not approve of torture . . . even of such an inhuman thing."

"But you do approve of results, Sire. The information you seek is vital to the Imperium." Cecilio gave a slight bow. "Nevertheless, I will use the lightest possible touch, gauging everything I do carefully."

Roderick warned, "We do not want this Navigator to die at your hands, or suffer."

Cecilio leaned close to the Emperor and lowered his voice. "Sire, with all respect we should not be having this conversation in front of the subject. Our methods should remain secret from him."

Roderick spoke loudly enough for all to hear. "No, I want Dobrec aware of his situation and the peril he faces. This Navigator must understand how necessary the information is to us." He nodded toward the Scalpel interrogator. "Very well, I authorize you to see what you can find out."

He stared ruefully at the creature in the tank, and the Navigator looked back with oversized eyes that seemed only remotely aware of the people around him, staring far past the Emperor, into the deepest and most uncharted regions of space and time.

The heroic reception from the citizens of Zimia was so overwhelming that even after four days of parades, speeches, and celebrations, the zeal had not diminished. Manford was pleased.

The Emperor had been forced to embrace him and lionize the brave Butlerian soldiers who had arrived at the perfect time to chase away Venport and his evil machine lovers. Settling in with the throngs at the capital city, rather than returning to his flagship in orbit, Manford had inflamed the crowds. And he kept them energized.

The swelling crowds had taken over empty homes and apartments, pushed themselves into temporary shelters, commandeered spare rooms in large family units, and set up communal sleeping tents across the palace plaza—whatever they needed to do. It was all perfectly justified and necessary.

If anyone from Zimia grumbled about the conditions, Manford merely spread his hands. "Good citizens of the Imperium are willing to make sacrifices for the future of humanity. After all, if we had not saved you from Venport's siege, your city would be in smoking ruins and you would all be dead. You can endure some small inconvenience to welcome your saviors."

Manford knew he was exaggerating his own importance, but the Emperor could not pretend that Salusa Secundus would have survived without the Butlerian intervention. And Manford did not intend to let him forget it. Roderick Corrino might not be as weak as Salvador had been . . . but Manford was not weak either.

After the three cymeks had attacked Lampadas and killed Sister Woodra, Manford's devoted followers howled for blood. New converts had rushed to his ranks, and even more joined after Venport's invasion of the Imperial capital. That dangerous man, his monstrous Navigators, his insidious machines, and his terrible cymeks had to be eradicated from the galaxy!

But not everything could be blamed on Directeur Venport. Even as the struggle for the human soul continued across the Imperium, a smaller-scale disaster occurred on Salusa Secundus. Far from Zimia in the southern lowlands, a large flood broke the banks of a Salusan river delta, and the rushing water devastated several trading settlements and river communities. Thousands were killed, tens of thousands displaced. The Emperor rushed to send emergency crews with temporary shelters and medical supplies. The suffering was extreme.

Empress Haditha announced that she would lead the relief efforts, calling upon the citizens of Salusa to contribute their work and supplies. She showed her strength and leadership by rallying support from all quarters. Manford found it admirable, but it was none of his concern.

And then Roderick came to see him. Tens of thousands of Butlerians were camped throughout the palace district, and Manford received him there like a visiting dignitary. The Emperor made his appeal. "I have work for your people, Manford Torondo. If you truly care about the well-being of humankind, then your followers can assist the flood victims. I will provide transportation to take them as humanitarian work crews."

Manford maintained a neutral expression, but he knew exactly what Roderick's real intent must be. The Emperor wanted to use this mundane catastrophe as an excuse to disperse the huge crowds of Butlerians, to get rid of them. No, he and his followers would not be deceived so easily.

"The flood victims are suffering, Sire, but that disaster was clearly an act of God," Manford said. "Those people must have been machine sympathizers. I would be cautious about helping them, because they likely deserved their punishment." He nodded as if to reaffirm his own conclusion. "Thank you, but my followers will stay right here, at the heart of our glorious capital. Surely you have enough trained home troops to handle a civil matter such as this? Weather events are rather commonplace, are they not?"

The Emperor looked angry on many levels, but Manford just smiled placidly at him. Anari Idaho stood like a statue, not questioning Manford's decision. Unable to coerce him, Roderick and his entourage departed.

~≈~

THE FOLLOWING DAY, as Manford sat propped on cushions under the rippling fabric of his pavilion, he contemplated his next steps. Butlerians filled the palace square on the west side of Zimia, and tens of thousands of believers strained the city's resources, but everyone would share the burden for the common good.

"'The mind of man is holy.'" He always found the mantra calming.

Manford knew the restless crowds could easily be driven to violence, and he fully understood the necessity of occasional mob celebrations as a pressure-release valve, although the last event in Zimia had gotten out of control. The death of the Emperor's young daughter had been an unfortunate tragedy, but at least the poor girl was a martyr.

That realization gave him an idea that brought a broad smile to his face. Perhaps if Manford presented it that way, the Emperor and Empress would forgive him. . . .

Anari had arranged for Manford's pavilion to be set up not far from a four-meter-high bronze statue of Emperor Faykan Corrino. Manford looked up at the statue, both impressed and offended by the towering figure. Faykan had been a hero at the end of the Jihad, and he certainly deserved to be celebrated—but not deified. Maybe someday there would be similar statues of Manford, though. He'd certainly done as much for humanity's future as Faykan had, and arguably more. . . .

He adjusted the cushions, felt a warm breeze on his face. He was making an impact here, but his goal was not to relax and enjoy the sunshine. After what the demon Venport had done—both on Lampadas and here—he knew he had to move against Kolhar as soon as possible. But even the Emperor was afraid to risk a military assault against VenHold headquarters. Deacon Harian wanted to unleash the Butlerians in a rampaging mob, not caring how many would be slaughtered, and Manford knew his followers would fight to the death no matter the odds. But he wanted to *win*, not just create another long list of martyrs. He needed some way to guarantee a victory. He prayed for a miracle.

Anari approached him, accompanied by a nobleman Manford did not recognize. The man wore expensive clothes, a rich green cloak, a gold-embroidered vest, and flowing pantaloons. A pie-shaped hat rested on his blond curls, making him appear more effete than handsome, but his eyes were open wide in adoration as he greeted the Butlerian leader. The man removed his hat and held it against his chest.

Anari provided the introduction. "Manford, this is an important Landsraad leader, Udorum Pondi from Gillek. Lord Pondi is a fervent convert to our Butlerian cause."

The nobleman stepped forward, as if he didn't know whether to fall to his knees or simply bow. "I am honored to meet you, Leader Torondo, and totally amazed. To be perfectly honest, my heart might burst."

Manford nodded, accepting the enthusiasm. It was not the only time he had received such accolades, and he always liked to listen to them.

"I was one of the first noblemen to take the pledge on behalf of my entire planet. We swore not to interact with evil machines. We cut off all dealings with Venport Holdings. We purged our cities, removed any hint of dangerous technology. I memorized the speeches of our beloved martyr Rayna Butler, and I listened to each of your recorded rallies. I read all of your writings and took them to heart. I want my planet to remain pure, even though we suffered greatly after we were cut off by the VenHold embargo."

"I wish I had many more like you." Manford's comment made the man's expression light up. "Many of us have suffered. Suffering is part of life—but humanity suffered far worse under the thinking machines."

Pondi wasn't finished. "Yes, yes, Leader Torondo! I also spoke out on behalf of our cause at the Landsraad Hall, but there are those who don't wish to listen, nobles with weak convictions. I'm not even convinced about Emperor Roderick's dedication, but I know I can trust you." He looked away as if ashamed. "I feel soiled by what I recently discovered on Gillek, but it is too important to ignore. I must turn it over to your hands. Such terrible weapons! Only you can be trusted to know what to do with so much power, Leader Torondo."

Anari looked at him intently, gave Pondi a meaningful nod. Manford was intrigued. "And what is it you've found?"

"During the purge of my planet, we ransacked technological vaults and discovered things that had been hidden away for decades, maybe even a century or more. What we found there . . ." Pondi shuddered, and tears began to pour down his cheeks. "I'm not worthy to keep it. Such a resource must be yours."

"What is it?" Manford repeated.

"A dangerous stockpile placed there for use against the thinking machines, but never deployed. They are intact. Perhaps . . . perhaps you can use them to save us all?"

Manford was growing impatient. "*What* things?"

Udorum Pondi looked up. "*Atomics*, Leader Torondo. A large stockpile of atomics from the Jihad. Enough warheads to destroy an entire thinking-machine world." He began to stammer. "I—I believe they can be better used for the Butlerian cause, under your guidance. If you will do me the honor of accepting them."

Manford's throat went dry, and he kept his voice steady. "Yes, Lord Pondi, I believe we can put them to very good use."

　　　　　　　　　　　　　　　　⚬⚬⚬

Is the ally of an outlaw also an outlaw?
—DRAIGO ROGET, Venport Holdings analysis,
Obligations and Alliances

A s a business leader, Josef could not let Venport Holdings be vulnerable to any single point of failure. Even after the seizure of his galactic banking operations, he still had wealth in places that the Emperor couldn't touch. And, given time and increased production, he would even rebuild his lost spice stockpile. He would not give up.

He didn't fool himself, though: He had been damaged severely but not defeated. No, he would find a way to grow strong again. The planetary shields and guardian ships would keep Kolhar safe, and all those additional warships on Arrakis should ensure that his hold remained firm there. Spice was the first and most important piece of the puzzle.

His operatives on numerous planets, particularly those with black-market connections, had scrounged alternative financing and secured temporary high-interest loans to keep VenHold functioning. Josef was forced to send some of his trading ships to service Butlerian-dominated planets, despite his prior edict to cut off the fanatics until they recanted their foolishness. Now, he could sell goods at exorbitant prices to those distressed people, while the extraordinary profits allowed him to maintain his defenses on Kolhar and to dispatch further shipments. His situation was no longer about the bottom-line profits that he could keep, but about survival, and making the money he needed to accomplish that. Too much was at stake—not just for him, but for the future of civilization.

A spice transport from Arrakis landed with a meager cargo load, barely a quarter full. Josef and Cioba went to meet the laborers who unloaded the packages of melange from suspensor pallets. He smelled the rich cinnamon aroma, which reminded him of all the scattered spice mixed with blood and smoke from his raided stockpile. When he looked at the paltry manifest, his heart sank.

"We are restoring our operations in the desert, Directeur," said the dusty captain. "Combined Mercantiles is sending out four new fully equipped harvesting teams, and we've put all the commandeered Imperial equipment to work. The next load will be more substantial, sir."

Josef gave a brusque nod. "It better be. This shipment isn't enough to fulfill a fraction of our commercial obligations, so we're reserving all of it for the Navigators. They must be our priority right now."

Cioba agreed. Norma Cenva had been vanishing more frequently and seemed more agitated and less comprehensible than usual. Perhaps by giving this entire shipment of melange to her Navigators, Josef could provide her with some reassurance.

He paced on the landing field, feeling frustrated. "I need this embargo to end. It disrupts commerce for everyone. How do I make Roderick Corrino listen?"

Josef's wife still favored the garments of the Sisterhood that had trained her. Cioba stood now in black robes that clung to her in the breezes. "In order to negotiate, there must be communication. But the Emperor will not talk with you directly—especially after your siege of Salusa. Therefore, you need an intermediary."

"And who will speak for me?"

Cioba pondered for a moment. "When Salvador banished the Sisterhood from Rossak, you gave aid to them, assisting them in setting up the new school on Wallach IX, furnishing them with transport as well as modular buildings and supplies."

Calculations raced through his mind. "Yes, their entire order survived because of me."

"I think it's time for me to go to Wallach IX and remind the new Mother Superior of the debt the Sisterhood owes us. At VenHold we need whatever allies we can get." She faced him like a soldier about to do battle. "I will speak with Mother Superior Valya. What would you ask of them?"

Josef suggested, "I want them to act as intermediaries, to talk to Roderick on our behalf. I don't want this feud with him, and I don't want to be Emperor! Roderick can have his damned throne, provided he becomes a suitable leader."

"Manford Torondo will never allow the Emperor to make peace with you," Cioba cautioned. "He has his own agenda."

"Then we will have to get rid of him—that much is obvious." He fumed. "In fact, it would solve most of our problems."

While supervising the unloading of spice, Josef and Cioba were surprised when Draigo Roget approached them from a landed shuttle. "I have a report for you, Directeur," he said. Stepping up to the dusty spice transport, the Mentat came to attention and quirked his lips in a small, uncharacteristic smile. "Fortunately, it is good news this time."

"Statistically, there has to be good news now and then," Cioba said.

"I just intercepted a report that EsconTran tried to keep secret. They lost one of their largest cargo transport ships due to a fatal navigational error."

Josef couldn't control how thrilled he was to hear this. "A true disaster, then? All hands lost? All cargo lost?"

"Everything, Directeur."

He smiled. "Excellent. Once again emphasizing how foolhardy it is to use any transportation company other than the VenHold Spacing Fleet. The half-Manford keeps flying in his spacefolders without Navigators, claiming that God will protect him. If only that little worm would disappear in a navigation mishap." Josef drew a deep breath of the bitter, fume-filled air.

"According to my Mentat projections, Directeur, if the Butlerian influence were removed, the Emperor would be more amenable to adjusting his position. He would owe you a tremendous debt."

"Mentat, you don't have to convince me that we need to eradicate the barbarians," Josef said. "Do you have a report on the cymek plans? I gave instructions for those battle machines to be made ready as soon as possible."

Draigo clasped his hands together behind him as the trio walked away from the spice transport. "That is my next piece of good news," he said. "The Denali scientists have nearly finished constructing the full cymek army and training the Navigator brains to guide them—one hundred additional units, as you specified, ready for your conquest of Lampadas. We will require no more than another two weeks."

Josef considered the news. "Considering how much havoc a mere three cymeks were able to cause, more than a hundred of them could level the planet."

The Mentat nodded. "Ptolemy is quite eager to move against the Butlerians. He submitted a detailed military assault plan for destroying Lampadas, and we are ready to present it for your modification and approval. Very soon, we will be capable of overrunning that defenseless world."

"The only problem is, the half-Manford and his barbarians are now ensconced at Salusa Secundus." Josef scowled. "I would much rather unleash all of my forces against Lampadas. Roderick may not believe this, but I respect the Imperium. I believe we should build it up, not tear it down . . . if I can just find a way out of this tangle."

"In the meantime I will see if the Sisterhood can assist us," Cioba said.

He smiled lovingly at his wife, then sighed. "We will be ready to attack Lampadas as soon as Manford goes back there. I don't doubt the Emperor is desperate to be rid of them, and he would undoubtedly consider it a favor if I do the work for him . . . but our timing has to be right."

One of the key aspects of being human is to experience and enjoy
human contact—the meeting of hearts and minds, the touching of bod-
ies, of skin. How I have missed that! I haven't felt human in so long.
                                        —ANNA CORRINO, the Denali Diary

A nna had waited for this moment—for Erasmus—and her anticipation
    was intense, but somehow she kept herself calm in his presence, knowing
that he appreciated being in control. He had trained her carefully during the
many months he had been her constant companion, the voice whispering in
her ear, and more.

In his new body Erasmus was the perfect male form, as if sculpted by a classical
master from those hedonistic days before the Time of Titans. The face resembled
Gilbertus Albans, but the *person* was completely different: Erasmus, her friend
and protector, the one who understood Anna better than anyone else. After her
mind had been twisted by the Sisterhood's Rossak drug, she had never thought
anyone would understand her again. But Erasmus did, and always had, even
before revealing himself as a disembodied, whispering voice in the first phase of
their relationship, advising her and asking probing questions.

But now he was *real*, standing before her in a form so handsome that her
eyes ached. She could only gaze briefly at him because a thin sheen of tears soft-
ened the image. "Just walk with me, Erasmus." She took his hand—his hand of
real, tangible *flesh*.

He appeared to be comfortable and in control of his new body. Together, they
strolled through the corridors of the laboratory domes, passing workrooms, paus-
ing to look at the hangars where immense cymek walkers were being refurbished
and armed for their impending assault on Lampadas.

When Erasmus clasped Anna's fingers, she felt electricity tingling through her arm—not electricity from the robotic gelsphere that held his memories and personality. No, this was the electricity of physical contact, the spark of a long-anticipated touch.

Anna had a spring in her step as she led him along, but when he stopped to stare at the enormous walkers, Erasmus had a distant, admiring look in his borrowed eyes. For a long time now, he had been telling her about the cymeks and the Synchronized Empire. He liked to talk about his magnificent villa with its slave pens and laboratories on Corrin, before the humans wiped it out in a barbaric atomic attack. Anna wondered what he thought now when he looked at these new cymeks.

She looped his arm around hers. "I want to show you so many things. I've waited a long time for this moment."

"As I have waited. Every sensation in this body is new and noteworthy." His voice sounded different coming from a natural, human throat. It had a rich and sonorous quality that sounded very much like Headmaster Albans.

"And if you are going to be human, you need to experience everything possible—in the way humans experience those things," she said. "I can show you, if you let me be your guide. I want to be special to you."

"You are already my special one, Anna." He looked down at her with a blank expression for a moment, and then the face shifted into a warm smile, as if Erasmus was thinking of how to manipulate a flowmetal robotic body but didn't yet understand the nuances of an expression made of flesh.

He raised his hand so he could stare in wonder at the palm. He flexed and unflexed the fingers. "So many lines and patterns on my fingertips and palm. I don't understand the code, and I wonder at the biological necessity of such randomness and infinite perfection. This also merits further study . . . a study of myself, instead of someone else. Thank you for bringing me here, Anna. You are a very important part of my instruction and growth as a sentient being."

While the Denali engineers kept working on the cymeks, Anna guided him away with her. They entered the sterile laboratory vault that held the enlarged and distorted brains of failed Navigators, the mutated gray matter holding many more cellular ripples than a normal human brain. As a bodiless memory core, Erasmus had expressed interest in the Navigator brains, and Anna had often taken him there so that he could observe with his optical sensors.

Now, though, he was there in person. "What a magnificent sight," he said.

Nearly a hundred enlarged brains hung inside their fluid-filled tanks—whether resting or contemplating, Anna didn't know. Fifteen tanks were missing from their slots, because those Navigator brains were out testing new cymek walkers, practicing combat and manipulation skills for the ultimate assault on the Butlerian homeworld. "I would like to explore these specimens further, conduct interesting experiments. Maybe I could link up to the communications conduits, so I can converse with them."

That was not at all what Anna had in mind. "But not right now—there's something far more important." When she took both his hands, her heart was pounding. She knew what she wanted, but was afraid to ask for it. Her breathing was shallow, and the sterile air burned her nose and throat. She leaned closer, touching the muscles of his body, holding his hands, and then she released one of them and ran her fingers across his chest. It felt so good to touch someone again.

"There are many more parts to being human, Erasmus dear, experiences you've never had. I want to be the first. I want to instruct you."

"I'm sure I will find it most interesting," he said.

She stopped him from talking further by pulling his face close and kissing him. It was her first kiss in a very long time, and the first for Erasmus, ever.

For several moments his lips remained motionless, but she stroked the side of his face and kissed him again. She let her eyelids fall closed, then forced herself to open them again so that she could look into his eyes. Erasmus had a perplexed, even amused expression, a glint that traveled all the way from his memory core.

Around them, the Navigator brains didn't seem to notice at all.

She felt the solidity of his body as she wrapped her arms around him. Anna kissed him again, and slowly he began to respond as if it were a learned experience. Then she broke away. "You will enjoy what I have to offer, I promise." She took his hand and led him out of the laboratory vault.

Understanding her intent, he said, "I am what humans call a virgin. This will be a valuable experiment."

When they had sealed themselves in her chamber, she pulled off his laboratory jumpsuit, even ripping some of the fabric in her eagerness. Although she had watched this body grow from a small lump of flesh into a finished naked body inside the biological tank, it was still a delicious discovery as she pulled away his garments now.

Erasmus had studied human history and witnessed sexual relations over the years. He had kept innumerable human slaves in his laboratory pens. "I'm familiar with the mechanics of the procreation process, and have read much of the mystique about sex, but my knowledge has always been objective, never subjective."

She pulled him down onto her narrow bed and crawled on top of him. Erasmus allowed himself to be pliable in her hands. "Not procreation, Erasmus. *Lovemaking.* And I want to make love to you now."

She had to take his hands and make him start removing her clothes, then she guided him to touch her body, to run his hands over her shoulders, her back, her breasts. At first, he simply followed instructions, but she encouraged him to be imaginative. As a lifelong researcher, Erasmus certainly understood the possibilities of experimentation.

Anna felt as if her world had become bright and soft again. She hadn't taken a lover since Hirondo Nef, who had made her promises, told her lies, seduced her, filled her with silly dreams. Salvador had ruined that relationship, although Anna now realized—thanks to a careful analysis by Erasmus—that Hirondo had only been using her, taking advantage of her. Anna knew that no one had ever really loved her before this, not in the way she wanted and deserved. No one understood her as much as Erasmus did.

He spoke little as she continued to kiss him, and massaged his back. Her every move, her every gesture went into a database, and he catalogued it along with what he knew about human romance and sexuality. Though he was a thinking-machine mind, the body was fully human and it knew how to respond.

⤋

ERASMUS STORED EVERY sensation. This was indeed a new set of unusual experiences—made even more instructive, but also baffling, as he chronicled the joy and ecstasy on Anna's face, her adoring expression after they had finished the biological activity.

The sensual movements had a ritualistic, prolonged manner that did not seem to be a particularly efficient means of reproduction, taking much longer than was absolutely required. Nevertheless, it was a fine example of the experimental possibilities the new body offered him.

Afterward, she lay close beside him, kissing his cheek and stroking his hair. Erasmus didn't entirely understand this epilogue, although he had read about it in countless romantic poems and stories. She didn't seem to want more from him, only this nearness. Because it seemed to be an essential part of the activity for her, he held her and said nothing.

"I love you, Erasmus," she said.

He filed away all the data of his new experiences.

In an objective analysis of the life and accomplishments of Vorian Atreides, it is surprising that he did not demand more for himself.

—HARUK ARI, historian of the Jihad

After leaving Chusuk and beginning to spread rumors that he would go to ground on Corrin, Vorian Atreides had one more important matter to take care of. If the Harkonnens left him alone, he would be surprised yet content, but if they came for him—as he expected—he intended to be ready.

When he arrived at Salusa Secundus, he was surprised to see so many Butlerian warships in orbit as well as huge crowds encamped in Zimia. But his business was with the Emperor, not the antitechnology movement.

He announced himself to spaceport security and asked to see Emperor Roderick, hoping the new ruler was an improvement from petty Salvador, who had caused Vor so many problems. He did not hide his identity, though—for this occasion he needed to be the legendary Hero of the Jihad, not a man trying to erase his past.

He intended to ask a favor, for Willem's sake. In all his years—centuries, in fact—of service, Vorian Atreides had asked for very little. His request would not threaten the Imperium, but it mattered a great deal to him.

The guards searched him at the entrance to the Palace, checked his identity papers, and then looked at one another in startled confusion.

"Yes, I am Vorian Atreides," he repeated his name. "I am confident the Emperor knows who I am. As do you, I assume?"

The guards placed him in a comfortable holding room and told him to wait. It was not a particularly auspicious welcome for a man of his stature, but Vor understood the caution. Because of a recent VenHold attack on Salusa and the chaotic influx of so many Butlerians, Imperial security had been increased to the highest levels.

After six hours, he was escorted from the holding chamber with profuse apologies from Chamberlain Bakim. The man greeted him cordially, apologized again, and led Vor away from the Palace to the Hall of Parliament in the center of the capital city, where the flags of noble houses hung from the golden-domed building and all around the large central square.

The chamberlain took him to Roderick's well-appointed Parliament office, where the Emperor was pacing beside his desk. Roderick Corrino gave him a strong handshake and said, "I regret the delay in seeing you, but the Imperial capital has recently been under siege—in more ways than one." The Emperor sighed, ran his hands through his own hair. "With all the turmoil in the Imperium, I thought you were long gone, making a quiet life for yourself."

"I stayed away, Sire—as your brother commanded. Emperor Salvador made that a condition before he would agree to protect Kepler against raids by slavers. I did as he asked, and tried to let history swallow me, but as it turned out, my own history would not leave me alone."

The restrictions had created much heartache for him, making him leave Mariella and all of his extended family on Kepler, but Salvador's insecurity was not to be disputed at the time. Vor drew a breath, met the Emperor's gaze directly. "I promise I will depart swiftly and cause you no further trouble, Sire. I came here to beg a favor. I hope you will grant it."

Roderick sat down, looking cautious, and dismissed the chamberlain, who hurried off to other duties. "That's better than you challenging me for the throne. I've had enough of that in the past week." The attempt at witticism fell flat, and he grew serious. "I have always admired your war record and sense of duty, Vorian Atreides. You are a genuine hero, and we have few enough of those. But these are not the best of times to ask for favors."

"It is small enough, Sire. A family matter—in fact, you can ensure the future of my family."

An aide came to the door, signaling the Emperor. "The pilot of your flyer reports that all is ready for the inspection flight, Sire."

Roderick turned. "Join me, and we can continue our conversation on board. It will be good to get away from Zimia and the mobs down there." Vor followed the Emperor out into the corridor, while he continued to explain, "We recently had a flood disaster, and the Empress Haditha is managing relief efforts, but in my position I am expected to fly over and inspect. It will rally greater support."

Vor was concerned. "Do you need my assistance, Sire?"

The Emperor considered for a long moment. "Your advice might be helpful, but the legendary Hero of the Jihad could distract our work crews. Let's have a look together, and we can talk further."

An escort contingent led them to the roof level of the Hall of Parliament, where a large Imperial flyer awaited them, with the Emperor's dark-robed Truthsayer, Reverend Mother Fielle, standing at the ramp. As the two men boarded the craft, Vor looked sidelong at her and suppressed his smile. This was an opportunity he could not pass up, and he would be sure she had important information to send back to the Sisterhood school. . . .

As the engines hummed and the aircraft prepared for takeoff, the men entered the Emperor's main stateroom as Fielle trailed them. The Imperial flyer had a customized interior with posh fabrics on the walls, and inset crystal glowglobes. In the central salon, uniformed attendants were laying out a meal on a table with two place settings. While Fielle remained unobtrusive on one side of the cabin, in her Truthsayer mode, the Emperor motioned for Vor to take the seat opposite him.

Roderick explained more about the flood. "A week ago we had a freak summer storm. Several major settlements in a river delta were flooded, thousands died, and many more were displaced. Haditha is already out there with the first wave of recovery crews. It's something she is quite capable of managing, while I am supposed to concern myself with more important Imperial matters. Even so, I want to tour some of the worst areas."

Vor nodded. "For those affected, a local disaster can be as significant as a galactic one."

"I face enough galactic disasters, too, but I am certainly glad my wife is in charge down there. I wish the Butlerians would make themselves useful in the relief efforts, but Leader Torondo does not seem inclined to let his people help." His face darkened. "Ever."

The aircraft lifted off so smoothly that Vor barely felt the motion. Staff brought plates of sliced meats and bread, and the Emperor relaxed as he ate. The flyer cruised away from the capital city like a huge bird, and soared out over the lush Salusan landscape.

Roderick set his fork down. "Tell me the answer to something that has long raised questions in my mind. House Atreides could have been one of the greatest and wealthiest noble families in the Landsraad, if you had asked for that. Faykan was ready to give you anything after the Battle of Corrin. No one would say that you are a man lacking in ambition. Why would you just . . . discard it all, throwing away the potential of your Great House?"

Vor took a drink of fresh juice from a wide-bottomed glass. "I never wanted that kind of wealth or power, Sire." He glanced over at Fielle, and the Truthsayer simply nodded to Roderick, acknowledging that he truly meant what he said. The Emperor did not seem to doubt it, regardless. "I had enough of grand gestures and countless lives depending on my every decision. I just wanted to be a normal man again, at least for a while."

Vor pictured the opulence of the mansions on old Earth, when he had lived among the thinking machines. He thought of his father, General Agamemnon, the cymek who had laid waste to countless planets . . . and pondered how many fortunes he himself had made and lost in his extended life.

"At times, that sounds wonderful to me. I never wanted the throne either." Roderick nodded with respect. "The Imperium shall forever be grateful to you, Vorian Atreides. Yes, if your favor is within my power, I will grant it. I lift all the restrictions my brother imposed upon you. Travel wherever you wish, live where you'd like—is that what you want?"

"Thank you, Sire. But my request is even more straightforward than that."

Already several hundred kilometers away from Zimia, the Imperial flyer cruised over a sweeping valley. When they reached the flooded river zone and flew low, both men peered out upon the devastation. By now the surging river had receded, leaving destroyed houses, land vehicles, and boats in its wake. Dead farm animals lay strewn on the ground. From above, they could see antlike teams of rescue workers digging in the sediment, setting up temporary settlements and relief camps.

The Emperor pondered the view gravely as the craft cruised over the swath of devastation. He finally looked up at his guest. "What is it you need me to do for you?"

"Sire, I want my descendants to have the opportunities that should be their birthright. I think I have earned the right to request this. They are Atreides, with a proud and distinguished heritage. They should be treated as such, even if I would prefer to disappear myself."

Roderick flashed a wan smile. "I want the same for my son Javicco. I hope the Corrino line keeps the throne for more than a few generations, but that will depend on how well I steer through these perilous times. So many forces are trying to tear the Imperium apart right now." He pushed aside the rest of his meal and stared out the window as the flyer circled into the foothills, where another village had been damaged by mudslides. "What family do you have? I believe there are some on Kepler—?"

"And they are perfectly content. I have no wish to draw them into Imperial politics. But one descendant from my Caladan line—a young man named Willem—has become especially important to me. Right now he is on Chusuk recovering from injuries, but I would like to arrange a place for him on Salusa Secundus. Give him a chance, Sire. He's intelligent and pleasant, but he has suffered recent tragedies, partly because of me, and I'd like to make it up to him.

I can deposit all the funds he needs to support himself, if you can find an op-portunity for him at court? A respectable spot among the new arrivals?"

Roderick seemed relieved that the request was not far more significant. He gave a quick wave. "I can't remember the last time I had a problem so easily solved. Of course I grant your most reasonable request. The Imperium owes you much more than that, and my court could certainly use the qualities of an Atreides."

Vor thanked him. The inspection flyer completed its circuit as they looked down at the flooded areas, the recovery crews, the temporary shelters, the large refugee towns. Roderick smiled wistfully, as if thinking of Haditha down there in the thick of the efforts.

When the craft finally headed back to Zimia, Roderick said, "I will dispatch more resources, so Haditha has everything she needs. In fact, if the Butlerians won't help, maybe I should command some of the nobles to join the effort."

Vor smiled. "With the Butlerians I suspect you may be inviting more trouble than it's worth."

"Many things are more trouble than they're worth." Roderick looked intently at him. "The Butlerians . . . Josef Venport—how would you deal with two extremes pulling my Imperium apart? If you were Emperor?"

Vor sat back, smiled thinly. "That is precisely why I never wanted to be Emperor, Sire."

The Emperor's shoulders fell slightly. "Manford Torondo and his followers are dangerous and destructive, yet they did save me from Venport's siege. But now they won't leave. Under other circumstances, I would ally myself with Ven-port Holdings, but that man murdered my brother and tried to overthrow my throne." He shook his head. "Haditha wants me to negotiate with him, but how can I try to reach a resolution with someone like that? A murderer on one hand and a madman on the other."

Vor frowned. "Negotiations are often conducted between rivals. Which solution holds the best future for the Imperium?"

"The solution that eliminates both extremes."

As the aircraft returned to the rooftop landing zone, the Emperor reiterated his promise to make a place for Willem. "Will you be here to introduce young Willem when he arrives? It would increase his standing if a Hero of the Jihad vouched for him in front of the other nobles and courtiers."

Vor did not look at the unobtrusive Truthsayer, but was aware that the woman was listening intently. "I'm afraid not, Sire. I doubt if I will ever see Willem again, in fact. I am about to undertake a dangerous mission, one that I must handle alone." But Vor's plan to lure the murderess, and perhaps her sister as well, all depended on whether Truthsayer Fielle reported to Mother Superior Valya . . . and he felt certain she would.

"I need to go where the Harkonnens won't find me. I'm sure you will understand, Sire, that I cannot discuss details even with you. I must vanish."

"You've earned the privilege," Emperor Roderick said. "I wish you all the best."

Eventually, Vor would reveal his destination, but not in the manner anyone would expect, and not until the proper time. Secretly, he had hired two operatives to plant a rumor after his departure that he was on Corrin, when he was assured of already being there. Knowing that Fielle had Sisters in the palace and in the government buildings, he had set it up so that the rumor would begin in the Imperial Court, and from that talkative throng it would spread outward, so that Fielle would be sure to hear it.

And as soon as the Emperor's Truthsayer learned of the rumor, Valya Harkonnen would be informed soon afterward.

Vor would be ready. . . .

It is not wise to beg some people for mercy. It only makes them less likely to grant it.
—"The Personality of a Madman," critical article against
Manford Torondo, redacted

In his pavilion among the encamped Butlerians in the central plaza, Manford Torondo used his muscular arms to pull himself off his sleeping pallet. The night was still dark around him. If he pressed the issue, he was sure he could have forced the Emperor to grant him opulent visitor's quarters in the Palace, but Manford was among his people out here. He could sense their energy all around him, their wild enthusiasm, their absolute devotion to him.

And soon he would call them to action.

Even with so many thousands of his followers crowded together, Manford felt alone now that Anari Idaho was gone. Following Manford's command, she had traveled with Lord Udorum Pondi in a Butlerian spacefolder, to inspect and quietly retrieve the secret atomics from his planet. When she came back with the unexpected treasure, Manford knew exactly what he was going to do with it.

In the meantime, though, he felt incomplete without her.

Although he could have summoned hundreds of eager helpers, Manford was capable of getting around on his own. He slid onto a custom mobile chair that his aides had placed here for him. Rolling the chair forward, he parted the pavilion curtains and looked out into the starry Salusan night. The capital city blazed and bustled even in the hours before dawn, but most of his followers were quietly asleep in the camp.

Around him Manford could see the Imperial gardens, coiffed trees and colorful flowers, statues of Jihad heroes lining the wide main path. Manford respected those champions who fought against the thinking machines. If only he could have been alive in those glorious days, when the enemies of humanity had been obvious to all. . . .

At the head of the plaza, far more prominent even than the statue of Emperor Faykan Corrino, towered the Three Martyrs—the most important icons of humanity's freedom: the religious leader Iblis Ginjo, Serena Butler, and her martyred child, the baby whose murder had sparked the entire war.

Looking at those legendary figures, Manford recalled the many planets his Butlerian followers had stormed. So many populations were yet to be saved from their own temptations, and Manford would press and press until they capitulated. For their own good.

As soon as Josef Venport was disposed of—oh, Manford could not wait to use his unexpected stockpile of atomics!—the rest of the Imperium would fall neatly in line. Then his sacred work would finally be done.

Along with Anari, Manford's most trusted military advisers were developing plans to smash Kolhar. He was certain that Emperor Roderick would be delighted to hear of this, and would give his blessing, no doubt secretly hoping the Butlerians would be decimated as well. Roderick Corrino's true feelings were not well concealed.

Manford had decided that the Emperor didn't need to know about the forbidden atomics. Roderick's approval was not necessary.

But Manford also had to convince the Emperor to ease the resentment he and his family felt toward the Butlerians. At least his Truthsayer had verified that Manford was innocent in the matter of Anna Corrino, but Roderick would still not forgive him for the accidental death of his young daughter.

But that would change very soon. Manford had concocted a way to honor little Nantha, something that the Imperial family would appreciate.

The Butlerian leader remained awake and alert for hours, enjoying the quiet peace of his own convictions while his hordes of followers slept. Inside the pavilion, without Anari to scold him, he surreptitiously reread parts of the Erasmus journals that he kept hidden. After he finished, he locked away the volumes again, then watched the dawn light suffuse the sky. . . .

Deacon Harian entered his pavilion with a breakfast tray and Manford's favorite pungent tea. The bald man was surprised to see Manford up. "Are you troubled? Did you get enough sleep?"

"Enough. I am just anxious for our unveiling today. The Emperor will be so pleased."

Harian frowned. "Will he?"

"He'd better."

As the camp stirred and people emerged, Manford sent out a crier to call for the Emperor's attention. Imperial guards emerged from the Palace, looked curiously at the activity, and retreated inside, no doubt to report to Roderick.

Manford relaxed and finished his tea. Harian had already rallied the dozen burly followers he would take with him.

Out in the sculpture gardens, a team of Butlerian workers struggled on the main path, carrying two heavy loads that were covered in scarlet and gold cloths. Manford smiled to himself. Roderick Corrino and his wife would be thrilled when they saw the extraordinary gift he had commissioned from his artisans, as a gesture of peace.

Curious gardeners, site functionaries, and half a dozen Imperial guards hurried to stop Manford's followers, but the workers moved forward anyway to deposit their enormous burdens, paying the guards no heed. The encamped Butlerian followers drew together.

Manford called for attendants to carry his chair up to a raised platform, from which he had a good vantage of the sculpture garden. He looked up at the Palace balcony, waiting for Roderick to emerge.

In a gruff voice, Deacon Harian commanded the work teams, guiding them as they erected one of the heavy objects beside the Three Martyrs. They removed the covering cloth to reveal a sturdy block of carved stone. A pedestal. Using serviceable pulleys and a great deal of sweat and straining, the workers wrestled the stand into position. Manford's stoneworkers had cut the pieces to fit tightly against the existing monument, because this new statue definitely belonged beside the Three Martyrs.

By the time the stone pedestal was in place, Emperor Roderick emerged on the high balcony, joined by Haditha, who had returned from the flood zone. Normally, his appearance would have been greeted with cheers, but today the people in the plaza were intent on the activity below.

Manford signaled, and Harian directed his helpers to position the second, much larger object, using an intricate network of ropes and pulleys and twenty muscular workers. Somehow, the concealing fabric remained in place; Manford did not want the Emperor and Empress to see the glorious object . . . not yet.

When the pieces were in place, Harian turned back, waiting for the final signal. Manford glanced at the Palace balcony. Emperor Roderick was not smiling, but that would soon change.

One of the Butlerians raised a long trumpet to his lips, and four others joined him in a stirring fanfare from the glorious Jihad. When the music faded, Manford spoke into a concealed voice amplifier, so that his words boomed out. "When tragedy occurs, those responsible must acknowledge it and atone. Let us always remember those who gave their lives for a more perfect world." He raised his hands. "Emperor Roderick Corrino and Empress Haditha, please accept this gift from me and my followers. With your help, we will keep humanity safe for the future and preserve our sacred, collective soul. 'The mind of man is holy.'"

In a roaring response, his thousands of followers intoned, "'The mind of man is holy.'"

Manford was brimming with so much emotion that he had to blink back the tears. He felt hope, pride, and deep satisfaction.

At his signal, the workers pulled away the concealing fabric to reveal an impressive new statue of a young girl in a royal dress and the tiara of a princess of the realm. Her face was achingly sweet and innocent. "There have been many martyrs in our struggle, but this one we must never forget. Together, we acknowledge and revere your beautiful fallen daughter Nantha Corrino!"

The crowd burst out in resounding applause, and Manford felt proud of what he had done.

On the high balcony of the Palace, Roderick stood like a statue himself, while Haditha grabbed his arm for balance as she reeled. Manford knew she must be overcome with love and appreciation.

This was his best way to show remorse for what had happened to the helpless girl, who had been caught in a Butlerian rampage festival. This grand gesture would make everything right.

From the balcony the Emperor stared, rendered speechless—presumably with gratitude. He held his wife as the other children joined them on the balcony to see what the fuss was about.

Throngs of people were streaming toward the gardens from all sides to view the new statue in its place beside Iblis, Serena, and baby Manion. Manford shouted into the voice amplifier, "Let there be *Four* Martyrs now! We will erect similar statues to little Nantha across the Imperium, so that everyone can know of the innocent blood that was spilled to save the soul of humanity. Nantha Corrino will live forever in the hearts of all good people."

The Emperor and Empress pulled their children back inside from the balcony, and Manford watched them, puzzled by their strange and unexpected reaction. But it didn't really matter, because his followers had already picked up the celebration. They would mark this day with the importance it deserved.

⇌

AFTER THEY STAGGERED back inside, holding each other, Roderick and Haditha slumped onto an antique Gustavian bench. They could still hear the maddening cheers outside. Roderick tried to be strong as he held his wife, but he trembled as much as she did.

Prince Javicco was distressed and confused. "Why would he make a statue of Nantha? Didn't that man kill her?"

"Yes, Javicco," Roderick said. "He killed your sister . . . and now he thinks this will make us forget."

Haditha wept quietly, pressing her face against the side of his neck. The other children gathered around the bench. Of his own initiative, young Javicco closed the balcony door, but they could still hear the mobs celebrating . . . mobs just like the one that had killed Nantha.

Their daughter represented only one drop of all the innocent blood the fanatics had spilled, and Manford Torondo had made a terrible mistake by reopening that wound.

Worse, the damned Butlerian leader had placed the Emperor in an untenable position. Roderick could hardly demand that the statue of his daughter be removed. Yet each time he looked out from his balcony, he would see the larger-than-life stone figure of his little girl, a constant and painful reminder of their loss. Did Manford think that would make the pain go away?

As Haditha continued her quiet sobbing, Roderick struggled with how to respond to this debacle. He couldn't refuse to acknowledge the statue, but he couldn't embrace the vile Butlerian leader over it, either. In every direction, more and more damage was being done.

Finally, he rose to his feet and took his wife's hand, both of them heartbroken as he kissed her gently. The taste of salt tears was on her lips. "I will destroy him," Roderick said. "This I swear to you."

She nodded. They both knew that Roderick couldn't just evict Manford and his followers from Zimia or the potentially violent mobs would turn on him, even in the capital city. When the Butlerians had saved the planet from the VenHold siege, Roderick had unwittingly fallen into a partnership with the fanatics.

But the Emperor had to be stronger than all the others.

"Your brother allowed the Butlerians to dictate his decisions," Haditha said, "and he let Josef Venport expand his power base far beyond that of anyone else in the Imperium. But you're a more skilled Emperor than Salvador ever was." She squeezed his hand. "You should have been born first."

Even though he knew this was true, he would not admit it. "My darling, the universe does not function on wishes. I need to rule with what I have." He went over to the closed balcony doors while Haditha gathered Javicco and the girls. "I will find a way to have the statue moved, so that we aren't forced to see it every day. I don't want to remember Nantha that way."

"Announce that you will move it to a more public place," Haditha suggested. "We can form a school in our daughter's honor, and the statue can be a monument in front."

Roderick smiled at the possibility. "I knew you would find a way, my love."

His thoughts wandered into regrets. If he had forced the issue earlier and convinced Salvador to abdicate, maybe he could have kept the Butlerians from mayhem. Then the riots would not have happened, and Nantha would not have been killed. Nor would the millions of other innocents who fell victim to Butlerian purges on so many planets. But that was all hindsight.

The universe does not function on wishes.

With the exception of independent robots such as myself, thinking machines do as they are programmed to do, which makes them efficient and predictable. Human beings often require additional incentive. I am investigating the concept of gratitude.

—ERASMUS, New Laboratory Journals

Ready to finish preparations for the Lampadas attack, Draigo returned to Denali with many responsibilities—projections to follow, prototypes to study and evaluate. He would ensure that all was ready when Directeur Venport gave the word.

For convenience he had moved into Noffe's old office, which the Tlulaxa administrator no longer needed since becoming a cymek. Although most of the projections were already in his mind, he reviewed Ptolemy's plans and concurred with the details. The well-armed ships of the VenHold Spacing Fleet and the big army of new cymeks should easily be sufficient to overrun the enemy. The barbarian fleet was old but nevertheless impressive, and after the siege of Salusa, they would no doubt feel cocky and overconfident.

Josef Venport was also overconfident, however, and Draigo needed to make certain the numbers added up.

Walking with unsteady steps, like a newborn animal trying to acquire a sense of balance, Erasmus arrived at the door hatch of Noffe's former office, leaning heavily all the way on Anna Corrino's arm. She held him up more than seemed absolutely necessary. He was still learning the precise functionality of his new body. "I must speak with you, Mentat. I have something to offer."

Anna nodded, as if extremely proud of him.

Since the cells from Erasmus's clone body had originated from Headmaster Albans, the features naturally looked familiar to Draigo, and he could not suppress an uncomfortable shiver. But this body, animated by the robot's mind, had an entirely different affect. The man might look very similar to Headmaster Albans, but they were not at all the same person.

"I am listening," Draigo said.

"With my human body I am finally able to consider new experiments and perform research I was previously unable to do. I revel in the marvelous possibilities," Erasmus said. "As I continue my assessments, however, I realize that I owe a number of debts. I owe Venport Holdings for my rescue and sanctuary, I owe the Denali scientists for the work they continue to do, and I owe Directeur Venport personally. I am also obligated to you, Mentat Draigo Roget."

"I see you have acquired a sense of personal responsibility," Draigo said.

"I'm teaching him to be grateful," Anna said. "I am certainly happy to have him with us."

Erasmus continued in a voice that sounded much like that of Headmaster Albans. "The sensations and experiences in this biological body are remarkable and largely unexpected. For that I am . . . exceedingly thankful. You, Draigo Roget, are personally responsible for saving my memory core—just as Gilbertus earlier saved me from the ruins of Corrin. You protected and preserved my gelsphere—and therefore all my knowledge and experiences—after the Butlerians overran the school on Lampadas."

"Don't forget that I helped save you too," Anna interjected.

Erasmus worked his facial muscles, eventually forming a frown. "And I have already expressed my gratitude to you. I am accomplishing a different objective now."

She looked away, scolded.

"And what objective is that?" Draigo asked, thinking about how very peculiar this situation was. "To thank me?"

"To provide something of tangible value. Many Denali scientists believe my knowledge will lead to a breakthrough, but unfortunately thinking machines were not adept at innovation, and as a result we lost the Jihad. Hence, I doubt if I can help in any creative fashion. Any technologies I might offer would pale in comparison with what you already possess."

"Then what is it you have in mind?" Draigo folded his arms across his chest.

Erasmus looked at him with the eerie eyes of Headmaster Albans. "Although I have inspired no theoretical breakthroughs, I can offer brute force right now."

"In war, brute force can indeed be useful." He nodded for Erasmus to continue.

"In the final days of the human war against the Synchronized Empire, the evermind Omnius dispatched many robotic war fleets, which spread out to numerous systems. Most of those machine battleships fell into silent inactivity when the Omnius copies were shut down."

"Venport Holdings already located many of those abandoned robot ships," Draigo said. "We refurbished the vessels and consolidated them into our commercial spacing fleet."

Erasmus said something that surprised him. "I know of an undiscovered battle group: forty robotic warships that were shut down en route to a battle that was already lost. Would you like to add them to VenHold's resources?" His lips formed a smile that he had apparently practiced. "Perhaps they would be helpful in your fight against Lampadas."

Draigo felt a thrill as possibilities cascaded through his mind. "I am sure the Directeur will be quite interested, provided you can find them."

Erasmus continued. "You are aware that Denali was once a cymek base. Long ago, this robot fleet departed from here and was shut down shortly thereafter; it has been dormant ever since. I have the exact location. With minimal effort you could retrieve the ships, recondition them, install new weapons, and even add foldspace engines if you desire. The vessels are yours."

Anna slid her arms around the robot's waist and hugged him.

Draigo was already projecting many effective ways to deploy a whole new battle group. "That would be a most acceptable gesture of gratitude."

IT FELT GOOD to be experimenting again. That was the primary reason for the independent robot's existence. Spending the past eight decades as nothing more than a disembodied gelsphere, Erasmus had been unable to perform the exciting work he wanted to do, and he'd had to content himself with mere thought experiments, as well as subtle psychological manipulations and schemes—which, while valuable, were not nearly as satisfying as genuine, tangible action. He'd also focused on surviving, and had accomplished that.

Now, in his flesh-and-blood form, Erasmus could walk wherever he wanted, touch anything he wanted, even eat food, and he could at last return to his research. He stood in the laboratory chamber that held the disembodied brains of failed Navigators. The brains fascinated him, enlarged and evolved, supposedly examples of *superior* humans, although even "superior" humans were a far cry from the capabilities of thinking machines.

He looked at the rows of tanks, all of them being prepared for installation in powerful cymek walker forms. They seemed to contemplate the meaning of their existence.

"You've been staring for an hour," Anna said. "We should go somewhere, do something."

"I am doing something," he said. In bygone days, as a prestigious robot on

Corrin, he had dissected, stimulated, and tortured his share of human brains. "I am considering experiments to perform."

Anna stepped closer. "Can I help?"

He pondered, choosing the right answer. "Of course." That was all she needed to hear.

Anna Corrino herself was one of his greatest experiments, proving how much he could achieve in manipulating, shaping, and developing her damaged personality. But he was mostly finished with her. Now he wanted to poke and prod the Navigator brains.

Although Anna had seemed bored and impatient only a moment ago, once he brought her into his work, she felt more valuable. With her assistance he prepared several initial tests. He gave her instructions, and she scurried off to obtain equipment for him.

He selected three living brains to experiment on, and when Anna brought him long, thin needle probes with electrified ends, he went through an extended process of trial and error to locate and stimulate the primary pain receptors in the Navigator brains. With thoughtrodes connected to each specimen, he took readings, adjusted his work, and promptly discovered how to torment the subjects.

He had done this many times before on human brains, but these mutated and supposedly evolved specimens were behaving the same way, with the same primitive responses at the base level of the brain. Even though the specimens did not have a physical form to thrash and scream, which would clearly demonstrate the agony they experienced, the thoughtrode readings did not lie.

"Are we getting the right results, Erasmus?" Anna asked.

"Disappointing ones," he said, and Anna's face fell, as if he had criticized her. "It's not you," he added quickly. "It is a failing of the brains themselves."

He reached out to grasp another tank, pressing his hands against the curved plaz wall and lifting it up. The next subject.

"What are you doing?" asked a sharp voice.

Erasmus turned to see Dr. Danebh scowling at him. His own human reactions nearly made him drop the brain container. But he managed to control himself. If the brain tank were to shatter on the laboratory floor, it would be a waste of an experimental subject.

"I am performing scientific research," he replied. "Is that not what this facility is designed for?"

The Tlulaxa doctor gave him a look of consternation. "Those brains are to guide cymek walkers in our attack against the Butlerians. Denali isn't a facility devoted to pure research, but to develop weapons against Manford Torondo. That is our priority. Don't damage our resources."

Erasmus accepted the justification. "Very well." He put the canister back in its slot and told Anna to return the other three to their places. "I believe I have learned everything necessary here."

He shook his head, imitating a gesture he had learned from observing humans. "Considering the primitive responses the subjects have demonstrated, I can understand why these are *failed* Navigators."

The one who makes a suggestion is often at a disadvantage compared with the one who listens and considers it, especially if there are conflicting personal goals.

—RODERICK CORRINO, advice to his brother Salvador

Valya continued to monitor the progress of her Sisters, especially the stubborn Orthodox ones. Apart from a handful of discards who had needed to be killed, most were successfully retrained, both physically and mentally. The Sisterhood was once again strong and stable, under her able leadership.

Ninke, though, remained a question mark. And a big one.

Sister Deborah stood beside Valya on the practice field, watching hundreds of trainees going through their solo routines, including the spunky and determined Gabi. They kicked at the air and struck imaginary targets with stone-hard fingertips, moving fast. Together, they perfected the combination of skills from Valya's Swordmaster education, the techniques she and her brother Griffin had created for themselves, and the Sorceress Way. Though closely packed together, the frenetic trainees did not touch one another, but landed gracefully in their proper combat positions, as if choreographed.

"They are making some progress," Deborah reported.

"Not enough for the standards I have set." Valya had found that it was never wise to offer too much praise, which might encourage some trainees to be satisfied with less than their absolute best. She raised her hands to pause the session, calling out, "I've seen good improvement, but *good* is less than *excellent*. A Sister must attain the pinnacle of human abilities, physical and mental. That is why Mother Superior Raquella founded our order.

"I have selected the best among you to undergo more intensive mental training, to add balance to your fighting abilities. You will need those mental skills to advance the Sisterhood into the future, as you will be taught important psychological tools, emotional shaping, and even Truthsaying for those of you who have the ability."

After she motioned for them to continue practicing, Valya focused on Ninke, while the former Orthodox Sister went through high-order defenses in which she countered complex attacks in sparring sessions with Gabi. Despite Ninke's stocky, muscular build, her movements were lithe. Her broken arm had recovered sufficiently that she trained with the others, showing only a slight favoring of the other arm.

Valya raised her eyebrows and turned to Deborah. "What is your assessment of Ninke?"

A small twitch of a frown turned Deborah's lips. "Since being released from the medical center, she is one of the standouts in both the physical and mental arenas. The injury may have made her reconsider her rebellious attitude."

"But is she loyal?"

Deborah could only shrug. "She professes to adhere to our philosophy, yet even with my careful observation, I can't ascertain her loyalty to *you*, Mother Superior. Without question, Ninke is loyal to the Sisterhood—but her degree of devotion to your new methods is not so clear. I doubt if she will ever be as faithful to you as she once was to Reverend Mother Dorotea."

Valya's brow furrowed in displeasure. "Just as there are degrees of love, so too are there degrees of devotion and loyalty. How much loyalty do you think is necessary for our purposes?" She watched Ninke continue to fight, wondering whether the woman was worth keeping, or if it was safer just to cut their potential losses and get rid of her after all.

As if sensing she was being singled out, Ninke stopped her routines and let Gabi catch her breath. She turned to face the two observers, her expression openly hostile. Valya stared back at her coolly, and spoke sidelong to the Sorceress. "Her blatant display of emotion shows a lack of mental toughness."

Ninke wrapped herself in utter calmness and casually glided toward the observers through the frenetic, fast-moving trainees without brushing against them. She faced Valya. "Mother Superior, I survived the hazing you imposed on my faction, and I completed all the demeaning tasks you made me perform. Because of your grudge against us, my fellow Orthodox Sisters have been beaten and injured—some even killed. But I am still here."

Valya instinctively tensed. "Those others were more valuable to the Sisterhood as examples of what happens to people who disobey me. I believe my methods have been effective."

"And me?" Ninke sniffed. "Of what value am I to you?"

With a stiff smile, Valya said, "When your faction betrayed us and nearly destroyed the Sisterhood, you committed treasonous acts. But I see potential in you, Ninke, so I have given you a second chance. Will you take it, or spurn your opportunity?"

Ninke lifted her chin. "I have proved myself enough. Sometimes an injustice must be addressed with more than words or acquiescence." She dropped into a fighting stance, her muscles loose and poised, her eyes hyperalert. "And this is one of those times. Accept me now as I am, or kill me."

The rest of the Sisters halted their practice, some of them aghast. Deborah stepped out of the way as Valya and Ninke began to circle each other. Ninke glanced to her left, which Valya interpreted as a deception, so she prepared for a strike in the opposite direction, but the other Sister whirled around exactly where she had looked, a double feint, and sprang straight at Valya and struck out at her. Valya used her own reflexes and combined fighting techniques. She felt a ripple of air as Ninke missed her. Barely. Ninke did not favor her injured arm at all, so the hesitation she'd shown in using it earlier must have been faked.

But when Valya spun to launch her own attack, the other woman was unexpectedly there facing her. Ninke struck the Mother Superior in the center of her chest with a hard kick. Valya bent her knees and let herself fall backward to soften the impact, then sprang back out of the combat area to better prepare for her opponent's next move.

In one blur of motion after another, the other Sister showed that she understood something of the advanced fighting methods, but Valya spotted patterns in Ninke's interpretation of the Sorceress Way. Patterns that reflected her inexperience.

Valya went on the attack, following the other woman's precise moves like a shadow. She surprised Ninke and drove her back with a series of kicks, fist thrusts, and hard elbows, ending with a stunning blow to the side of the head. Then Valya took her down with a strike to the knees, pinned her to the ground, and pressed two fingers against a nerve in her neck, rendering her helpless.

In the adrenaline rush, Valya could have killed Ninke on the spot, but decided to spare her life. She released her hold on the pressure point and backed away, then astonished Ninke by helping her to her feet.

Trembling with anger, ready to continue fighting, Ninke faced Valya. "I am loyal to the Sisterhood, Mother Superior," she said in a defiant voice. "And I will fight our enemies. Are you an enemy of the Sisterhood? Or should I focus on a different one?"

Valya smiled. "Your comment is as unexpected as some of your fighting moves." She nodded quickly. "I am the Mother Superior. I am not now, nor have I ever been, nor will I ever be, an enemy of the Sisterhood. We already have enough enemies." She raised her voice, so the others could hear. "Ninke, your punishment is over, the past is forgotten. Now it is time for us to unify into a strong force—a vital, yet nearly invisible, part of the Imperium."

Ninke moved back among the other women on the practice field, where she resumed her energetic routines with Gabi. "Yes," Valya muttered to Deborah as they continued to observe. "We certainly have enough outside enemies to keep us busy."

⁓

WHEN CIOBA STEPPED off the VenHold shuttle on Wallach IX, returning to the Sisterhood school after such a long time, she was glad to see her black-robed colleagues awaiting her. Though her original training had taken place on Rossak, this still felt like a homecoming.

Cioba had chosen to wear the white robe of a Sorceress, calling attention to her rare genetics. She was proud of her heritage, and now she hoped to make these women the allies of Venport Holdings, even though they were already working more closely with the Imperial Court . . . though not always to VenHold's benefit, from what her sources had reported to her.

As she crossed the landing field toward the main school buildings, Cioba noted that the gathered Sisters stood poised, as if they were a security detail in addition to a reception committee. Among them, the moon-faced Sister Olivia stared at her guardedly. "You have come alone?"

Trying to understand the unexpectedly stiff attitude, Cioba said, "I came alone, but I am pleased to find myself among friends now."

A small smile broke through Olivia's wary expression. "The Emperor has clamped down on your husband's company, and we know VenHold recently attempted to lay siege to Salusa Secundus, an attempt that ended in a debacle. It is dangerous for us to have you here, or to have any dealings with Josef Venport."

"The Emperor took severe and unjustified actions to harm us, but Venport Holdings is strong and will survive. We need the advice and assistance of the Sisterhood, however. That is why I have come." Cioba glanced around. "I must see Mother Superior Valya about an important matter. Please, Olivia?"

With a softening expression, Olivia gestured toward several large new buildings under construction. "The Mother Superior monitors the work daily. Come with me."

Olivia led Cioba up a stone-paved path to the main buildings. While Josef had given them the initial classroom structures that helped the Sisterhood make their start here, the Mother School seemed to be thriving now on this remote world, going into a major expansion phase. Would Valya remember to show gratitude for what Venport Holdings had done for them?

The landing field had a new terminal structure, larger than the previous temporary one. A male construction crew moved a prefab building on a rolling framework to a new foundation, while workers installed windows and doors in two large new dormitories that had stone walls and red tile roofs.

"This school is different from our cliff city on Rossak, but it is going to be beautiful," Cioba said. "Raquella would have been pleased."

Olivia led her to the young Mother Superior who stood in front of the stone building, talking to a man in a tan work suit who made notes as she spoke. Although Valya noted Cioba's arrival, she remained engrossed in her discussion until she dismissed the contractor.

Cioba was married to Josef and was a vital part of Venport Holdings, but she had been raised and trained in the Sisterhood, so her allegiance to the Mother Superior was deeply ingrained. Raquella's successor was not an easy woman to know, with complex, sometimes contradictory ambitions and a wall around her.

When Valya turned her attention to Cioba, she spoke bluntly, "I am surprised you came here, Cioba Venport. The Emperor would pay a fine ransom if we delivered you to him—a small sacrifice on my part to obtain a great deal of influence."

Cioba had hoped for a cordial conversation, and negotiations. She even wanted to visit her daughters Candys and Sabine, who were being taught here. But in light of Valya's aggressive comment, she shifted her entire approach. "With respect to you, Mother Superior, I would advise against that. I am a Sorceress and a Reverend Mother. If you were to treat me so disrespectfully, it could create a new rift in the Sisterhood—just when you are trying to heal an old wound."

Valya turned away to look at the construction activities. "Even so, your coming here entails great risk for us."

"Perhaps, Mother Superior, but I am certain you have ways to prevent the escape of the information. I am here to ask you to take another risk, on my husband's behalf. Just as he took a big chance himself when he helped the Sisterhood after we were disbanded by Emperor Salvador."

Valya arched her dark eyebrows, looked deeply apprehensive. "What would you ask of us?"

"The Sisterhood could serve as an intermediary to resolve the dispute between Josef and Emperor Roderick. Negotiating peace would bring stability to the Imperium and place both the Emperor and VenHold in your debt."

Valya narrowed her gaze. "The Emperor has confiscated all VenHold financial assets and seized their banks across the Imperium. Your husband recently laid siege to Salusa Secundus and retreated in defeat after the Butlerians drove him away. What possible advantage would the Sisterhood gain if we were to strengthen ties with Venport Holdings?"

Cioba forced calm upon herself. "That is an inaccurate assessment of events, Mother Superior, but keep in mind that VenHold still controls significant economic assets in other areas. Josef went to Salusa not to conquer, but to force an end to the dispute."

"And the reason he retreated so suddenly? I don't feel as if we have received all of the information on that."

"I am not a military tactician," Cioba said, with the most enigmatic smile she could muster.

Valya gave her a wry smile in return. "All right. But as for the 'dispute,' I believe it began when your husband assassinated Roderick's brother—murdered an *Emperor*."

Cioba struggled to find a way to break through the Mother Superior's stony resistance. "Salvador Corrino was a volatile and dangerous man. Do not forget that he slaughtered many Sisters on Rossak. Whatever my husband's actions, you have to agree that the Imperium benefits from a more stable Emperor."

The young Mother Superior gazed at her dispassionately, not seeming to care about her problems. "Agreed, and that is why the Sisterhood has strengthened ties with Roderick Corrino, the Imperial Court, and many Landsraad nobles. I do not wish to jeopardize that."

Cioba continued doggedly, "Because of Roderick's grievance against Josef, the Butlerian fanatics have been gaining influence and power at the expense of reason. I know you have no great love for the Butlerians, Mother Superior. Think of the damage the Orthodox Sisters caused to our order, how they nearly destroyed us!"

"Yes, but that is an internal matter to the Sisterhood, and it has been resolved." Valya gave a grudging nod. "However, I do agree that we would all be much better off if the dispute were to end. One retaliation leads to a counterretaliation, which leads to another, ad infinitum. But I have well-placed Sisters in the Imperial Palace, including Fielle as the Emperor's Truthsayer. Those women are required to serve both the Sisterhood and the Emperor to the best of their abilities."

"Sometimes at cross-purposes, though."

"The Sisterhood's purpose is paramount." Valya's dark eyes were hard.

"The Sisterhood's purpose is wide-ranging," Cioba countered. She hoped this cryptic statement was enough to remind Valya that Cioba knew about the Sisterhood's hidden computers and their extensive genetic records. In fact, Cioba herself had arranged for the secret VenHold transport that had retrieved these computers and records from the Rossak jungles. "For the good of the Imperium, we must force a wedge between the Butlerians and the Emperor.

Venport Holdings can do that, and only my husband has a military force sufficient to oppose the fanatics. He calls on the Sisterhood for assistance. You can
serve as an intermediary between Josef and Roderick, finding a way for them to
become allies."

Valya crossed her arms over her chest. "Helping Josef that way would bring
the wrath of the Emperor *and* the Butlerians down on us." She shook her head.
"No, Sister Cioba. After the setback we suffered on Rossak, I don't think that's
wise. As Mother Superior, I will not place our order between another collision
of titanic forces. Too dangerous for us. The Sisterhood must remain neutral in
this matter."

Valya dismissed her and walked briskly off to the main complex, accompanied by Deborah, leaving Cioba alone, stunned and disheartened by the aloof
dismissal.

⸎

WHEN VALYA RETURNED to her offices, she received a surprising intelligence report that made her pulse race. Fielle had rushed a coded message directly to her from the Imperial Court, news that she knew the Mother Superior
would want right away. *Yes, Fielle knows me all too well.*

Vorian Atreides had gone there to meet with Emperor Roderick on Salusa,
and after the hated man left, the Truthsayer had been able to gather important
information. There were strong indications that he had gone to Corrin, and
that he thought he could hide there.

He was wrong.

In this vast and infinitely complex universe, danger is always present. For an ordinary person, the challenge is to determine the pitfalls and how to avoid them. Like other humans, I am not perfect, but my pre- science elevates me to another level of consciousness.

—NORMA CENVA, recorded comments

Sometimes the revelations of prescience came to her unbidden, but the uni- verse had so many variables, far beyond even her comprehension. Reality itself was imperfect and unpredictable.

Like other Navigators, her expanded prescience allowed her to see safe path- ways through and around countless star systems. In this sense the universe was hers and available to her, as much as she wished to explore, and she wanted to give the universe to her Navigators. But the universe was not exactly a safe place.

Troubled, she gazed out upon the Kolhar field of Navigator tanks with ten- der feelings, letting her thoughts run through countless possibilities. These were her children, she was their creator. And this maternal sense, this undeniable love for her creations, was stronger than any feeling she held for her great-grandson. She worried about Josef's welfare, but he had caused his own problems.

Due to the commercial embargo the Emperor had imposed throughout the Imperium, many of her Navigators had been withdrawn from their great space- faring ships, and remained here in their tanks. Now, with the spice stockpile on Arrakis destroyed, vital melange supplies were curtailed. Even though Josef had increased harvesting to higher levels with all his teams, there still was not enough spice for her or for her Navigators.

Because of the feud with Roderick Corrino, her Navigators were suffering. Josef had withdrawn so many of his commercial ships that only a handful of Navigators were still active, and being cut off from foldspace travel caused them great distress. They reacted as if the universe had been stolen from them. Norma did her best to stabilize the damage, to coax and comfort her Navigators; to balance the situation as much as possible she redistributed some of the limited spice gas, strengthening those who needed it most.

Conversely, without VenHold commerce, the Imperium itself was straining. Unrest brewed among populations that did not receive their regular shipments of vital commodities; countless addicts were longing for melange, just as her Navigators were. Prices had skyrocketed.

Though Norma usually remained aloof from human concerns, she could see the crisis building, and feared that inaction would result in violent repercussions. People did foolish things, and she worried that Josef's enemies would soon take rash actions as a result.

And those actions could adversely affect her Navigators.

Manford Torondo hated what they represented, and his followers had slain one of her precious children on Baridge. Now, Emperor Roderick held Dobrec hostage as a research specimen on Salusa Secundus. Both of these leaders were desperate, superstitious . . . and dangerous.

In the fractured map of prescience, she had foreseen the possibility of a Navigator being kidnapped, but the greater disaster of the wrecked spice bank on Arrakis had blinded her at the time. She had not rushed back to Kolhar soon enough to prevent the loss of Dobrec.

Now, her thoughts tangled in knots. She gazed beyond the field of Navigators, extending her mind's eye far out in space toward Salusa Secundus, which was the heart of a psychic storm she was feeling. She could sense the tension in Dobrec's mind there, the crisis he faced as the Imperial interrogator pressed him more and more strenuously. Prescience provided her with few clear details, but she learned enough to realize that the captive Navigator would not survive.

Even from Kolhar she could visualize the secret underground laboratory, the prodding, sampling, and tormenting that was being inflicted on Dobrec—all in a clumsy attempt to understand what no mere human could ever comprehend. Yet the Scalpel interrogator understood techniques that no Navigator knew, techniques that no Navigator could resist.

Norma felt hollow inside.

Emperor Roderick Corrino might be a moral man in the human sense, but Norma's morals were not the same as his, nor Manford Torondo's . . . nor Josef's, for that matter. Yet all of those men, in their righteous cocoons, professed to be taking actions for the proper reasons.

Because of who she was—and *what* she was—Norma's obligations were greater than herself, greater than those men and their goals. The captive Navigator created an immense problem for her.

In the far-distant tank, Dobrec drifted, trapped, but Norma could see only visual echoes of his presence. The Emperor would do anything to understand

Navigators, to find a way to strike against Venport Holdings. Roderick Corrino did not comprehend the great danger of his decisions, nor did Josef understand what he had provoked. And Manford Torondo, especially, did not know the terrible consequences of his actions, or actions that were to come.

She could not rescue Dobrec because of all the soldiers the Emperor had stationed to guard the laboratory, but she could help him in another way, show him how to take an infinite and necessary journey. . . .

Through her agitated awareness, Norma sensed the dark storm coming, a menace to her Navigators that was greater than any peril they had ever faced. The danger loomed over all of them on Kolhar, over all of Venport Holdings . . . over the future itself.

The threat and terror were crippling. She had no answer. Norma felt as if she were drowning inside her isolated tank. She felt . . . helpless. And the threat was coming *here* to Kolhar. And soon.

In a frantic attempt to understand, she reached out with the tendrils of her remarkable mind, probing, searching. . . .

Grant me the proper weapons and I will conquer the soul of humanity.
—RAYNA BUTLER, final public rally on Kellimor

After she returned from Lord Pondi's planet, Anari Idaho's report was exactly what Manford had hoped for. With her own eyes, the loyal Swordmaster had seen Pondi's stockpile of atomics, doomsday weapons like those that had been used to wipe out the thinking machines.

But not all of the warheads had been used in that ruthless holocaust, and a planet-killing reserve had been set aside on Gillek. The nobleman was far too frightened to keep it there, and he was such an eager convert to the Butlerian movement that he had offered it all to Manford—who knew exactly how to make use of such unexpected bounty, and strength. It was just what he needed against Venport and his supposedly impregnable stronghold on Kolhar.

Over the course of several days on Pondi's planet, Anari and her team had worked under cover of darkness to remove every one of the atomics. As she prepared to depart with her prize, the nervous nobleman had remained behind, bowing, weeping with happiness, thanking Anari for relieving him of such a terrible burden. Her Butlerian spacefolder raced back to Salusa Secundus with a full arsenal of forbidden atomics, and when the ship slipped in among Manford's fleet, no one guessed how much destruction she carried in the hold.

Proud of her accomplishment, Anari shuttled down to rejoin the ever-growing hordes camped in Zimia's palace square. Manford was relieved to have her back, and not just because of the news she brought. He was a far stronger leader with his Swordmaster present, and not merely in the physical sense. He could never have asked for a more perfect bodyguard, nor a better emotional bulwark, a stabilizer.

After Anari delivered her oral report in a low voice, close to his ear, Manford heaved a long, ecstatic sigh. Looking toward the towering Imperial Palace nearby, he narrowed his gaze. "I would prefer to keep this knowledge away from our dear Emperor Roderick. It does not concern him, and he has already shown that he is unwilling to take difficult but necessary actions. Therefore, *we* will use the atomics against our mutual enemy. And we will win. Anari, I am certain that Roderick Corrino will thank us."

Both he and the Emperor were determined to crush Directeur Venport and erase his cursed technology, but Manford didn't entirely trust Roderick's convictions. While weak-willed Salvador could be pressured into doing what he was told, his brother had an unfortunate habit of thinking for himself.

Anari warned, "The use of atomics is strictly forbidden—particularly atomics against humans."

During the long days of waiting for her report, hoping for the best, Manford had already thought through the consequences. "The use of thinking-machine technology is also forbidden, and Venport is clearly guilty of violating that. He sent *cymeks* to Salusa Secundus! I will use one anathema to destroy another. Thinking machines tortured and enslaved us for centuries, but remember that atomics *liberated* us. There is no moral equivalency." He flushed as he thought of the glorious mission that lay before them. "After we wipe out Kolhar, if Roderick is too upset, I will explain that we did it to avenge the murder of his brother. If there is still too much uproar about our method, we can be contrite and beg forgiveness." He smiled, nodding to himself. "I don't expect it to be overly difficult, though. Roderick also gets what he wants."

"*If* we succeed," Anari said. "Remember that Kolhar is the most heavily defended planet in the Imperium. Despite our atomics, we could suffer heavy losses."

He looked at the sprawling encampment of Butlerians all around him. "We have plenty of blood to spend." He gestured to Anari, having already made his plans. "Take me to the Imperial Palace. I will inform the Emperor that we intend to conquer Kolhar, and all my followers will depart immediately. He doesn't need to know more details."

He had many warships in orbit alongside Roderick's Imperial Armed Forces, including the hostage fleet that Admiral Harte had recently brought home. All those fighters were happy comrades for the time being . . . but Manford knew that the Butlerians had overstayed their welcome. The Emperor wanted them to leave.

When Manford returned after defeating Directeur Venport, though, his followers would never leave. They would be here to stay.

⋙⋘

EMPEROR RODERICK SAT with Haditha in his private suite in the Palace, reading the unexpected handwritten message from Manford Torondo. The Butlerian leader announced that his entire fleet would depart for Kolhar, "to do what must be done. My forces are sufficient and my followers are determined. We will break through Venport's defenses and lay waste to his entire planet."

It was welcome news indeed.

He caught his breath as he handed the message to his auburn-haired wife. "I will tell Manford he has my blessing. The Butlerians will surely be slaughtered in the attempt, but they might still inflict considerable damage on Venport." He tapped his fingers on the ornate bloodwood table. "Both sides may decimate each other."

Haditha finished reading and set the note aside. "Manford must know that, though. He seems altogether too confident. Or foolish."

"They can't depart from Salusa swiftly enough, as far as I am concerned." Although the Butlerian ships had made no overt threat against the Imperial capital, Roderick knew they could just as easily turn against Salusa, and maybe even attempt a coup. "I don't trust Manford Torondo any more than I trust Directeur Venport."

By now, he had decided that General Roon's strike force had been lost somehow. Admiral Harte's hostage battle group from Kolhar consisted of slow FTL ships that could not compete with even the old-model Butlerian fleet. Roderick had a plan for Harte's ships, though—one that would be effective against the Butlerian homeworld, provided they were not totally destroyed at Kolhar. Either way, he felt confident that the Butlerians would be defeated.

The Emperor was supposed to possess the strongest military force, bar none, but during the course of his reign Salvador had let the fleet degenerate into corruption and incompetence. Salvador had become too dependent on the VenHold Spacing Fleet for transport, which left his military nearly helpless when Directeur Venport betrayed the Imperium.

Roderick stifled a groan. His brother had weakened the throne in ways that would take generations to repair . . . if House Corrino survived that long.

In the meantime, Roderick had signed extended contracts with EsconTran and other foldspace shipping companies to transport his peacekeeping ships around the increasingly restless Imperium. But only VenHold had Navigators, and so far Roderick's scientists had not been able to poke, prod, or analyze the answers out of their captive specimen. . . .

Roderick struggled with the turmoil. An Emperor could not be tossed back and forth like a toy between the Butlerians and Venport! Soon, though, if the clash at Kolhar was bloody enough, the problem might resolve itself. . . .

BEFORE MANFORD AND his followers departed on their "holy mission," the Emperor announced a day of celebrations to make the Butlerians feel appreciated. Their rallies seemed surprisingly restrained, because apparently they were saving their rage to be unleashed against Venport.

When Manford was ready to shuttle hundreds of thousands of followers up to his fleet in orbit, Roderick and Haditha gave the warships a grand send-off. They waved from the Palace towers as ship after ship lifted into the sky.

"Good riddance," Roderick muttered. He didn't really appreciate the Butlerians at all.

Haditha squeezed his hand. "Do you think they really could conquer Kolhar?"

"Faith and blind fanaticism are not sufficient weapons. I only hope the Butlerians inflict mortal damage on Venport's forces before they themselves are destroyed."

That would remove both of the annoying thorns that had been tormenting him.

When receiving an unexpected gift, a wise man does not ask too many questions. Only the foolish person assumes that a gift is simply a gift, and that there are no implied obligations.

—DIRECTEUR JOSEF VENPORT, Venport Holdings
consolidation memo

Erasmus was true to his word. After allowing for the vagaries of positioning and more than a century of drifting, Draigo's scouts found the thinking-machine fleet exactly where the independent robot had said it would be. Forty bulky battleships hanging in space, dark and cold, but intact.

Once scouts tagged the robot fleet, Draigo gathered a crew of Denali engineers and technicians to assess, inspect, and reactivate the thinking-machine vessels and pilot them back to the research planet.

Erasmus asked for permission to accompany the recovery team, but after Draigo considered multiple worst-case scenarios he concluded that he did not trust the robot enough: If given access to all those machine ships, Erasmus might just be tempted to seize them for his own purposes. Though his memory core now resided in a vulnerable biological body, Draigo chose not to take the risk.

A Navigator had brought the recovery team out into deep space, where the tagged robot fleet drifted, and now Draigo paced the piloting deck in silence, studying his prize. The Navigator in the tank behind him made no comment.

The Denali chief engineer, a tough woman named Hana Elkora, joined him on the deck. "I can't wait to get my hands on those. Over the last ten years I've refurbished two dozen old thinking-machine vessels and added them to the Ven-Hold commercial fleet—but never so many at one time." Clearly pleased, she put her hands on her broad hips, as if considering all the hard work ahead. "This is a real treasure trove. Good thing the barbarians didn't find them first. Those fanatics would have blown up perfectly good vessels without even attempting to salvage them."

Draigo nodded. "What matters is that we have these warships, assets we can either turn against Manford Torondo or use to defend Arrakis or Kolhar."

"Damned right, and we'll get right to work," Elkora said. "By now I know the usual machine booby traps, and I am more than familiar with lumbering old robot engines. We'll get these ships going one at a time and fly them back to Denali. Even with just faster-than-light drives, you should start receiving the new vessels within a week."

As the Mentat stared at the dark hulks floating there, he began counting and cataloguing them. "Directeur Venport will dispatch carrier ships with spare Holtzman engines to be installed. We can turn these wrecks into spacefolders in no time."

"I'm ready to get to work," Elkora said.

"All of us are."

⤙⥟⤚

AN INITIAL CREW made their way aboard the first of the mothballed vessels. They used generators and battery packs to reactivate the rudimentary life-support systems, which the thinking machines had installed only for transporting human slaves. After several hours, the engineers managed to make the machine ship sufficiently habitable, and more workers came aboard in insulated suits and breathers.

Draigo and Elkora entered the echoing vessel, noting metal corridors and chambers and very few amenities. Aboard, they found hundreds of deactivated robots and combat meks. The ominous machines stood where they had frozen, burly and fearsome units. The Mentat stood in front of one motionless metal figure, examining its reinforced arms and legs, the integrated weaponry.

"These things are just junk," said Elkora. "You always find them aboard abandoned robot ships. We can dump them out the airlocks—if you want us to bother with that."

"Do what you feel is necessary." Draigo continued to stare at the combat robot, as if challenging it. It was vastly different from Erasmus in his new biological body. "Cleaning out the garbage is not your priority. Remove the ones that get in the way, a minimum amount to save time. We can always dispose of the robots at Denali, where we have more manpower—pile them on the surface where the old cymek bodies rusted for decades."

"Understood, sir. My team will take it from here."

Feeling an odd compulsion, Draigo reached out to touch the exoskeleton of the combat mek. He thought of how much fear the thinking machines had pounded into the human psyche for so long.

He found it curious now, with the threat of the Butlerians and the repercussions from Emperor Roderick himself, that these thinking machines were no longer the greatest threat to civilization.

We may try to solve the problems of the Imperium, but to a large extent our future is in the uncaring hands of Fate. We must make our own way, constantly calculating and recalculating the odds of success.

—HADITHA CORRINO to her husband, after
consulting with a Sister Mentat

The Butlerian mobs had left Zimia, racing off to what would likely be their bloody, suicidal annihilation at Kolhar, but the Emperor remained troubled. Would it really be so easy to get rid of them? And to get rid of Venport?

When Roderick opened his eyes, moonlight filtered through the merh-silk curtains of his bedchamber. A disturbing dream had awakened him, and he could not dismiss it from his thoughts. Next to him, Haditha slept soundly on the wide bed, and that gave him a measure of comfort.

He recalled seeing her for the first time at a grand ball in the Imperial Palace. He had been a young prince, while she was the younger sister of one of the ladies in waiting in his father's court. He'd noticed her in the throng of nobles with her long auburn hair and classic patrician features, wearing a white gown with a ruby-pearl necklace. As if drawn by gravity, he had moved closer to listen as she talked with a young man in a formal suit. She seemed so very much alive in contrast with other people around her.

Haditha had glanced in his direction, flashing a smile meant just for him. Later that evening, after an embarrassing incident when Salvador got too drunk and slipped on the dance floor, Roderick approached her again, and they strolled arm in arm through the palace gardens. It had been magical.

At the time, although he was the second son of Emperor Jules, Roderick had not dreamed of taking the throne, but he *had* envisioned being with Haditha for the rest of his life. It had felt so right. They had seemed destined to be together. . . .

Now, as Roderick slipped out of bed in the moonlight, she opened her eyes and gave him that warm smile he'd first seen so long ago. He leaned over and kissed her tenderly. "It's all right. I'm just thinking about what's going to happen when the Butlerians arrive at Kolhar. Manford has no idea what he'll face there, though I will not mourn much if Venport wipes them out."

Haditha sat up, brushing her hair out of her face. "Manford is a hateful, obsessed man, but he is dangerous, and we can't assess what his fanatical followers will do. Maybe *Venport* won't know what hit him." She saw his troubled expression. "Do you want someone to talk to?"

"You're always my best adviser, but I need time to measure my own thoughts. Go back to sleep. I won't be long."

Leaving the bedchamber, Roderick Corrino walked down a short corridor to the sanctuary of his private office. Once inside, though, he felt a strange compulsion. He unlocked a side cabinet and brought out the eerie flowmetal cape that the scavenger had given him from Corrin. The garment was cool to his touch and shimmered with alien magic. As he held the cape up to a glowglobe and watched the hypnotic play of lights and colors on its faceted surface, he wondered if it had really once belonged to the evil robot Erasmus.

The metallic fabric shifted, seeming to move of its own volition. Taking a deep breath for courage, he wrapped it around his shoulders, feeling it flow and adjust itself to his upper body. He secured a clasp, then examined himself in a wall mirror. The cape looked rather elegant on him, but he felt oddly guilty, as if some taint in it might corrupt him, turning him into a twisted, demented creature like the notorious Erasmus. But for all its marvels, the thing was just a cape. It could do no harm now.

In the dream that had awakened him, Roderick had seen himself wearing the flowmetal cloak as he rode through the streets of Zimia at the head of an Imperial procession . . . with an army of thinking machines behind him. He had not been himself. He had been Erasmus.

Now, as the tattered details of the dream dissipated in his memory, he remained disturbed. The Butlerians decried all advanced technology and refused to consider any useful purpose that would outweigh the risk, but Roderick was not so adamant. There had to be situations in which computers and work-saving equipment could be used by people—and *controlled* by people, as Venport insisted.

He removed the unusual article of clothing, returned it to the cabinet, and locked it inside. It was only a harmless, inanimate thing, yet he felt strangely reluctant to admit to anyone that he had tried it on.

THE NEXT MORNING, he and the Empress traveled to the military base outside the city where Admiral Harte's soldiers had been stationed. With the departure of the Butlerian fleet, Roderick had pounced on the opportunity, issuing new orders to Harte. He could permanently render the fanatics impotent.

The fleet of Imperial warships would undertake a slow, quiet mission—insurance against the out-of-control Butlerians, insurance against whatever happened at Kolhar. They would lock down Lampadas . . . maybe even without spilling a single drop of blood.

Standing together on a high walkway, Roderick and Haditha observed the hundred newly landed warships that Directeur Venport had held hostage aboard the carrier. The old vessels were spaceworthy and perfectly appropriate for this new, secret deployment. They possessed enough weaponry that they could be an intimidating force under the correct conditions, aided by the element of surprise. When the surviving Butlerians returned to Lampadas, they would not be in any condition to put up much resistance.

Ordinarily, Harte's peacekeeping fleet would have been delivered to their destination by a large foldspace carrier—such as the VenHold vessel that had seized them. The ships could fly using standard faster-than-light engines, although that would take them weeks to reach a destination. On this occasion, for security, it was tactically worth taking this amount of time.

The landing field was abuzz with activity as Harte's battle group made preparations for departure. Roderick paused on the walkway to point out to Haditha one of the vessels being prepared: a long, sleek warship with a wide forward viewing area. "That was my father's flagship. When I was very young, Emperor Jules took my brother and me aboard to tell us of its glorious history. So many stories about it."

The Empress smiled at him. "With good fortune, there will be new stories to tell, and they will be added to the Corrino legend."

"I suspect we're going to have a big success. I like our plan. It just might work."

The two had developed the idea together. Since the Imperial Armed Forces could no longer rely on VenHold foldspace carriers, they had decided to dispatch these reliable FTL ships quietly and slowly to Lampadas, where they could keep watch on the Butlerians. If Manford and his followers survived their confrontation at Kolhar and returned to Lampadas, Admiral Harte could keep them bottled up there. Better yet, if Manford's forces were decimated, then Harte could simply neutralize the last sparks of the fanatical movement.

"It's a perfect backdoor maneuver," Roderick said. "Since these ships are not carried aboard a spacefolder, they will arrive unnoticed outside the Lampadas system, and Harte can wait there until the time is right."

One possibility: If Manford did somehow manage to destroy the VenHold headquarters on Kolhar, the Imperium might have no more Navigators. That added even more urgency to the interrogation of the captive Dobrec. Roderick very much needed his Scalpel investigator to extract answers from their only Navigator specimen. He was anxious for progress, but had heard no recent report from his underground research lab. While he and Haditha observed Admiral Harte's preparations for the fleet's departure, Roderick sent a message to the research facility, insisting on answers.

For the next hour, the fleet assembled for the big launch. The old flagship began to move laterally on an immense transport mechanism that delivered it to a takeoff area. Other vessels lifted off to a rendezvous point in Salusan orbit, from which they would quietly depart on the long voyage to Lampadas.

But just as Roderick and Haditha were about to return to the Palace, a messenger arrived with grim news. "Directly from Administrator Athens, Sire!" He handed over a message cylinder. "I believe it is bad news, very bad. . . ."

Needing privacy, Roderick dismissed the messenger, cracked open the cylinder, and cursed when he read the message inside. He felt as if the floor had dropped out beneath him. "Our Navigator is dead," he said to Haditha. "The lab administrator insists Dobrec was questioned carefully and gently, all according to my command, but the creature just died anyway, as if . . . as if of his own volition." Roderick shook his head in dismay. "He *willed* himself to stop living, and took his secrets with him."

She gripped his hand. "I'm sorry. I know you were hoping for a breakthrough."

As much as he wanted the Butlerians to defeat Josef Venport, he could not afford to lose VenHold's knowledge and resources.

He sent an immediate response to the facility. "Prepare the specimen for dissection. We must learn everything that we still can."

It is a sad joke of fate that barbarians can so quickly destroy what civilizations took centuries to build.

—DIRECTEUR JOSEF VENPORT on the evacuation of Kolhar

With dimensional space rippling around her tank, Norma Cenva hurtled back to Kolhar, driven by the adrenaline of prescience. Urgency and desperation echoed like thunderclaps in her mind. With a crack of displaced air, her sealed chamber reappeared on its central dais in the field of Navigator tanks in the middle of the night.

Something terrible was about to happen. Not even Josef's defenses could prevent the approaching threat. The Butlerians were coming here to destroy, and they would arrive soon.

Bright stars shone through cloud veils in the dark sky. Around her, more than eighty tanks sparkled in reflected monitor lights and suspended security glowglobes. Some tanks were occupied; others were empty.

A powerful sense of alarm pulsed through her. Her children were threatened—all of them! She had to evacuate the ones still undergoing transformation, and get the true Navigators to depart on their own before it was too late. Only she could fold space with her mind; all other Navigators required the use of Holtzman engines. She had to get them aboard spacefolders and take them away.

Norma sent a summons to the Navigators aboard the orbiting VenHold ships, informing them that she was retrieving all of the Navigator tanks, taking them to safety before the impending holocaust.

There was no way she could stop it.

Her announcement caused great anxiety and consternation, but they listened. Thankfully, they paid close attention.

As she began to help her Navigators, Norma realized that Josef was also in danger, and she decided to warn him personally. But evacuating all of Kolhar would never be possible. There was not enough time.

Norma was fond of her great-grandson, whose personality reminded her in some ways of her late husband Aurelius Venport, back when she had been merely human and capable of that sort of love. Aurelius had always cared for Norma, even when her own mother considered her a freak. He had given the young woman everything she needed or wanted as she transformed into this incredible being.

Even today, long after Aurelius's death, Norma continued to evolve. Josef and his powerful commercial empire had made it possible for her precious Navigators to become what they were today. She needed him. It only made sense, logically and emotionally, that she had to protect Josef as well.

Recognizing the consequences of her own actions, Norma realized that she was herself partly responsible for this catastrophic chain of events. By prematurely withdrawing the VenHold fleet from Salusa Secundus, she had given the Butlerian leader a boost of perceived power while making her great-grandson look weak, cowardly, and vulnerable.

Now, she intended to make up for it by saving him. As soon as Norma knew that the rescue of her Navigators was under way, she went to warn Josef.

※

IN THE SILENT hours of the night, Josef lay intertwined with Cioba in their spacious private dwelling. Even as he dozed, his mental wheels did not stop turning.

His wife had just returned from Wallach IX with her disappointing news that the Sisterhood refused his overtures for a rapprochement with the Emperor and an alliance. That angered Josef, after all he had done for them when *they* were outlaws. He made up his mind to withdraw his daughters from the school, not wanting to risk the Sisters using them as hostages.

The news from Draigo Roget had been much better. The robot Erasmus had revealed the location of forty intact thinking-machine battleships adrift in space. Denali engineers were repairing them now, and Josef had already dispatched a hauler with Holtzman engine upgrades for all of them. They would make his VenHold fleet significantly stronger. . . .

The crack and thump of displaced air woke him immediately. Josef sprang out of bed and landed in a crouch on the carpeted floor. Cioba also came alert, and they stared at the cumbersome tank that had just appeared in the open area of their bedroom.

Josef wrapped a sheet around himself. "What is it, Grandmother?" He knew

Norma followed her own capricious thoughts. Perhaps she had recalled some concept she wanted to discuss with him, heedless of the hour or place.

"I came to warn you." Norma's voice sounded distorted, beyond that of an ordinary human, containing a tangential otherness. "Remove your ships from Kolhar," she said. "There is little time. Leave immediately."

He was fully awake now, but not pleased. "Kolhar is our fortress world. How can we be in danger?" He thought of his well-armed guardian ships, the layers of heavy shields that embraced the planet.

"The Butlerians are coming, Josef, a huge force of them. They will destroy you."

He was so surprised he couldn't even laugh. "Those primitive barbarians could never break through our advanced defenses."

"Heed my warning, Josef. Trust my prescience. My Navigators need to be evacuated." Norma's ornate vault vanished in a rush of displaced air, leaving Josef and Cioba confused and alarmed.

"She's been behaving strangely," he said, "ordering one evacuation after another."

"At Salusa, she sensed that the spice stockpile was being raided—and she was right," Cioba pointed out. "We have to trust her."

"Even with her prescience, we arrived at Arrakis too late," Josef said, feeling a sudden chill. "I have no idea what she's worried about this time, but if she wants us to leave, I think we should."

While he and Cioba dressed themselves and grabbed a few possessions, Josef sounded an alarm for all spaceport operations and ground troops. He increased the planetary shields and called for VenHold warships to take a defensive posture—only to discover that Norma had already withdrawn two large fold-space carriers from orbit and brought them down to the Navigator field.

Taking a fast groundcar, he and Cioba raced out to the valley, which was in turmoil. Dazzling glowglobe security lights blazed in the air, shining down on the two landed spacefolders that covered the barren ground. Enhanced suspensor fields added structural integrity to the vessels that were normally meant for open space rather than the stress of a planetary gravity field.

The cargo hatches were open, and uniformed VenHold employees used antigravity clamps and suspensor rigs to move the tanks containing the proto-Navigators. They wrestled with one at a time, keeping the melange gas supply connected to the tanks.

Josef was shocked to see such a large-scale evacuation. One breathless Ven-Hold worker with a stubble of beard spoke to him. "We are moving as swiftly as possible, Directeur—as ordered."

"By Norma?" Josef asked, trying to calm himself.

The man didn't seem to know. "We were given only one hour. Both of these carriers have to be loaded and ready to depart. Our Holtzman engines are on standby. The Navigator on deck is preparing to fold space without even leaving the surface. I don't know how that's—"

Cioba interrupted, "Has anyone been told the exact nature of the danger?"

The frantic workers could not answer, but they continued to load the Navigator tanks with great haste, clearing the eighty sparkling tanks.

"The planetary shields are in place," Josef said, but even he wasn't convinced it would be enough.

Norma's tank appeared on its dais, overlooking the mostly empty Navigator field. "We depart in moments, Josef. Join us. We are beneath the shields now, but will reappear above them."

"How can I just leave everything behind—my industries, spaceport, ships, construction yards?"

"You have no choice," Norma said, "if you wish to live."

Josef looked at Cioba, then they hurried aboard the nearest carrier. The rest of the Kolhar workers hunkered down to defend themselves against a threat they had not even seen yet.

Once the great ships were sealed, the Navigators simply winked them out of existence, disappearing from the ground and reappearing in far orbit above Kolhar, bypassing normal dimensional paths to get around the planetary shields.

But even in orbit, they were far from safe.

⟨⟩

MANFORD TORONDO'S FLEET appeared without warning.

The faithful aboard had been drilled en route from Salusa Secundus, and every person knew their role. The captains of the 115 ships fully understood Manford's plan.

At first, his faithful had been horrified to learn about the stockpile of atomics that Anari had distributed among their vessels—atomics exactly like the ones that had devastated so many thinking-machine worlds. Despite the current prohibition against such doomsday weapons, the Butlerians did relish the idea of bombarding the headquarters of the machine lovers.

Manford knew that Directeur Venport had no chance against such an onslaught, but he also knew that his forces could not afford a prolonged space conflict against superior enemy warships. He had to saturate Kolhar with the atomics and then leave as quickly as possible.

When his Butlerian spacefolders emerged into real space and accelerated toward the planet, he looked across at Anari, who was staring through the windowport at their destination ahead. The Swordmaster contacted the other captains, then gave him a hard grin. "Only two of our vessels were lost in transit, Manford—navigation errors. Acceptable losses for a mission such as this. We have no need of the monster Navigators Venport uses. Your followers are blessed, and we are destined to achieve a great victory today."

"Indeed we are, Anari."

Manford was familiar with the history of Serena Butler's Jihad, the climactic bloodbath of atomic devastation that wiped out countless Synchronized Worlds, and he had supplemented this knowledge by reading the Erasmus journals, which recounted the horrific final attack on Corrin. Manford knew exactly what was about to happen now—and looked forward to it.

Impossibly, though, someone had alerted Josef Venport ahead of time. The devil's defenders were ready, a fleet of warships with weapons activated, and the planetary shields increased. Two large VenHold carriers appeared high above the planet, evacuating, but he was focused on the heavily armored vessels standing between him and Kolhar.

Under normal circumstances, Manford's fleet would have been cut to ribbons in a full-fledged battle. They could not have breached the orbital defenses with conventional weapons, much less destroyed the planetary shields. But Manford had something the Directeur would not expect.

As VenHold warships opened fire on his fleet, the Butlerian leader smiled.

Anari gave the ominous order. Manford's first five vessels surged forward to launch atomic projectiles, paying no heed to the VenHold battleships standing against them. The nuclear warheads detonated in the atmosphere like small, brilliant suns. Energy shock waves swept the VenHold ships aside like a child scattering unwanted toys.

Like incandescent battering rams in space, three more strategically fired atomics stunned the last effective Kolhar defenses, and the planetary shields began to go off-line.

Manford took a moment to enjoy what he was seeing as the rest of his holy fleet charged into the open wound. "Unleash our warheads—every single one. I do not want any survivors left on that accursed planet, human or animal. The whole place is contaminated."

These powerful weapons would grant him a glorious victory, but they also made him feel soiled. Yet, he could think of no more satisfying way to dispose of them all.

The next wave of atomics obliterated the planetary shields above VenHold's industrial facilities, and Manford knew that his fifty remaining warheads would be more than sufficient to finish the job.

THE TWO VENHOLD carriers pulled away, rescuing all of the proto-Navigator tanks as well as any refugees who had rushed aboard at the last moment. Josef watched in horror as massive detonations wiped out his defensive ships and planetary shields. Then explosion after explosion blistered the surface of Kolhar and eradicated the spaceports, cities, outposts . . . and all living things.

"Atomics!" Cioba cried. She squeezed her husband's hand so tightly he thought she might break his bones. "I can't believe that even the barbarians would dare!"

A few defensive VenHold ships managed to limp away, and some of the Butlerian forces broke formation to pursue them like ravenous hyenas.

Josef's thoughts went wild. Such weapons were utterly forbidden in the Imperium. *Atomics!* Emperor Roderick would never have authorized this strike— Manford Torondo and all his followers would now be shunned, banished from imperial society.

Or . . . would Roderick gloss over the horrendous war crime as the price of vengeance? Josef was sickened. Did the Emperor even know about this?

The VenHold spacefolders began to accelerate as they escaped. With waves of detonations behind them, Josef knew there was nothing he could save on Kolhar. The planet would be a radioactive wasteland, uninhabitable for decades. He didn't want to think about the death toll down there.

Josef had the Navigators send messages to any remnants of his fleet, and tell them to join him where he was going. He needed to go someplace safe where he could think—and plan his counterattack.

"Take us to Arrakis," he said. "We'll be safe there. For now."

All this obsession with the biological activity of procreation! I do not understand it. Humans are preoccupied with the smallest nuances of sex, almost elevating it to a form of religion. But then, I have never really understood religion, either.

—ERASMUS, Secret Laboratory Notebooks

Anna Corrino remained by his side every day, talking about the most trivial matters, engaging in seemingly endless conversations, so that Erasmus longed for the times when he had been in full control of their relationship. Back at the Mentat School, he had expended a great deal of effort to shape her to be this way, to reconfigure her malleable mind so that she was focused on him. Instead of this, he wished for the frustrating, but intellectually challenging, resistance of a strong woman like Serena Butler.

Anna also required frequent reassuring physical contact from him. Even when she could see him standing right next to her, she would touch his arm, as if she didn't believe he truly existed in this form. From a psychological standpoint, Erasmus understood the need of a damaged person, but the distractions were beginning to interfere with the progress of his other important experiments.

In order to have some time alone and undisturbed, he found himself concocting tasks to keep Anna busy. He sent her off to collect the former human names of the failed Navigator brains in their tanks, which took her hours. It was not necessary, or even interesting, information, because he didn't care about their prior identities, or personal histories.

After Anna returned with a full list of names, he asked her to find out which planets had been the original homes of the exiled Denali researchers; many were Tlulaxa, but others came from different planets that had also been oppressed by Butlerian fanaticism. Again, he had no use for that information, but she went off to do whatever he asked, and found the people to direct her to the records. It kept her happy to think she was contributing to his research. This task took her two days, and Anna completed it with such dedication that he realized he could perhaps rely on her for real work.

Erasmus also wanted to travel to the recovery operations with the old robot ships, but Draigo Roget would not allow him to leave the research planet. He was able to review Hana Elkora's reports, however, and allowed Anna to look over his shoulder. He found her presence irritating, but wanted to see what she could do that was worthwhile, and also knew what the emotional consequences would be if he told her to leave him alone.

After studying this experimental subject for so long, he understood that poor Anna needed such reassurance. Not only was her mind unstable and fragile, but her self-esteem could be easily manipulated—as Erasmus himself had done many times during their unusual relationship. For her sake, he tolerated Anna's behavior and tried to learn from it, in his continuing analysis of her damaged psyche and emotions. He had, after all, initiated her intense attraction toward him in the first place.

Erasmus had pulled on Anna's heartstrings long before she ever saw his new body, and he was beginning to understand the consequences of those manipulations. He studied her adoring expression, her dreamy eyes, and knew she would do anything for him. Even though he had no quantitative way to measure her emotions, he realized that she loved him.

Thinking back on his centuries of interacting with humans—captive slaves, lab subjects, even a number of turncoat collaborators—Erasmus realized that never before had anyone truly loved him in a romantic way. That was an interesting revelation, and warranted further study.

Yes, Gilbertus had been loyal and dedicated, a true friend. After witnessing his cruel execution, Erasmus comprehended part of the range of human emotions. He'd felt genuine grief, even despair over the death—and anger and a desire for vengeance toward Manford Torondo and his Butlerians.

But love . . . love was something different. A very complex emotion, with many aspects—like looking into the most complex facets of a diamond.

Now, inside one of the laboratories, Tlulaxa scientists were monitoring a fresh Navigator brain. All the protected brains in their canisters had just become inexplicably agitated. None of the researchers could understand why, not even Ptolemy or Noffe.

The scientists were likewise becoming agitated. "The Navigator brains have to be prepared," Ptolemy said. "The cymek attack force must be ready for launch—we need to rely on these brains to destroy the Butlerians."

Erasmus found their consternation amusing. He worked the muscles in his face to form a smile. "Perhaps they just need the appropriate stimuli."

He had been practicing the subtleties of human facial expressions. The real face he had now was far more sophisticated than his best flowmetal body in the old days, as it provided him with precise motor skills and involuntary muscles. To her credit, Anna had helped teach him to smile and laugh, poking and prodding his face as if it were a mask of clay. Even in his robot body, he had been able to imitate laughter, but this was different—and it actually felt good.

Now he reacted to Anna's intent expression. She was watching him, instead of the scientists, who were ignoring Erasmus in their angst over the agitated Navigators. So he shifted his focus to her, touched her arm, and gave her his best imitation of a heartfelt smile. She beamed in response.

He had already learned so much in assessing sensations from his nerve endings—the simple satisfaction of breathing and eating, tasks that even the youngest human infant could perform, but which no machine had ever done before. Even this damaged woman had taught him much.

He had also determined that the sexual act was quite pleasurable, objectively speaking, although Anna wanted to engage in intercourse far more often than was necessary for his research purposes. Plotting his own sensations on a curve, he developed a pattern to the sexual activities and did his best to model and measure her own responses. There was quite a significant variation each time, though.

Knowing she wanted his attentions now, he led Anna away from the preoccupied scientists. She seemed extremely pleased that he would take the initiative. For his own part, Erasmus devoted a section of his mind to considering further experiments he could perform on the Navigator brains. They were certainly interesting subjects.

But first he had sexual obligations; otherwise, Anna would not leave him alone. It was an investment in overall efficiency.

Always before, Erasmus had interpreted romance as an example of human illogic and inefficiency. Once, he had quipped to the machine ruler Omnius that if robot manufacturing lines required such a complex and unpredictable mating dance before reproducing a new combat mek or worker robot, the thinking machines would never have spread beyond a single world.

But at this time, as he continued his series of physical experiments with Anna Corrino, he began to grasp some of the nuances. From his many years on Earth, Erasmus had memorized a wealth of human writings, including a series of well-regarded professorial handbooks on sex. He accessed that information and put those techniques into practice, much to Anna's delight. His new biological body, though, did not have the stamina of even a common robot form, and he finished long before completing the steps in the opening chapter of the first handbook.

Afterward she clung to him anyway, snuggling close. "You are the ideal lover, Erasmus. You were made just for me. Everything is so perfect! We're sheltered in this dome, away from the Imperial Palace and planetary wars, away from everything . . . just you and me. Oh, how I wish we could stay here forever!"

"Forever seems longer than necessary." He knew that the Denali facility had been created for the purpose of developing weapons against the Butlerians, and Erasmus fully intended to avenge the death of Gilbertus. But he knew that if he revealed this priority to Anna, he would hurt her feelings, and that would be counterproductive.

As he pondered, she surprised him by asking, "Do you think we could have children?" She propped herself up on an elbow and turned her bright blue eyes on him. "I'd like to have a baby. Just think of what sort of son or daughter we could produce!"

Erasmus rose from the bed in alarm. He had accepted his biological body without fully considering the implications of sexual intercourse. If Anna were to have his baby, that would be an unnecessary complication, a time-consuming distraction. He'd dealt with babies before in his experimental laboratories, and had never enjoyed being around them. And he was sure that the experience of childbirth and the pressures of motherhood would damage Anna's already fragile psyche.

She pressed, "I could be a good mother, I know I could. Wouldn't you like to be a father? Doesn't that sound exciting?"

Erasmus remembered Serena Butler, the human female he had admired as an intellectual sparring partner. The thinking machines had taken her prisoner while pregnant, and he had learned much about humankind from her. But after giving birth to the needy, crying, helpless baby, Serena's personality changed. She became argumentative and far less interesting. That baby ruined the close and intimate relationship they'd had. The child had, in fact, become such an interference to his goals that Erasmus finally threw the disruptive infant off a high balcony. . . .

No, he did not want children of his own, but he was wise enough to keep such comments to himself. "I'll have one of the Tlulaxa doctors test you immediately. They can verify whether or not you are pregnant."

With a contented smile, Anna lay back on the bed.

Erasmus worked to keep a reflexive expression of concern off his face. If Anna Corrino were indeed carrying a fertilized embryo, he would order the Tlulaxa doctors to terminate it quickly and quietly, before she knew it was there.

Opposing powers and ideologies will lead to inevitable clashes, but even with vast ideological differences, rational minds can invariably find common ground, given sufficient incentive. It is not possible, however, to negotiate with a madman.

> —DIRECTEUR JOSEF VENPORT, statement to
> VenHold Spacing Fleet on the evacuation of Kolhar

Arrakis remained a hardscrabble world with rugged inhabitants who had learned how to survive there. Now the desert planet would be Josef's sanctuary, and he damn well wasn't going to let anyone strike him here. After fleeing from the holocaust, he ordered the recall of all of his remaining forces to protect the spice operations as well as his refugee Navigators and other Ven-Hold personnel.

He still could not wrap his mind around what had happened: Kolhar was destroyed! The Butlerians had used forbidden atomics!

In warfare, in business, and in politics there were rules of civilized behavior. In humanity there were expectations. But these savages were not civilized; they barely qualified as human. After seeing what they had done, Josef was even more convinced that the half-Manford and his insane followers would destroy the human race if left unchecked. Mankind had accomplished too much over the millennia, built too much, created too much to let a wild mob tear it all down. Josef knew that he *had* to win this war.

And if Emperor Roderick would not stand up to them, then Josef would have to find some way to do it himself. He refused to let the march of history simply head off a cliff.

Manford had bombarded a settled planet with nuclear weapons, bringing about a catastrophe as had not been seen since the end of the Jihad. The madman! Such weapons were as reviled in the Imperium as the thinking machines themselves. Did Manford think the Emperor would simply ignore this? Roderick would be forced to turn against the Butlerians now.

Josef clung to that hope. This would be the tipping point indeed—it had to be.

He was wounded to the core, and not even Cioba's well-practiced Sisterhood skills could begin to soothe him. He took comfort in telling himself that he would send his large force of cymek war machines to Lampadas, where they would exterminate every last one of the antitechnology fanatics. In fact, he thought with a razor smile, once he overwhelmed that planet, he would make it his new headquarters. An eye for an eye, and more.

"You underestimated your enemy," Cioba said as their flagship drifted in Arrakis orbit, joining the other defensive forces there.

"I underestimated the extent of their madness; that was my mistake. I will never discount their state of mind again. I would rather destroy them down to the last follower than try to understand their motives."

As Josef gazed out at all the ships he had rescued from Kolhar, thanks to Norma's prescient warning, he knew they would form a formidable defense here. His ship captains had orders to immediately attack and destroy any Butlerian vessel that dared to approach the desert planet.

Josef could not overlook the possibility that the legless leader might have more warheads.

He could not tell whether even these remaining ships would be sufficient to defend Arrakis if Emperor Roderick decided to launch a full-scale invasion to recapture the spice operations. Josef didn't know what to believe anymore. The universe had gone berserk.

Were the Emperor and Manford Torondo working together as part of a secret plan? Had Roderick himself authorized the use of atomics?

No, that Josef could not accept. Roderick Corrino was not perfect, but he was still the man Josef had hoped would restore civilization. And the use of atomics would unravel the fabric of society, including everything House Corrino stood for. Roderick would never have authorized their use. It was unimaginable.

Josef suspected the Emperor didn't even know how the Butlerians had destroyed Kolhar. He had probably been told a lie. But the man needed to understand what the fanatics had done.

"My Navigators require ships," Norma Cenva said from her tank. "My Navigators require spice. You know this, Josef. We have been hurt badly."

"We hold Arrakis, Grandmother, and I do not intend to lose it. This will be our base of operations now, the most defended planet in the Imperium. You will have your spice."

"We rescued scores of Navigators from Kolhar, and I will guide and nurture them," Norma pressed. "Others will require vessels. The universe is ours—if you provide us with ships. With Navigators and ships, your fleet will be stronger."

Josef smiled as the solution came to him. "I'll have the ships for you soon. They are at Denali—another forty ships, old thinking-machine vessels. At this moment they are being fitted with Holtzman engines. When ready, each one will be guided by a Navigator. Is that acceptable?"

She drifted in her tank. "I will send Navigators to Denali to retrieve them. Yes, forty more ships are a step in the right direction."

⟶⟵

AS THEIR SHUTTLE descended to Arrakis City, Josef sat beside Cioba, trying to control his anger. He would not lose any more ground. He would put an entire crew of his rescued Kolhar employees to work in the spice operations and increase production at all costs. He would find more VenHold ships to add to the defenses that were already here. Arrakis would be utterly secure.

He growled, "I lost my banks because of the Emperor, and I lost Kolhar because of the barbarians. I will *never* give up my spice operations here!"

"No, my husband." Cioba sounded confident. "We will not."

His company had suffered a giant blow with the destruction of the spice stockpile, but Josef had ordered his Mentat administrators to dispatch all harvesting teams. They had scoured the Arrakis City repair yards and placed every available piece of factory equipment into service, even the older, inefficient harvesters. Josef intended to rebuild his supplies of melange, and his fortune. Once he satisfied the desperate Navigators, any surplus would be sold at exorbitant prices to the wealthiest addicts in the Imperium. Under the circumstances, it appeared to be the only way VenHold could restore its finances.

The Arrakis City spaceport was relatively calm after the VenHold crackdown on the Imperials and black marketeers, but it was still a lawless zone. Smugglers had begun to encroach on the new spice operations again, but Josef would put an end to that quickly and severely. He could no longer afford to be tolerant. He put all of his operations on high alert.

He and Cioba arrived at the fortress headquarters of Combined Mercantiles, whereupon he summoned Rogin and Tomkir. Josef sat tensely in the meeting chamber. "I need to leverage the disaster we just suffered on Kolhar—to open the Emperor's eyes." Even in the hurricane of defeat and devastation, Josef Venport could see opportunities.

Cioba and the two Mentats looked surprised, but he did not doubt himself. "Think about it. Manford Toronto just changed this conflict in a fundamental way. He stepped over a line that should never have been crossed. Suddenly, *we* are the victims, the horrendously wronged party for all to see. What that madman did at Kolhar exceeded his worst crimes on other planets. This was a crime against humanity itself." Josef's voice rose. "By using forbidden atomics, the half-Manford shows that he must not be allowed to exist in any civilized society. Yes, I know Emperor Roderick hates me, but he must be made to hate *this* more."

He looked around the room. "We have to make him see that I am not the threat he should fear most. I am the reasonable alternative who will ensure stability and the future of humanity." He turned to Cioba. "I've got to talk with Roderick Corrino face-to-face and clarify the situation for him. It is critically important."

"But you have already asked for that repeatedly," Cioba said. "He never agreed. You tried to force him to concede with your siege of Salusa, and now he will not even talk with you."

Josef took her hands in his, giving and receiving strength. "Then we have to change his mind—and for that I need you."

"Me? How can I help?"

"You were trained in the Sisterhood. Even if they spurned our offer of an alliance, *you* can still use the skills you learned. Go to Salusa and find a way to deliver a message to Roderick. Tell him I request a détente meeting, here in orbit above Arrakis. It is not exactly neutral ground, but considering recent events, I will not make myself any more vulnerable. He can bring whatever security he deems necessary. But we must have a discussion."

"Will he listen?" asked Tomkir.

"Manford Torondo just proved he is a mad dog with no respect for the laws or morals of humankind. How many more atomics do the Butlerians possess? Enough to threaten Salusa Secundus itself? What is to stop them from unleashing atomics on the capital world if Manford is displeased with the Emperor? Roderick knows it is a valid possibility. No matter what the Emperor thinks of me, surely he'll be more frightened of the Butlerians." He flashed a hard smile. "I'll offer to destroy Manford Torondo for him, if he will grant me amnesty." In fact, he would relish the job.

Cioba pondered. "What if the Emperor still believes you want to take his throne?"

Josef placed his fist on the table in the conference room. "No one but a deluded fool would want to be the Emperor of the Imperium. Roderick himself never wanted it, and I don't want it either." He beseeched Cioba. "Make him see that. Convince him that this is a sincere offer and not a trick."

She rose from the table. "I shall do my best, Josef. I'll use everything I learned from the Sisterhood—and Fielle can affirm the truth of my words. If Norma Cenva will guide a ship, I'll depart for Salusa immediately."

If you perceive that a person holds power over you, whether or not it is true, then your weakness is very real.

—MANFORD TORONDO, final Lampadas rally

The atomic cleansing of Kolhar had blistered the face of the planet and erased Venport's machine contamination. As far as Manford was concerned, the nuclear blasts had forever ended the hubris of that godless man. Venport was on the run, and soon he would be completely defeated. Any VenHold remnants elsewhere in the Imperium would be hunted down and dealt with as a matter of priority.

After that was accomplished, Manford would solidify his political influence and ensure that Emperor Roderick ruled with the proper mindset. The soul of humanity would be saved, at last.

Sitting in a custom chair at the window of his office on the fourth floor, Manford's heart swelled with joy. He had not felt such perfect satisfaction in a very long time. The spirit of Rayna Butler must be watching over him with pride, and he kept her beautiful icon painting close.

As his victorious Butlerian ships returned to Lampadas, the size of the crowds astonished even him. So many people! More than half a million souls had gathered from all across the world, and more had emigrated from other planets, just to be closer to him. Warm tears filled his eyes, and his heart pounded as if it might burst from his chest.

Beside him, Anari Idaho gazed out the window at the incredible gathering, as if vindicated that Manford had finally received his due. His look-alike double wanted to go out to be seen by the public, to "take the risk" among so many people, but Manford knew there was no real danger to his person. He sent the body double away and out of sight; the real Butlerian leader would face his followers himself.

Even after such a resounding success at Kolhar, Deacon Harian remained grim. "There will be hell to pay because of the atomics. The Emperor will not ignore it, and people will hate what you have done."

"Some have always hated what I do, but I do what is necessary anyway."

Anari added, "The battle for the human soul is not an easy one. We will silence those who complain too loudly."

Manford left unsaid: *Even Emperor Roderick.*

Now, when he looked out the high window at the throngs crowded across Empok, their faces uplifted in a delirious hope of glimpsing him, he knew that every one of them would forfeit their lives in service to his goals—Rayna Butler's goals. By carrying her eternal message, he possessed a weapon far more powerful than atomics.

Uniformed men stood around the Butlerian headquarters. So many pilgrims had arrived in recent weeks that guards had to drive the supplicants away, sometimes using brutal measures. New converts and avid recruits flocked to Lampadas, filling the city to capacity, straining its resources. Manford had returned from the cleansing of Kolhar with tens of thousands of additional followers who had joined him at Salusa Secundus.

Beside him at the window, Anari stared across an endless sea of faces. "You can feel the waves of their devotion, Manford. They want you to lead them to more victories. They want you to save them."

"I will save them, in whatever way I can. Our numbers swell with every triumph."

His clashes with Venport had been an extremely effective recruiting tool. The ultimate victory of the Butlerian movement was all but ensured now, but Manford secretly wondered what he would do after he won this struggle for the soul of humanity. Alas, the war would never be completely won, for humans would always be weak and unreliable, and their doubts would open them to new dangers against which Manford would have to protect them.

Anari continued to stare. "Of all your followers on planets across the Imperium, you know that I am the most devoted." She turned to him with those wide, guileless eyes that seemed to open straight to her faithful heart.

"I've never harbored any doubts of that, Anari." He wondered why she felt any need to remind him of her dedication. "No one else comes close."

Deacon Harian bustled back in with sweat glistening on his bald pate. "Security informs me the crowd is getting restless. They clamor to see you. They *need* to see you."

"Then I shall give them what they require. I'll both inspire and calm them." He did not reveal his concerns, though. These people were angry and ready to do something, anything. After Kolhar, their emotions burned like a wildfire that could slip out of his control. He needed to direct the explosion away from himself, somehow.

He remembered what had happened during the rampage festival in Zimia. The death of little Nantha Corrino had damaged the trusting relationship he should have had with the Emperor; no memorial statue, however large, would make up for it. The victory at Kolhar would not last these Butlerians for long. They needed to be unleashed elsewhere.

Anari fitted the saddle-harness onto her shoulders and lifted him without the necessity of asking permission, then settled him into place. She looked up at him. "Are you ready to receive their applause, Manford?"

"Yes. It is what they need."

The Butlerian security troops cleared a path, and announcements rippled across the city. With Deacon Harian beside them, Anari strode out of the head-quarters into the sunlight and the roar of the adoring crowd.

Earlier, Manford had reconsidered bringing out his stand-in for at least the beginning of the event. The designated body double looked very much like him, a man so devoted that he'd voluntarily let his legs be amputated so he could serve the Butlerian cause. The duplicate was his public face in dangerous situations.

But today Manford knew that his followers would have noticed the subtle difference in his appearance and voice. They needed him in person. That other legless man, the backup, could be used under lesser circumstances, where he was only seen from a distance or inside a carriage, but not here. Today, on this momentous occasion, no cheap substitute would do.

A thunderous wave of cheers buffeted him on Anari's shoulders. Manford raised his hands, and the thunder grew even louder.

For a moment, unwanted thoughts about Erasmus and his forbidden journals slid insidiously into his mind, intrusive images of the diabolical thinking ma-chine that had enslaved and tortured so many humans. Erasmus had loved to stand before throngs of oppressed captives. But Manford knew those downtrod-den people had never cheered the evil machine like this. Erasmus had never been beloved; he had simply been feared.

He remembered what the robot had written. "Humans are a resource, a tool, a weapon—but only if used properly. I continue to study methods of manipulat-ing their emotions, their biological programming. At best they are flawed tools and weak weapons. But there are so many of them."

There are so many of them.

Manford smiled at the crowd of admirers. He spotted Headmaster Zendur and scores of new, approved students from the reformed Mentat School. The rest of these followers came from other worlds, pilgrims who journeyed to Lampadas to prove their devotion for him. This planet could not support them for long. They would have to be unleashed elsewhere, and soon.

"My friends and followers," he said, "you gladden my soul. You make me certain that we will win the final battle."

The tumult of cheers died to a surprisingly quiet murmur. His voice was broadcast on speakers across the city. It was abhorrent advanced technology, he knew, but necessary, and Manford had given a special dispensation to the Committee of Orthodoxy, asserting that such communications systems were vital to the Butlerian movement and therefore approved.

"I am here to announce an important victory on Kolhar, where our forces dealt a fatal blow to Josef Venport and his enclave of machine lovers." The rest of his words were drowned out in another tidal wave of sound.

He would not mention the atomics for now.

From his shirt he removed the small painted icon that he kept with him at all times: Rayna surrounded by an angelic aura. His gaze lingered on it. "Rayna Butler would be proud of what we've accomplished, but our great struggle is not yet over. I need you more than ever, all of you. Even though we have crushed the stronghold of our greatest enemy, we must make certain Emperor Roderick guides humanity on the proper path. And I am the one to show him."

More cheers, which lasted several minutes, during which time Manford could not talk, and could barely think. Though Anari stood as still as a statue, he felt her grow tense beneath him.

Finally the crowd quieted enough for him to continue, "Some of you may be required to become martyrs—and that is a glorious privilege." Manford quoted an ancient rebel. "'The tree of liberty must be fertilized with the blood of martyrs.' Before going back to the Emperor, we will seize what remains of Venport Holdings, the ships in his Spacing Fleet, the monstrous Navigators. We will put an end to all known VenHold operations. Only then will we go to Salusa and make the Emperor see what we have accomplished. He dare not oppose us." Manford smiled at them, and the roaring of their voices went on and on.

Anari had not heard this plan before. In a voice only for him, she said, "It will be a slaughter if the Emperor does not clear the way for us to enter the capital peacefully. A slaughter on both sides."

Manford nodded, knowing that even a slaughter would be to his advantage. "The more of us who die gloriously, the more recruits we will gain."

I have never been attracted to a person's pretentious demeanor. A gaudy surface often obscures a hidden agenda. Rather, I trust the quiet, unassuming person much more than one who constantly needs to re-mind others of his accomplishments and embellish them.

—EMPEROR RODERICK CORRINO

After two weeks, Hana Elkora and her salvage team at the mothballed thinking-machine fleet managed to reactivate the FTL engines of twenty-five of the forty vessels. Meanwhile, Elkora had directed a skeleton crew to fly the robot ships back to Denali, one by one, where the rest of the repairs and refurbishment were completed. Kolhar had already delivered shipments of Holtzman engines immediately after Draigo sent his request, and the foldspace engines would be installed while the ships orbited the research planet.

Elkora had ejected thousands of deactivated robots that cluttered the decks of the reclaimed ships—"taking out the garbage," as she called it—while hundreds more were found and removed during the final operations at Denali, and all the robots were simply dumped near the laboratory domes, where they would be left to rust in the corrosive atmosphere, just like the old cymek walkers. The Mentat was proud of his progress and felt eager to report to Directeur Venport.

And then Draigo learned what had happened at Kolhar.

USING A SMALL spacefolder, Norma Cenva quietly delivered Cioba to Salusa Secundus. With her perfect mastery of coordinates, the Navigator woman deposited her passenger in a secluded meadow on the outskirts of Zimia. Cioba could see the magnificent buildings of the capital city a short distance away, and a gravel footpath just ahead led her to a groundcar road and the Imperial Palace. The walk took her an hour.

Crowds moved toward the Palace like iron filings toward a magnet. Dressed in the robes of a nondescript Sister, Cioba made her way with a clear sense of purpose until a trio of Imperial guards stopped her from entering the main archway, demanding to know her identity.

"I am Sister Cioba, and I have business with the Emperor's Truthsayer. Surely you recognize my robes?" Although Mother Superior Valya had refused to use her own influence to resolve the dispute, Cioba hoped that Fielle would help arrange for a brief conversation with Emperor Roderick. The Sisterhood owed her that, at least.

It took Cioba most of the day to navigate the labyrinth of the city-sized Palace among thousands of functionaries. At sunset, after contacting several other Sisters for guidance, she finally located Fielle in the echoing south hall. The large-statured Truthsayer greeted her with a cautious smile. "You take an enormous risk by coming here. After your husband threatened Salusa, the Emperor certainly has no great love for him."

Fielle must know that this was not a social call. Trying to suppress her agitation, Cioba said in a crisp voice, "I had to come here. The Butlerians have committed unforgivable crimes against humanity. No matter how the Emperor feels about my husband, he must be made to see who the real enemy is. Please help by arranging for me to speak with him, just briefly. I need him to listen to me."

The Truthsayer frowned, sensing her urgency as well as the truth in her words. "I suggest an indirect but more effective route. I might be able to arrange for you to speak with Haditha."

The Emperor's wife came within the hour, curious but wary. Fielle led her to a sitting room where Cioba waited. Seeing her, Haditha became tense and guarded, but Cioba preferred it to the vengeful anger that would have come from Roderick. This might be her only chance.

The two women looked at each other in silence while the Truthsayer stood as an intermediary, neither interfering nor helping. "I shouldn't be talking with you," Haditha said. "Roderick has declared your husband a fugitive from Imperial justice. Josef Venport assassinated his brother."

Cioba gave a slight nod. "And your husband has done everything in his power to destroy us and bankrupt Venport Holdings. We can't always excuse the actions of the men we love. When two such forces collide, the collateral damage ripples throughout the Imperium. Far better if they were just to talk, don't you think?"

Haditha remained stiff. "Why should Roderick listen to him? Why should he trust anything your husband has to say?"

"Because Josef is not your greatest problem." Cioba didn't hesitate, driving home the most important point. "The Butlerians have used forbidden *atomics*!

They brought on a holocaust that utterly destroyed Kolhar. Do not be blind to the true enemy of civilization."

Haditha reeled, astounded by the news. Watching her, Cioba immediately realized that the Empress had had no prior knowledge of the Butlerian plan. Although it was possible that Roderick had kept his collusion a secret from his wife, Cioba didn't think so. She had always believed that Manford acted on his own and did exactly as he pleased.

On one side, the Imperial Truthsayer nodded to Haditha, affirming the truth of what Cioba had just said.

Cioba marshaled her emotions and continued as if issuing an official report. "Manford Torondo bombarded our planet with an entire nuclear stockpile, without warning. Our cities were obliterated. Only a few VenHold ships escaped, rescuing Navigators and some of our personnel, but we still suffered a great loss of life—from *atomics*, my Lady! My husband has withdrawn to Arrakis, where he has gathered all his remaining defenses as a secure stronghold."

Haditha's voice was less steady now. "Your husband laid siege to the Imperial capital. He threatened our city with cymeks—*cymeks*! The Butlerians saved us. They rescued the Imperial Palace and my family."

"Josef did not come here to overthrow the Imperial throne. He did not come to destroy or remove Emperor Roderick from his rightful place—he came with a show of strength, so the Emperor would negotiate with him. Despite appearances, we were not driven away by the Butlerians at all—the VenHold fleet was forced to withdraw due to . . . unforeseen circumstances that had nothing to do with the arrival of Manford Torondo's ships."

She leaned forward, adding with great passion in her voice, "My husband just wants to talk with yours. Josef is a leader of industry, Roderick is the leader of the Imperium. They should be allies against the barbarians that mean to destroy our way of life."

Haditha was pale, shaken. Her voice trembled. "The use of atomics has not yet been verified. I have only your word for it—and even though you may believe what you are saying, you could have received erroneous information."

"Nothing erroneous about it. I saw the attack, barely escaped. Send a scout to the ruins of Kolhar," Cioba said. "Or better yet, wait for Manford to crow about his victory."

Fielle turned to the Emperor's wife. "She speaks the truth, my Lady. There is no hesitation in her words."

Cioba played her next card. "Manford has used atomics once. Does he have more warheads? If so, will he use them against us on Arrakis?" She met Haditha's gaze with her steely eyes. "Or will he keep some in reserve, knowing that he can't manipulate your husband the way he manipulated Emperor Salvador? What is to stop him from using atomics on Salusa?"

Cioba could see that her words had struck a raw nerve. She didn't need to argue further; Haditha knew full well what the fanatical leader was likely to do. Making a great effort to sound reasonable, Cioba said, "Josef asks for the Emperor to meet with him in private, in a safe, neutral place where they can discuss a resolution."

Haditha let out a sound of quiet disgust. "Why should Roderick trust the man who killed his brother any more than he trusts the man who killed our daughter?"

"I assure you, my Empress, Josef only wishes to run Venport Holdings and earn his way back into the Emperor's good graces. Let us join together to solve our mutual problem: Manford Torondo."

Haditha gave her a shrewd look. "What neutral place? Here on Salusa?"

Cioba shook her head. "The Emperor has put a price on Josef's head, so he will not leave Arrakis, which may be the only place he is safe, his last true stronghold. He suggests a meeting aboard a neutral ship in orbit over Arrakis, with as much security as the Emperor cares to bring."

"Your husband overwhelmed our Imperial peacekeeping forces there and still holds them hostage."

"Josef has always been a pragmatic man. Perhaps their release could be a gesture of good faith."

The Truthsayer spoke up. "I should point out, Empress Haditha, that having such a meeting here on Salusa would be problematic for a different reason. Directeur Venport would be seen, and word would get back to the Butlerians that the Emperor met with him. We dare not risk that."

Cioba could see that the Emperor's wife understood the logic of the argument, but a commotion occurred at the doorway before she could reply. Imperial guards escorted a flushed Roderick Corrino into the small sitting room.

The Emperor strode in and turned his gaze on Cioba like a weapon locking on a target. "I can hold you hostage and order Directeur Venport to surrender. How much does he value you? I would be curious to see."

Haditha spoke up. "Listen to what she has to say, Roderick."

"Her husband is a traitor and a murderer." The Emperor's face darkened. "He threatens the Imperium. He threatens *me*—"

Haditha cut him off. "The Butlerians used *atomics*, Roderick. They destroyed Kolhar."

Unexpectedly, the air shifted in the room, and the crystalline glowglobes flickered and dimmed. Norma Cenva's tank appeared on the open floor so suddenly that everyone staggered backward.

Norma's otherworldly voice came through the speakerpatch. "Emperor Roderick Corrino, you captured one of my Navigators. You tested him and interrogated him. Now Dobrec is dead. He gave up his will to live."

The accusation hung for a moment, and Roderick struggled to respond.

Norma continued, "Now Butlerian atomics have incinerated all Navigator facilities on Kolhar." She drifted in the tank with an accusatory stare and attitude. "Stability must be restored. Commerce must return. We need a constant supply of spice from Arrakis."

Her large face pressed against the viewing port. "Emperor Roderick Corrino, I personally guarantee your safety if you travel to Arrakis to meet with my great-grandson, as he asks." Her voice grew louder, booming. "This crisis must be resolved."

Roderick shuddered visibly at the sight of the Navigator woman staring at him, and Cioba added quietly, "*Please* meet with my husband, Sire. It will change the course of the Imperium, will *save* the Imperium."

The Emperor grudgingly listened as Cioba and Haditha explained the request for a secret détente session over Arrakis. When they were finished, he exchanged a deeply communicative look with his wife, and Haditha gave the smallest of nods.

Roderick glanced at Norma's tank, then said to Cioba, "I do not trust Josef Venport after what he has done, but Norma Cenva . . . is something else entirely. It is still a gamble, but I will go."

Is there no end to the impetuous nature of the young, you ask? Ah, but if their brash actions ceased, civilization would lose a vital resource. The secret is to harness that energy for good purposes.

—FAYKAN CORRINO, first Emperor
after the fall of the thinking machines

As Willem Atreides recovered from his injuries, he learned to his dismay that Vor had abandoned him on Chusuk. Bringing Tula Harkonnen to justice was supposed to have been their joint mission!

During his weeks of recuperation in a luxurious guest house at the Royal Bach Palais, the young man was restless even with the constant attentions of Princess Harmona and her excellent staff. He was impatient to be on the move again, to rejoin Vorian. He could not let his ancestor do everything himself.

Harmona obviously wanted him to stay. He longed for a normal life and a beautiful companion, thinking of her caring, charming personality as much as her physical beauty. She was everything he could have asked for, and more . . . but first he had a job to do. For Orry.

A paunchy male servant brought a tray of food for him and left it on a table in the sitting area. Willem thanked the man, though he didn't feel much like eating. Feeling edgy, like a caged animal, he paced around the main room.

He and Vor had almost caught Tula Harkonnen, but now Vorian was pursuing her alone, without Willem. *She killed Orry! I will not be left behind!* He'd spoken of this to anyone in the palais who would listen, but Harmona's personal physician was just as firm in requiring him to remain here, so that he could heal. Well, he had healed enough by now. Even with his undeniable feelings toward Harmona, he could not continue day after day in this velvet-lined prison. He might have forced the issue and left anytime he wished, but he had no resources of his own, and no ship that would let him follow Vorian Atreides.

He had only a written note from him, instructing him to remain safe on Chusuk until he received further word. Safe! His brother was dead and the murderer was still on the loose. "I intend to draw out the Harkonnens," Vor had written.

Each day became more difficult than the previous one. Harmona was aware of his growing frustration, and they discussed his concerns. Each night he went to bed with troubling thoughts whirling through his mind, and lay awake for hours. In the mornings, he felt weary, with nothing resolved.

But he did enjoy his time with the princess, and Harmona was almost, *almost* enough to make him forget. Yet there were too many unresolved issues for him to drag her into his uncertain life. He had to ensure that Tula Harkonnen paid the price she owed.

But apparently Vor had mentioned going to Corrin, luring them there, facing his enemies, and keeping Willem safe . . . a plan that did not require Willem's participation. Not if he had anything to say about it!

After knocking lightly, Harmona entered, wearing a maroon dress embroidered with the silver treble-clef crest of House Bach. Yet before she could even greet him, he stood and announced his decision in a firm tone. "I'm going to Corrin. That's where Vorian went, and I can't let him finish this without me."

She looked at him with concern, but not surprise. "You're not in peak condition yet. You should remain under a doctor's care for a few more weeks."

"I have been under his care for too long as far as I'm concerned, and now I am recovered enough. I'll try to be careful, but I won't let my injuries slow me down if I see Tula Harkonnen. As an Atreides, I have no choice after what she did."

"I know." Harmona nodded sadly. "House Bach can provide the funding you need, and I'll make the arrangements to send you to Corrin." She sighed. "I just hope and pray you will come back to me."

❧

BEFORE LEAVING SALUSA, Vor had liquidated another secret account to purchase a small spaceworthy ship, an antique from the Jihad era. He felt right at home in the vessel, and it reminded him of his beloved old craft, the *Dream Voyager*, enough that he mentally christened this one the *New Voyager*. The name was strictly for his own amusement, not marked on the hull or anywhere else; he kept the ship inconspicuous and managed to fly away with it unregistered, thanks to a large bribe. It was money well spent.

Despite its age, the craft was well maintained, and he was familiar with its inner workings. The *New Voyager* did not have Holtzman engines, but used a familiar workhorse FTL drive. If he'd been in a particular hurry, he could have bought passage aboard a larger EsconTran foldspace carrier. But the delay served his purposes. He had told his operatives to wait for two weeks before spreading the rumor in the Imperial Court that he'd gone to Corrin. By that time he would have arrived, and his preparations would be complete.

Pain echoed in his heart as he arrived at Corrin again. In his long lifetime he had lived so many years on so many worlds, experiencing loves and families and losses, but Corrin—the heart of the former Synchronized Empire—was where he had spent much of his youth, as a human with special privileges granted by his thinking-machine masters. Much later, Vorian Atreides had led the human forces back to destroy the place. Corrin was also where Abulurd Harkonnen had betrayed the Army of Humanity during the crucial moments at the Bridge of Hrethgir. That disgrace, that cowardice, had been the spark of the Atreides-Harkonnen feud.

Yes, it was fitting for him to be here now . . . and to lure the Harkonnens here.

After inoculating himself against residual radiation from the old atomic attack, he landed the *New Voyager* in a cleared area not far from the largest settlement. He donned protective filmgoggles against the harsh light of the red sun, and emerged into what had once been the glorious machine capital. He carried a satchel filled with clothing and small weapons that he might need to use in a pinch. If Valya or Tula came after him here, he needed to be ready.

Omnius's prime city had been flattened in the nuclear blasts, but many twisted towers of exotic materials remained as silent sentinels over a dead empire. Strange, stunted flora struggled to grow on the destroyed landscape, achieving no more than feeble footholds. It would be centuries before this planet would thrive again, if ever. His skin tingled as he remembered his youth in this place, before he went away and fought in the Jihad, before the holocaust here. This stark, haunted landscape still had an aftertaste of humanity's suffering. . . .

It was an unsettling homecoming. Everything he remembered here had been blasted into rubble more than eight decades ago—destroyed by *his* ships in the Army of Humanity. Even so, he had a strange, powerful feeling of belonging under the red giant sun. It would be fitting for the blood feud to end here.

If he could end it.

As Vor explored, heading toward the large settlement he had noticed in the ruins, he perspired under the harsh sunlight, but gradually grew acclimatized.

Scavengers now lived in the rubble in a makeshift settlement, and he introduced himself to a hard-bitten woman called Korla, the self-anointed Queen of

Trash, the planetary leader. She had a dirty face, a tangle of black hair, and a stained, patched-together radiation suit that looked more suitable for a burn pile than for daily use. An unusual, silvery flowmetal cape curled around her shoulders, as if the garment were alive.

Several thousand ragged, worn-looking refugees scraped out a living on Corrin. The wreckage of the once-great machine cities contained riches and oddities for those who were willing to risk the effort to find them. Many were working the piles now, using tools to drill and dig.

Vor gave his real name, because he wanted to be sure the Harkonnens could follow the clues. It was clear, though, that neither Korla nor any of the other scavengers believed he was truly the legendary hero of the Jihad. The Corrin scavengers didn't much care about a newcomer living there, though, so long as he posed no threat.

The real threat would be coming directly after him.

The husky-voiced leader led Vor up a rough, sloping pile of black slag. From the top of the mound, they saw scavengers mining scraps of flowmetal, using cutting tools and pulsing electronic devices. A pasty flow of the strange metallic substance oozed out of a cut the crew had made; Vor remembered the flowmetal used by the most sophisticated thinking machines long ago, but he had never seen these wild, unruly remnants.

The Queen of Trash nodded toward the group. "Our devices tune the collapsed flowmetal underpinnings to resonant frequencies, and that makes the substance mobile. Working together, my teams can coerce it into containers for shipping. It'll be worth a fortune, if we ever resume regular trade throughout the Imperium again."

That evening, Korla invited Vor to dine with her in an underground dwelling formed out of the frozen flowmetal to create a cavelike, sheltered place. The two sat at an irregular black table that had been shaped by cutting and grinding tools. Vor could hear the soft whirring of recirculating fans in the background.

"I don't know why you came here, Vorian Atreides," Korla said, making his authentic name sound like a fine joke, "but I assume you'll tell me who you really are whenever it pleases you to do so. For now, whether you call yourself an emperor, a prince, or a legendary war hero, you're one of us."

After dinner, the scavengers led him through a maze of dim, hermetically sealed tunnels beneath the wrecked city. Vor would make himself a simple and basic home here, and would wait for his trap to spring.

He had no idea how long it would be before the Harkonnens took the bait, but he felt confident that they would.

Vor did not think Valya would arrive with a large force. Even though the two of them were sworn foes, as the leaders of their respective noble families they should engage in a one-on-one personal combat between them, to settle every-thing. Honor and tradition dictated that.

But, to play it safe against someone who hated him so much (and now he felt the same way toward her), all evening long Vor had been looking for places to set explosive charges throughout the tunnel system—tiny, undetectable devices that only he could detonate, if they were needed.

The enemy of my enemy can still betray me.
The enemy of my enemy can still kill me.

—EMPEROR RODERICK CORRINO I

Thirty well-armed Imperial spacefolders arrived at Arrakis, bearing the Emperor on his secret mission. He hoped it would be a great enough show of strength to intimidate Josef Venport.

Roderick Corrino was uneasy about the proposed meeting with Directeur Venport, but the session could not be avoided. And since a fast scout ship had just brought him images verifying the destruction of Kolhar—it was true, the madman *had* used forbidden atomics!—Roderick knew that the Butlerian transgression required a strong and decisive response. No wonder Manford had seemed so confident, so cocky when he'd departed from Zimia with all his followers. It would only be a matter of time before he flooded back to Salusa Secundus with a large entourage, to make further impossible demands.

Roderick also realized that Josef Venport had never before been so weak, so backed into a corner. This might be the Emperor's best chance. He understood the wealth of possibilities that Venport Holdings had to offer, yet he wrestled with a silent, important quandary: How could he get control over the vital commercial spacefolders and the esoteric Navigators, and still get rid of Venport?

By careful arrangement, they would hold the secret détente meeting inside an empty, orbiting cargo container that had been verified as neutral to the satisfaction of both sides.

Despite Venport's difficult situation, Roderick doubted if his own Imperial military forces could defeat these remnants of the VenHold Spacing Fleet in battle, if shooting started. He feared a ploy from the Directeur, some deception meant to lure Imperial defenses away from Salusa Secundus. Maybe Venport intended to slip in and conquer the capital world once and for all, as he had tried to do before.

Yes, his Truthsayer had verified what Venport's wife claimed . . . but Cioba was one of the Sisters too, and Roderick could not be certain what tricks of artful deception she might know, or exactly where her loyalties lay. Or Fielle's, for that matter.

On the other hand, Kolhar was indeed destroyed. Atomics! There could be no denying it. Manford Torondo was indeed a worse threat to civilization than Venport.

It was a risky balancing act for the Emperor. With his defenses stretched paper thin, Roderick felt very exposed, yet he did not dare permit Josef Venport to see any sign of weakness.

He took as many warships to the meeting as he dared, leaving as substantial a guardian force in fixed orbit above Salusa as possible. Admiral Harte's fleet of slow-moving warships had already departed for Lampadas, where they would await their opportunity, and during that journey they were entirely out of reach of communications. They could not be recalled to reinforce defenses over the Imperial capital; the moment they activated their FTL engines and surged into space, they were beyond the point of no return. Unfortunately, Harte was expecting most of the Butlerian fleet to have been wiped out at Kolhar—but now Roderick knew that Manford's ships had emerged from the atomic attack mostly unscathed. When the Butlerian warships returned to Lampadas, they would presumably be as powerful as ever. Harte would not be ready for that.

Now it was more imperative than ever that the Butlerian fanatics be contained, or destroyed—before they could unleash another atomic attack, perhaps against Salusa next time. But to ally himself with a man like Venport . . .

In deciding to partner with either Torondo or Venport, the Emperor was faced with a Hobson's choice. Both alternatives were very bad, and presented their own large risks.

Roderick's nostrils flared as he remembered how Venport had stood smiling before the new Emperor's throne after the coronation, saying he was ready to get down to business, knowing all the while that he was responsible for Salvador's death. Then, once the treachery was revealed, Venport fled like a cowardly worm, whisked away by Norma Cenva. . . .

Now when Roderick entered the improvised meeting chamber in the orbiting cargo hauler, accompanied by his guards and Truthsayer, the Navigator woman's tank was already in the room. He knew that Norma's priorities were far beyond his understanding. Despite the distraction of the large tank, Roderick focused his entire attention on Josef Venport. His enemy.

The reviled Directeur had already seated himself at the negotiating table, his cinnamon-brown hair perfectly combed, his thick mustache trimmed, his eyes narrowed and intense. "Thank you for joining me, Emperor Roderick Corrino."

Roderick stood in front of the table, not yet deigning to sit down. "At least you acknowledge my rightful title this time."

"I acknowledged it when I went to swear loyalty to you at your coronation, Sire. I meant it then, and I mean it now—provided we can come to a reasonable agreement."

VenHold security troops were lined up at the back of the room, while an equal number of tense Imperial guards waited nearby, weapons at the ready, but Roderick doubted there would be any violence during this discussion. That was not Josef Venport's way. He preferred to do things behind peoples' backs.

Roderick took a seat across from him while the Truthsayer remained standing at his side. She frowned, as if trying to assess whether or not Venport was lying. The Emperor said, "I remind you that we still have your wife in the Imperial Palace as insurance, should you attempt any treachery."

Cioba had agreed to the arrangement, understanding the wisdom of it, though she would rather have been at her husband's side. The Emperor had made it clear those terms were not negotiable.

The Directeur placed his elbows on the table. "Surely you can see that your real enemy, our *shared* enemy, is Manford Toronto and his bloodthirsty mobs. They bullied, twisted, and manipulated your brother. They rampaged through the streets of Zimia, burning and looting. They killed your daughter. They overthrew the Mentat School on Lampadas and murdered or kidnapped your sister. And now they've destroyed my planet, using forbidden atomics." Venport leaned over the table. "How much more convincing do you need, Sire? You know full well they will turn against you next, if you don't do exactly as they say."

Noncommittally, the Emperor said, "I agree that the Butlerian mobs are cause for great concern, and their use of forbidden atomics—even against you—makes them infinitely worse. It is apparent that they would bend any rule, break any law, to achieve their aims." Roderick folded his hands in front of him on the negotiating table. "And their aims are not generally aligned with those of the Imperium. I can see that."

Venport smiled in obvious relief. "Exactly as I have always maintained, Sire. We must work together. I can be your greatest ally, if we find a way to put this unpleasantness behind us."

"*Unpleasantness?* My brother is dead because of you. The *Emperor* is dead because of you!"

Venport lifted his hands in contrition. "I understand your outrage, Sire. It was truly an unfortunate turn of events. Salvador's death was never my intent, though I admit I wanted to remove him from the throne in order to stop the damage he was doing, the weakness he was bringing upon the Imperium." He used his most reasonable businesslike voice. "I know you saw it yourself, Sire. You are nobody's fool."

"He was my *brother*," Roderick insisted.

"Sadly, my operatives were far too enthusiastic. I meant for them to take Salvador to a safe, sheltered place and hold him in temporary exile. I hoped I could convince him to abdicate in favor of your leadership. Let us be blunt, Sire— you are far more suited to the Imperial throne than he ever was." The Directeur shook his head. "But the plan went wrong. A sandworm came unexpectedly, and the harvester could not be evacuated in time. I offer my deepest apologies, and I ask you to suggest any appropriate fine as compensation. I want to make this right between us."

Roderick glanced up at his Truthsayer. Fielle had been watching the Directeur and listening to his words, and she gave an almost imperceptible shake of her head. Venport was lying or at least distorting something in his favor, just as Roderick had suspected.

The Directeur continued, "You've already seized the assets of my interplanetary banks, Sire, and a vast stockpile of melange here on Arrakis was obliterated." He narrowed his blue-eyed gaze. "I assume you had something to do with that?"

"I'm sure it was just an unfortunate accident, like the one that killed my brother," Roderick said, his voice dripping with sarcasm. "A situation that went further than I'd intended. Perhaps *my* operatives were too enthusiastic."

Norma spoke up from her tank. "So much spice was destroyed . . . a setback to my Navigators. And it was unnecessary. End this squabble." Her unusual voice seemed to carry a heavy undertone of threat. "If you do, the universe will be secure."

"You brought a military force to Salusa Secundus and placed the Imperial capital under siege," Roderick continued, as if listing the man's crimes. "You threatened my citizens and my rule. You used cymeks, and yet you rail about atomics? If the Butlerians hadn't arrived at the right time, you might have brought down the Imperial throne."

Venport folded his arms across his chest, squirmed, then put his hands back on the table. "Only because you forced me to, Sire. I never wanted to rule in your stead. Even the actions I took against your brother were because I wanted *you* to rule the Imperium. Not me. I know you are wise and competent, but you forced me into an untenable situation." The Directeur slumped back and glanced at Norma's sealed tank, as if beseeching her for advice.

Glancing at Fielle, Roderick saw that these words were true. Venport didn't want to be Emperor.

Emperor Roderick knew what the loss of Kolhar meant to Venport Holdings, and he knew that the company was nearly bankrupt after the seizure of their financial assets across the Imperium; the destruction of their spice stockpile had only made matters worse. These VenHold ships above Arrakis and his assets on the ground might be all the Directeur had left to his name.

Roderick assessed his nemesis, judging that Josef Venport was not yet defeated, but near it, and on the ragged edge of desperation. The Emperor intended to press his advantage. "And how do you propose to make amends?"

"Manford Torondo and his Butlerians committed serious crimes of their own, and I trust they will be punished. But who will do the punishing?" The business mogul's eyes narrowed. "I can help with that, Sire. Let us find a way to resolve our differences, and get back to business as usual."

Business as usual! Roderick fought to keep the disgusted expression off his face. *The man acts as if he wants to be friends!* He remained silent.

Venport pressed, "How can we end this feud, Sire? Please give me your ideas, and I will do everything in my power to meet your terms."

A strong Josef Venport would never have made such an offer. Roderick squared his shoulders and looked the Directeur straight in the eye. "Take care of my Butlerian problem—completely and immediately. Then, and only then, will we talk."

He knew that Venport didn't have enough ships or weapons to face off against the Butlerian throngs. Even if Manford had no more atomics to use against Venport, the fanatics could absorb appalling losses and still call it victory. But they would be weakened . . . perhaps weakened enough by the time Admiral Harte's slow fleet arrived.

Venport's answer surprised him, though. "It would be my pleasure to take care of that for you, Sire. Consider it done. We will level Lampadas, just as Manford obliterated Kolhar. Except we won't use illegal atomics."

Josef rose to his feet, went to the Emperor, and extended his hand, but Roderick merely gave him a curt nod. "We will talk again—if you succeed."

While lashing out against an insult can provide a certain gratification,
a long-anticipated and carefully planned revenge is far more satisfying.

—DIRECTEUR JOSEPH VENPORT, private
conversation with his wife, Cioba

Now that he had the Emperor's blessing—rather, his command—to destroy Manford Torondo and his barbarian followers, Josef felt vindicated as well as recharged. He gambled that Roderick would be true to his word, and if this was the price for putting the personal conflict behind them, Josef would gladly pay it. He had already wanted to eradicate the Butlerian vermin for his own reasons. He had intended to go after them with or without the Imperial sanction.

Obviously, the Emperor realized the necessity of eliminating the fanatics, even if he used VenHold to take care of the dirty work. This was truly a perfect solution, but the Emperor had no idea what kind of weapons VenHold could bring to bear against the Butlerians.

According to Draigo, their force of cymek warrior forms was ready to launch from Denali—more than one hundred battle machines with perfectly configured Navigator brains—not to mention the forty refurbished robot ships, which were ready to be placed into service as well. Josef intended to station those new warships at Arrakis, refusing to weaken his grip here while he went to Lampadas. No one would dare to challenge him.

And after their atomic attack on Kolhar, Manford and his savages had gone home to their primitive planet, where they were completely vulnerable.

Yes, this plan was indeed coming together nicely. Once they were back in the Emperor's good graces and the antitechnology cancer had been excised, the Imperium would be strong again. VenHold and *Josef* would be strong again! Then he could come back and resume his spice production with a vengeance.

First, though, the Manford-devil had to die, and that was a task Josef anticipated with great relish.

Leaving Arrakis, the VenHold fleet arrived at Denali, the base from which Josef would launch his surprise attack on Lampadas. Since the laboratory domes could not support the many thousands of extra inhabitants, most of his personnel remained aboard the orbiting ships during the two days of staging. Josef traveled down to the surface to meet with Draigo, Ptolemy, and Administrator Noffe, so that they could finalize the assault against Manford Toronto.

They were more than ready.

He also wanted to see Anna Corrino, his last bargaining chip. If all went well with this operation and Emperor Roderick was true to his word, Josef wouldn't even need her. Her brother still did not know that he had her there, safe but held hostage . . . much as Cioba was on Salusa Secundus. Once Manford was destroyed, if Roderick made amends and remained true to his word, Josef would be pleased to return his sister to him, unharmed.

Everyone would be friends again.

If the Emperor betrayed him, Anna would make an excellent human shield, as a last resort.

When the shuttle landed in the darkness in front of the clustered lab domes, he felt a thrill of fear and excitement to see five fearsome cymeks striding noisily toward them through the caustic greenish mists. As a sealed-environment sleeve connected the shuttle to the laboratory domes, Josef watched the immense walkers march along on patrol. Each of Ptolemy's redesigned mechanical warriors was more heavily armored than earlier models, carrying more weaponry than any cymeks that had fought during Serena Butler's Jihad. These were invincible.

Josef smiled to imagine how Manford Toronto would react upon seeing a large force of such battle machines land on his doorstep. . . .

During the détente meeting, he'd gotten the impression that Roderick considered him weak and wounded, perhaps even defeated, but Josef would surprise him. The Emperor had no idea about this Denali installation or the cymek army just waiting to be unleashed.

Venport entered the dome wearing formal business clothes, and Draigo was there to meet him. "Directeur, the cymek walker forms are ready, as are the Navigator brains to drive them. We are prepared to strike the Butlerians, on your command."

"The command is given," Josef said, sounding pleased, "in the name of the Emperor himself. Roderick finally recognizes the true scope of the threat posed by the fanatics. Prepare the cymek drop-pods and begin loading the Navigator brains. We are readying our warships in orbit. This will be a total, unrestrained attack, with no mercy and no survivors—not after what those monsters did to Kolhar. I want to launch for Lampadas as soon as possible. The half-Manford is there now, crowing about his victory. This is our chance to obliterate him."

The Mentat nodded. "We know he's used atomics—so we must consider that he might have more when we go against him. But I suspect that he will be hesitant to use atomics anywhere near his own homeworld. It would foul his nest."

"I was thinking the same thing."

"Also," Draigo said, "the forty refurbished thinking-machine battleships have already been dispatched to Arrakis, as you ordered, where they will hold firm against any incursion. Your operations there are secure."

"Excellent. Soon enough we will resume full spice production, expand our commercial routes with more Navigator ships, and bask in the Emperor's high regard . . . in an Imperium without the silly Butlerians." He allowed himself a satisfied smile. "We may be at the beginning of a new golden age after all."

While the Mentat conferred with Noffe and Ptolemy, Josef went to see Anna Corrino. He needed her to do something for him, as insurance. While he waited in the main admin office, Josef reviewed the initial Lampadas foray, during which a mere three cymeks had caused so much damage. He could only imagine what a powerful force of them would do against a world full of unarmed primitives.

Two figures appeared at the waiting room door, lovely young Anna Corrino and a muscular man who looked like an idealized reproduction of Headmaster Albans. Surprised, Josef rose to his feet. "You are Erasmus? This is your new body?"

The man lifted his arms and flexed his fingers, as if still marveling at himself. "I am, and it is."

Anna Corrino grasped her companion's arm. "Erasmus is one of us now. He is my lover and my true love. Thank you for keeping me safe here with him, Directeur Venport."

Josef gave the young woman a reassuring smile. Anna's primary mental damage had occurred on Rossak at the Sisterhood school. Afterward, she had been sent to be trained among Mentats, in the hope that Headmaster Albans could reshape her thoughts and make her normal again. When Draigo Roget whisked her off to safekeeping on Denali, Anna had been frightened, but he managed to convince her that the laboratory domes were a sanctuary against the turbulence in the Imperium. Anna seemed not to understand her value as a hostage.

Now she pressed herself against the biological body of Erasmus. "We are so happy now."

Josef smiled back at her. "Good, then there is something I need you to do for me. I think your brother is concerned about you. Would you record a message for me? We should reassure him." *For insurance.*

"My brother?" Anna's brow furrowed, as if trying to remember. "Which one—Roderick? Or Salvador?"

Josef kept his voice smooth and gentle. "I'm afraid Salvador suffered an unfortunate accident. He is dead."

"Oh, that's right—I forgot. A sandworm gobbled him up." She shrugged. "Salvador ruined my love affair with Hirondo and sent me to the Sisterhood school."

"Roderick is Emperor now," Josef said. "I'm sure he wants to know that you are safe. I would very much like you to record a holo message to reassure him. Could you possibly do that for me?"

"Of course, as long as I don't have to leave Erasmus." She slipped her hands around her companion's arm.

"No, I want you to stay safe right here, for as long as is necessary."

Erasmus's brow furrowed as he worked through the implications. Finally he looked at Josef. "I understand. He is right, Anna, it is very important that we say what your brother needs to hear. I will help you make the recording so that it says exactly the right words."

"Thank you. Record it as soon as you can." Josef looked into the human eyes of the independent robot, and a strange understanding passed between them. Erasmus was probably devious enough to develop a more effective recording than any Josef would have constructed, and it was obvious that Anna would do anything for him. "I'll review it when you're finished," Josef added.

Interrupting them, Draigo arrived at the office door, accompanied by two cymek carts carrying brain canisters. "The walkers are being loaded and shipped up to orbit now, Directeur. All Navigator brains have been briefed on the attack plan against Lampadas. Ptolemy and Noffe are eager to go."

Anna brightened. "Will you kill Manford Torondo?"

"We most certainly will," Josef promised.

"I'm glad. He's a monstrous, cruel man. He cut off the head of Headmaster Albans. Actually his Swordmaster did it, but Manford gave the order, so he's responsible." She frowned, reliving the event. "If you kill both Manford and Anari, that would be best."

"We intend to," Josef assured her. Anna seemed happy with the answer.

*For every scientist who dedicates his life to helping humanity, there are
ten thousand fools who are just as willing to destroy.*

—PTOLEMY, Zenith Archives

T he warship sensors were connected directly to Ptolemy's brain via
thoughtrode, so he was able to study the entire planet as the VenHold
fleet approached Lampadas. Manford Toronto was down there, the man who
had inflicted so much pain, suffering, and *ignorance* on the human race.

The last time here, when Ptolemy was accompanied by only two other cymeks,
they had dropped down to cause mayhem and kill a single target. Although the
latter objective had failed, they had learned much about the planet's vulnerabilities. Now this full-scale, Imperially sanctioned operation would mount a frontal
assault on the dangerous fanatics—using cymek walkers and advanced warships.

There would be no mercy, no peace talks, no prisoners taken. The Butlerian
infestation would be exterminated in their own nest.

Directeur Venport had said it best. This was a sentence to be carried out in
order to guarantee the future of human civilization. The titanic cymeks and the
bulk of the VenHold Spacing Fleet would be enough to do the job.

As the ships closed in, Ptolemy, Noffe, and the brooding Navigator brains
installed themselves in gigantic cymek walkers, each one an arsenal in itself.
When the preservation canisters were locked into place, the cymek brains
tested the thoughtrodes. The spiderlike walkers would be an agile and unstoppa-
ble army, ready to raze the city of Empok.

As the cymek drop-pods prepared to launch, Ptolemy wondered if he would
feel pleasure once he avenged Dr. Elchan, or just a sense of closure to know he
had at last done something for his friend and all the others the fanatics had
harmed.

When the armored containers were loaded in the launching bay, Ptolemy's external sensors showed him the adjacent pods containing Administrator Noffe and the other Navigator cymeks. They would smash the Butlerians like a hammer. Ptolemy swiveled his optical sensors to watch Directeur Venport enter the bay. The business leader stood proudly next to the cymek pods, with the black-garbed Draigo Roget at his side.

"You will launch as soon as we enter planetary orbit," the Directeur said. "Cymek forces will take care of the ground battle, while our fleet will have its hands full fighting the barbarian warships."

"Those old Butlerian vessels are no match for our shields or weapons," Draigo said, not in a boastful manner, just stating a Mentat analysis. "But it will be a tactical challenge, considering the size of their fleet. We are risking everything on this."

"With the Emperor's blessing," Venport said.

While he made sure that Arrakis was well defended, Venport had left only a skeleton crew behind at Denali, since the secret research outpost was secure in its isolation. Once they eliminated the Butlerian threat, the research station's reason for existence would go away, and Ptolemy looked forward to the day when he and Administrator Noffe could focus on other scientific work to help humanity.

"We will accomplish the mission, Directeur," Noffe said through the pod's speakerpatch. "Given the level of resistance that Lampadas is capable of mounting, we will not fail."

"I wish I could be down there myself," Venport growled, "but I'll do my share of destruction up here."

Alarms sounded as the VenHold fleet entered Lampadas orbit. The antique Butlerian warships scrambled to respond to the unexpected arrival. They blasted away in a pell-mell barrage without any tactical coordination. Explosions rumbled through the hull of the VenHold carrier, and Ptolemy's sensors detected energy discharges, but none of the enemy strikes penetrated the shields. Manford's defenders were like a child having a tantrum, growing more desperate when it didn't get what it wanted.

Draigo said, "We should launch the cymeks now, Directeur."

Venport's eyes gleamed with anticipation. "Yes, we need to do that."

Connected to his fellow cymeks through external sensors, Ptolemy watched armored pods tumble out of the bay doors of other carriers, dropping through intermittent, timed gaps in the Holtzman shields. Finally Ptolemy felt his own pod launch.

Speeding down through the atmosphere like a meteor, Ptolemy scanned upward to watch the VenHold fleet begin its clash with the Butlerian ships. Already, three of the enemy vessels were damaged or destroyed.

And it was just the beginning.

⟨≈⟩

ANARI IDAHO BURST into Manford's office, her eyes uncharacteristically wide in panic. "Venport has come for us—we are under attack by his fleet! They've opened fire on our ships in orbit."

Startled, Manford quickly concealed the Erasmus journal he'd been reading behind a pile of other papers. His rush of guilt vanished when he saw her look of urgency. "Venport?" he said. "But we obliterated Kolhar—what can he possibly have left to fight with?" He scowled. "I didn't know he was even still alive."

Deacon Harian strode into the room, his face flushed. "Apparently, he had more assets than just Kolhar, and now he intends to get his revenge."

Anari nodded. "Venport's ships have dropped more than a hundred armored projectiles through the atmosphere, just like the ones we saw before. I believe they are cymeks—and they are on the way down to Empok."

As if to confirm her statement, the projectiles began to crash around the city, and Manford felt a sickening chill. *We used atomics against him, and now he turns thinking machines against us.*

Anari reached down to grab him. "Let me take you to safety in the deep tunnels, Manford. I'll seal you in an armored room and guard you myself. We'll send your body double outside—"

"You will not!" He shook free of her grasp. "The demon machines are our greatest enemies, and I will not hide while Venport's monsters lay waste to my world. Now is the time for me to guide my followers—I will rally them!"

In a stern voice, Deacon Harian said, "Leader Torondo, this is the reason your body double exists. Let that expendable man take the risk. Anari can carry him into battle."

Manford was growing angry. "Millions of my followers came to Lampadas for *me*, to be my weapons in the fight for the human soul. Now is the time I need them most, and I won't let them be led by a counterfeit. Enough! There will be no further discussion."

Outside in the streets, the crowd was roaring like a beast. Some fled in panic with no safe place to go, while others tried to form a solid defense against the cymeks that emerged from their crash pods. Manford could hear explosions and the heavy grating sounds of mechanical limbs, humming pistons, and thudding footfalls—far too close. The giant walkers began to march.

"Take me out there, Anari. My faith is strong enough to face down these demons."

She looked torn. "But I swore to keep you safe, Manford."

"Then don't allow any harm to come to me."

Anari's thoughts and loyalties seesawed, and finally she secured her shoulder harness in place and lifted him onto it. Then she grabbed her sword and carried him out into battle.

WITH THE MENTAT at his side, Josef returned to the bridge of his flagship, which Norma herself had guided to Lampadas. Like birds of prey, more than two hundred VenHold ships had arrived at the Butlerian planet. Now, the enemy vessels standing against them were exactly what Josef had expected, the same ragtag vessels that had appeared unexpectedly at Salusa Secundus . . . the same ones that had bombarded Kolhar with atomics.

He would show the fanatics that reckless enthusiasm could not make up for the combined shortfall of inadequate shields and out-of-date weapons. Emperor Roderick would be pleased . . . as Josef himself would be.

By the time he and Draigo reached the bridge, the cymeks had been deployed on Lampadas, and above them the space battle was already under way. Josef expected to mop up the skirmish quickly; it was his task to take care of the barbarian ships in orbit.

The Butlerians shot projectile weapons at the VenHold fleet, and Josef frowned in annoyance as the bridge deck vibrated from the buffeting of explosions against his ship's shield. After watching the outnumbered ragtag ships closing in like small, overconfident guard dogs, he said, "Cut them to ribbons."

With Mentat focus, Draigo studied the warship positions, made a quick assessment, and issued instructions. With short, staccato sentences, he directed specific VenHold vessels to take designated positions and open fire. In less than fifteen minutes, seven enemy vessels had been destroyed and three others so severely damaged that they reeled away from the fight.

No, this would not take long. Josef drew a deep, satisfied breath.

Though he didn't issue additional commands for the time being, he sat back in the captain's chair, observing and enjoying. Down on the surface, Ptolemy and the new cymeks should be having an easy time mowing down the savages.

Beside him, Draigo gave a surprised gasp, and the command crew shouted. In an unexpected tactic, four Butlerian ships drove at full speed toward a large VenHold carrier in a suicidal charge. The Butlerians fired a spray of projectile weapons, hammering and hammering the VenHold shields in a frenzied effort, until the single ship's defenses were overwhelmed. When the VenHold shields finally failed, three of the enemy ships peeled away at the last moment, while the fourth continued forward, accelerating like a battering ram. It plowed into the spacefolder, and explosions scattered the debris of both ships.

Josef stared in disbelief. After a moment's assessment, Draigo said, "We're heading into the den of a madman—I am not surprised he would encourage the use of suicide tactics against us."

Josef's skin crawled as he looked around. "It might be worse than that. The half-Manford was willing to use atomics against us at Kolhar. What if he uses atomics again? We thought he wouldn't use them on Lampadas, not wanting to foul his own nest. But we might have been wrong."

The Mentat's answer was swift and cold. "We will find out soon enough."

Josef leaned forward. "Put all our ships on high alert to watch out for warheads being launched, and prepare for evasive action if necessary. He's not going to catch us by surprise. In the meantime, close ranks and open fire. Destroy as many of those ships as you can. They can't launch atomics if their ships are wiped out."

As soon as the VenHold fleet turned their weapons against the fanatical forces, the outnumbered Butlerian ships fell, one after another, slaughtered like cannon fodder. With each vessel he destroyed, Josef chalked up another bit of revenge for what these savages had done at Kolhar.

In addition to atomics, the barbarians had found ways to reveal even more aspects of their insanity, and they suddenly demonstrated one such tactic: The antique ships had been outfitted with old-style lasguns, a type of energy weapon from the time of the Jihad. Lasguns were known to interact violently with Holtzman shields, resulting in an energy release equivalent to a small atomic warhead. Thus, lasguns had been removed from any scenario in which shields might be present. No one wanted to take the risk of complete mutual destruction.

Except the Butlerians.

One fanatic ship fired a lasbeam directly at a heavily shielded VenHold vessel—intentionally—and the lasgun-shield interaction triggered a vaporization shock wave that disintegrated both the VenHold ship and its Butlerian attacker.

Appalled, Josef let out a wordless shout, rising to his feet. "This is insane!"

In the uproar on his bridge, even Draigo could barely keep his calm. "Lasguns, Directeur! If all the Butlerian ships are outfitted with them, they won't even need atomics against us."

Josef choked out the words. "They are completely mad!"

A second enemy ship fired a lasgun beam, triggering another blinding detonation that wiped out a VenHold warship while simultaneously eliminating itself. It was total mutual destruction, one Butlerian vessel for each VenHold vessel . . . and the fanatics were willing to accept the losses.

The Mentat was coldly analytical. "We outnumber them, Directeur. If they continue the attrition until nothing remains of their forces, part of our fleet will still remain."

"But that's not acceptable to me. We would lose half of our fleet before we obliterated the enemy." He shook his head. "It's insanity. We can't defend against such attacks. I won't accept that way of winning!"

Another lasgun burst, two more ships annihilated.

The Mentat made a swift projection. "Then the only way for us to survive is to cease using our shields, Directeur."

"That would leave us entirely vulnerable!"

"Vulnerable to *damage*, Directeur. But a lasgun-shield interaction guarantees annihilation. If we drop our shields, we eliminate their greatest advantage."

The VenHold fleet dispersed in an urgent partial retreat, spreading their ships farther apart to mitigate collateral damage caused by the pseudo-atomic explosions. Josef clenched his fists. "Damn it, drop our shields—but go on the offensive. Use all the weapons we have, full force. I want to make the barbarians wither."

❦

WITH THE THRUM of pistons and hydraulics, and the sound of weapons locking into firing positions, Ptolemy rose on his segmented walker legs. He felt the crackle of the electrafluid that kept his brain functioning. He was strong and alert as he strode into battle. He felt *invincible*.

Manipulating his multiple legs, he charged into Empok, where he saw throngs of people like ants from a stirred-up nest. Every member of that crowd was his enemy, every deluded fool who had flocked to Manford Torondo's call. Their spreading ignorance was a weapon of mass destruction.

Ptolemy could not forget the vicious fanatics who had surrounded his laboratory on Zenith, smashing his experiments and destroying his research; and with a simple nod from Manford Torondo, they had burned Dr. Elchan alive. The legless leader had sounded sickeningly paternal when he spoke to Ptolemy afterward: "It was necessary for you to learn your lesson."

Now, Ptolemy intended to teach a lesson of his own.

Throughout the city he saw columns of smoke rising as other cymeks attacked. Explosions leveled buildings, leaving only tumbled walls, fire, and rising dust. Flame-cannons ignited entire neighborhoods. His auditory sensors picked up screams of pain, angry shouts, and the delirious panic of the fanatics. Ptolemy had the option to silence the distraction, but he found it strangely stimulating.

Marching forward, he launched a volley of explosive projectiles toward individual homes. He stalked after the milling crowds and sprayed them with acid hoses, leaving hundreds of people writhing and smoking in the streets, their skin melting. One man staggered away, clawing at the jelly that ran out of his oozing eye sockets; he dropped to his knees, vomiting acid, as his whole body collapsed into a wreckage of smoking meat.

Ptolemy's flame-cannons incinerated the savages, and some of them continued to run for surprising distances before they collapsed into a horrific smoking tangle. His blasts of heat were so targeted and intense that skulls exploded as the brains inside boiled into steam. Then he widened the nozzle and mowed down crowds of hundreds at a time.

Swiveling his head-turret, Ptolemy saw dozens of cymeks wreaking similar havoc. Not far away, Noffe's walker smashed a clock tower with a thundering noise, then plowed through the rubble to crush a warehouse and a school before scampering over the ruins.

To Ptolemy's astonishment, though, he saw more than a thousand Butlerians rush *toward* one of the cymeks, not caring how many were massacred on the way. Only a small percentage of the mob made it to the walker body, where they used hooks and ropes to attach themselves, climbing onto the giant cymek like parasites.

Ptolemy realized that swarms of the people were also racing toward him. He blasted them with explosives, incinerated them with fire, burned their flesh with acid. A round orifice on his torso belched poisonous smoke and nerve toxins. In his immense form, he thundered forward, killing everything in his path.

It was exhilarating.

Still, the fanatics raced toward the cymeks, throwing away their lives for no purpose. The foolish Butlerians kept coming, and Ptolemy slew thousands of them.

Yet, tens of thousands filled the losses, and kept coming.

Death does not diminish the power of the truly faithful. The strength of a martyr is a thousand times the strength of a mere follower.

—MANFORD TORONDO, Lampadas rallies

The cymek walkers marched forward like monsters from the greatest nightmares of mankind, smashing buildings into rubble, slaughtering crowds as if they were massed insects.

Even so, Manford went out to face them. Bravely, he rode high on the shoulders of his Swordmaster. He showed no fear, because fear was a weakness—and thousands of his followers thronged around him. They did not flee from the deadly machines, but instead rushed defiantly toward them. With so much faith and strength all around him, Manford did not feel weak. Not at all.

Wearing a powerful voice amplifier, he shouted the familiar mantra to rally them: "'The mind of man is holy!'" They took up the call and turned it into a battle cry.

More than a hundred cymeks unleashed an array of appalling weapons against his valiant followers: fire, acid, poisonous smoke, explosive projectiles. Thousands of victims lay strewn across the city, smoking, melting bodies, writhing unrecognizable forms, nameless. *The faithful. The martyrs. The blessed ones.* The only shield the Butlerians had was their numbers and their powerful faith—something even demonic thinking machines could not defeat.

From Anari's shoulders, Manford waved his arms and shouted for his Butlerians to press forward. The mob flooded ahead without hesitation, knowing that the lives they expended before the mechanical monsters were not a wasted effort, but more sparks in a rising conflagration. Even surrounded by explosions, horrific screams, smoke and blood and terror, Manford felt fully alive and energized. "Tear down those machine demons!"

Anari raised her sword in front of her and strode forward. During her training on Ginaz, she and her fellow Swordmasters had practiced against combat meks, but those had been much smaller programmed robots, with computer minds. The fact that the cymeks were driven by traitorous human brains made these enemies much worse, far more dangerous.

The terrible battle machines destroyed everything in their path and kept going, but Manford had over a million followers here. Any number of sacrifices was acceptable, so long as the cymeks were destroyed and Venport was defeated.

Additional Swordmasters in the throngs now joined the fight, trained fighters who led countless believers in the biggest surge against the cymeks, a tidal wave of simple weapons and flesh slamming against the machine walkers. Wild and desperate people clung like bugs to the nearby warrior forms; they climbed up the segmented legs to reach the main turrets.

Deacon Harian accompanied a pair of Swordmasters, shouting as they led a mob of thousands down a side street and up onto the rooftops. They intercepted and attacked a cymek walker that rumbled close. Its flame-cannons and artillery projectiles destroyed the nearby buildings, but did not kill all of the people—at least not yet.

The two Swordmasters led the close-in attack, throwing ropes and grappling hooks so they could swarm the war machine. The mob members carried makeshift weapons: crowbars, clubs, and metal pikes; some even had small explosives. Those who managed to get close enough could sweep in under the flame-cannons and artillery projectiles. First, only a few made it, but then dozens of fanatics reached the core of the cymek walker, climbing its metal sides. As their numbers increased, they detonated explosives at the articulated joints of the walker, exploiting weak points.

One of its legs broke off at the joint, and the enormous apparatus groaned and collapsed. On the ground, the crippled walker flailed in a semicircle as it tried to stabilize itself. Seizing their chance, Deacon Harian and the two Swordmasters dismantled a second leg with explosives at the joints, and that kept the machine on the ground. Although it still fired detonating projectiles in desperate random directions, enough of the attackers survived to rip open its turret and expose the disembodied brain in its protective canister. They pulled the thoughtrodes free and tore the brain canister loose. Unguided, the walker body simply froze in place.

Deacon Harian lifted the brain canister and gleefully threw it to the ground below, where the infuriated mob smashed the naked Navigator brain into a pulp of biological residue.

As Manford guided Anari into the thick of the attack, he saw another group of ingenious Butlerians using heavy ground vehicles to pull steel cables. Dozens of them swooped under another walker form and used the cables like webs to entangle and trip the machine. When the cymek was slowed sufficiently, the Butlerians swarmed forward and overwhelmed it, despite heavy losses.

As a last defense, the entangled cymek belched defensive clouds of poisonous gas that settled over the oncoming horde, killing the faithful. But when breezes dissipated the smoke, a new crowd swept forward, and enough of them scrambled aboard the cymek to destroy its guiding brain.

Seeing the destruction of two cymeks, Anari brandished her sword, letting out a wordless battle cry, as Manford shouted orders from her shoulders. A wave of Butlerians howled alongside. She charged ahead, carrying Manford in search of another enemy. His throat was raw, his voice hoarse from shouting.

Riding on her sturdy shoulders, Manford could feel the spirit of Rayna Butler within him, and he touched the icon painting of her that he kept inside his shirt. He knew they would win here today. Even if victory cost the lives of thousands of Butlerians for every single cymek they destroyed, he would pay that price without hesitation.

Yes, he had that many followers to spend.

Anari must be feeling the energy within her as well. She jogged ahead, leading throngs of enraged Butlerians down a wide street and around a corner, where they came face-to-face with another looming cymek. The demon machine rose up on segmented metal legs.

With a smile, Manford faced his nemesis.

⤜⤏

IN SPACE OVERHEAD, the battle continued, with suicidal Butlerians using lasguns against the Holtzman shields before Josef could spread the word among his fleet to drop those defenses. The lasgun-shield interactions triggered a succession of pseudo-atomic blasts, which wiped out seven more VenHold vessels, and an equal number of their own, before Draigo's frantic message circulated. "VenHold ships, drop shields! Drop your Holtzman shields!"

Josef reviled the barbarian tactics, but was not surprised by them. As soon as all shields were down, he observed, "We are no longer vulnerable to instant annihilation, but we'll still be battered by the barrage from their conventional weapons."

"Mathematically, Directeur, our numbers of ships and weaponry are far better than theirs, and our hulls are strong enough to withstand a fair amount of damage," the Mentat said. "We should still succeed."

"I don't care what it takes to finish the task," Josef growled. "Destroy those warships before the enemy imagines he has achieved some kind of victory."

"I am happy to do so, Directeur." The Mentat guided their flagship forward, while transmitting to the rest of the spacefolders as they closed in on the Butlerians. Despite their limited technology, the enemy ships caused an inordinate amount of damage to the VenHold attackers, proving tougher to destroy than expected.

Draigo frowned, staring at the screens. "I'm afraid they have an advantage, Directeur. Since the Butlerians know we will not employ suicidal tactics or fire lasguns at them, they have maintained their own shields, while we are vulnerable."

"Then increase our bombardment," Josef said. "Overwhelm their shields. We have the power."

"The task is more difficult, Directeur, but not by an impossible amount."

Using their superior weaponry, the VenHold ships were relentless, pummeling and pummeling the fanatics. On one Butlerian ship after another, the defenses collapsed under the barrage—and waves of weapons fire destroyed them. Their fleet dwindled.

Even so, knowing that Josef's attacking ships lacked shields, the Butlerians pushed forward in an increased opportunistic frenzy. Their old-model warships could withstand several minutes of constant hammering before their shields failed. The barbarians grouped their ships and hurtled forward at full speed, like a salvo of gigantic artillery shells. They rammed into the unprotected VenHold hulls and destroyed three more of Josef's ships.

His throat went dry, and his pulse pounded in his temples. "They are all mad!"

"Directeur," the helmsman yelled. "Incoming ships!"

Josef looked up to see three suicidal vessels hurtling toward his flagship. "Evasive action—get us out of their way. But keep firing. Take out their shields."

The oncoming enemy ships glowed like comets as their shields deflected the play of weapons fire, and they blindly accelerated toward Josef's flagship. He braced himself, realizing that his vessel could not lumber out of the way in time.

"Grandmother!" he shouted at her tank. He knew she was watching the shifting battlefield. "Now!"

Suddenly, thanks to Norma, his spacefolder was in a different place, jerked sideways to the other side of the space battlefield. "Too many Navigators lost, too many of our ships damaged," she said. "We must destroy this enemy."

He exhaled a long cold sigh of relief. "Yes, Grandmother. They certainly deserve to be destroyed. I'm trying to do just that."

Even if the Butlerians proved to be more difficult to kill than expected, he would not retreat until the job was done.

ON THE GROUND, no matter how many of the savages Ptolemy gassed, burned, or shot down, they kept coming. He drew little satisfaction from his rampage, but he continued forward nevertheless, tearing a wide swath of destruction through Empok.

The Butlerian fanatics were like a plague, and their numbers seemed infinite. Where did they all come from? Tens of thousands, hundreds of thousands, maybe a million or more. They surged forward like cockroaches, crowding the cymeks with utter disregard for the appalling casualties they suffered. The streets were piled with bodies.

In disbelief, Ptolemy had watched them scramble over their own dead and take down one of the Navigator cymeks, dismantling its body, smashing the brain canister. In even greater horror, he'd watched them bring down other walkers with wrecking bars, wedges, cutting tools to dismantle a single joint or protected cable. Some attackers used primitive explosives at key vulnerable spots, while other rabid swarms simply used astonishing numbers and unchecked fanatical energy. They fell upon the cymeks, including Administrator Noffe!

In alarm, Ptolemy crashed his way toward his besieged friend, intending to roast these vermin by the thousands, but he was too far away to reach him in time. Noffe's walker form stalled under the weight of tens of thousands of Butlerians, many wielding crude weapons, and then they got to the administrator's brain canister.

Noffe had sacrificed so much already, and now in this pivotal fight for the future of humanity, the mob took him down. Through the communications link, Ptolemy heard Noffe's panicked mental screams until the ruthless barbarians cut off the thoughtrode contact and crushed his preservation canister.

Those screams had sounded much like Elchan's. . . .

Now, as Ptolemy thundered forward, infuriated and unwilling to stop, he came upon an even larger, swelling crowd. The mob was like a mindless organism with a single deadly goal. The people swarmed out of side streets and thoroughfares, climbed the remnants of burning buildings, and threw themselves from rooftops onto the cymeks.

Confronted by this new throng, Ptolemy's enhanced optical sensors spotted a familiar man riding on the shoulders of a female Swordmaster. The Butlerian leader looked confident and arrogant, as if he had the situation under control. The roar of the mob was deafening, but Ptolemy focused all of his hatred on Manford Torondo.

The Butlerian leader was shouting in a ragged voice that sounded like a thin and insignificant squeak, but he had a voice amplifier. "We will destroy you, demon—and all of your mechanical brethren! Our faith is a shield that you cannot comprehend."

The response of his people was deafening, primal.

Years ago, as a diligent scientist in his original laboratory, Ptolemy had felt insignificant and helpless, unable to defend himself. He now felt stronger than ever. His cymek body was nearly invincible, his weapons powerful, and his anger unquenchable.

Ptolemy amplified his voice, even though he doubted the Butlerian leader would remember him. "Manford Torondo, you and your followers must pay for your crimes against humanity—and I am the one to call in that debt!"

Manford had time to yell in a scornful voice. "You talk about humanity? You, a monster?"

A single blast from Ptolemy's flame-cannon or a drenching spray of caustic acid would have leveled the entire mob and incinerated the legless fanatic. But instead, he wanted to make Manford feel as helpless as the man had made him feel on that terrible night years ago. This was too personal a vendetta for Ptolemy to use a weapon of mass destruction.

Feeling elation, Ptolemy skittered forward on his mechanical body with swift, spiderlike grace made possible by the advanced thoughtrodes that he and Dr. Elchan had developed long ago. That was fitting. Ptolemy's optical sensors were focused on the Butlerian leader and his Swordmaster. He swept sideways with one of his claw-ended legs, smashing Anari Idaho aside like a tiny toy.

This knocked Manford out of his harness, throwing him violently to the ground. Ptolemy reached forward and snatched up the hated leader by his torso, even though the vile man tried to escape by scuttling away on his hands.

In the air, Manford squirmed and flailed his arms, looking so weak, so helpless. Ptolemy lifted him high even as the Butlerians screamed in rage and panic. With his visual enhancement, Ptolemy recorded the look of disgust on Manford's face. He wished it were fear instead, but realized he was witnessing the bravery of fanaticism, Manford's willingness to become a martyr. Ptolemy didn't care about that, he just wanted the man dead.

"For the future of humanity," Ptolemy shouted through his speakerpatch. "For the blood of all your victims!" He reached up his second clawed hand, holding Manford Torondo with both mechanical arms in front of the raging crowd, dangling him over them. The fanatical leader yelled something, but his words were drowned out in the howls from the Butlerians.

"And for Elchan!"

It was like a child ready to pluck the wings off a fly.

FAR BELOW, STILL grasping her sword, Anari lurched to her feet, coughing blood and looking upward in horror. She knew that something was broken inside her, but she didn't care about her own pain. She screamed, spraying red from her mouth. "No, not Manford!"

As if they had been paralyzed all at once, tens of thousands of Butlerians gasped in an instant of sickening silence.

In the last second Manford looked down at his loyal Swordmaster and companion, with an expression of deep love and a beatific acceptance of his fate. His loyal Swordmaster remembered something he had said to her once: *The strength of a martyr is a thousand times the strength of a mere follower.*

Then the cymek ripped Manford apart and threw the bloody remnants—torso, arms, entrails, head—in different directions.

A person who is willing to admit defeat is simply unskilled at redefining the situation.

—DIRECTEUR JOSEF VENPORT,
address to surviving scientists at Denali

After a long slow voyage, Admiral Harte's fleet of old-style FTL ships had arrived at the outskirts of the Lampadas system, unseen. In accordance with his orders from the Emperor, Harte directed his ships to stand down and wait in communication silence, setting a trap to be sprung when the time was right.

His crew deployed stealth-wrapped recon satellites, scout buoys, and shielded picket ships to monitor Lampadas and the Butlerian fleet that had returned from attacking Kolhar. He had been surprised to see so many of their warships intact after their assault on VenHold's fortified headquarters. Both Emperor Roderick and Harte had assumed that the Butlerians would be decimated, if not completely destroyed. His fleet was supposed to be no more than a mop-up operation.

But Manford Torondo's forces had returned home, looking only slightly bruised—and far too strong for his ships to fight in a head-to-head battle. And if he attacked the Butlerians and failed to eradicate them completely, the fanatics would retaliate in ways the Imperium might not survive. No, it was better to be cautious until he understood the complete situation.

And so his fleet monitored the planet, gathering information, looking for an opening. His powered-down ships hung in the outer darkness for days.

On the flagship he met regularly with his team of tactical specialists and space combat experts. Harte had all the advance information he needed, including comprehensive data on the Butlerian fleet's abilities and weaknesses. The Emperor had given him great latitude in his orders, instructing him to look for an opportunity—and if one came up, to pounce on it.

Then such an opportunity appeared. The VenHold Spacing Fleet arrived unexpectedly and launched a full-scale attack against the Butlerians on Lampadas.

"Battle stations!" Admiral Harte shouted. Across his gathered warships, officers ran to their posts; weapons grids powered up, artillery launchers loaded.

But Harte told them to wait. They hung silently in position, observing the clash in Lampadas orbit.

Long-distance surveillance showed the escalating space battle. Detonations vaporized pairs of warships at a time, both Butlerian and VenHold; some of Manford's ships engaged in suicide runs, ramming and destroying opposing vessels so easily that Harte had no choice but to conclude that the VenHold fleet was, for some incomprehensible reason, *unshielded.*

The VenHold ships fought back with great fury, destroying one Butlerian vessel after another. The Admiral sat back in astonished satisfaction as the two enemies of the Imperium tore each other apart. "They are doing our work for us," he said to his adjutant.

Like spectators at a sporting event, Harte's crew observed the battle for hours. Manford's fleet was decimated, and the VenHold vessels—reeling despite their victory—had suffered severe damage because they refused to use their shields.

Harte narrowed his gaze. Only a few Butlerian ships drifted in orbit, their crews undoubtedly bloodied and weak, and the damaged VenHold ships were completely vulnerable. He could not pass up such a chance.

Harte felt his anger rise toward Josef Venport, the man who held the Admiral's ships hostage for months . . . the man who had laid siege to Salusa and tried to overthrow the Emperor. Venport was an enemy of the Imperium, just as the Butlerians were.

When dispatching this slow, silent fleet from Salusa Secundus, Roderick Corrino had given Harte full authority to act, and now his decision was clear. The chance to finish off Venport was right there in front of him. "Attack!" Harte shouted into the fleet comm-system. "Go in with weapons blazing."

Maintaining communications silence afterward, his surprise fleet accelerated down toward Lampadas from the edge of the solar system. The VenHold ships might have been able to pick them up on long-range sensors, but Harte was confident no one was looking in his direction. He would catch Directeur Venport completely unawares.

And if any Butlerian ships were still fighting, Harte's battle group would "accidentally" destroy them, as unintended collateral damage. The Emperor had made it clear that it was necessary to eliminate both Josef Venport and Manford Toronto in order to build a strong Imperium. Harte's preference would be to leave no survivors on either side.

Emperor Roderick would give him a medal.

Coming in from behind, mostly unseen, his fleet of restored Imperial battleships blasted their way into the reeling remnants of the space battle. With their combined firepower, Harte's ships destroyed ten unshielded VenHold vessels in the first two minutes.

The comm-lines burst into life with the remnants of the Butlerian fleet declaring, "We are saved! The Imperials have come to rescue us!" Harte ignored the irony, and then Directeur Venport demanded to know who these new attackers were.

Umberto Harte took great pleasure in responding to Venport. "It is an old friend, Directeur. Remember Admiral Harte? By order of Emperor Roderick Corrino, your life is forfeit as a criminal and traitor to the Imperium." He turned to his weapons officers. "Continue firing until the job is done."

⤜∾⤏

AS THE CYMEK tossed the pieces of Manford's mangled body to the streets, Anari screamed and sobbed at the grisly sight. She dropped to her knees and pounded her fist into the ground, ignoring the pain of her shattered ribs and internal bleeding. Her grief ignited a torch of anger and vengeance.

For Manford!

Energized by the memory of their beloved leader, she rose to her feet. Her eyes were bright and fiery, her expression fixed like a mask. Years ago, she had given her life over to Manford, had sworn to protect him. She had failed her master, the worst of all possible failures—he was dead.

She let out a wordless howl, gestured with her sword. Anari didn't need to give instructions. She merely yelled, "For Manford!"

Tens of thousands of impassioned Butlerians charged forward screaming his name. From across the city, hundreds of thousands joined them. Sweaty, wild-eyed, some burned and bleeding from fighting the cymeks; one man had a broken arm with a splintered bone protruding from his skin, but he seemed to use the pain as euphoria and staggered forward howling his challenge. The sweeping crowd ran into the fray without a care for their own survival, chanting, "Manford! Manford! Manford!"

Against such numbers, even the strongest armor and advanced cymek weaponry could do nothing. The screaming fanatics surged onto Ptolemy's cymek walker and scrambled up the blood-smeared metal limbs. They broke apart the legs with wrenches and cutting tools, dismantled the cab, blew open the turret, and yanked out Ptolemy's brain canister.

Howling and screaming, they held up the transparent cylinder, grabbed it and passed it from one set of hands to another. They were bloody, their fingers torn, their nails ripped off from clawing at the metal machine. But they had their enemy now, their prize, the one who murdered Manford.

They lifted Ptolemy's canister high. It was disconnected from sensors and the speakerpatch, so he could not even scream. With a resounding roar of victory, they smashed open the seal, poured out the blue electrafluid, and dumped the naked pink brain onto the ground.

Thousands of brutal feet stomped until Ptolemy was no more than a thin splattered smear.

⊱≋⊰

AS THE RISING tide of fanatical outrage surged across Empok, the crowds understood how to achieve their ultimate victory. As if possessed by the spirit of Manford himself, Anari led the infuriated followers in wave after wave of destruction. They all knew what to do. In their righteous rage, nothing could stop them.

Hundreds of thousands of Butlerians took down every last one of the rampaging cymeks. The fanatics paid an unspeakably high cost in blood—but they won.

Letting the mayhem continue on its own, Anari went back and wept over the torn remnants of Manford's body. She cursed herself for failing to die in his place. *She* should be the one torn apart. Manford should still be alive!

Now, in her terrible misery, she understood exactly how Manford had felt when he held the mangled remains of his beloved Rayna in the wake of the assassin's bomb blast. Yet Manford had used that anguish and fury to become a bright new flame, the next leader of the Butlerians.

A position he could no longer hold.

Anari touched Manford's blood-soaked shirt, felt a hard, flat object inside, and drew out the stained icon painting of Rayna Butler surrounded by a halo of purity. He had treasured this, carried it with him every waking moment. Anari Idaho clasped the icon against her breast, feeling a warmth of love, and knowing exactly what Manford and Rayna would want her to do now.

The Butlerians needed a new leader.

⊱≋⊰

SHAKEN BY THE surprise arrival of the Imperial ships, Draigo Roget scrambled to the flickering tactical console of the flagship. "We are betrayed, Directeur." Harte's fleet had plunged in from nowhere, opened fire on their unshielded ships. "The Emperor is attacking us."

"But we are here on Roderick's own orders!"

The Mentat said, "They hit us right when we were most vulnerable. A masterful treachery."

The realization sickened Josef. "The Emperor sent them here to crush us while our shields were down and our backs were turned. Get those shields back up!"

Harte's attack caused enormous damage to Josef's flagship in the brief moments before the crew could reactivate their Holtzman shields. Meanwhile, on the live feeds from his cymek army down below, he was appalled to see one warrior machine after another go off-line, destroyed by hordes of savages.

Josef ordered his warships to ignore the pathetic scraps of Manford's fleet and open fire on the Imperial vessels instead. They responded, but Draigo gave a grim Mentat assessment. "After the space battle, our weapons are mostly depleted, Directeur. Even our restored shields are far weaker than they should be. We have suffered great damage."

Under concentrated Imperial fire, one more VenHold ship fell, its hull ripped open and engines blown off-line; the dying vessel drifted, a dark hulk in space among the other wreckage.

Josef tore the words out of his throat. "These—losses—are—*unacceptable!*"

Norma Cenva's voice blared across the static and sparks of the flagship's bridge. "My prescience did not warn me of this attack. Now too many of my Navigators are lost and we must retreat."

Josef knew she was right. Admiral Harte intended to wipe them out—and had the weaponry to do so. Their shields were weakening, and their depleted weapons were no match for this large unexpected force. They had been cheated by the Emperor himself.

At least his vessels were faster, since Harte's ships did not have Holtzman engines. "Tell your Navigators, Grandmother! Withdraw whatever ships remain."

"They will expect us to go to Arrakis, Directeur," Draigo said.

"Arrakis is well protected—no, we should go to our Denali stronghold, where they'll never find us. Grandmother, set our course."

The Imperial fleet continued to fire, causing more and more damage, and Josef needed to buy just another few moments as the Holtzman engines built up enough power to fold space.

He had one last card to play. It would be a close thing.

He transmitted a parting shot designed to make the Emperor think twice. "Admiral, you should know that Anna Corrino is safe in my custody. Her life is in my hands. Consider your next actions with extreme care. Unless you cease firing immediately, the Emperor will never see his sister again."

On the comm screen, Harte was livid, but he did call off the continuing weapons barrage. "Directeur, I demand—"

The Imperial ships withdrew for just a moment, and it was enough time. The flagship's Holtzman engines thrummed as Josef spun to face the Navigator tank. "Now, Grandmother."

All the remaining VenHold ships vanished.

A person's sense of balance is measured by how he handles the unexpected. The ability and will to survive in the face of unforeseen challenges is one of the most admirable of all human traits. Thinking machines cannot begin to understand it.

—GHAN MUMBAI, philosopher of the Jihad

Under the ruins of Corrin where he had made his new home, Vor awoke to the sound of screaming—many people in terrible agony. He was instantly alert. Had Valya Harkonnen come here with assassins?

The screams! As he bolted out of his sleeping chamber into a connecting tunnel, he experienced a bright flashback from the first century of the Jihad: There had been an explosion below decks during a space battle, and backwash fires had caused emergency bulkhead doors to seal the engine compartment. Vor and his fellow soldiers had tried unsuccessfully to free the trapped engineers, and they heard the screams of the men and women being roasted alive for ten of the longest minutes of his life. . . .

This sounded just as horrific.

His reflexes kicking in, Vor ran toward the screams with no thought for his own safety. He had survived countless challenges in his life, but merely surviving was not enough. Vorian Atreides had been programmed to help others.

In the dimly lit tunnels, numerous doorways led to sleeping compartments, and more of the ragtag scavengers began to emerge as he ran by. Vor didn't answer their shouted questions, asking him what was going on, couldn't take the time to reply. He just kept running toward the screams, his mind churning with his own questions. Had the Harkonnens launched a military attack on Corrin? Would they strike the entire settlement just to get at him?

But would Tula or Valya be so blatantly destructive? He didn't think so. *They would want to get me. Personally.*

The screams continued outside, and it occurred to him that this might be a trap, designed to lure him out. He ignored the worry.

Ahead, a strange glow shimmered from where a stairway descended to the larger and deeper main tunnel. He peered down to see a river of silvery liquid gushing through the lower tunnel like flowing metal blood, a living substance that pulsed like a mindless amoeba . . . and frantic scavengers were caught in the powerful flow. Like drowning victims, they flailed their arms and yelled for help. Some wore protective suits, but most were vulnerable. The malicious quicksilver engulfed them. Even as they struggled to get away, the powerful flow seemed to fight back, pulling them under.

Choking on the thick, bitter tang in the air, Vor scrambled down the stairs to reach the trapped scavengers. Their resonance extraction operations had somehow broken down the flowmetal and left it unconstrained. Now it seemed to be on a mindless rampage.

A wiry woman in a protective suit floated toward him in the current, struggling to stay above the surface; her face was covered by a half-mask breather. Boxy equipment floated alongside her, a set of the resonance manipulators that Korla's people used to extract flowmetal from the ruins. A deep mining team must have triggered this unexpected backlash, and Vor didn't know how it would ever stop.

The desperate woman yelled something that was muffled by her mask. She reached out to Vor, and he grabbed hold of her gloved hand. Because she was coated with a film of flowmetal, his grip nearly slipped off, but he clenched tighter and used his other hand to grab her by the elbow. He hoisted her onto the stairway, where she shuddered, dripping silvery liquid and retching.

Another man fought against the thickening metallic flood, struggling to reach Vor. But a swell of the flowmetal reached up to engulf his head and sucked him under the shimmering, quivering surface. The man's screams fell silent.

Two more scavengers were swept past in the flow, still struggling, followed by a dead woman floating facedown, all of them well beyond his reach. The flowmetal pulled the bodies along in a powerful current, lifted them up, and compressed around them like a tightening fist. The men cried out, but their voices were overwhelmed by the sound of cracking bones.

Heaving deep breaths on the precarious stairs, the woman Vor had rescued said, "We hit a big flowmetal vein, and our resonators started a cascade. It broke underground barricades and flooded out—much more than we could handle. Sometimes the damned stuff seems alive!"

Since this had once been the central city of the evermind Omnius, Vor realized that perhaps the flowmetal *was* alive, in an eerie, machine way. Two more bodies drifted past, already crushed by the flowmetal, their arms and legs twisted at unnatural angles.

The silvery, glowing river made a scraping, grinding noise as it surged through the tunnel like a force of nature, and in a matter of minutes it was past, leaving wreckage and corpses behind. The tunnel was empty now, except for oozing patches that clung to the walls and shining puddles on the floor. Vor felt great sadness that he had not been able to save more of the victims.

Beside him, the rescued woman shuddered with exhaustion and fear. Vor looked behind him to see other bedraggled people crowded at the top of the stairwell, just watching him. Korla stood with them, wearing her scuffed jumpsuit and flowmetal cape.

The rescued woman looked in fearful revulsion at the flowmetal staining her outfit, then shook her head. "Thank you. I'm Horaan Eshdi."

"And I am Vorian Atreides."

"Maybe you truly are him," Korla boomed out. "The real Vorian Atreides might have done something like that." Her expression went dark. "This is the worst disaster we've encountered, but not the first. Last year another flowmetal surge collapsed an entire section of the tunnels, killed twelve of us."

As the scavengers regrouped, Vor was astonished to hear his own name called over the comm that each of the workers carried—a familiar male voice. "Calling the settlement ahead. Vorian Atreides? Vorian! I know you came here. I see your ship."

"There's a small drop-shuttle on its way down from orbit." Korla checked her comm, frowned at Vor. "Just landed."

The group of scavengers climbed out to the surface of the blasted world, where the night had a ruddy tinge from the backscattered light of Corrin's red sun. Around them, the ruined city seemed to be shifting and moving, like boulders in a slow, glowing lava flow.

Korla peered all around her, saw the lights of the landed shuttle, and barked into the comm, "Who's calling? Identify yourself out there."

Vor could make out a suited figure picking its way carefully over the unstable ground. An answer came over the comm, "My name is Willem, and I'm looking for Vorian Atreides. I'll pay a large reward to anyone who can direct me to him."

At the offer of the reward, the comm-system filled with "helpful" scavenger voices. Vor stiffened, worried that Willem had left his safety on Chusuk. He had wanted the young man to stay away while he faced the Harkonnens himself and ended the decades-long feud. Was it so terrible for Willem to have remained behind with Princess Harmona? But Vor should have known Willem would never be satisfied with a passive, comfortable role on the sidelines. He sighed.

The young man waved to him, trudging over the rubble toward the group of scavengers, and Vor realized he was glad to see him anyway. When they came together, he said, "It's dangerous here."

Willem's eagerness would not be shaken, though. "That's not much of a welcome! I came a long way to see you. You abandoned me on Chusuk."

"To recover from your injuries—with a beautiful woman."

Willem seemed embarrassed. "I am fully recovered. And Harmona is waiting for me, waiting for us to finish the work we have to do."

"I left a message for you to stay away."

"I decided to ignore it." Willem grinned. "And if you were me, you would have done exactly the same thing. I need to be here with you—if they're coming for you. You're luring the Harkonnens here."

Instinctively, Vor glanced up at the starry, red-tinged sky, but saw no sign of any approaching craft. If Willem had tracked him down this quickly, then maybe the Harkonnens would not be far behind.

The young man lowered his voice. "You're setting a trap, aren't you?"

"Yes, but it's my responsibility to spring it. You have a future, and can still have a family. I made arrangements for you on Salusa Secundus, at the Imperial Court. The Emperor will personally give you a position—all you have to do is show up." His voice took on a pleading tone. "Go live your life, a normal life. Let me take care of this."

With a stubborn shake of his head, Willem said, "Not alone. You always spoke to me about Atreides honor. I'm not going to abandon you. I couldn't live with myself if I did."

Vor looked at him for a long while. This young man was, after all, an Atreides, and Vor had made him understand all the honor and tradition of that name. Willem was doing exactly what he would have done himself. How could Vor possibly send him away?

"All right, then I can use your help."

The mass deaths and injuries that occurred in this place were tragic, but necessary. We must move on from here. My Imperium is now a better place.

—EMPEROR RODERICK CORRINO,
surveying the battlefields of Lampadas

With the death of Manford Torondo and the subjugation of Lampadas, the backbone of the Butlerian movement had been broken. Exactly as the Emperor had hoped.

As soon as the swift courier arrived at the capital planet, Roderick commissioned an EsconTran spacefolder to transport his ornate ceremonial barge and Imperial entourage, along with a strong force of peacekeeping troops that would remain behind on Lampadas. He would meet with Admiral Harte, while the last few fanatics were still reeling from their utter defeat.

Most of the surviving Butlerians were on Lampadas, but he knew there were others around the Imperium, little clusters here and there, and some planetary officials who had been sympathizers—and might still cause problems. He'd seen the intelligence reports. But any fanatics remaining would be nothing compared with what they had been under Manford Torondo. There might be a few brushfires to put out, but no more.

Roderick made the triumphant announcement from the Imperial Palace before he departed, encouraging independent traders and couriers to disseminate the news across the Imperium. The barbarian movement would now crumble, and Admiral Harte would keep the core of the surviving fanatics bottled up on Lampadas in the meantime. How long would it take for the rest of the planetary leaders to renounce their antitechnology vows and open themselves to unrestricted trade again?

All was as it should be. Manford Torondo was dead. Josef Venport was defeated.

And Roderick Corrino was Emperor. He had an empire to rebuild and new interstellar business consortiums to develop.

After making his bargain with the Directeur, he had not intended for
Admiral Harte to attack the unwary VenHold forces from behind. It seemed a
deceitful, even dishonorable move, and Josef Venport surely believed that the
Emperor had betrayed him, but Harte had been completely cut off from communication. There had been no way to stop him.

But now Roderick knew about Venport's own added treachery, that he had
kidnapped Anna. Admiral Harte had passed along the stunning threat Venport
had issued just before escaping justice yet again. All the months that Roderick had
worried about his sister, feared for her life, sure that she had been murdered . . .
and Venport had known all along!

He has my sister! One last bargaining chip, one last knife that had been
thrust in the Emperor's side. That could not be tolerated.

First, he and his Imperial forces would ensure that the subdued Butlerians
were under adequate control, with their homeworld locked down so that the
fanatics could cause no further trouble. Then he would set about finding where
Directeur Venport had gone to ground.

When his entourage arrived in the Lampadas system, Roderick went with
Admiral Harte down to the war-torn surface where the survivors had just begun
to pick up the pieces. In devastated Empok, they were greeted at the ravaged
landing field by an Imperial color guard in spotless uniforms, carrying bright
banners. It was in strong contrast to the destruction around them, with the city
in ruins and buildings burned or smashed to rubble.

The Emperor and the coolly professional Harte stood watching the crisp
performance of the guards, while Manford's leftover followers looked shell-
shocked. Roderick Corrino was their Emperor, and these people of Lampadas
could devote their energies to giving their service to the Imperium. They no
longer needed Leader Torondo.

The Admiral was impeccable in his dress uniform, wearing a chest full of
colorful ribbons. Roderick intended to give him more commendations once
they all returned to Salusa, but the job wasn't finished yet. The Imperial battle
group still had to mop up the remnants of Josef Venport's fleet and find Anna—
wherever they had gone.

Roderick had already sent a scout ship to the spice operations on Arrakis.
Though the Directeur had visibly increased his defenses with a cordon of
impressive thinking-machine warships to withstand any Imperial action, Josef
Venport was not there himself—nor was Anna. The quick, clandestine survey
had made it obvious that the Imperial Armed Forces couldn't fight those

intimidating battleships—not yet. And although the spice industry was valuable, the Emperor had a far more important goal.

He has my sister! The Directeur must be hiding in some other bolt-hole, and Roderick would uproot him there, once he discovered where it was.

The commander of the color guard separated from the rest of the troops and stepped in front of the Emperor, maintaining a long salute, while the two flag bearers spun their scarlet-and-gold Corrino banners. The battered Butlerian survivors looked on without enthusiasm. The air reeked of smoke, dust, and blood.

Roderick returned the salute with a brief, concise motion, as did Admiral Harte. When the color guard performance was concluded, the Admiral led him into the devastated city. Imperial soldiers helped the survivors put out the last few fires and spray down the powdery toxic residue from the poison clouds spewed by cymek walkers.

The main effort was to gather and bury the bodies, for the corpses outnumbered the living by a wide margin. The wrecked cymeks were motionless, giant mechanical monsters defeated by the sheer force and fanaticism of countless martyrs.

The Emperor felt a chill go down his back as he grasped just how many Butlerians had given their lives here. His momentary sympathy for the victims was tempered by the realization of how much unbridled power the movement had wielded. These people had killed Nantha, and had used atomics, despite the strict prohibitions in the Imperium. Manford surely would have turned against him before long.

Yes, it was good they were defeated.

The Emperor and the Admiral reached the site where the Butlerian leader had died, and the smashed cymek walker that had killed him now looked like a slain dragon. The surviving fanatics had been building a haphazard shrine from the rubble, but without guidance. Roderick could sense their despair, but also their remaining fervor, which made him uneasy.

Manford had always talked about the power of a martyr, and if at all possible the Emperor had no intention of letting the man become one. What was next, yet another statue erected next to Nantha's? He vowed to quench this spark before it became a flame, to ensure that the Butlerians remained broken.

Dirt- and soot-smeared, Anari Idaho moved away from the growing cairn of rubble being laid at the shrine site. The Imperial soldiers demanded that she surrender her sword in the presence of the Emperor, but she stiffened, obviously insulted. "I am a Swordmaster of Ginaz. I have never relinquished my weapon before, not even in the Imperial presence."

"But you will today," Admiral Harte insisted.

After a long, grudging standoff, she handed her sword to an Imperial soldier, then faced Roderick proudly, as if she were his equal. "Sire, after such a tragedy, our followers are pleased that you have come to commemorate the fall of our blessed leader. Manford faced the demons that haunt all of us, and in the end his noble fight destroyed him. But not his memory."

Roderick frowned at her statement and attitude. "Manford died, as did a great many here on Lampadas, and my next priority is to mete out justice against Directeur Venport." Upon her look of satisfaction, he continued in a much more stern voice, "But I did not come here to mark the death of Leader Torondo. I came to impose order and to accept the formal disbanding of your movement."

Anari rocked back at the unexpected response. Anger flashed in her eyes. "Surrender, Sire? But we have always fought on your side—on the side of humanity."

"The Butlerians changed that when they used forbidden atomics to destroy Kolhar. That alone carries a sentence of death under Imperial law. Manford is no longer alive to face the war crimes tribunal I intend to hold on Salusa Secundus, but his followers have committed many crimes against humanity."

Anari trembled with rage, and the Imperial soldiers tensed, ready to shoot down the Swordmaster if she made a move against him. "Crimes *against* humanity, Sire? Our every action was for the *welfare* of humanity, to save the human soul from the temptation of thinking machines."

"And for the sake of humanity, we must strengthen the Imperium. Because these people have suffered so severely, I will forego the need for a formal surrender ceremony from you, but know this: I will *never* allow the Butlerians to become an unruly mob again. The last of you will remain here on Lampadas, and will be watched closely."

Roderick gestured to Admiral Harte, and they continued the inspection, leaving Anari behind at a makeshift shrine the Emperor would order destroyed, and then find a way to keep people from restoring it.

Swordmasters had always been honorable, and Anari Idaho had been flawlessly loyal to her master. Perhaps Roderick should send her off to Ginaz, where she could continue to serve, but cause no further trouble.

The Butlerian capital was a wasteland, and Roderick could only imagine the fierce battle that had occurred here. He shuddered to think of the power of that mob. The growing shrine around Manford's death site made him uneasy, and he would take action to stop it quickly.

His staff took orders. "To show my Imperial generosity, I will send construction teams to rebuild Empok, funded by my own treasury." He knew Haditha would approve. "We'll raze the old city, burn all the remnants. I want nothing left of the place where Manford fell: no memorials, no statues, no rallying point. They will have a whole new Imperial-class city on this spot."

Admiral Harte nodded.

"And the job isn't finished. We still have to force the unconditional surrender of Directeur Venport—and get Anna back. Continue the investigation and interrogations, Admiral. I need to know where he went."

The fall from complete triumph to abject defeat is a great distance, but can take very little time.

—DIRECTEUR JOSEF VENPORT, personal log, Denali laboratories

It was a full-blown retreat—Josef could think of no other way to say it, no way to sugarcoat it. He couldn't label it as a "commercial setback" or "disruption of trade activities." This was completely different.

The universe had gone mad, yet he refused to admit defeat.

He'd been hammered by fanatical Butlerian suicide runs, maniacs who used atomics, who fired lasguns at shielded ships. And then, just after he had crushed the fanatics, *Imperial* ships attacked him in the lowest form of treachery. Betrayed by Roderick Corrino—the man Josef had personally placed on the Imperial throne. *I should have known not to trust him.*

It was a bitter pill to swallow. Josef had devoted his efforts and his fortune to *saving* civilization, and now they were trying to destroy him from every quarter. To hell with them all! He would find a way to come back on his own terms.

After Admiral Harte's shameful, backstabbing attack, the remaining Ven-Hold ships had reeled away, heavily damaged. Dozens of Josef's wrecked vessels had been left around Lampadas, as he had been unable to retrieve the crippled vessels from orbit. Another terrible loss . . .

When his fleet regrouped around the secure site of Denali, Josef ordered his engineers to make as many repairs as possible. The secret Denali laboratories had been designed for research and development rather than heavy assembly, but they were the only option he had. The main Kolhar industrial facilities were nothing more than radioactive slag.

But his people had always been innovative, breaking rules and achieving the unexpected. They would do so again. He needed his fleet back in shape and ready to fight.

Standing next to a pale Draigo Roget aboard the flagship, Josef kept shaking his head in dismay. This was the low point of his entire life and career. "The Emperor made a bargain with me. I destroyed Manford exactly as he instructed me to do. I wanted to put the Imperium back together. "

"Apparently, Emperor Roderick had plans of his own," Draigo said.

Josef felt his face burn. "At least now he knows that I hold his sister hostage. He has always made this disagreement personal, and I've just made it more personal yet. If he doesn't come to terms now, maybe I'll send her back to Salusa, piece by piece . . . to pay him back for this betrayal."

But it was an empty threat, and he knew it. Anna was his last asset, the only remaining lever he could use to move Roderick.

He felt a chill as he remembered that Cioba was also being held on Salusa. What would the Emperor do to her if anything happened to Anna? Josef knew that his wife was incredibly resourceful, not just due to her Sisterhood training but also because of her Sorceress blood. He was sure Roderick Corrino would underestimate her, and he hoped Cioba would get herself to safety. He worried about her.

Not long ago, Josef had expected to return here victorious, with the Butlerian problem resolved and VenHold restored to the Emperor's good graces. As soon as Josef had restored business as usual to the Imperium, without the anti-technology fanatics, he had even considered offering Denali scientific advances to the Imperium at large, in the name of progress and prosperity for all of humankind. He would have delivered Anna Corrino unharmed, a bargaining chip no longer needed, a peace offering. That should have ended the dispute.

But Josef had killed one irrational fanatic only to be betrayed by another. It was time to reassess, and take an entirely different tack.

His remaining ships orbited high above the poisonous atmosphere of Denali. Josef's throat felt raw from shouting his outrage, and even his Mentat remained silent now, internally making projections, trying to find some alternate way to recapture the lost prominence of Venport Holdings. Josef ransacked his own mind, because he'd always been able to find solutions. But he came up empty now.

Norma Cenva swam in the orange gas inside her tank, showing agitation. "My prescience is flawed—I did not see the attack coming. Now its shock waves clamor in my mind. My Navigators . . . so many harmed or killed! We must protect spice operations on Arrakis. The Emperor will seek to seize them."

As Roderick understood the magnitude of the VenHold setback, he would indeed move against the defensive forces on the desert planet. That was what Salvador had tried to do in the first place, and he had died in the attempt.

He nodded grimly. "You are correct, Grandmother. Without spice, and without our Navigators, I could never rebuild Venport Holdings." He turned to Draigo. "Mentat, tally our remaining assets, and determine how much more we can spare to protect Arrakis. Send what we can to guard the spice—everything that is not absolutely vital to our survival here. I will not let him have the melange. So long as we don't lose Arrakis, I can make VenHold strong again."

"Protect my Navigators," Norma said from her tank. "Protect the spice."

The Mentat offered his assessment. "I propose we send half of our functional warships to stand firm at Arrakis."

"Won't that leave Denali vulnerable?"

"We will still keep fifty ships here, but the secrecy of this installation is its greatest shield."

He nodded. "Yes, that's the best move."

The Directeur had always recognized that business itself was a war. He had fought many commercial battles and vanquished countless opponents. Now, with the faintest of smiles, he remembered capturing the Thonaris Shipyards from his shipping rival Celestial Transport.

Now Josef had sustained one massive defeat after another. Was he to blame? Was it due to his own hubris, his own extreme pride? His financial assets had been stolen by the Emperor, and Norma herself had blocked an easy victory at Salusa Secundus in a failed attempt to save the spice bank on Arrakis. Even so, Josef had agreed to do as the Emperor asked, destroying the Butlerian savages, only to lose even more in the process when the Imperial forces turned against him.

Now that he had time to reflect, Josef saw how he'd been the Emperor's pawn. Roderick had cleverly pitted Venport Holdings against the Butlerians, letting them tear each other apart, which left House Corrino as the true victor. He needed only to finish off whatever remained after the battle of Lampadas.

Trying to look at the situation objectively—which was not at all easy under the circumstances—Josef could almost admire the man's adept planning and execution. But this was not over, not yet.

Nevertheless, he still felt unsettling concerns, and his mind kept imagining ways that Roderick could still harm him. Denali was secure, hidden, and protected—but even so. . . .

"No one knows of this planet's existence," Josef said. "But we can't be too confident. Admiral Harte has access to the wreckage of VenHold ships lost in Lampadas orbit. The Emperor's experts could comb through them, scour the foldspace records, study the automated logs, our security measures." He locked gazes with the Mentat. "Somewhere among all those clues, what if he discovers the location of Denali?"

Draigo remained silent as his sophisticated thought processes churned through the available data. "The Emperor does have Mentats of his own." Finally, he nodded. "That is a valid concern, Directeur. We should prepare for the worst. It is short of a certainty, but the Emperor's forces may still be coming."

Uneasy, Josef issued orders for all personnel to repair his remaining ships, salvaging weapons systems, rebuilding Holtzman engines and shields. He had to get ready for his next move . . . as soon as he figured out what that would be.

THE DENALI SCIENTISTS were stunned to hear about the defeat of all the cymeks and the deaths of Ptolemy and Noffe. In an emergency meeting, Josef summoned his lead researchers so they could inventory the defenses available, should Denali be attacked. The Tlulaxa researchers, who had done such an excellent job growing a biological body for Erasmus, were pleased with the breakthroughs they had achieved over the years, but could offer nothing on a scale that might stand against an Imperial assault of the planet.

Josef assigned Draigo to manage the scientists and inventory the projects under way in the research domes. Except for a handful of patrol machines left behind, the cymek army had been destroyed, and the Directeur's instructions were to focus only on the projects with the best destructive potential.

The Emperor might well be coming.

Denali's recent efforts had been devoted to developing and building the Navigator cymeks—a brute-force army designed to combat the primitive Butlerians on Lampadas, not to fight a well-organized Imperial space fleet. Now, the research teams scrambled to find a way to protect this facility. On another occasion, Josef would have been glad to see them so motivated. This time, however, it was desperation, and he didn't like the feeling.

An eager Erasmus approached Josef, offering to help. "May I review the battle images transmitted by the cymeks?"

Josef gave him a curious, skeptical look. "Why would that be relevant? We lost all the cymeks on Lampadas, and have only a few cymeks left here, not enough to stand against the Imperial Armed Forces."

The robot regarded him with his new biological eyes. "I wish to observe the massacre because I saw the Butlerians execute Headmaster Albans, my friend and former ward. I would find it inspirational to watch them die."

"I understand completely." Josef granted Erasmus full access to the laboratories and support buildings, hoping he might suggest some innovative strategy that even Draigo Roget had not considered. Seeing the gleam in Erasmus's eyes, he knew the robot understood that if Denali fell, he himself would surely be destroyed. Josef pressed, "We have to find some other weapon we can use to defeat Roderick."

Erasmus said, "There may be something we can use."

Josef raised his eyebrows. "Did my researchers stumble upon something without telling me about it?"

"When the forty thinking-machine ships were brought here, hundreds of fighting robots were discarded on the surface of Denali. Some of them have already corroded into nonfunctionality, but I've seen others, and they might still be repaired. I can reprogram them remotely." His bright eyes held a strange, intense expression. "If Imperial troops should land and make a ground assault, those combat meks could be our last line of defense."

The Mentat pointed out, "If Imperial troops penetrate our orbital defenses and begin a ground assault, Directeur, then we have already lost."

"And if that happens," Josef said, "we have nothing to lose, and I'll damn well want the robots, just in case." He turned to Erasmus. "Do it. Do what you can."

Anna Corrino glided into the chamber, smiling, her attention centered on her beloved Erasmus. She seemed oblivious to the tension. As Erasmus reviewed the violent images of the cymek massacre in Empok, she came up behind him and kissed the back of his head. "I missed you so much."

Josef watched her. Despite all of Denali's defenses, this young woman might be the best asset he had left.

One does not beg the universe for mercy.
—TERF BRAKHERN, a wandering minstrel of the Jihad

Though she was Mother Superior with responsibility for the entire Sisterhood, Valya was also a Harkonnen military commander on a vital personal mission. So much of her life had been focused on one man, one target, that his loathsome face came to her in nightmares.

Vorian Atreides.

Now, thanks to a direct report from Truthsayer Fielle, as well as additional rumors, Valya knew where the Atreides fox had gone to ground: out in the old remnants of the thinking-machine empire, at Corrin—the very planet where he betrayed and disgraced her ancestor, Abulurd Harkonnen. It was a particular insult.

But the man couldn't hide from her. Valya had found him. For Vorian Atreides, there was no refuge, anywhere. Tula's bodyguards had left the job unfinished on Chusuk, because those Sisters had not understood the true import of that enemy. Valya would not make that mistake.

She could have dispatched a team of anonymous killers to hunt him down—there were enough skilled assassins on Wallach IX to take care of the matter easily. With their combined new fighting skills, they could have overwhelmed him, no matter how hard he fought. But this mission was not something Valya Harkonnen wished to delegate. She needed to be there herself, to see Vorian's fatal wounds with her own eyes, to dip her fingers in his warm blood and watch him die.

And Tula ought to be there as well, to witness the long-awaited satisfaction for her family. It would be her sister's reward for her remarkable service in killing

Orry Atreides . . . a young man who was of no consequence, except that his murder had hurt Vorian to the core.

Her operatives on Salusa had intercepted a trader from Corrin who came to deliver valuable salvage from the machine world; when pressed for information, the trader tried to convince the Sisters in the Imperial Court to pay him for the information they wanted about Vorian Atreides. The Sisters gave him a small fee and promised much more as they immediately dispatched him to Wallach IX so that he could speak with the Mother Superior.

The grinning trader offered Valya all the details she needed, acknowledging that Vorian Atreides was indeed in the settlement on Corrin, even including a sketch of the intricate tunnel system where the scavengers lived . . . where her target was in hiding. Even better, she learned that Orry's brother Willem had now joined Vorian there. Good, that would neatly wrap up all the threads of her vendetta.

As a final loyalty test, Valya ordered Sister Ninke to dispose of the talkative trader, since she could not risk anyone warning Vor that they were coming. The former Orthodox Sister passed the test with skill and discretion.

Now Valya had everything she needed. . . .

After careful consideration, she designated Sister Deborah as her alternate to run the school, and then handpicked Sisters who would join her on her mission to Corrin. It would not be a massive military operation, but a surgical strike with a single goal in mind. The threat this one man posed was not to be minimized, but she was confident in herself, and in her fellow Sisters.

Then she used the school's funds to charter a compact spacefolder, which quietly departed from Wallach IX.

After reaching Corrin, the spacefolder remained above the dead machine planet, while three small shuttles dropped down and flew in over the night side. Each craft carried five expert fighters, adepts in the consolidated combat style that she had developed personally; four of them were also Truthsayers.

The Atreides didn't stand a chance. Three teams, together but separate, each backing up the others, each looking for alternate ways to kill the target and block any escape. Valya led one squad, accompanied by a surprisingly determined Ninke, and an oddly reticent Tula, who had been quite moody of late. Valya insisted that she take heart, saying, "It will all be good again once he is dead."

"No, it won't," Tula retorted. "You've said yourself it will never be like the old days. We Harkonnens have lost too much."

"But we have not lost our honor. We will destroy these bastards—mark my words, Tula. We *will* win."

The younger woman looked pale. "Do we still have our honor if we win like this—by sneaking in to kill men who are only trying to stay away from us?"

Valya nodded somberly. "If we do nothing, we will have lost our honor. You must understand that."

"Part of me does, and part doesn't." Tula looked away, then back at Valya. "You've wanted this for such a long time."

"Since I was a small child, years before Vorian murdered Griffin." Valya was disturbed by her sister's lack of enthusiasm. Even so, she knew she and her fellow commandos could defeat their enemy. When they got back to Wallach IX, she would make sure Tula underwent rigorous guilt-erasure training. The girl had to be cured of this nonsense.

As they landed outside the dark ruins of the former machine capital, the shuttle sensors mapped out the main scavenger settlement, the largest concentration of inhabitants on the surface. According to the trader and his sketches, that was where Vorian had gone to hide. Valya stared intently through the green-tinted gloom of her light-enhancement lenses.

The three squads of women emerged at separate staging points outside the scavenger settlement, so they could move across the landscape and converge with no warning. As soon as they disembarked, the teams moved through the night, closing in on the ruined city. Fifteen deadly fighters in three teams against a pair of victims: redundancy to make absolutely certain they were successful. Valya carried a dagger at her waist, for the finishing touches.

Leading her own squad, she slipped a protective mask over her face, as did the others, completing the seal of their slick black suits. Tula was behind her, silent and ready, as well as Sister Ninke, the Truthsayer Cindel, and a tough and spunky young Sister Gabi. Valya confirmed her connection with the two other five-woman teams on her private comm, and they streamed forward with hardly a sound, like deadly shadows.

Approaching where they knew Vor had taken shelter, according to the intelligence from the bribed Corrin trader, Valya and her team came upon a landed ship, a small personal vessel of a vintage design. Valya called up the information that the trader had given them, and confirmed that this ship belonged to Vorian Atreides. His personal craft.

Motioning her Sisters to a halt, they circled the ship warily, scanning it. She didn't think the man would sleep inside, but still felt a chill to know it was *his*, that he had been here. "This is what Vorian Atreides will use to escape from us if we don't kill him in the tunnels. He'll try to get away." She paused, ran her dark eyes over the outside of the craft, staring at the engines, and then directed her Sisters to open the cabin, easily bypassing the minimal interlocks of the access hatch.

"We have to make sure he does not survive if he tries to slip away from us," Valya said. She nodded to Ninke and Gabi. "I assume you know how to rig the engines? Sabotage them? It is one of the skills I believe both of you have learned."

The two women went to work—it was done easily enough.

Later, as they glided through the ruddy night toward the entrance to the underground settlement, the ruined machine city gently shifted and rumbled. "Be careful," Valya said in a hushed voice. "The ruins seem unstable."

"We need to find the warrens where they are hiding," Ninke said in an edgy voice. "We'll dig them out and stab them through their hearts."

Valya appreciated her intensity and dedication. She and the other commando Sisters did not know—nor did they need to—the details of the Harkonnen-Atreides blood feud. As far as the Sisters were concerned, their Mother Superior had issued instructions, and they would follow.

As they glided among the mounds of rubble and jagged silhouettes of once-towering structures, Sister Gabi suddenly slipped and flailed. The base structure shifted, rose up, and seized the young woman. A pool of flowmetal swirled in the slag at Gabi's feet, and a swell of silver gushed up like the arterial blood of a machine. The well-trained Sister remained silent as she struggled to get free, using her bodily training to control her screams as the mobile, quicksilver substance pulled her down to her waist. The other commandos rushed to help her.

Fighting hard, Gabi grabbed on to an extrusion of black metal in the rubble. Ninke seized hold of her arm and pulled, trying to extract her.

None of them made any sound that might draw attention. Even Gabi, despite facing the prospect of death, did not cry out as the flowmetal tightened around her hips, crushing her body. A starburst of blood came out of her open mouth, and her expression sagged into agony and horror—still silent—before the flowmetal lurched again, pulling hard, and sucked her under.

After Gabi was gone, the quicksilver pool became placid, hardening into nondescript slag that did not show even a ripple of movement.

The survivors stared, and Tula looked sickened. Truthsayer Cindel and Sister Ninke were both troubled and hyperalert. Valya gave them a moment, then turned her back and impatiently urged the group forward. "There are still four of us, and two other teams. Do not let down your guard," she said. "Vorian Atreides is dangerous too."

No secret is kept forever, and a hiding place is often exposed through overconfidence.

—Sisterhood axiom

Following Roderick's command that the fugitive Directeur Venport be found at all costs, Imperial experts combed over the wreckage of the VenHold ships, hoping to find clues. In the days since the space battle over Lampadas, Admiral Harte's troops had rounded up any surviving VenHold crewmembers, and seized some Navigators that remained alive but weakened in their damaged tanks. The captive Navigators died soon afterward, without revealing any information.

The sophisticated logs in the ships' navigation files contained a wealth of foldspace data, but the databases self-destructed upon inspection, killing more than twenty of Harte's best forensic technicians. One of the wrecked vessels was damaged sufficiently, though, that the purge routines failed when they were triggered, which left some information for the investigators to dig into, study, and dig into some more. From this, they were able to infer a set of mysterious coordinates for an unremarkable system that contained no known habitable planets. The Denali system.

But Roderick needed to be certain.

The captive VenHold crewmembers seemed a more likely source of viable information. Salvador had enjoyed the game of torture, using his adept practitioners to ferret out unwilling revelations, but Roderick had been loathe to use the same tactics. Now, however, he decided to do whatever was necessary for the sake of the Imperium. And for his sister.

First, he sent Fielle to interrogate the prisoners, hoping the Truthsayer could learn something important. On Admiral Harte's flagship, only an hour ago, she had finished questioning all of the captives. Venport's employees refused to speak, and even the best Truthsayer could not determine the truth or lie of silence.

When Fielle proved unsuccessful, Roderick agreed to send in the team of Scalpel interrogators led by Robér Cecilio. In a chamber below decks on Harte's flagship, Cecilio and his team busily worked on the employees. The pain expert seemed to want to make up for his failure to learn anything from the captive Navigator he had probed in Zimia.

Roderick stayed aboard his plush barge, not wanting to watch what they were doing, but his imagination disturbed him too much. Unable to wait any longer, he shuttled over to Harte's ship, where he was led down to the secure decks. Escorted by Admiral Harte himself, he walked reluctantly toward a closed door at the end of a corridor. He heard muffled screams, but took a deep breath and kept going. He needed to know.

He felt glad that Haditha wasn't here.

As if expecting him, Robér Cecilio stepped into the corridor, closing the door behind him. "Sire, you instructed me that speed was more important than subtlety. I was pleased to operate without any restraints this time."

The Emperor assessed the black-robed man, then stared at the closed door. He could hear no noises on the other side now, wondered if any of the VenHold prisoners were still alive. "Yes, and the results? Do you know where he is hiding?"

"I am confident that the first five captives had no information to reveal, but several others finally provided a star-system name and astronomical coordinates. A planet called Denali. They say it is the site of a top-secret VenHold research facility."

This confirmed the information from the half-damaged navigation database in one of the stranded VenHold ships.

He stepped around the Scalpel interrogator, entered the sealed chamber. The room smelled of blood, urine, and terror but he was even more sickened to see the VenHold employee: he was horrifically broken, most of his skin flayed, his arm and leg joints in all the wrong places. Cecilio proudly went to the unconscious victim and prodded him, as if he considered this wreck of humanity to be a trophy. The eyelids flickered, didn't open.

"Sire, I'm convinced that the subject's information is accurate—and consistent with the revelations from three other prisoners."

Though Roderick was disturbed to see such mangled remnants of a human being, he had to reassess what actions he considered necessary and acceptable. It was a matter of priorities. "Thank you, Cecilio." He turned to Admiral Harte. "Denali?"

"Sire, I had an aide look it up in archives from the League of Nobles. Denali appeared in the old records as a small planet with a poisonous atmosphere . . . possibly an old cymek base, but not confirmed. Never settled, never even noticed as far as the records showed."

The Emperor nodded. "A poisonous planet for a poisonous man." That was where Roderick would go.

RODERICK RUSHED AN Imperial communiqué back to Salusa, summoning the bulk of his armed forces on two foldspace carriers so he could bring an overwhelming fleet to Denali. He intended to snuff out his last major enemy.

When the Imperial battleships arrived at Lampadas, Roderick studied a screen in the main salon of his barge, with Admiral Harte standing beside him. "A handful of ships will be enough to keep the remaining Butlerian fanatics under control here, Sire," Harte said. "They have nothing. Better to devote our main force to fighting Venport, who is still a threat."

Harte's forces had already commandeered any damaged but functional Butlerian ships and pressed them into Imperial service as well. Without Manford Toronto, the fanatics were disorganized; Anari Idaho was a Swordmaster, not a true leader. The Butlerians were fewer in number now, and too weak to pose much of a concern. The problem was mostly solved.

Ironically, Josef Venport had done exactly as he'd promised: He had taken care of the fanatics and killed their commander. And the Butlerians, in turn—with the timely and unexpected assistance of Admiral Harte—had caused significant damage to the VenHold threat. A crackdown on Denali would wrap it all up, and Venport would not know what was coming.

"The Directeur is not yet sufficiently defeated," Roderick announced. "We will leave some of your FTL ships here to monitor the Butlerians on the ground, but I am taking the rest of our fleet to finish the job at Denali."

Harte followed Roderick out of the barge's luxurious main salon. "The Butlerians will wish to join us so they can continue their fight against the Directeur. Since his cymeks killed Leader Toronto, they loathe him more than ever."

"I forbid their further involvement," Roderick said. "The Butlerians no longer dictate my actions. We will achieve our own victory, Admiral—an *Imperial* victory. And then we can end this terrible mess, once and for all."

The glory of love.
The nature of love.
The foolishness of love.

—ERASMUS, attempts at poetry,
New Laboratory Journals, volume 2

Inside the laboratory domes, Anna followed Erasmus wherever he went. She drew strength from being in his orbit, but her constant presence bothered him more and more, especially now that he had to concentrate on urgent preparations for the defense of Denali. Not surprisingly, she seemed not to understand the magnitude of the crisis, and he did not have time to explain it to her now.

During his initial observations of Anna at the Mentat School, he had catalogued her mood swings and biological obsessions. Now that he was with her physically as well as conversationally, his comprehension of the young woman's needs had grown. She had given him a great deal to ponder, ideas for subtle follow-up research, but none of that was important now. He actually found her irritating, even though she could not be blamed.

Under normal circumstances, the independent robot would have enjoyed the opportunity to conduct even more experiments on Anna's emotions, but in light of the current crisis facing them, such esoteric studies were a lower priority. In all probability, with the persistent prying of the Emperor's operatives, a vengeful Imperial fleet would soon discover Denali. Then they would be in deep trouble.

Since Erasmus's own survival was on the line, he did not like the uncertainty.

Anna trailed after him from one laboratory to another as he watched the scientists working with greater desperation than before. She touched him often, smiling and chattering, and it was all he could do to concentrate. Fortunately, she had already recorded the necessary video message for Venport to use as a bargaining chip, if he ever needed to hold her up as a human shield.

During the Jihad, Erasmus and Omnius had used many thousands of human shields at the Battle of Corrin, but it had not proved a sufficient deterrent. Anna was only one person, and a damaged one at that. Knowing this, the independent robot had to find another way to save them.

Many of the discarded combat meks taken from the thinking-machine fleet had been left on the surface of Denali, just like the original cymek walkers, and Erasmus had sorted out the most viable ones, to wipe their basic programming, and to recharge some of their weapons systems. In times past, such fighting meks could wreak terrible damage upon undefended human populations. Here at Denali, though, there was little chance of a ground battle, so he did not expend a great deal of effort on the possibility. He had many of the still-functional robots sent to equipment hangars on standby, however, just in case.

The machines were not hardened against the corrosive atmosphere, but he readied as many as he could, then devoted his attentions to larger-scale possibilities. He had a planet to defend, and all the resources of Venport Holdings. It reminded him of when Omnius had allowed him to dabble in any research that interested him. It was good to have a body again.

He also oversaw the frantic development of small, self-targeted missiles that could soar into orbit and hover beside an enemy ship, then pass slowly through its shields unhindered; once through the barrier, they would accelerate to explode into the hull. That seemed a promising approach, but developing a useful arsenal of such weapons would require extensive testing and prototype iterations. And Denali had no time.

Nevertheless, Erasmus reviewed the plans and suggested modifications. One of the researchers was clearly suspicious of him because he was a former thinking machine, but Erasmus frowned with his human face, forming an expression that was becoming more and more natural to him. "You distrust me, but I challenge you to use your logic. Even if I were as evil as you think I am, it behooves me to help save us all—myself included. I have as much at stake here as anyone does."

The scientist muttered, "But what happens afterward?" Dismissing the robot, he turned his attention back to a workstation beside him, where a second designer was modifying an electronic detonation mechanism. Erasmus bent closer to see.

Feeling ignored, Anna clung to his arm. "Come, there's something important I want to show you."

Even as Anna talked with him about inconsequential things, he used part of his brain to upload and memorize not only the shield-penetrating missile design, but also several other promising concepts that were, alas, still in the blueprint stage. There was no time to develop and implement them. Unless the Emperor took far longer than expected, these alternate weapons systems would never be constructed before it was too late.

Fortunately, Erasmus could process more than one problem at a time. Holding in his mind the projects he needed to review, he followed Anna as requested. Moving down the corridors, she told him about her fogwood tree back on Salusa and an old woman named Orenna who had been like a mother to her. She rambled on about memories from her childhood, including a favorite meal she had eaten for her ninth birthday celebration.

Erasmus dismissed all of her comments as he continued his military analysis.

When they reached their private quarters, Anna sealed the door, threw her arms around his neck, and kissed him on the mouth. "I've been with you all day, yet I still miss you! I want to feel your body against mine." Laughing, she peeled off his tunic and discarded it. "We can use those manuals you remember from old Earth." She ran her palms over his muscular chest.

Erasmus responded to her kisses, but remained focused on how soon Emperor Roderick might discover the location of Denali, and how quickly these facilities could produce a meaningful number of the shield-penetrating missiles.

Disappointed that he wasn't undressing her, Anna removed her own clothing and stood naked before him, waiting for him to admire her. He knew what she was expecting, so with a distant part of his mind, he formed words to tell her what she wanted to hear. "You are very beautiful, Anna, and I am pleased to have you as my lover."

Elated, she pulled him onto the bed with her, and although he performed as expected, most of his computer mind was devoted to continued analysis and projections. He developed another possible modification to the slow-missile design and also considered an improved set of autonomous instructions to the combat meks he had recently reprogrammed outside the domes. Every small thing added to Denali's defenses.

While Anna fussed over him, he went through the obligatory physical motions, but she seemed to sense his distance. Straddling him, she placed her hands on his shoulders and leaned close so that he was forced to look at her. "Make love to me!" she insisted, even though he had been doing so for the past half hour. "I want your whole focus, just like I'm focused on you. We belong together."

But he was frustrated by her interference, and made her roll off of him. "An Imperial fleet may be coming to destroy us, and I am busy trying to prepare our defenses. You and I have experienced intercourse in numerous varieties. I've already catalogued the experiences and sorted the data. There is no need to continue this. Other things are much more important. What is the point of repeating an experiment so many times, especially a successful one?"

She scrambled off the bed and stared at him with wide eyes that quickly filled with tears. "An *experiment*? No need to continue this? What do you mean?"

Erasmus couldn't understand. "Were you not satisfied? I believe I performed well enough. We are finished for now. Other concerns are much more important."

She raised her voice to a shout. "We're finished for now? An experiment? That's all I am to you? Don't you understand? I love you, Erasmus."

"Of course, I am sure you do."

Anna's knees buckled, and she collapsed to the floor. "You don't feel anything for me? I've given you my entire heart and soul, everything I have. I thought you were my perfect lover, but I . . . I'm just an *experiment* to you?" She wiped tears from her eyes and grabbed her clothes as she stumbled for the door. "Other things are more important? With your new body, I thought you wanted to have human emotions."

"Yes, that is one of my priorities, but right now, I cannot be delayed by biological needs. The mind is superior to the body. Can't you understand that?"

She retorted, "I thought you felt deep love for me—but all you learned was how to lie better!"

Erasmus pondered her outburst for a moment. "How have I lied?" Tapping into his memories of Gilbertus's execution, he compared his experiences, his memories, his . . . feelings toward Anna, such as they were. He didn't fully understand them. He had a definite fondness for her, but she obviously felt much more strongly toward him.

Tears welled up in her eyes and ran down her cheeks. She didn't bother to wipe them away, and just permitted them to flow. He found this curious, but only for a moment before he turned his attentions elsewhere, as he needed to do.

He wondered if this was the place where he should apologize to her. He decided he would have to deal with that later, when it was a priority.

In a serendipitous coincidence, two other ideas about the robot reprogramming clicked together as his gelcircuitry continued to process. A possible solution! "I cannot spare any time for our personal interactions right now." He grabbed for his own clothes. "I must speak with the weapons scientists."

Sobbing uncontrollably, Anna bolted out into the corridor and ran toward one of the now-empty cymek hangars. He assumed she would huddle by herself and cry until she was red-faced and swollen-eyed. He could deal with that later. Right now, Anna's capricious emotions reminded him of Serena Butler decades ago, and her constantly crying baby.

With Anna no longer distracting him, he had the space and privacy he required, and the ability to concentrate on vital matters.

Vorian Atreides knew that the best way to avoid attackers was to remain constantly on the move. A hunted man should sleep in a different safe house every night and move from job to job, planet to planet.

In this case, though, Vor was both the pursuer and the pursued. He wanted the Harkonnen assassins to come here, and he needed to kill his enemies before they got to him. Willem's arrival complicated the situation, but he could depend on his young companion as well. Willem was eager to fight at his side. Too often in his life, Vor had tried to go it alone. Now, the pair worked and planned together.

They were ready.

Korla's scavengers had few sophisticated systems inside their outpost in the rubble, but the people were security conscious, guarding their own possessions. In order to keep peace among her workers, the Queen of Trash had installed sensors and alarms throughout the underground warren, even in sections damaged by the recent flowmetal instability. Her people had to worry more about stealing from one another than about any outside threat, since few visitors came to Corrin. Yet there was little of portable value here, except for what they themselves excavated.

Out of an abundance of caution, as soon as Willem joined him, Vor began choosing new and secret quarters for them, never spending more than one night in each place before moving on. On a wild and ungoverned planet such as this, it was hard to say how many people knew their whereabouts at any given moment.

Vor intended for Valya and Tula Harkonnen to find him—but on his own terms. He didn't want to be blindsided, as they had been on Chusuk. Vor and Willem were lucky to have survived that; next time, he needed to see the enemy coming.

Without notifying Korla or anyone else, Vor used a specialized tool to unlock a chamber he knew was unoccupied—the home of one of the dead miners from the recent flood of liquid metal. He left their previous quarters locked so that a casual observer—or a dedicated assassin—would think they still lived there.

After the other scavengers were asleep, he and Willem took their meager belongings and moved quietly in the darkness. Vor also left tiny monitoring devices on the tunnel walls, particularly just outside his former chamber, which would alert him to any tampering. He had spent several weeks preparing for the eventual attack, building up secret defenses, even implanting tiny but powerful explosives in inconspicuous places, as an added surprise.

Feeling momentarily safe in their new hidden room, Vor sat on a wall bench, taking first watch while Willem caught some sleep on one of the bunks. After three hours, he would awaken the young man, and they would switch places. The darkness around them was illuminated only by the faint glow of a holo display that transmitted a projection of the tunnels. At present, it showed only the dim, empty passageways and numerous sealed chambers where the scavengers slept.

Vor checked the weapons kit secured to his waist; Willem had one of his own in a storage alcove next to his bunk. Each kit contained a knife, a projectile pistol, compact tools, and a pry bar.

Vor liked this room because it was one of several that had an emergency escape hatch on the rear wall. When he'd broken his way inside and checked the rear exit, he was quite satisfied. The back hatch led out into an adjacent tunnel and up to the desolate surface.

On the bunk, Willem fell into a fitful sleep, but Vor remained alert, staring at the motionless holoprojection of the tunnels. Watching.

❧

OUTSIDE, THE REMAINING members of the Sisterhood squads slid invisibly through the ruddy gloom, converging on the scavenger settlement. The women had discovered numerous ways into the warren settlement, but now they focused on a rarely used venting system that granted them access to the tunnels.

When Valya, Tula, and two other commando Sisters passed through a nondescript hatch into the deep protected rooms below, Tula entered before her sister. Valya glanced behind her into the brooding night, then entered and closed the hatch quietly behind them. The team descended into the complex, reaching the corridors of barricaded sleeping rooms.

Working with nimble fingers, Sister Ninke used tools to disconnect the crude alarm system from the first sealed door. After finishing, she stepped back to let one of the other commandos open it carefully. Even with the security systems disabled, the old salvaged door squeaked.

Inside the dim room, two figures stirred, men who reacted to the unexpected noise, but not fast enough. In a blur, Cindel fell on the first man with her dagger, while Valya slipped past them and killed the second man. The men hardly uttered any sounds. Valya could not afford an alarm being sounded now.

Illuminating a small handlight, Tula shone a glow into the faces of the two victims, but both were older, dark-skinned men. Neither was an Atreides, but Valya had not expected the mission to be so easy.

Moving through the room, she opened the opposite door that led into the larger complex. Down the passageway, she spotted other stealthy figures moving. Good, another of her commando squads had already gotten inside, and moments later she received a signal confirming that the third one had entered as well. They began the full search.

Now they could all hunt, and soon the task would be completed. They would find the two Atreides quickly enough.

❦

AFTER SITTING MOTIONLESS, awake but drifting into a meditative state, Vor snapped to full awareness when he saw a flicker of motion on the holo-image. Sleek, dark shapes were moving through the enclave—where they definitely did not belong. He nudged Willem, put a hand over the young man's mouth as he awoke, and pointed at the display.

Willem silently grabbed his weapons kit from the alcove. Vor already had his. They were both ready. The two men watched the female shapes glide like oil through the tunnels to converge outside Vor's previous room. The dark figures paused, regrouped, and then forced their way inside.

Vor gripped his weapons, knowing that the chamber was empty. Moments later, the dark-garbed women were back outside, huddling together in obvious confusion. Then they began hunting again.

"Be ready," he whispered. Willem was perspiring and breathing unevenly as he tried to keep himself calm. "I knew they'd come."

The images were dark and indistinct, but Vor decided one figure clearly re-sembled Tula Harkonnen; if it *was* Tula, then Valya might be with her, to make certain the attack was successful. He was hoping for that.

Watching them, he decided to take action of his own. He had planned for this. Counting down the seconds, he touched a trigger to activate explosives he'd implanted in the walls. The roar of the detonation sent shock waves through the tunnels. On the portable screen, he saw dark-clad bodies slamming into the walls . . . and then sections of the unstable tunnels sliding down in collapse.

Korla and the rest of the scavengers would be awake now. Vor needed to take charge of the crisis.

In the flickering projection on the damaged imager, Vor saw several of the strangers lying motionless, while others bounded away. He had not expected to kill them all; this was just the first step, but he was ready to deal with them. He counted three bodies, wasn't sure who they were, but hoped . . .

Willem looked at him with shining eyes. "For Orry."

Vor nodded. "Let's go."

One of the surviving women discovered the implanted imager. She scanned the device, followed the signal, and then plucked it out of the wall. Just before the holo dissolved into a smoke of static, Vor saw her point down the tunnels toward his hiding place. The commandos raced along the passageway, heading in his direction. Then the screen showed nothing but static.

Cursing, Vor grabbed his companion's arm and pushed him toward the rear escape hatch and out into the side corridor. Willem gasped as they ran, "Did you see them? What sort of weapons do they have?"

"I don't know exactly, but I don't like what I saw."

Underground alarms sounded; bright amber lights strobed inside the stair-wells. Vor and Willem fled in silence. Reaching the last doorway at the top of the steep stairwell, they burst outside onto the rubble-strewn surface. Under the starry night of Corrin, the rough landscape appeared even more otherworldly than in daylight. Vor hurried Willem to the other side of a slag pile, where they hid. His ship wasn't far away, out in the open, but he had no intention of running now that he had lured the Harkonnens here.

Before long, he heard a voice call out. "Vorian Atreides, this is Valya Harkonnen. Your traps and tricks can't stop us. Enough running. It's time to face the justice you deserve—to bring honor back to our house and death to yours."

Vor and Willem both withdrew compact projectile pistols from their weap-ons kits and prepared to fire.

"You could keep hiding," Valya shouted, "or you could come out and accept our challenge. You know that's the way it's destined to be, Atreides—us against you. Do you accept, or are you cowards?"

In the moonlight, Vor spotted the two Harkonnen women in dark single-suits, while four other women emerged behind them. He wondered how many more there were.

He could see how much Willem wanted to fight them, win or lose. Vor felt the same—but what about the other Sister commandos out there? Valya had undoubtedly brought the best with her. He doubted if Griffin's sister would truly accept a fair duel, without reinforcements to interfere if he and Willem were to get the upper hand.

And the two Atreides were here alone.

Before he could respond, Vor heard many more voices—men and women. In the moonlight he saw the burly form of Korla of Corrin striding out, garbed in her shimmering flowmetal cape. Many angry scavengers accompanied her, well armed with large projectile rifles. Their powerful illuminators bathed the stark area in bright light.

"Who the hell are you?" Korla demanded of Valya and her companions. Her unkempt, patchy black hair gave her an even wilder appearance than usual. "And why are you here?"

Valya looked at her haughtily. "I am the Mother Superior of the Sisterhood. I have a rightful vendetta against two fugitives you are harboring."

"And I am the ruler of this world, and we care nothing about your laws or your vendetta," Korla growled. "This is Corrin."

"I issued a challenge to Vorian and his ward. The Atreides must pay for Vorian's crimes against my House. My sister and I will fight them in personal combat and settle this dispute here and now—without your interference."

When Korla turned, her flowmetal cape flickered and twitched. "This is my world, and I'll interfere in any damned manner I like."

Vor emerged from concealment with Willem beside him, drawing their attention. "Korla of Corrin, if we can count on your people to prevent those other women from attacking us, we'll face the two who challenge us. It's what they want . . . and what I want. I see no other way to end this bitter feud. The Harkonnens have hated me unjustly for eight decades. But the reality is here nonetheless, and I am prepared to deal with it."

Korla snorted. "And what did he do to deserve such anger? Is he a lover who jilted you?"

Valya's face flared with disgust. "He killed my brother Griffin."

Knowing it would do no good against her hatred, Vor stated simply, "I did not harm your brother. He was my friend. I tried to save him."

She looked sick. "You lie, Atreides."

Surprisingly, Sister Cindel, the Truthsayer, frowned. Her brow furrowed. "Mother Superior . . . he is telling the truth. There is no falsehood in his statement."

Vor lifted his chin, remained where he was. "As I said, I didn't kill Griffin." He fully expected her next to charge him with falsely accusing Abulurd Harkonnen of cowardice at the end of the Butlerian Jihad, but for some reason she didn't mention that.

Valya swayed, as if suddenly trying to recover her balance, but then her own determination made her straighten. "I still do not believe it. Vorian Atreides has poisoned my own Truthsayer."

"I expected nothing else from you," Vor said. He couldn't even feel disappointed. "You're so set on revenge."

"We are both going to fight you!" Willem insisted, glaring at Tula. "You *did* kill *my* brother."

The Queen of Trash looked around at her people. Just behind her, Vor also spotted the wiry woman he had rescued from the flowmetal flood. Horaan Eshdi's eyes shone in the light of the illuminators. "We have little enough entertainment here," Korla said. "Let's watch them fight."

The scavengers muttered agreement.

Vor stepped forward with Willem at his side. Valya and Tula Harkonnen stood together, with the other dark-garbed women arranged behind them like primed weapons. Vor thought the remaining Sisters might be able to break through any resistance the scavengers tried to mount, but the number of people and weapons would at least make them think twice. Korla's workers tightened ranks around the other Sisters, even pushing them back.

For now, the tableau was Vor's to command.

Holstering his projectile pistol, he whispered to Willem, "They are able to move in a blur and use techniques you have never seen." He strode toward Valya, suspecting that she carried concealed weapons, but he had his own as well. He had never expected this to be a fair fight.

Curiously, Tula hung back, so Vor motioned for Willem to do the same, even though the murderous young woman was the one they had been hunting all along. He heard the low voices of the scavenger crowd, but the other Sisters remained where they were, blocked from the combat arena.

Vor saw no reason to delay. This confrontation had been coming to a head for years. As the red-giant dawn tinged the sky, he and Valya circled each other slowly and warily, crouched in fighting stances on the rubble of the once-great machine city.

The duel consumed his awareness, sharpened his senses. He watched his nemesis with intense concentration, saw a muscle twitch in one of her arms, but did not react. She was testing him. He discerned what could be a dagger concealed at her hip. He had no doubt Valya would use it if she saw the opportunity.

Valya darted toward him, and he slipped sideways quickly to let her pass, but he did not whirl to face where he thought she should be. Instead, remembering the tricks Griffin Harkonnen had used during their combat, he dropped to the ground and rolled in Valya's direction before popping back up to his feet, hoping that he had chosen correctly.

Somehow, Valya materialized several paces to his left. For an instant that lasted no longer than a caught breath, she seemed to wait for him to make the next move.

Behind him, to his concern, he realized that Willem and Tula were beginning their own combat. Vor had fought Tula once at an inn on Caladan just after she murdered Orry. Vor had barely survived the confrontation. He feared for Willem's life now, but he could not let his attention stray from his own opponent.

During his flicker of hesitation, Valya flung herself into the air, and kicked him in the middle of his chest. Vor staggered backward. When she charged toward him to finish the attack, he savagely kicked her legs out from under her. Valya crashed to the ground with a look of surprise and irritation on her face.

Vor's chest screamed in pain, but he kept his expression neutral and eyes alert as she bounded to her feet, ready to go after him again. Looking up from her apparent vulnerability, she spoke in a strange, throaty voice: "When I come toward you this time, *your muscles will freeze.*"

At her eerie, commanding tone, Vor suddenly found he could not move. It was as if his body had turned to stone, a frightening, uncontrolled sensation. By concentrating, though, he managed to break free of whatever strange hold she had inflicted upon him. Realizing that the attack was only in his mind, he forced it aside. Valya's look of confidence faded as she saw him slide to his left, on the move again and ready to counterattack.

Just then the sharp report of a projectile gun rang out, and Valya saw her sister fall. She whirled and let out a sudden cry. "No!"

Tula writhed on the ground, and Willem loomed over her, his projectile weapon drawn and his face dark with hatred. Blood flowed from her left shoulder, and one arm hung useless. Tula struggled back to her feet, drew a dagger with her good arm, and faced him defiantly. Her face showed anger and pride . . . but also something else, something softer?

"What kind of monster pretends to love a man just to murder him?" Willem demanded. "My brother loved you—a *Harkonnen!*"

Valya snarled and tried to lunge toward her sister, but Vor threw himself against her to stop her from interfering.

Willem raised the projectile weapon again.

When he arrived above the dark, mist-shrouded research planet, Roderick was pleased with the impressive fleet he had assembled on such short notice. Venport would not possibly be expecting them.

The foldspace carriers emerged, and the swarm of Imperial warships dropped out of the enormous holding bays and raced toward Denali, side by side. They were ready to fight.

From the bridge of Harte's flagship, Roderick was surprised to see that Directeur Venport had assembled an unexpectedly robust defensive net, considering how many warships he had lost at Lampadas, as well as the force he had diverted to protect his Arrakis operations.

The Emperor stood with his hands behind his back. "Apparently he did not assume he was safe hiding here after all."

On the bridge beside him, Admiral Harte offered a small smile. "The most important part, Sire, is that our ships outnumber theirs, and we have greater overall firepower. It will be a challenge, but we will defeat them."

Roderick hoped the Admiral was right. He was uneasy that they had left Salusa more vulnerable than he would have liked, but his real enemy, the last remaining thorn in his side, was right here in front of him. As soon as Venport Holdings was broken, Roderick could create a new commercial network to conduct trade throughout the Imperium. He envisioned a golden age, without Butlerian resistance to common technology and without Josef Venport's ruthless business practices.

Much blood had been shed already, and it would not be an easy victory. Scars would remain for a long time.

"Don't underestimate them," Roderick warned. "If Venport has weapons laboratories down there, he may well have surprises for us." Now that the man had been betrayed, wounded, and backed into a corner, he would be enraged, desperate, and unpredictable, and that made him especially dangerous.

Harte said, "Our shields are up, Sire, and the VenHold ships ahead of us also have full Holtzman shields." He paused to let the import sink in. "At Lampadas, Sire, the Butlerians used lasguns to fire upon shields. It was sheer suicide . . . but what if Venport is desperate enough to resort to such tactics?"

The Emperor shook his head. "Not a chance. The Directeur may be ruthless, but he is neither irrational nor suicidal."

Like a noose tightening around Denali, the Imperial fleet closed in. The VenHold ships displayed arrays of glowing weapons ports as they prepared to make their last stand. The clustered ships hung motionless in orbit, and Roderick waited for Venport to acknowledge that he had lost, though the Emperor did not hold much hope for that.

He has Anna down there. Roderick was sure Venport would try to use her life to buy his own.

Impatient, he opened a broad channel. "Directeur Josef Venport, if you surrender yourself and deliver my sister unharmed, we can end this without further loss of life." He realized this situation was a complete turnabout from when VenHold ships had placed Salusa Secundus under siege. "If you wish to prove your mettle by fighting us, it will be a bloody battle, but most of the blood will be yours. Make no mistake about it, we *will* prevail. As a logical businessman, you should know when to cut your losses."

Venport finally appeared on the screen, speaking to them from a sealed chamber in the laboratory domes below. He was dressed impeccably, his reddish hair perfect, but Roderick noticed his face looked somewhat haggard. The Directeur narrowed his blue-eyed gaze, showed a flash of anger. "Manford Torondo was willing to speak any lie, provided it met his needs—I expected that of him. But you broke your word as well, Roderick Corrino. We had a deal. I used my company military force to crush the Butlerians, and then your fleet attacked us when we were weakened. Why should I trust anything you say after that betrayal?"

Roderick pressed his lips into a firm line. "Admiral Harte was out of contact and operating under previous standing orders. When his fleet arrived at Lampadas, he was unaware of our bargain. His attack on you was truly the result of an unfortunate misunderstanding. I did not intend it to happen, and I might even have been willing to apologize." He hardened his voice. "Until you revealed that you have been holding my sister hostage, that you knew where she was all along. You should not be so ready to point your finger at me, Directeur." He raised his voice, speaking with the authority of an Emperor. "Let me speak to Anna. Now."

Venport appeared unimpressed. "Your sister recorded a message for you. Listen to her own words." Without further preamble, he transmitted a recording.

On the screen, Anna smiled at the imager. Yes, it was her, and she appeared to be inside one of the Denali domes, with a cymek work area behind her. She looked healthy, well cared for, even content. Her brow furrowed in a frown as she leaned closer. "This is a message to my brother. Dear Roderick, I am here and I am safe. Directeur Venport keeps me safe, keeps close watch on me." She smiled pleasantly. "More important, I'm *happy*. My lover is here on Denali! Everything is wonderful, and Directeur Venport says I can remain for as long as I want. In fact, he insists." Her eyes flicked back and forth. "Though I do miss you. Please come and visit."

The recording ended and was replaced by Venport's face. In a sharp voice, he added, "As you can see, your dear Anna is safe for now. You should thank me—one of my operatives rescued her when the barbarians took over the Mentat School. They would surely have killed her, while I have only held her here for her own protection, showing her every courtesy. I planned to deliver her to you as a goodwill gesture, but then you set out to destroy me. If I am as desperate as you believe I am, then don't force me to harm her. Discontinue your aggressive posture, withdraw your ships, and come down with an unarmed party to negotiate an end to this crisis."

He cut off the transmission abruptly.

Roderick stewed, said off-line, "Maybe we should pull back and give him a moment to breathe. He must come to realize that his best option is surrender."

Reverend Mother Fielle stood beside them, having carefully watched Josef Venport. "He does have Anna Corrino hostage, and I believe she is unharmed thus far. In that, I detect no deception. She is his only bargaining chip, so he will not hurt her, Sire. You can push him harder."

Admiral Harte agreed. "It is dangerous for you to show weakness now. This should be our final battle against the most dangerous man in the Imperium, now that Manford is dead. Venport will not harm your sister. He knows that if he *did* there would be nothing to stop us from wiping out everything he has." Harte wore a determined expression on his flushed face, and he held up a clenched fist. "We can defeat Venport Holdings, seize the Directeur, and end his threat to the Imperium." He forcibly straightened his fingers. "I apologize for being so outspoken, Sire. The decision is yours, of course. The Directeur held me and my troops prisoner, so this is also personal for me. Too personal, it seems."

Roderick nodded. "It's all personal, Admiral. And that man has escaped too many times for me to underestimate him again." He remembered how Venport had strolled into the Imperial Audience Chamber to congratulate him after the coronation—knowing all the while that *he* had assassinated Salvador. Norma

Cenva had whisked him away the moment his crime was exposed, and Venport could escape just as easily now. Like a greased worm.

But Roderick wouldn't let him.

From the Admiral's flagship, which had once been Emperor Jules's grand flagship, Roderick gazed out at his large Imperial fleet. "After all that man has done, I will not give him a way to save face, and I will not withdraw and send in an unarmed team as if we are merely negotiating a trade deal! The time to be reasonable is past, and I will not show weakness. Venport has made himself as much an enemy of the Imperium as Manford Toronto ever was. We have the upper hand. Let's finish this."

Admiral Harte straightened, looking pleased. "He's right below us—we can easily destroy the laboratory domes from orbit."

"My sister is down there, Admiral. She's an innocent and always has been. We can't just carpet bomb the domes. Under the circumstances, I want a surgical strike."

Harte nodded. "You make it more difficult, Sire, but it can be done. First, though, we need to neutralize his warships in orbit."

"In that, Admiral, you may proceed with all the resources at your disposal."

The Sisterhood school teaches that love is dangerous, which I have always found puzzling. Obviously, there is a great deal about this emotion that I do not understand.

—ERASMUS, final Denali Notebooks

Invasion alarms rang throughout the laboratory domes, but Anna was already running away. She did not care about political problems or space fleets. Her world had fallen apart. Sirens summoned everyone to their posts, and military transmissions from the VenHold fleet in orbit warned of an imminent attack. Denali personnel raced through the corridors in a panic.

But Anna was too absorbed in her own misery. She pressed her hands to her ears, ducked her head, and continued to run, uninterested in the crisis. In her state of mind all the noise sounded like mocking laughter, faceless shouts that seemed to taunt her with a merciless twisting of the knife.

Her heart was not just broken; it was shattered. Her mind was already a fragile construct held together by cobwebs and memories, and now it had curled up to hide from the reality she could not bear to face. She had surrendered her heart, her soul, her deepest self to Erasmus. She had unleashed her passion, shared every feeling with him. And she had been fooled, betrayed.

It was entirely her fault. She was aware that Erasmus was cold and unfeeling, an evil thinking machine, but Anna had cheated herself into believing he had changed. She had saved him from certain destruction during the fall of the Mentat School, and thought he felt something special for her in return. She thought she had repaired the robot's dark spirit and healed him with love, helping him understand what it meant to be a human being.

But he viewed everything she had done for him and given him as nothing more than an experiment. An *experiment!* She felt so violated. He said he was finished with her, had no time for her. Other concerns were more important.

Back when she was a young girl on Salusa, Emperor Jules had forced her to watch brutal public and private executions—"for her own good," he said—but those horrific experiences had scarred rather than strengthened her. Her brother Salvador had also tormented her, stealing every chance at happiness she might have had; then he'd sent her away to the Sisterhood on Rossak, where she thought she had friends, where Sister Valya had been her companion. But Valya had manipulated her too, tricked her into taking the "agony" poison that destroyed her mind. It was another experiment!

In her own family, Anna had once believed that Roderick, at least, truly loved her, that he was on her side. Yet he hadn't wanted to deal with her eccentricities either, so he sent her away to the Mentat School.

Too many people had taken Anna's heart, crushed it in an iron grip, and then abandoned her.

Erasmus was supposed to have been her closest friend of all, her lover, her true love. She had devoted herself entirely to him as the lifeline that kept her damaged mind together. Isolated here on Denali, at least she had him, and for a short while it had been paradise for her. She had been deliriously happy.

But now it was all smashed to bits. Erasmus's flippant dismissal showed her that, once again, she had been tricked by her soft heart. He was no better than Hirondo, the lover her brothers had sent away from her on Salusa Secundus.

Erasmus had destroyed their relationship, and Anna had no one else. None of the scientists or laboratory workers were her friends. Even old Lady Orenna back on Salusa—the closest person Anna ever had to a mother—was dead. Anna had nothing left . . . only her despair, hopelessness, and bitter memories.

How many times could she be destroyed before it was enough? If this present crisis wiped out the whole Denali facility, it might be a blessing for her.

As the deafening alarms continued to ring, Anna staggered away with tears streaming down her face. Hot, wrenching sobs tore at her chest, but no one paid the slightest attention to her misery.

Eventually, she stumbled into an empty cymek hangar. Except for a few left-over walkers still patrolling the blasted landscape outside the domes, the cymek army was gone. Manford Torondo and his fanatics had destroyed the machines on Lampadas. Maybe the Butlerians had come to Denali now, and that was what the alarms were all about.

She knew the invaders would want to kill Erasmus, as they had killed so many other thinking machines. After what she'd been put through, she didn't care if they tore Erasmus apart and dissected his gelcircuitry brain. The thought horrified her for a moment. If she saved him, maybe he would change, maybe he would apologize. A flare of hope shot higher within her, but crashed down again. She had been such a fool. She saw that clearly now. It was no mistake.

He was an evil robot, just as the Butlerians had always claimed, and she felt repulsed to have fallen in love with such a heartless, calculating monster. Erasmus had intentionally jabbed and twisted her feelings in order to create emotions for him to study, as if she were one of the specimens in his laboratory!

Alarms continued to shriek, and VenHold workers scrambled to defend Denali. Anna vowed she would never let anyone hurt her again, and couldn't think of a pain greater than the raw and jagged ache that was tearing her apart from the inside. She had only one decision to make now, a choice that was hers and no one else's.

Inside the cymek hangar she looked outside through the broad windows, at the swirling, greenish mists. In the darkness the drifting fog looked so peaceful, so soothing. It would embrace her if she came into contact with it. She would breathe the mist into her lungs and would drown in its lethal embrace.

She went to the airlock and closed herself inside. The cautionary interior alarm was drowned out by the racket in the domes.

Princess Anna Corrino ignored the warnings, opened the outer hatch, and staggered out into the poisonous air of Denali.

⁓⬧⬩⬩⬧⁓

AS HE ASSESSED the newly arrived Imperial fleet and calculated their weapons versus the VenHold defenses available on the Navigator-guided ships in orbit, Erasmus realized that this facility was in serious trouble. Alarms continued to shriek. He had hoped for more time to work on developing effective new defenses, but the most interesting concepts were no more than design specs or, at best, untested prototypes.

His computer mind focused on the problem; Directeur Venport would want his assessment as soon as possible. Just like dear Gilbertus, Draigo Roget had helped him understand the overall political situation in the Imperium, explaining that Venport Holdings had more enemies than just Manford Torondo.

Erasmus had taken pleasure in seeing the Mentat's clean and ordered thoughts—made possible, he knew, by the logic techniques he himself had developed for Gilbertus to share. The people on Denali were natural allies, thrown together to develop ways to fight the Butlerians, but now their enemy was the Emperor himself. And they would all have to fight together in order to survive.

Over the course of his existence, Erasmus had forged a number of unorthodox alliances; some had been effective, while others surprised him in the wrong way. The failures—particularly Serena Butler and the young Vorian Atreides—were usually caused by unpredictable human behavior. Their species frequently disregarded the straightforward statements they called promises. Emperor

Roderick Corrino had broken a promise to Josef Venport, and now it looked certain that Denali would fall.

The Tlulaxa scientists had grown Erasmus a new body, as requested, but it had taken sweet Anna Corrino to show him the complexities and nuances of being human. Anna had helped him understand the odd and esoteric feelings caused by biological influences and chemical changes. After analyzing the young woman for a very long time, at last he thought he was beginning to understand.

Both before and during the Jihad, as a robot in a beautiful flowmetal body, he had studied hundreds of thousands of experimental subjects, building a database of observations. But those had always been external analyses, and now with this human form grown from the cells of Gilbertus, he could experience the sensations directly.

Anna had expected so much from him—more than he could give—and he knew she was disappointed. That troubled him as well, because he wished he could grasp those emotions he had admired for so long.

Alas, he simply had no time for them now. The priority was obvious: Denali was under attack. He analyzed the array of Imperial ships and prepared to make a quick report to Directeur Venport.

The VenHold ships standing in defense of Denali were going to be problematic, he realized. Norma Cenva would not sacrifice her precious Navigators even for the survival of this research facility. She was irrational about her creations, and she held significant influence over Josef Venport. That meant the available battleships were not expendable, no matter the strategic advantages, which limited the robot's plans.

He calculated that if the Directeur sacrificed all the large VenHold spacefolders in a massive attack, they could possibly defeat or at least drive back the Imperial fleet, despite being outnumbered. At least it allowed him to formulate a plan in which the surviving scientists and personnel on Denali—including himself and of course Anna—could get away. That was paramount.

If he and Anna escaped, they might continue their studies elsewhere. Perhaps then he could develop into a full-fledged person, but such things took time. In the past few months, he had learned more about humanity than he had in his entire existence before that. He had embraced sadness and guilt over the death of Gilbertus, and genuine rage toward Manford Torondo and the Butlerians—and, yes, satisfaction, even glee, when he viewed images of the Butlerian leader being torn to shreds.

And then there was Anna, with her caring and her love. She fawned over him, which at times was oppressive and annoying, but she meant well, and he was certainly fond of her. No, it was more than that. The intensity of his emotions might eventually become what she called love. In fact, he'd been told that love was a spectrum, with varying degrees of feelings in a variety of situations. He thought he might just be someplace on that spectrum.

In a desperate attempt to bargain with the Emperor, Directeur Venport had broadcast Anna's cheery recording that Erasmus had so carefully crafted for her. Roderick must love Anna as well, but love from a brother was a different variety of that particular emotion, although Erasmus didn't quite understand the difference between the passionate love Anna directed toward him and the close familial love she felt toward a sibling. Or the respectful love that Gilbertus had held for him.

That was another thing to investigate when he had the time and opportunity, when there were no interruptions and no alarms. . . .

In a flash of insight, Erasmus realized that he had hurt Anna with his curt dismissal—hurt her terribly—when she only wanted to love and be loved in return. That was not so much to ask. He paused to review his memories of her distraught expression, her abject despair as she'd fled into the corridors. Hurting her had been unintentional on his part, and not part of any experiment. He had simply been preoccupied with more important things.

She had been so devastated, though, that Erasmus felt . . . sad? Guilty?

In the past, the robot would simply have filed away those observations for later assessment, but he didn't wish to hurt Anna, didn't want to make her sad. He wondered whether this incident might have damaged her irreparably. She was such a fragile specimen.

And she had become more than a mere experiment, much more.

Perhaps he should explain himself to her, and sooner would be better than later, especially if Denali fell and Imperial forces took over the laboratory domes. He didn't wish to miss that chance. Although he did have defensive suggestions for Directeur Venport, he decided that his priorities should now be in finding Anna Corrino. It didn't seem logical, but it did seem right.

He returned to their quarters, but she wasn't there. That did not surprise him, because she had run away sobbing. Likely she was hiding somewhere, and all the shrieking alarms must be frightening her. She would want Erasmus to comfort her, and he had learned techniques to do that. He would apologize to her, which should theoretically be effective.

Erasmus searched in the various laboratories without success and finally went to the cymek hangar, only to find it open and empty. The airlock light was activated, showing that it had been used in the last minute or two. He frowned, then linked into the data from the observation imagers and pulled up the most recent recordings. On screen, he watched Anna stumble into the hangar, weeping and disoriented. She clasped her hands to her head. She looked utterly wretched.

Then, to his astonishment—no, the emotions felt different from that. Was it horror? Or disbelief?—Anna entered the airlock and exited into the caustic atmosphere of Denali. The alarm tone that signaled an unauthorized use of the airlock seemed completely irrelevant amid the urgent background clamor.

Erasmus had been a robot for his entire existence, but knew how delicate Anna's biological form would be. She could not survive long out there in that unbreathable mixture of gases.

The airlock had reset itself, and he wished he had his powerful flowmetal body, or even one of the more cumbersome combat meks that had once held his memory core. He scanned the exterior imagers and saw that Anna had gone no more than a hundred steps from the building. He watched her drop to her knees, then collapse and fall forward.

There was no time to summon help. Erasmus felt a wrench of strange pain inside his chest . . . anguish and fear. There was no time! He had to act.

He strode into the airlock, sealed it, and began the cycle, ignoring the alarms. Anna was only a few steps away, but she was outside. His wonderful body, grown from the cells of Gilbertus, had its weaknesses, but his ward had a strong physique and should last long enough. The Tlulaxa could always grow him another one, but right now he simply had to rescue the frail Anna—pick her up and carry her back to the airlock. Once inside the habitable zone, she could receive treatment at the Denali Medical Center. She would make it. She had to survive.

He could see her through the windowport in the airlock door. She lay blanketed by the greenish-gray mists, but she wasn't moving.

The airlock door opened at last, and Erasmus bounded out onto the surface. He ran at a good pace—he knew how to run. He had been exercising and testing the limits of his muscles. His physical form would no doubt be damaged by the hostile air, but Dr. Danebh or one of the other Tlulaxa scientists could fix that. He wasn't concerned about himself—he was worried about Anna.

But the searing acid inside his mouth and nose was uncomfortable, and very disturbing. He held his breath as he ran, but before he could find her, he had to gulp in more air. Biological imperative. When he choked in a breath, it was like swallowing a river of fire. The caustic fumes charred his lung tissue with shocking pain, and his eyes burned as if someone had thrown a handful of hot sharp needles into them.

Erasmus reeled. His plan to run and retrieve Anna was quickly falling apart. Even with his running start, after a few steps he could barely see. He coughed and sucked in a deep breath, which made the situation much worse. His skin began to blister and burn. Even the fabric of his garment turned brown and began to smoke, but he kept struggling his way forward. Three additional steps. Then two more—closer to Anna. He could almost reach out and touch her.

With some difficulty he made it to Anna's side. Erasmus dropped to his knees next to her, lifting her small body. She twitched and coughed, her body wracked with spasms. Her eyes were milky white and already burned into blindness by the acid air.

Erasmus could barely see her because his own vision was blurred and burning, but he held her, cradled her.

He spoke, his words ragged and raw. "Anna, I did not mean to hurt you." Each breath he took caused more and more damage, as if he were being hollowed out from inside. He didn't know if Anna could hear him, but still he spoke the words. "I am terribly, terribly sorry. You are my love. You taught me what is important in life."

When Anna coughed, dark, smoking blood dribbled from her mouth. As if she could sense he was there, she reached out to touch his face. He strained to hear her voice, but her words were little more than a racking, faltering breath. "My Erasmus—"

Anna Corrino died as he held her. Erasmus pulled her closer against his biological body, knowing his own bodily tissues were failing. The deadly atmosphere would eat away his flesh, his bones, but he thought his brain, the gelsphere core, would survive. Anna was already a burned and disfigured form, but even his sight of her melted into a blurred mix of colors, then black, as he lost his eyes.

Erasmus thought only of how beautiful Anna had looked when he'd made love to her earlier as she had taught him, the delicate, lingering touch of their lips. Since the scientists would have to grow another body for him, maybe they could find enough viable cells to clone Anna, too.

If anything remained of Denali and its research labs.

If anyone ever found him.

When he tried to move, Erasmus found that his muscle control was gone. His limbs failed him. He tried to get to his feet, but collapsed, sprawling on the ground beside Anna. Deep in his memories of human literature and song, he thought about the legends of star-crossed lovers dying in each other's arms. And he appreciated Anna's last words to him.

His own name.

Reassessing now, Erasmus thought that he might truly have loved Anna in the best, most pure way possible; somehow, in simulating love he had attained more than his expectations, without realizing it. He understood now that love had made him do something foolhardy by rushing out here into the deadly atmosphere. Against logic, he had assumed he could just return to the dome after saving her.

Anna had said the Sisterhood taught that the emotion of love was dangerous, and now he had an inkling of why. There was much more to learn about many things, but he might never again have the opportunity.

Around him, his physical body smoked and bubbled, the acids scouring away his borrowed flesh, eating down to the bone, then wearing down his skull and collapsing the structure that supported the gelcircuitry sphere. Through it all, Erasmus's thoughts kept swirling, and he pondered that this fate was not at all what he had expected.

When the biological shell finally dissolved, exposing his memory core to the destructive gases, he was shocked to feel his thoughts melting away, dispersing, disintegrating. Finally, the acids destroyed the gelsphere, erasing every last vestige of Erasmus, down to the final question mark.

The alarms throughout the Denali domes were intended to inspire a sense of urgency and determination in a crisis, yet the primary result was to cause a panic. Josef had to grit his teeth and calm himself so he could think straight. He couldn't let himself appear intimidated in front of the Emperor.

As the Directeur of Venport Holdings, he had the best minds at his disposal; he represented the future of civilization, the triumph of reason over barbarism. He had hoped Roderick Corrino believed the same, but now he knew the man was simply prosecuting his own personal vendetta.

Despite the setbacks, despite betrayals from every side, Josef knew there had to be a solution. He had to find a way to win—and with Anna Corrino he could at least force the Emperor to talk.

Josef had settled into the offices that had once belonged to Administrator Noffe as a place to concentrate. Draigo stood at silent attention beside him; even the Mentat was at a loss to suggest a clever solution.

"We have to find a way out of this," Josef said. "How do we stand up against the Imperial forces? How do we fight? There are more geniuses consolidated on Denali than on any other world in the Imperium, and I brought them here for a reason."

The black-garbed Mentat nodded. "Yes, Directeur, and they have a substantial incentive to remember why they are here. But most of your geniuses are theorists, not military strategists. They develop ideas."

Noffe's old desk, built to accommodate the Tlulaxa administrator, was too small for Josef, but he sat at it anyway. "We are under threat *right now*—there's no time to play with esoteric ideas."

Frustrated, Josef shut down the automated alarms, and an ominous silence fell over the complex of domes. "That racket wasn't helping. My people are already tense enough. I need everyone to concentrate." He looked around, impatient, and his stomach clenched. "Where is Erasmus? He was supposed to deliver a report. I expected him to offer solutions—for his own survival if for no other reason."

Draigo frowned. "The robot is usually reliable. I will send out inquiries."

For the hundredth time, Josef wished Cioba were here. His wife was like a rudder to his drifting ship. With her Sorceress blood and Sisterhood training, she might figure a way out, and at the very least, her presence and guidance might have inspired him to come up with a viable solution. But she was far away now, and he wanted her to be safe. She was better off on Salusa. He was sure she would escape if anything happened to him, and then fold herself back into the Sisterhood.

The people on Denali did not have the option to slip away, though. This would have to be their last stand.

In orbit, the Imperial ships did not back down. Instead, they loomed in a threatening posture with all weapons activated. Before they opened fire, Roderick broadcast again. "Directeur Venport, I demand to see proof of life before I even consider negotiations. Let me speak with my sister."

Judging by the Emperor's image on the comm screen, the man had not slept recently. His Truthsayer stood at his side, so Josef could not lie; fortunately, he did not have to. "Sire, your sister is safe and comfortable here—completely oblivious to the events taking place, and the danger she is in. I have not told her how you betrayed me. Her safety now depends on your actions."

The Emperor's eyes were bloodshot. "Show her to me, and I may decide not to annihilate you."

Josef watched the Imperial forces close in overhead. Numerous VenHold ships prepared to face them, but many of his vessels still needed repair after being damaged at Lampadas. They were not in top fighting condition.

Josef had to buy time. "Easily done, Sire. I will get Anna. Then we can finally negotiate an acceptable solution." He cut off the transmission and looked at Draigo. "There, the Emperor has shown his weakness. Send Anna Corrino to me."

BUT THE YOUNG woman could not be found. Anywhere.

Draigo sent a summons over the laboratory-wide intercom system, and when she did not respond, he made a priority broadcast. "Anyone who has seen Anna Corrino, please inform us. It is most urgent."

Still nothing. They couldn't find Erasmus, either. Their searches turned up no sign of the independent robot.

Josef raised his voice. "I don't understand. These are self-contained domes! How can they be missing?"

Draigo redoubled the search efforts, calling on all scientists, engineers, and security troops to inspect every corridor, ransack every chamber. The Mentat surrounded himself with display screens and reviewed every surveillance recording, scanning through records at the accelerated speed of his mind, absorbing multiple lines of input.

Anna Corrino was not difficult to spot in the recent images. Draigo noted that she looked distraught, walking unevenly and weeping. He watched her enter the cymek hangar and pass through an airlock to emerge in the outside air—to her certain death. Even more astonishing, Erasmus rushed after her only a few minutes later. Both of them had gone outside unprotected.

Draigo considered the ten patrol cymeks that remained at Denali, leftover walker forms that had either been under repair or otherwise not ready to join the Lampadas assault. But the machine bodies were functional enough to march around outside. He instructed the patrol cymeks to circle the domes and find where Anna and Erasmus had last been seen.

Adjusting the input to his screens, he watched as the big walkers searched the area just outside the domes, crisscrossing the rugged terrain. Their imagers used different portions of the spectrum to filter out the poisonous fumes and to cut through the dark gloom.

In minutes, two cymeks came upon a pair of human-shaped stains. Even the residue had mostly been eaten away by the acid mist, leaving only silhouettes and bone fragments. The cymeks took high-resolution images, zooming in.

Draigo's thoughts and projections spun ahead, but he already knew the terrible answer.

One of the cymeks reached forward delicately, as if testing the dexterity of its large mechanical hands. It reached into the larger stain and scooped out a silvery-blue sphere—or what remained of it: the memory core of Erasmus. As the cymek lifted it, the sphere collapsed and oozed out as a synthetic gelatinous-metallic substance that dripped onto the ground.

Draigo closed his eyes. Their hostage, their only bargaining chip to prevent certain defeat, was dead—along with Erasmus.

❧

WHEN HE OPENED the channel to Emperor Roderick in his flagship, Josef knew that his own survival, the future of VenHold, the distant spice operations on Arrakis—everything he had—was on the line. He had made his calculations and saw that his remaining Navigator ships could still put up a good fight, as could his handful of patrolling cymeks. He could defend against a frontal assault by Imperial troops, but only for a time.

It wouldn't be enough, and he couldn't fool Roderick for long.

Right now, he had to make the Emperor believe him, and he had to believe it himself, so he could lie and buy valuable time. Or, he could try to be evasive so that the Truthsayer would not detect his falsehood, giving him a chance to find a way to escape. Maybe during the melee he could fly off in a private ship, leaving it all behind. The Venport legacy would carry on somehow, although it might be hidden in the shrouds of history.

With a stony expression, he faced Roderick Corrino on the screen. The Emperor looked extremely displeased when he didn't see Anna there. "I demand to see my sister immediately."

"I would like to oblige you, Sire, but she is presently unavailable," Josef said in a maddeningly calm voice. "She cannot talk with you." It was the truth. He had to be careful with his choice of words.

"If you cannot produce her, then you are bluffing. We will commence firing on your ships in orbit and continue until Anna becomes 'available.'" The Emperor reached forward to sign off.

"Wait!" Josef cursed his abrupt response, knowing it revealed too much. He caught a subtle flicker in the Truthsayer's expression as she stood next to Roderick. "Your sister is my most powerful leverage. We both know that. And your Truthsayer can hear that I am not lying—Anna came willingly to me. She wanted to be here. I did not coerce her to come here in any way."

Fielle paused, looked uncomfortable. "He is telling the truth, Sire."

Josef snapped, "Withdraw your ships and deactivate your weapons so that we can talk like two businessmen."

"I am *Emperor*, and I am here to mete out justice. When will Anna become available?"

Josef tried not to speak an outright lie but could only come up with, "I cannot say."

Sister Fielle interrupted, asking in a sharp tone, "Will she *ever* be able to speak with us?"

He tried to think of a way he could answer truthfully. "I won't reveal more of my situation. Withdraw your ships, Sire."

Roderick raised his voice in a demand. "Is my sister still alive?"

Josef's pulse raced now. He felt his cheeks flush. Any answer would be a lie, and any hesitation would also reveal the truth. He reached forward to terminate the transmission just as Fielle turned to the Emperor. "Unfortunately, your sister is dead, Sire. Josef Venport's behavior confirms it, beyond any doubt."

Roderick's face fell. His voice came out cold and hollow. "Damn you, Venport!"

Almost immediately, the bombardment began.

There are more ways to win a battle than anyone can teach you.
And even more ways to lose.

—VORIAN ATREIDES

Tula had been shot in the shoulder, and in Valya's moment of sickened hesitation, Vor could have sprung at her and taken her down. Willem's projectile weapon was pointed directly at the young woman's head as she stood in front of him, holding a dagger, and bleeding. One twitch of his finger would kill her.

But Tula faced him, not blinking, not defiant, seemingly not even afraid. She waited with a certain courage and nobility, as if ready to accept her fate, whatever it might be. Yet only months ago she had committed a heinous, cowardly act by murdering Orry.

Watching the tableau, Valya froze in horror, obviously realizing that if she attacked Vorian now, then Willem would kill her sister. The pause was only a few seconds, but it seemed to stretch out forever. Vor sensed something unusual in the air, something unexpected. Was this hard and vengeful woman's concern a reflection of her love for Tula? Was the Sisterhood's leader even capable of such an emotion?

"If you wish to kill me, Willem Atreides, I cannot stop you," Tula said, "and I understand why you're doing it. The terrible pain of your loss justifies your revenge . . . just as the pain of Griffin's loss justified our actions. No matter who killed him."

The comment surprised Vor. The Harkonnens had been rationalizing their hatred toward him for generations, finding one reason after another to continue the feud against a straw man from the past. None of that, though, warranted the slaughter of an innocent young man on his wedding night, just because of his name.

"But if you kill me," Tula continued with a ragged edge in her voice, "you'll also be killing an Atreides. You see, I am carrying Orry's child."

Willem recoiled. "You're lying!"

Vor felt a sick jolt. Was this a desperate trick to save her own life?

Valya looked at her sister in horror. "It can't be true!"

Tula smiled sadly and shifted her body, causing her to wince in pain from the bleeding wound in her shoulder. She gazed at Valya and said, "But it *is* true, dear sister. I was actually fond of Orry, so even though I followed your command to murder him, I made love to him first." Her voice hitched, but she forced herself to keep speaking. "When I returned to Wallach IX, you congratulated me for what I'd done . . . but you never met Orry, did you? You didn't know him. I saw the obvious goodness in him. But even so, I did what you commanded me to do—for you and for House Harkonnen."

"I refuse to believe this!" Valya stared at her sister in complete revulsion.

Vor felt no sympathy for the iron-handed Sisterhood leader, nor for gullible young Tula. All he could think of was the blood-spattered bed and the innocent, slaughtered Orry. "You didn't show any regret when you scrawled your words on the wall in his blood."

"Valya told me what to write," Tula said. "I just delivered the message."

Though Willem still pointed the projectile weapon at her, his hands trembled now. Tula continued to gaze at her sister, as if the young Atreides were not there at all. She pressed a hand against the ragged shoulder wound as she said, "Valya, you know I'm not lying when I say I am pregnant. And you know it is Orry's child."

Standing among the Sisters, Cindel nodded, but Valya did not even look in the Truthsayer's direction. The Mother Superior was white, her eyes narrowed, her breathing fast. Vor thought she might even lash out and kill Tula herself—and he would have to stop her. Not to protect Tula . . . but for the baby. An Atreides baby.

Ignoring her sister and the other female commandos, Tula dropped the dagger on the rocky ground with a punctuating clatter. She climbed to her feet and faced Willem, spread her arms. "Get it over with, if that is what you need to do. For Orry's sake, take me as a sacrifice, and then be done with this. For the Harkonnens and the Atreides."

"She's telling the truth," Valya said, and the words struck Willem like a slap. "She *is* carrying his baby." She screamed at the sky, "My own sister is carrying an *Atreides* child!"

Still poised to spring, Vor spoke a warning to Willem, who kept his weapon pointed at Tula's head, "Take great care to make the correct decision here. If you kill Tula, you could be killing your own brother's child." His gut also told him that Tula was telling the truth, and that it was not a trick. It was too real; her expressions and behavior were too real. She was with child. Vor did not want Atreides blood on their hands—and Valya didn't want to spill Harkonnen blood.

He took a cautious step toward the young Mother Superior, thinking there might be another way out of this. "I am the one you want. I'm the one you've always wanted. I caused Abulurd's downfall after the Battle of Corrin and forced his exile to Lankiveil. I was there when your brother Griffin died, even if I did not kill him. End your vendetta against the Atreides here and now, and take it out on me instead. After this, give Willem the freedom to live his own life—so that your sister and her child can be safe."

"Why should I listen to you?" Valya's eyes were steely.

Vor gave her a cold smile. "We still have something to settle." He felt no fear, paid no attention to the other Sister commandos who had come here to kill them, didn't care about Korla or the fascinated scavengers watching the scene now. "I will face you here—as Griffin and I once faced each other in the sietch on Arrakis, before we put aside our differences. But I need assurances of Willem's safety."

The Queen of Trash interrupted them. "I'll make the arrangements on his behalf. Vorian Atreides did well enough with us here, even saved some of our own. We'll see that young Willem leaves unharmed, with no interference from these women."

The Sisters had a chartered spacefolder in orbit, and with the *New Voyager*, Vor had his own way off the planet, if he survived. Korla would see that Willem made his way to Salusa Secundus—but Vor had to defeat Valya first.

Willem finally holstered his weapon, and Tula nearly collapsed from her bleeding wound. While Vor and Valya continued to face each other like hair-trigger weapons, one of the commando Sisters applied a field-dressing medpack to Tula's injury. The lean, older Sister looked up and gave her assessment. "She needs more care than I can give her here, Mother Superior Valya. We need to get her back up to the main ship."

"Not yet," Valya said. She turned once more toward Vorian. "She will want to watch this. She needs to see it."

Vorian's world focused on his deadly opponent, and he crouched, ready to fight for his life. He reconsidered the wisdom of that, because he knew that even if he defeated Valya Harkonnen here, even if it was a fair fight in front of witnesses, he was sure she would want revenge after all . . . that she might never let Willem live his life in peace.

"I am the one you blame for all that has gone wrong with House Harkonnen," Vor said in a strong voice, hammering the point home. "I am responsible for everything—isn't that the conclusion you reached? If my life is the only payment you'll accept for that debt, then come and take it."

He saw only one way that the Harkonnens would ever relent. He had been prepared for this all along.

In a lightning-fast move, Valya lashed out and struck him, knocking him off his feet. He scrambled back up, but she was a dervish, unleashing years of pent-up hatred and blame. He counterattacked, but could hardly land a blow against her. When he did strike a hard blow in her midsection, she brushed it off and redoubled her attack. Her fighting skills were far superior to Griffin's, and obviously superior to his own.

Coughing blood, Vor looked up and saw a murderous glint in Valya's dark eyes. He spoke through bloody lips, "When you kill me, will you finally be satisfied? Will each of our Houses be whole again?" He needed to make her see the folly of her obsession. He was like a man on his deathbed, trying to right a lifetime of wrongs, real or perceived.

"Stop this, Valya," Tula pleaded. She looked gray-skinned, and the right half of her dark suit was soaked with blood.

But Valya came at him again.

From blow after blow, Vor saw red static around his vision. His head rang as she smashed her open palms against his temples, but they were not mortal blows. In the roar inside his ears, he could hear the Corrin scavengers shouting, calling for him to beat her. He was certain Valya intended to kill him. If he just allowed it, he could end this feud. He'd had a long life, and he was weary in so many ways.

Valya slammed him down to the rubble, threw herself on top of his prone form, pummeling him. He used all his skills to block her repeated attempts at a deathblow, but his energy was waning. Pain erupted from a dozen different injuries, any one of them nearly crippling.

On one side, Willem was shouting in dismay.

Valya knew the most lethal places to strike a human body. She was hurting him intentionally, trying to make him suffer, short of killing him. Finally, he sensed her whole body change, and she coiled for the final deathblow. She would strike like a sledgehammer and cave in his skull.

And Vor was ready for it.

Truth and honor are the allies of the righteous.
Desperation and deceit are the allies of the morally weak.
—ANARI IDAHO

E mperor Roderick's sudden salvo took the crews aboard the damaged Ven-Hold ships by surprise. Kinetic projectiles slammed against enhanced shields, and even though they failed to penetrate, the avalanche of explosive shells overloaded some of the shield generators that had been under repair since the battle of Lampadas.

As the barriers wavered, Emperor Roderick sat on his command bridge, flanked by Truthsayer Fielle and Admiral Harte. "Continue the bombardment on those ships. Their systems will fail soon, if we can keep firing." He turned to Harte. "With our inventory of projectiles, how long can we sustain the barrage at this intensity?"

The Admiral asked a young officer on the bridge, who responded, "We planned for this, Sire. Our ships carry weaponry that is disproportionate to their model. We can continue at this constant rate for seven hours. I cannot say whether that will be sufficient."

"We will have our answer sooner than seven hours." The Emperor felt an angry ache inside that sharpened his focus into an executioner's blade. Anna . . . such an innocent, naïve girl. He couldn't believe Venport would be so foolish as to kill her preemptively; therefore, something else must have happened. An accident? An illness? Some other tragedy? It didn't really matter. In any case, she was dead. Roderick knew that his sister had often been her own worst enemy.

While he could never forgive Venport for assassinating his brother, Salvador's stupid actions had brought about his own demise. Anna, though, was merely a pawn—a flighty girl with absolutely no understanding of the web tangled around her. Venport had taken her hostage for his own purposes, and now she was dead.

For that, Roderick vowed to obliterate the Directeur and everything he cherished.

The VenHold defenders fought back against the Imperial forces, launching a high-powered retaliation, but Roderick remained grimly determined. His fleet pressed onward. Occasionally, one of Harte's ships withdrew, but only if it had suffered so much damage that it could no longer function properly. Still, the rest of the Imperial fleet kept firing. He had learned that type of relentlessness from the Butlerians.

"Continue bombardment. Maintain maximum shields." Their invisible defenses were a complex, flickering pattern in which sections of overlapping Holtzman shields dropped to allow the launch of projectiles, then resealed the gaps with nanosecond timing.

Soon, some of the VenHold vessels—particularly the undamaged commercial ships that had come here at Norma Cenva's call—became adept at finding and predicting those nanosecond weaknesses, and a few projectiles managed to slip through and seriously damage two Imperial ships. Other shields were failing as well.

That only made Roderick angrier.

Admiral Harte turned to the Emperor. "If I might suggest, Sire—the laboratory domes on the surface are far more vulnerable to bombardment than these warships." His voice grew harder. "And since you no longer need to worry about protecting an innocent hostage, dropping suborbital explosives would destroy, or certainly imperil, Venport's operations. That is his weakness."

Roderick felt sickened. "That would bring a swift and decisive end to this, but I want Venport in shackles, dragged before my throne on Salusa. We can't just obliterate him from orbit, as satisfying as that might be. He should be convicted and punished appropriately in front of the entire Imperium, in a very public and painful execution." He nodded slowly, knowing how much Salvador would have enjoyed that. "Bombard only the landing facilities and the outlying domes. Those will be hangars and supply depots. Let him know that we can take him out at any time, unless he surrenders."

Soon, their missiles and bombs plunged down to produce precisely targeted explosions on the surface, and the relentless Imperial pummeling of the VenHold warships continued. Even the strongest shields had never been designed to withstand hours of nonstop bombardment like this.

The Emperor couldn't tear his gaze away from the tactical screens, waiting, *willing*, the enemy shields to fail.

As he watched, one of the VenHold ships finally did succumb. The shields flickered off, and the vessel exploded—a loss that must have dealt a severe psychological blow to the enemy.

Roderick spoke quietly to Fielle and Admiral Harte. "I learned a thing or two from Serena Butler's Jihad: Keep pressing forward, persevere, ignore the odds. Our determination, our sense of moral righteousness, and our refusal to admit defeat is stronger than any of the enemy's weapons."

He continued the surface bombardment and the saturation fire. Their defenses were weakening—Roderick could see that. Yet VenHold warships also obliterated three Imperial vessels and crippled two more. From his flagship bridge, Roderick watched it all unfold.

Just then, with a pop of displaced air and a small wave of pressure that swept across the deck, an armored Navigator tank appeared before the Emperor.

Admiral Harte shouted, leaping to defend Roderick. The guards on the bridge deck drew their weapons. Some of the crew scrambled out of their seats. But the Emperor remained cool. He rose to his feet from the command chair. He could see Norma's distorted form suspended inside the tank, floating in orange spice gas. He had faced her before.

The armored chamber ticked and clicked, adjusting to the new environment with a brief startling hiss, as an overpressure valve vented a cinnamon reek of melange. Roderick gestured for his guards to hold their fire as he stepped bravely up to the tank. "Norma Cenva, I did not expect to see you here."

The swollen head looked at him with oversized, unblinking eyes. Her lips moved, and her eerie, otherworldly voice came through a speakerpatch on the tank. "Many Navigators have died. My Navigators. Next, I predict you will move against Arrakis . . . the spice operations. I cannot allow that. This conflict must stop."

Roderick was not intimidated by her bizarre form. "This conflict will end when Josef Venport surrenders and pays for his crimes—not a moment sooner. He is responsible for his own situation, and for the harm your Navigators have suffered."

"Josef did harm your brother, and he did fail to adequately safeguard your sister. Anna Corrino was difficult to manage, and she took her own life."

The revelation hit Roderick like a punch in the stomach. He struggled for words. "Venport should never have kept her as a hostage."

"There are many things he should not have done." Norma hung there in silence, as if pondering. "For your Imperium, though, the Butlerians caused the greatest turmoil. Forbidden atomics destroyed Kolhar and my Navigator fields. I barely saved my children in time. Butlerian ships wiped out many of my vessels above Lampadas. Your battle group attacked us when we were vulnerable. Your scientists tortured and killed Dobrec. *You* are responsible for the instabilities as well, Emperor Roderick Corrino. This must end."

"I could not ignore the assassination of an Emperor!"

"Your family squabbles are not relevant. The universe is ours, but we must make the correct decisions here today. My Navigators must be permitted to fold space and explore the cosmos. They will create the commercial fabric that binds the Imperium together. My Navigators must be allowed to evolve, to the full extent of their destiny."

"I realize that your Navigators are not active participants in this conflict," Roderick said. "If Directeur Venport is defeated, I will save them. You and your collection of mutant humans will all be permitted to serve under Imperial control."

"My Navigators must fly ships. They must be free to travel across the Imperium and beyond. We need to make many more of our kind, and for that I must have melange. I cannot tolerate this harmful interference. Leave the spice operations intact and productive."

Wheels began turning in Roderick's mind as he realized that she was negotiating with him, but without Venport's knowledge. "As Emperor, I can ensure that your conditions are met. My Imperium also requires Navigators. I need safe and stable commercial shipping. If we consolidate the spice-harvesting operations on Arrakis under Imperial administration and flush out any smugglers there, you will have the constant flow of melange you need. To your benefit, and mine." He placed his face almost against the viewing port. "I will save your Navigators, Norma Cenva—but Venport Holdings must fall. That is not negotiable."

"How would you save my Navigators without Venport Holdings?"

He took heart from her apparent interest. "The VenHold Spacing Fleet is a good model, if it were under the leadership of anyone other than Josef Venport. Venport Holdings, as a company, must be dissolved. The whole Imperium must see that they have been defeated after defying their Emperor." He spoke quickly of ideas he had been pondering, and now that the opportunity arose, he seized his chance.

"I would endorse a unified and reliable spacing fleet of large ships guided without error by Navigators. I propose the creation of an independent Spacing Guild to serve commerce throughout the Imperium. Communication and transportation is the tapestry that binds our civilization together across countless planetary systems. Trade must be allowed to function unfettered by war or the threat of war. Under this new Spacing Guild, I will see that you have all the Navigators you wish, and all the spice you need." He hardened his voice. "But only if Venport Holdings is defeated and dissolved."

Norma hesitated, considering possibilities in her advanced mind. "Very well, I will remove the defenses around Denali. Your troops may land and do as you wish."

Fielle interrupted, "But Josef Venport is your great-grandson. You would betray him?"

"Josef is mortal and insignificant. On the great path of prescience, the future is spread out before us. I have foreseen a Spacing Guild such as you propose. Now we must make it happen."

Roderick's heart pounded. Could the solution be so straightforward, so simple as this?

Norma continued, "But I must have your word, Emperor Roderick Corrino. No more treachery." She amplified her voice so that it pounded across the flagship's bridge. "Vow, before your God and these witnesses, that no Navigators will be harmed, neither the ones that have been transformed nor those who are yet to undergo the transformation."

He crossed his arms over his chest. "You have my Imperial promise, and my promise as the noble head of House Corrino. *No Navigator will be harmed.* We have a bargain."

Without a word, Norma folded space, and her sealed tank withdrew with a clap of muffled thunder.

Roderick looked at Admiral Harte, drew a breath, and said, "All Imperial ships, stand down immediately. Cease firing on the VenHold vessels." His brow furrowed. "But continue our bombardment of the surface."

Less than five minutes later, without warning, every one of the original Ven-Hold defense ships circling Denali simply folded space and vanished, abandoning the laboratory planet, leaving it naked and vulnerable. It reminded the Emperor of what Norma had done with the VenHold fleet besieging Salusa.

Roderick smiled at the suddenly undefended installation. "Admiral Harte, dispatch our troops—thousands of armed soldiers in personnel carriers. Swarm the planet and arrest the scientists." He took a deep, agitated breath. "And bring me Josef Venport."

Things of great value can vanish in an instant.
—a saying of Old Earth

As Valya coiled to kill him, Korla's booming voice seemed to make time stop. "Enough! Step away from that man or you'll be suffering mortal wounds of your own."

Vorian lay battered and broken on the ground, expecting the next strike to be the deathblow. He was prepared for it. One way or another he had to stop this vendetta, even if it meant the end of his own long life. At least Willem could survive and thrive.

But Korla was preventing the end of the feud. "Let her finish me," Vor croaked.

"No!" Willem shouted. "Kill him, and I'll kill you."

"No," Vor said. "No, you won't. This vendetta has gone on too long, for too many generations. It has to stop here!"

The scavengers who had gathered to watch the duel now put an end to it. The hard-bitten workers who had survived so much hardship raised their brute-force projectile rifles and aimed them toward the surviving commando Sisters. They also had daggers at their hips and were ready to fight. If any of the Sisters moved, they would be gunned down. Although Vor understood that they would not surrender easily with their deadly fighting skills, the odds were not in their favor.

"That's enough, I said," Korla repeated. "Vorian Atreides leaves here alive."

Valya flashed a sharp glance at her. "We came all this way to kill the Atreides. I intend to do so."

"In life, we don't always get what we want," Korla said in a mocking tone. "You've had your fun. You've beaten him."

"Not enough."

"But I said it was enough," Korla answered, with a swirl of her flowmetal cape. "And I rule here, not you."

Valya seemed torn between her desire to kill Vor and her desire to make him suffer for as long as possible. She looked at all the deadly weapons pointed at her commandos, hundreds of armed scavengers against a handful of women. After reaching an apparent crisis in her mind, she pulled away from Vor, lifted her hands in capitulation, and sneered down at his broken form. "You want me to let him run away."

"Yes," Korla said.

"That won't put an end to it," Vor said.

"But I will not need to bother with it anymore. Go—get to your ship. Fly out of here before I change my mind."

Valya's dark eyes had a sudden unreadable gleam. "Yes, go. Escape in your ship, and we will keep hunting you." Then, looking over at the pregnant Tula, she added in a voice that made Vor's blood cold, "Besides, if I ever change my mind, I always have an Atreides I can kill."

Tula recoiled in shock, and Willem growled, "That's my brother's child. It belongs on Caladan, with my family."

"It is my child!" Tula said.

"It belongs to the Sisterhood," Valya snapped. "That will be good enough for me to know . . . and for you to know, Vorian Atreides. Even if you get away, you will always remember that I have your bloodline in my grasp, along with my own bloodline." She laughed. "I find that acceptable. Go to your ship. Get out of here."

Feeling his bruises, the cracks in his bones, the blood streaming down his face, Vor pushed himself up from the ground. He wiped blood from his mouth. "I'm your target, not another innocent person. Not Willem. Not an unborn baby." He turned to the young man, who stood seething. "I want you to go now, Willem— and be safe. Remember where I told you to go."

Willem interjected. "No, Vor, I'm coming with you now. We'll leave together on your ship."

He shook his head. "I put you in too much danger, and that will be the case for as long as you're with me. I go alone into my unknown future. For your own sake, for the sake of House Atreides, you've got to break away from me. Create your own life, and do well." He suspected Willem would want to return to see Princess Harmona on Chusuk before going to the Imperial Court on Salusa Secundus. "I've provided you with everything you need to succeed. You have leadership qualities. Use them."

Before Valya could declare another blood vendetta against Willem, Korla stepped forward. "Willem will stay here, under my protection, until these bitches are long gone." Her scavengers gestured with their weapons. Vor looked at the Queen of Trash, and she gave a brief nod. "Go, Vorian Atreides—take your ship. Fly to safety while we hold them here."

Oddly, Valya just smiled.

The scavengers, including Horaan Eshdi, kept their weapons trained on the frustrated Sisters. Korla said to Valya, "Once Vorian is away safely, you can all go back to whatever you call home. And don't bother us again."

Vor did not feel victorious. He just felt cold inside.

Bleeding from dozens of injuries, he glanced at Willem, whose face was filled with a plea. Vor knew this was the last time he would ever see the young man, and said to him, "I've tried to leave my past behind many times already. Maybe this time I will succeed." He limped off through the rubble, winding his way between the unbalanced spires and collapsed skyscrapers of what had once been the thinking-machine metropolis.

Though held back by all the weapons trained against her, Valya called out, "We will keep coming for you, Vorian Atreides."

He paused and looked back at her. "I know you will."

THE SCAVENGERS DID not lower their guard even after Vor departed.

Willem wanted to lash out at someone; he felt confused and dissatisfied. He was even more sickened by Tula than he had been before, this young woman who had conceived a child just before murdering his brother. What terrible things would the Sisterhood do to that infant, that innocent child? He had to find some way to save it . . . but how could he continue his quest to murder Tula, if she was the mother of Orry's child?

The scavengers waited, their weapons ready. Valya and the commando Sisters looked like bombs waiting for a spark to light the fuse. It was obvious that they didn't like to feel helpless.

"Well, this is a nice little standoff," Korla remarked.

With an intense, irresistibly evocative Voice, Valya barked, *"Drop your weapons."*

Startled, some of the scavengers did, and their projectile rifles clattered on the rubble. The other Sisters prepared to move forward in attack, but the remaining scavengers primed their weapons.

"Not another word from you!" yelled Korla. "You can command some of us with that witchery, but not all of us at the same time. And we'll gun you down before you can speak again."

Sheepish, the scavengers who had reacted to the strange vocal command grabbed their projectile rifles again and stood closer. More than a hundred deadly weapons remained targeted on the Sisters.

Willem squirmed, almost wishing they would make a move.

Vorian had been keeping the *New Voyager* nearby, and in less than ten minutes they heard the powerful takeoff engines building to proper levels. Willem gazed through the debris of broken buildings with tears stinging his eyes, watching for the ship to lift off, taking Vor to a new world, a new life.

How he longed to go with him! Yes, he understood the opportunities that waited for him at the Imperial Court, but he enjoyed being with the legendary hero who had become his mentor, and loved listening to his stories about the Jihad.

"As soon as I see him fly up to orbit, you're all free to go," Korla told the Sisters, crossing arms over her chest. "And we'll be glad to have you gone. Willem, there's a spacefolder due here in two days. I will escort you to whatever planet you like."

Frustrated, Willem mumbled under his breath.

With a rushing thrum of engines, Vor's personal ship lifted off the ground. The ornate, antique vessel climbed slowly and smoothly into the air. Once in orbit, the FTL engines would be engaged and the ship would leave Corrin and Vor's pursuers behind.

"We will find him again," Valya vowed. "We will always be watching." She stared at the ship with an angry expression on her face.

Willem bit off the words. "You've accomplished nothing. Vor's bruises will heal, and he's been good at eluding you—and everyone else—for a very long time."

"Maybe his fate will catch up with him," Valya said.

Suddenly, with a boom that cracked across the sky like thunder, Vor's ship exploded in midair. Its engines split open in a fiery geyser that ripped the hull apart. The fuel tanks ignited, adding a double, then a triple fireball.

Willem's mouth dropped open. He collapsed to the ground moaning, hardly able to speak or breathe. The scavengers stared upward at the expanding debris cloud, crying out in shock.

Large pieces of torn, burning wreckage tumbled out of the sky, pattering into the ruins of the machine buildings. In the sky, a blossom of smoke and flames spread out, then faded like spirits drifting away.

Willem began weeping openly, his hands clenched. He wanted to throw himself on Tula or Valya, but Korla saw his mounting violence and nudged him with the end of a projectile rifle. "Don't do what you're thinking, boy."

Mother Superior Valya stared up at the wreckage in the sky, her face a smug, satisfied mask. "There are many paths to victory. That was not my preference, but Vorian Atreides is dead. It's a triumph I can accept."

Willem seethed. These women must have found Vorian's ship and sabotaged it as a contingency plan, as they were closing in on the tunnels where he and Vor had hidden.

Korla was thinking the same thing. "Did you rig his ship to explode?"

Valya sniffed. "You have no proof of that, do you?"

Korla just glowered at her. The ship was barely a smudge in the sky now, all that remained of the legendary Vorian Atreides, the great Hero of the Jihad, the savior of mankind from the thinking machines.

It occurred to Willem that the Jihad had ended here on Corrin decades ago, and this was where the famous Vorian Atreides eventually met his end as well. Willem could not see any way to call it a fitting end for the greatest man he had ever met, or would ever meet. But some would undoubtedly say exactly that.

Valya skewered Willem with her gaze. "Watch yourself, Atreides pup. A vendetta that has burned so brightly for generations will not just fade away." Then she and her commando Sisters turned to leave, heading in the direction of the wreckage that had fallen from the sky.

Where some see treachery, others see opportunity. The definition depends on which side of the issue you are on.

—DIRECTEUR JOSEF VENPORT, final Denali logs

The pointless and unnecessary death of Anna Corrino, as well as the loss of Erasmus, had figuratively cut Josef's legs out from under him like a cruel parody of Manford Torondo.

With his fleet of Navigator-guided spacefolders, he had the largest commercial enterprise in the history of the Imperium. His operations on Arrakis produced and distributed spice to meet the hungry demands of addicted citizens as well as for Norma's Navigators. He had envisioned a golden age of advancement and prosperity, the ability for the human race to achieve its dreams. . . . He had also experienced the pitfalls: the clumsy leadership of Emperor Salvador, the ignorance and superstition espoused by the violent fanatics.

I could have saved them—saved them all. I could have kept humanity out of the dark ages . . . and yet they insist on marching blindly over the precipice.

All his work was collapsing around him, one huge section at a time, leaving him deeply wounded and isolated. His Denali scientists had come up with no new weapons to save the facility. The vengeful Emperor was tightening his military noose around the planet, willing to sacrifice his own battleships to break through the VenHold defensive cordon, while relentlessly bombing the surface. Josef held on, trying to find some last-ditch defense, hoping for a miracle.

And then Norma simply whisked away all of her Navigator ships, leaving Denali exposed.

The VenHold fleet that had been standing as the defensive barrier against the Imperial ships just . . . vanished into space! Then, with Denali suddenly unprotected, the Imperial fleet surged in.

Josef stared at the screen, unable to believe what had just happened. Norma had done the same thing to him at Salusa, and now he howled out her name, railing at her. "Why are you trying to destroy me?"

She did not respond.

Standing in the operations center of the main laboratory dome, he collapsed to the deck. After achieving so much, on such a huge scale, he had lost everything. He could not prevent Roderick's victory now.

The continuing bombardment from orbit targeted the area around the laboratory domes. Several explosions had wrecked the warehouses and habitation shelters around the perimeter; one blast destroyed a cymek walker as it patrolled the poisonous landscape. Without even delivering an ultimatum, Emperor Roderick sent down a flood of ground troops to take over the base.

Josef turned away from the images of the oncoming ships on the screens and faced his Mentat, who asked him, "Now that Roderick knows Anna is dead, he could simply carpet bomb this installation and kill everyone in the domes. Why take the risk of a ground assault?" Draigo pursed his lips and postulated, "It is possible he does not wish the collateral loss of life among the other Denali scientists. He may want to salvage and co-opt our research."

With a sinking feeling, Josef realized that he knew the answer. "No, it's because he wants to take me alive—to disgrace me and drag me before the highest court in the Imperium on trumped-up charges. For the time being, no matter what happens, he will let me live." His face burned with helpless anger. What a fool he had been to trust the Emperor! He muttered to himself, "I used to consider Roderick Corrino a reasonable man, but I'm willing to bet he will choose one of Salvador's barbarian execution methods."

His eyes stung, and he had trouble breathing. Considering the alternative, suicide might be a better option, but he wasn't ready to take that long, dark plunge. It was never an option that Josef Venport would consider. He didn't want such a disgrace to be his final act, the thing that people would remember about him. After all he had accomplished, all he had dreamed—what would Cioba think?

As the Directeur, he had handled multiple business, political, and military crises, always finding a way to juggle one of them against the others, to pull an unorthodox solution from the rubble of possibilities. But even he could not mitigate so many betrayals, so many disasters, so many inconceivable setbacks hitting him at the same time.

❦

HUNDREDS OF TROOP transports descended through the murky skies to alight around the Denali complex. The nine remaining patrol cymeks scuttled toward the troop carriers to attack them as they landed. With powerful walker arms, they ripped open the hulls, exposing the human crews to the deadly atmosphere. The last cymeks destroyed five transports, immobilizing and crushing them all, but more Imperial ships kept landing in a rocky open area within reach of the facility, and exo-suited soldiers stormed across the terrain toward the domes. These fighters for the Emperor were far more heavily armed than the Butlerian mobs had been.

As Josef watched on the screens in his office stronghold, he saw hangar doors open in two of the warehouse domes, and ranks of refurbished combat meks marched out onto the hostile landscape of Denali. Erasmus had reprogrammed the fighting robots out there. Even though the independent robot was gone now, the combat meks marched out of their own volition.

"Mentat, report," Josef said.

"Erasmus must have programmed them to respond in the event of a crisis," Draigo said. "Maybe to protect himself, or possibly more than that. Not all of the meks are operational—many were still in bad condition the last time he gave me an inspection tour."

"But some are functional enough." Josef felt a surge of hope as more and more of the combat robots streamed out to face the attackers. "Will they be enough to turn the tide?"

"Doubtful, Directeur," Draigo said. "But at least we have a chance at defense now."

The first wave of the exo-suited Imperial soldiers found themselves facing an enemy they had not expected . . . hundreds of burly, lurching combat robots. "Fighting meks!" a captain called through the comm.

The Imperial soldiers had been trained to expect a fight, though, and their commanders had not underestimated what exotic defenses the Denali weapons scientists might raise against them. The suited Imperial soldiers turned their heavy weapons against the mechanical army from the past.

The fighting meks pushed forward in an uneven surge, targeting both landed ships and fighters. Thanks to the caustic atmosphere, their body metal was tarnished and corroded; some of their segmented limbs hung useless. But they were relentless. The machines skittered forward like a nightmare from the Jihad.

Imperial pulse weapons mowed them down, but the corroded robots kept coming. Once the first ranks reached close combat, the meks began to kill the Imperial soldiers by gashing their protective suits or tearing off their breathing helmets. Even a minor breach of the seal was enough to make them collapse.

The Imperial soldiers fell back to the shelter of the landed carriers, and from there they mounted a defense against the combat meks. The landers themselves had offensive weapons that drove back the machine advance. Many of the corroded robots malfunctioned and were unable to keep moving forward. The Emperor's fighters picked them off from their defensive positions, holding firm with their concentrated barrage.

Over the course of several hours, the exo-suited soldiers suffered casualties, but they neutralized the majority of the fighting robots. Then they regrouped and charged toward the sealed laboratory domes, and proceeded to break into them.

FROM WITHIN NOFFE'S old administration chamber, Josef could hear the shouts as some of the airlocks were breached. The previously muted alarms came back on, and he felt cornered. Norma had abandoned him without a word of explanation, and he could not begin to grasp why she would do so. Was there another raid on the spice operations at Arrakis? He had already left so many of his defenses there . . . and he could sorely use them here at Denali.

Surely, Norma knew what Emperor Roderick would do to him once he was captured. She had to know she was leaving him to die. She simply couldn't be as oblivious and detached as she seemed. No, Norma had done this intentionally—abandoned him. His great-grandmother, his business partner . . . and after all he had given her, all the concessions he had made so that she could continue to develop her precious Navigators. Many people had turned against him, but *this* was the one betrayal Josef had never expected.

The universe is ours, she always said. But apparently she was content to have a universe without Josef in it.

Draigo returned to report that the last of the combat meks had fallen and that the occupying forces were now unhindered. The Mentat ran a hand nervously through his black hair. "I cannot project any viable option for our victory, Directeur—or for your escape."

Josef looked at the images being transmitted from outside. Imperial soldiers had already breached the hangar airlocks and overrun several laboratories. They were seizing Denali scientists and confining them in makeshift holding cells; some researchers were killed outright if they tried to flee or resist.

He was grimly pleased to see Tlulaxa scientists slow the advance of the Imperials. In one of the biological domes, they unleashed three prototype biomechanical borers—insidious lampreys with metallic teeth that lunged forward to attack the soldiers. Oh, if only those could have been manufactured in great numbers and then turned loose on a superstitious mob of fanatics! Josef had not imagined using the borers against Imperial soldiers, but the cornered scientists were desperate and resourceful.

In the end, though, it wasn't enough.

The biomechanical lampreys lashed and struck, chewing and tunneling. Three Imperials were killed, half eaten before the prototype machine creatures were neutralized. Then the enraged soldiers turned their weapons on the cowering Tlulaxa scientists and massacred them.

More suited troops kept pushing in through the laboratory domes, taking and holding one corridor after another, one chamber after another. They made their way methodically to the administration dome—and Josef had nowhere else to run.

As he and his Mentat stood together in the administration chamber, Draigo said to Josef, "Permit me to act as negotiator, Directeur. I will present myself as your representative and arrange to save our scientists and our important research. I may be able to salvage something out of this."

"You're talking about surrender," Josef said.

"I believe it is the only option. The question you must answer, Directeur, is whether or not you wish to be taken alive." It was a flat, cool statement, but Draigo's intent eyes burned into his.

"I am not going to kill myself, Mentat. That would be an admission of complete failure."

"Such was my guess, sir, yet I regret to inform you that I have no reasonable projection in which Emperor Roderick allows you to live. The timing of your death may be the only part that is in your control."

Ice ran down Josef's spine. "Go, Mentat—make your best deal. Save yourself and save something of my legacy . . . maybe the human race can use it after all, my innovation, my business models. You are an excellent negotiator." He took a breath. "I thank you for your years of service."

With a brisk nod, Draigo left the admin chamber. Josef sealed the door behind him, although the lock would never withstand a concerted effort to break through. Silent and alone, he sat at Noffe's old desk knowing this was the last remnant of his vast planetary commercial empire. He had been squeezed down to this, trapped and cornered.

He heard pounding on the barricaded metal hatch of the office, and the hiss of thermal cutters as they began to burn through the sealed lock.

His stomach clenched, and thunderous possibilities clamored around his head. He couldn't think of any other way out, but knew these Imperial soldiers would capture him, and he would be disgraced, every last vestige of his legacy destroyed.

And after all that, Roderick would put him to death, undoubtedly with a big celebratory event in the main square of Zimia.

The barricaded office door began to collapse, glowing red, metal dripping down the wall. His mind started to go blank. The end was near, and he had nowhere to run. His entire future and past had focused down to this one moment.

Suddenly, Norma Cenva's tank appeared in the chamber, crushing the chair that had only recently held Draigo Roget. The armored vault knocked aside the furniture, collapsed a shelf in the small office.

Josef showed no surprise or fear to see her there, did not even rise from his chair. He merely glared at her, his heart as heavy as stone. She had already shattered his last hope—what more did she want of him? To gloat? To explain herself in hopes that he would forgive her?

His voice projected the deep weariness and disappointment he felt. "I did not believe you would ever do it, Grandmother, but you destroyed me."

His heart ached as he longed to see his beautiful wife once more, but he knew that was not possible. No, he was deluding himself. He had nothing, at least nothing that could save him. Neither his money nor his spice could do it.

Now, for the first time, he finally felt defeated, with no way out. "I thought we shared a common dream," he said to her. "I gave you everything you needed, I fought to pave a clear future for human civilization, to save the Imperium . . . and instead of defending me to the last, you betrayed me." He smiled grimly. "You threw me to the Corrino lions."

Norma's swollen head came close to the observation windowport. "I have not destroyed you, Josef, nor have I abandoned you. My prescience showed me possible paths of failure, but I chose the one that would save my Navigators . . . and you."

"You're going to save me? Where will you take me, to Arrakis?" He lurched to his feet as he heard the clamor continuing through the connected laboratory domes. The cutting tools had almost opened the door. "You'd better be quick about it. This complex is overrun. Emperor Roderick will execute me. His soldiers will be here any moment, and his torturers will not be far behind."

Her voice was maddeningly steady. "There is no place in the universe for you to hide. No, I have a different solution."

"What are you saying?" He looked at the door, saw it caving in, heard the shouts of soldiers on the other side. "We're running out of time!"

Her voice came back to him as distant words, painfully slow. "Emperor Roderick made a solemn promise that he would protect all of my Navigators, that they would not be harmed. A new Spacing Guild is to be formed. The universe is ours."

"Good for you," Josef said, unable to keep the sarcasm from his voice. "You got what you wanted. How does that help me?"

"It is a significant loophole. Emperor Roderick gave me his word. It is for the best." Spice gas vented from her tank, and a small hatch on the side disengaged from its seals. "You must become a Navigator, Josef."

We must understand evil if we are to fight it, but only evil can truly understand evil. That is the quandary our souls must face.

　　　　　—ANARI IDAHO, new leader of the Butlerian movement

I n the ruins of Empok, the surviving Butlerians began to pick up the pieces so they could rebuild, although it seemed an impossible task. Anari Idaho quickly silenced any expressions of hopelessness or despair, however. Her voice was harsh, her face stern as she bellowed to the throngs, "Challenges strengthen us. Our great Leader Toronto would never have given up! Every breath spent complaining is a breath that should be devoted to work. We have much to rebuild here—so rebuild!"

Imperial teams came to Lampadas bearing supplies and workers, but Anari saw them for what they were: watchdogs, spies, and controllers. They meant to bottle up the movement on this planet. Her Butlerians were forced to tolerate the intrusion . . . for now. Until they grew stronger.

By order of the Emperor, the fallen cymek walkers were turned into monuments, optimistic declarations that the strength of the human spirit—the power of bare hands and complete faith—was sufficient to bring down even titanic nightmares. The cymek preservation canisters had been smashed, and remnants of the evil disembodied brains had been stomped into organic pulp; all else was burned so that no vile residue could contaminate the faithful.

Even defeated, though, these ominous wrecks made Anari shudder whenever she looked at them. Some Butlerians wanted to dump the components in the swamps near the Mentat School, but as much as she loathed what the machine monsters represented, she refused to do that. On this her feelings ran parallel with those of Emperor Roderick. From her standpoint, it was important for every Butlerian to see them and remember the horrors of unchecked

technology . . . a message that humans must never become lax in their vigi-
lance.

The Imperial reconstruction crews worked at cross-purposes with the natives,
razing the remnants of the old city. By strict Imperial command, the Butlerian
mourners were forbidden to erect a monument at the site where Manford had
fallen. Despite the increasing wails of grief from the people, the soldiers stood
firm and drove off any protesters. Anari was offended, but could see no way to
win that fight. Not yet. So she changed the rules and announced to the faithful,
"Manford is not a *place*. He lives in my heart and everywhere, and all of you feel
the same. Our monument for Manford is within our hearts, in the memories
we hold of him."

While heavy Imperial machinery crushed the damaged buildings, covered
up mass graves where countless lesser martyrs were laid to rest, and paved over
portions of the Empok battleground, Anari led a group of the faithful to the
battered warrior form that had been the Ptolemy cymek, the monster that had
murdered Manford. Using simple tools, they disengaged one of the pincer claw-
hands, still marked with Manford's blood. Holy blood.

Under cover of darkness, Anari had the grim relic smuggled back to Butlerian headquarters, where it sat, unwashed, for all to see. The dried bloodstains
were a simple reminder of painful but necessary sacrifices, and she did not let
them forget that Manford Toronto was only one of half a million martyrs who
had fallen on that horrific day.

Inside the headquarters building, the morning air was filled with the loud
and chaotic sounds of construction work. Heavy haulers and small hand wagons
carted away the residue of shattered buildings, thousands of tons of rubble. By
Emperor Roderick's order, they would build a new, simpler city.

Because of the numerous threats against his life, Manford had always kept a
body double who could make public appearances in his stead. On that terrible
day when the cymeks attacked Empok, Manford had refused to let the double serve
his destiny, and now Anari resented this man who looked so much like Leader
Toronto; he had failed utterly, for he remained alive while Manford was dead.

Anari had failed in the same way.

Now, the body double seemed too eager to fulfill his role again, and to broaden
it. "I can become a new Manford Toronto," he insisted. "Stronger than ever.
The people will know I've returned. They will believe in me."

"Only the gullible ones will. It's not a good idea."

He had come to her in Manford's old administration offices—her offices
now. She was annoyed that he had allowed himself to be seen, since the double's
very existence had always been a carefully kept secret. Seeing him had caused
a few ecstatic and terrified followers to claim that Leader Toronto's ghost had

returned to guide them, a spirit from beyond who could offer the truth and wisdom that the Butlerians sorely needed right now.

Anari angrily dispatched her own people to quash the rumors. She closed the curtains in the offices so that others could not glimpse him now.

Propped up on cushions, seated like Manford in a chair designed to accommodate his legless form, the double looked at Anari with a fiery determination in his eyes. She didn't know his original name, but his name didn't really matter. He had pretended to be Manford for so long that without his physical resemblance to the charismatic leader, he was nothing.

Deacon Harian—his forehead bandaged from a severe wound, and one eye blinded from the acid mists sprayed by the cymeks, his arm in a sling—was also in the office. Though he was just as determined to do something significant in the aftermath, he looked uneasily at the double. Anari would have to make the necessary decision, and she was perfectly willing to do so.

The surrogate said, "We have an opportunity now. You need me!" His voice sounded strident. "I will make the Butlerians strong."

She looked at him closely, but his face was wrong. Yes, the features were similar, but this was not Manford. Anari knew the real Manford more intimately than any other person, and this ambitious creature was a far cry from the man he resembled.

"You can use me," said the double, and now his voice took on a whining edge. "As Manford Torondo, I will lead the Butlerians back to prominence, and we will be stronger than ever."

"Your role *was* to appear to be Manford Torondo." Anari hardened her voice. "But you are not Manford. You were chosen for similarity of features and for your willingness to sacrifice part of your body, not because of any skill or charisma you possess."

Angry now, she stepped around the furniture that had once been Manford's. She kept her long sword lying across the surface of the desk so she would never forget who she really was. "We do not need you. Your appearance would only cause confusion and raise questions."

"I should have been there to die for him, I know that," mumbled the duplicate. "I tried, but Manford wouldn't let me. He ordered me to stay away."

Anari reminded herself that Manford's spirit carried on inside her, as well as inside his most loyal followers. That would have to be sufficient.

The look-alike's burning ambition disturbed her. It had been difficult enough to cover up and salvage the truth after so many witnesses in Arrakis City saw an earlier "Manford" shot in the head with a projectile pistol. Now, convincing the mass of followers that Leader Torondo still lived was impossible, since countless thousands had watched the real Manford ripped to pieces by the demon cymek.

"The Butlerians will move forward under my leadership," Anari said. "I will guide them myself, because I understand what Manford would have wanted. I know his true goals." She had never wanted to lead the movement, but perhaps not wanting it was a criterion for the task. Anyone who desired a position of such great power might not be worthy to have it.

The look-alike had a stubborn streak. "But I am trained! I am perfect for the job."

Anari corrected him. "You were taught how to read scripts. That is all."

"Don't you see?" the look-alike said. "We can say it was a body double torn apart by the cymek, not the real Manford! I'll become the real Manford!"

"It's not going to happen," she said, glowering at him.

With his one good eye, Deacon Harian regarded her, drank in the conversation, and saw where it was going. He gave her a slight nod.

The double continued, openly whining now. "But I made so many sacrifices. I gave everything I had to the movement, even agreed to have my legs amputated."

"Yes," Anari agreed, and picked up her sword. "And now you must make one more sacrifice. You are no longer needed." She strode closer to him and raised the blade.

He looked at her with terrified eyes and tried to scramble away, but without his legs he was not nearly as nimble as Manford had been.

Just as she swung the blade in a classic arc, she looked at the man's face and felt a disquieting shiver of recognition, for it almost seemed as if she were killing Manford. But Anari had already been responsible for his death once, and this man was just a pale, irritating imitation.

Her sword cleanly sliced off the duplicate's head, just as she had decapitated Headmaster Albans in front of the Mentat School. She took no great satisfaction in the task. With Manford dead and an empty hole in her soul, Anari doubted if she would ever feel real satisfaction again.

Still, she had to perform her duty for the human race, in Manford's memory.

Deacon Harian stood, accepting her decision. "Yes, it is better if you become the face of the Butlerians now. They don't need any further confusion."

She called in the bearers who had carried the legless man into the office and told them to take away the garbage. Deacon Harian followed them out. He gave her a quick glance, and Anari read his expression, knowing he would take care of the bearers as well, removing the last witnesses.

Yes, it was time to move on.

Manford had left her with a very heavy burden. She felt uncomfortable occupying this place that had been his sanctuary after the initial cymek attack killed Sister Woodra and destroyed his cottage. She didn't feel right usurping everything that had been Leader Torondo's, but she had to do it for the sake of the movement, for the sake of Manford and Rayna. If she didn't do this, the Butlerians would fall apart, and the efforts of those great and inspirational leaders would have been for naught.

Their space fleet had been almost completely destroyed in the battle, and the remaining ships had been seized by Emperor Roderick for his own fight against Directeur Venport. Anari suspected the Butlerians would never get their warships back again. Without access to space transportation, she and all of Manford's followers were mostly stranded on Lampadas, but that was fine for now. They could rebuild here and grow stronger . . . no matter how long it took.

Though she did not fully understand such things, she'd been told that Roderick had confiscated Butlerian financial assets on other planets to add to the Imperial coffers, claiming the movement's money as repayment of the debt incurred by this horrific war. These followers had already given everything of themselves, and hundreds of thousands had sacrificed their lives in the last battle.

Money was the least of their concerns, though. They would persevere. With massive numbers, they would persevere.

Alone in the haunted office, Anari began to look around, and discovered that one of the cabinets by Manford's desk was locked. She was aware he had kept secrets, but she knew what those secrets were anyway. And she realized what must be inside that cabinet. Her pulse quickened.

She used a tool to break the lock and pry open the cabinet door. Inside, she found three thick books that had long ago been taken from the devastated ruins of Corrin . . . laboratory journals written by the vile robot Erasmus.

Her skin crawled. She touched the top volume and quickly withdrew her fingers as if burned. But the journal called out to her like a hypnotic serpent, and she took it out and placed it on the desk. This book was evil, filled with poisonous thoughts. Part of her knew that she should immediately burn all three volumes, destroying those words so that the insidious writings would be erased forever.

But she paused, weighed down by confusion and doubt. Anari knew that Manford had secretly read these books. He had pored over them when he locked himself in his room, believing that Anari did not know. But she kept such a close watch on her beloved leader that very little escaped her notice.

Manford had found something worthwhile in these dangerous writings, something important. He had once told Anari that he intended to understand the evil of the oppressors of humanity.

She opened the first volume and began to read, finding dark chronicles of violent experiments, tortures of captive humans, psychological manipulations, all part of the robot's attempt to comprehend human emotions and motivations, although a demon could never grasp the human soul.

Anari's brow furrowed as she kept reading, page after page.

And yet . . .

Manford had made numerous notes in the margins, his own thoughts, responses, arguments refuting the robot's claims. And sometimes, appallingly, he actually agreed with Erasmus.

Anari closed the book and put it on top of the others. She would study the writings later, page by page, but she promised herself that she would not let them taint her. She would use the journals of Erasmus for her own purposes, just as Manford had. Yes, that was what she would do.

In a supreme irony, she and her reborn Butlerians would—through Erasmus—ensure that demon technology would never again run rampant in human civilization.

Denali was overrun, at last. The Imperial Armed Forces had suffered many casualties against the cymek stragglers and the corroded combat meks, but they had brought down the last of the battle machines before securing the entire domed facility. Now it was time to take care of loose ends.

Troops had breached the sealed laboratory domes and surged inside to capture the refugee weapons scientists. The soldiers had incurred more casualties in doing so, but now Denali was completely under Imperial control. All in all, Roderick was satisfied; he would have suffered far more significant losses in the space battle if Norma Cenva had not made her surprising bargain with him. All of her Navigator ships had simply withdrawn from the battlefield, leaving the VenHold laboratories completely vulnerable.

When Admiral Harte informed him that Denali was secure, Roderick descended to the surface to claim his hard-fought victory. All resistance had been quashed, and every one of the domes was under firm control, locked down by Imperial forces. Accompanied by his heavily armed escort, the Emperor took a military shuttle down through the murky clouds. He brought his Truthsayer along, but he remained silent as they rode through the bumpy air currents, lost in his own thoughts. He felt a sharp sadness over how much this conflict had cost him personally—Salvador, sweet Nantha, and now Anna as well.

But Roderick clung to his triumph. Both of his main enemies were now defeated.

The Butlerians were all but neutralized, their charismatic leader dead, most of their resources stripped away. Their fanatical core group was bottled up on Lampadas, where they would be closely monitored so that they never ran rampant across the Imperium again.

With the scheme Roderick had proposed to Norma Cenva, all the Navigator-guided spacefolders would form a politically unaffiliated Spacing Guild to ensure safe transportation throughout the Imperium. Never again would one power-hungry person place a commercial stranglehold on so many planets.

Directeur Venport had been broken, his trading empire disrupted, his vast wealth seized, and now his last stand had failed. Denali was under Imperial control—but that wasn't enough. Josef Venport himself had to face justice.

After troops escorted his entourage into the laboratory domes, Admiral Harte greeted him with a sharp salute. Uniformed soldiers marched them toward the administrative chamber where the Directeur had barricaded himself. This enemy had to meet the same fate as Manford: death.

A black-garbed Mentat stood coolly by, a prisoner, but seemingly unconcerned about his future. Draigo Roget had already made his own deal when he surrendered to the Imperial troops: He offered his services to manage the spice operations on Arrakis, under the umbrella of Imperial control. Roderick knew Norma Cenva would prefer such a smooth transition to a prolonged clash between Imperial forces—who knew little about harvesting and distributing melange—and the leaderless Combined Mercantiles crews that were still working in the deserts. Although Venport's pet Mentat would have to be watched closely for his loyalty, he was certainly competent to handle those operations. The complexities of the melange business would not be left to an amateur.

Draigo had cemented the deal by conceding an extraordinary percentage of the spice profits to be poured into the Salusan treasury. Fielle reminded Roderick that the Imperium's finances had long been weakened by Salvador's ill-advised decisions as well as numerous destructive misadventures with the Butlerians. A steady flow of profits from uncontested spice operations would be a swift and significant source of income.

As he stepped forward, Roderick looked around. "Where is Directeur Venport? I will see him for myself."

Admiral Harte looked uncomfortable. "There is a slight . . . uh, complication, Sire."

Roderick's nostrils flared. "What do you mean? Was he killed? I ordered him to be taken alive. He was the whole reason for the ground assault—otherwise I could have just turned the planet into slag, bombarding it from orbit."

"The Directeur has not been killed, Sire. But . . . Norma Cenva wishes to speak with you."

Roderick saw that the armored door of the administrator's chamber had been blasted aside. He wasn't surprised. Venport would have barricaded himself to the last: The Directeur was not a man to surrender, but in the end he had lost. The Emperor strode forward, climbing over debris, looking around for Venport.

Inside, the small office was dominated by Norma Cenva's Navigator tank. Thick clouds of swirling gas filled the box, but Roderick could see the familiar distorted form inside. Norma spoke before he could say anything. "You have your victory, Emperor Roderick Corrino. I withdrew my ships as promised, and thereby allowed you to conquer Denali. In return, you will form a Spacing Guild, and you will protect my Navigators. No harm will come to any of them. As you promised."

"Yes, that is what I promised," Roderick said in clipped words. "I am the Emperor, and I am true to my word." He looked around the room. "But I will not forgive Josef Venport. He is to be turned over to me so that he can face justice."

"You may not take him." Norma drifted closer to the viewing port. "Because in doing so, you would break your promise."

Roderick drew a deep breath. "I made my command clear. Venport is guilty of crimes against the Imperium, so his life is forfeit. I will not negotiate on this!"

"You already have. You made a vow in front of many witnesses. It was not open to interpretation. You have your victory here. You may have everything else on Denali, but you may not have my Navigators. You agreed."

Roderick was confused. "What does that have to do with Directeur Venport and his crimes?"

"Josef is now one of the Navigators you swore to protect." She stirred, and the cinnamon fumes swirled to reveal another figure inside the chamber with her. "He is currently undergoing his metamorphosis. I will help him in every way possible, and my prescience tells me there is a good chance he will survive."

The Emperor felt a surge of rage that this barely human woman had out-maneuvered him, tricked him. Josef Venport was *not* going to escape after the appalling things he had done.

But she said, "If you break your promise to me, I will take all my Navigators away, and our ships will never serve the Imperium. The universe is ours."

Roderick could not let this ruthless man escape without punishment for his crimes, for killing Salvador. He looked deeper into the tank and recognized his enemy, his face in agony and his clothes mostly eaten away by the harsh melange gas. Josef Venport writhed and choked, drifting in panicked circles as his hands thrashed. His fingers were splayed so widely in his suffering that some of the bones were obviously broken. His eyes were closed, and his face had a waxy consistency, as if portions of it were melting, changing his features. Much of his hair had already fallen out.

"You may not have my Navigators," Norma repeated.

And as Roderick looked at Venport's slow, horrific transformation, he thought he just might be satisfied after all. . . .

The priorities of truly great people differ markedly from those of lesser mortals.

—A voice from Other Memory

According to the witnesses on Corrin, Vorian Atreides was killed in the midair spaceship explosion. He was dead, and that was a good beginning. Vor had to start over, as if reborn. A clean slate—again.

His private spacefolder was a slower old-model vessel, much like the *Dream Voyager* he had flown for years. Vor knew all of the ship's systems, as well as its inherent flaws.

Beaten and bloodied, still alive but upset that he had not been able to end the feud, he had dragged himself back to his ship, as Korla and the scavengers demanded. They had promised to protect Willem, but by making him leave, the feud was not ended.

Entering the cockpit, swaying from the pain, Vor had inspected his ship, knowing all the systems so well, and as he powered up the engines, he had sensed something wrong . . . the subtlest fluctuation, a minor variance—which led him to inspect inside the energy-train console.

He saw that the *New Voyager's* engines had been rigged to explode in the air. While the ship had rested here, unoccupied, someone had sabotaged it, planted explosives set to detonate as soon as it gained altitude. He knew with a chill that Valya and her commandos must have set up this contingency just in case he happened to elude them. They had no intention of letting him escape alive.

As Vor bent over, angry, to disconnect the booby trap so he could fly away and claim his own small victory, he hesitated. Then he saw the rest of the solution.

He'd lived long enough with Harkonnen hatred that he knew their vendetta would continue so long as Valya and Tula thought he remained alive. Abulurd's bitter descendants would only be satisfied if they knew for certain that he was dead.

And so he ended the feud in the only way he could see. He had to die, as far as they were concerned.

He activated the ship's engines, while bleeding profusely over the controls, the cockpit, the deck—thanks to the injuries Valya had inflicted. The blood would add veracity: If any of the Sisters decided to scan the wreckage that fell from the sky—and they would, he was sure of it—his DNA would be there. They would be convinced he was aboard.

Even though post-Jihad humanity shunned all automated systems and computerized guidance, he knew crude methods of making the ship fly by itself—at least enough to take off and rise toward orbit, unguided. The *New Voyager* didn't have to go far to serve his purpose.

They would all see it with their own eyes.

Willem would be devastated—first losing Orry, and now Vorian. The two had grown quite close. In fact, the last time Vor had felt so paternal toward anyone was, ironically, with Griffin Harkonnen. But young Willem had to be just as convinced as the Sisters. His grief would be real.

Willem would survive, though, and he would recover from his grief. Vor had caused much sorrow in his life; this was just one more instance to add to his mental balance sheet.

But he would live with the guilt—and he would *live*. Because of that, the feud would be over, and Willem would have a life too. The young Atreides would go to the Imperial Court and make a good life for himself, the life he deserved . . . a life without a Harkonnen blood feud weighing him down.

Or so Vor hoped.

As the engines powered up and the ship prepared to take off under its automated guidance, Vor climbed out through a small access hatch, bringing supplies with him, then crawled away into the rubble.

From there, he watched his ship explode.

Afterward he ducked underground, finding a bolt-hole in the rubble, and sealed himself in. He would wait for several days, until it was safe.

⤚∽⤙

HE HID UNTIL he knew the scheduled trading spacefolder had come and taken Willem away. Finally, Vor emerged into the ruddy sunlight of Corrin, remembering how many years he had lived here, back when it was the thinking-machine capital.

He was done here, though. He wrapped himself with rags and a patchwork radiation suit, slipped into the tunnels he knew so well, kept himself among the shadows—as so many of the scavengers did—while the rest of them worked at excavating valuable items from the ruins.

Their next trading ship would depart in a week, with dozens of people aboard, and Vor intended to be among them. Horaan Eshdi, the woman he had saved from the flowmetal outburst, was surprised when he approached her among the groups of workers in the rubble operations, but also pleased to see him alive. "I need your help," he said, in a low voice.

"You have earned it," she replied. "Whatever you need."

When the next trade spacefolder arrived at Corrin, she helped him to hide his identity by giving him a salvaged wardrobe from one of the miners killed in the flowmetal flood. He muffled his face and wrapped his skin to protect against the harsh red sunlight. Horaan let him pass, looking haughty, attracting no questions. The scavengers didn't pay much attention to their companions as they moved toward the cargo shuttle that came down from an EsconTran ship.

Vor kept his head down as he climbed aboard with the group of boisterous traders. Out of the corner of his eye, he saw that Horaan had joined the group, but she stayed away from him now. Good. He did not need, nor want, any company. He felt the comforting rumble of engines as the shuttle took off, heading for the spacefolder. He leaned back against the bulkhead and closed his eyes.

He would make his way, independently. As he had done so many times before.

It was the price Vorian Atreides had to pay for the existence he wanted, the new situation he needed, after going through so much. And it was the price he had to pay for Willem's future.

After living for more than two centuries, Vor had grown weary of his old persona and all the baggage it carried. He craved something new and fresh, and a universe of options lay before him. It was like shedding his skin.

It was not only a matter of where he was going, but much more. He had many ideas, and plenty of experience, in knowing how not to be found. Out in the Imperium, after so much time, no one even thought to connect Vorian's face with the visage they saw in history books, on memorial statues, even on Imperial coins. He would make his way to other worlds, backwater worlds, where he might even find a Tlulaxa surgeon who could make cellular alterations to his face. And Vor would survive, for however long his life-extension treatment might last.

He could obtain different features through surgery, and an entirely different existence, but he would still be Vorian Atreides, always an Atreides, on the inside. He could hardly wait to step into the skin of the new person he intended to become.

Those who do not ask for a thing are much more likely to deserve it.
—Mentat teaching

Secure in his rule, the Emperor stood in his flowmetal cape outside the golden-domed Hall of Parliament. Now that he no longer needed to be concerned about the superstitious Butlerians, he wore the exotic cape as a symbol of pride and confidence, and to mark the victory of humans over machines in the Jihad. He did not fear thinking machines, nor fanatics.

He was the Emperor.

Empress Haditha, Crown Prince Javicco, and the younger princesses Tikya and Wissoma were at his side, gazing out on a sea of people spreading across Zimia's central plaza. Landsraad nobles flanked the Imperial seats, while behind them a wraparound screen concealed the real reason for the gathering.

Roderick squinted into the bright noon sunlight. Flags hung from government buildings around the square, fluttering in a gentle breeze. The scarlet-and-gold buntings of House Corrino were draped across balconies above, including the balcony from which Emperor Salvador had addressed his subjects on many occasions.

With the major crises solved in the Imperium, the city was in a celebratory mood. The Emperor and Empress were dressed in their formal attire of state—he wore a Corrino uniform with a scarlet sash across his chest, and Haditha a long gown of matching colors, along with Hagal jewels and her impressive crown, the crown that Salvador had rarely let his own wife wear. But Haditha was different; as far as Roderick was concerned, she deserved it.

As he waited for the cheers to fade, he glanced at Fielle, who remained close. His Truthsayer had certainly proved her worth in the last encounter against

Directeur Venport, and he valued her presence, although he wasn't sure how much he could trust the Sisterhood as a whole. In a fit of pique Salvador had disbanded their entire order, and it had been a mistake. Roderick saw that as allies the Sisters could be useful, and as enemies they could be dangerous, but they were so secretive and controlled that one could rarely tell which side they were on.

Such as Cioba Venport . . . She had come here because of her Sisterhood connections, but as the wife of an outlaw, she had been held on Salusa as a hostage. She had vanished shortly after hearing the news of her husband's defeat and was nowhere to be found. Was her loyalty to Venport or to the Sisterhood? One rumor suggested that she had fled to Wallach IX, although the Sisterhood denied it. If true, Roderick doubted if he would ever pry her loose from that insular school. But he would keep watching, and would not forget.

Right now, Fielle had been joined by Mother Superior Valya, the leader of the Sisterhood, who wore heavy, dark garments. Valya was astonishingly young for a role of such enormous importance, but her actions and mannerisms carried the weight of countless generations. Her face looked oddly bruised, the worst marks covered with obvious makeup.

The Mother Superior had come here to represent the Sisterhood—as well as her own noble family, House Harkonnen from Lankiveil—for the Imperial victory celebration. Valya had used influence and favors to request a place for her younger brother Danvis at court, so that he could enhance his family's visibility in the Landsraad. Roderick had granted the request.

Now, sitting in a reserved box seat, Danvis Harkonnen wore whale-fur finery from his home, though his clothes were several years out of style. The bright-eyed young man looked thin and pale, out of his depth, but Roderick found him to be fresh-faced and likable.

When the cheers dampened in anticipation, Roderick spoke in an amplified voice that carried out over the farthest fringes of the crowd. "This gathering makes me recall the celebrations under my grandfather Faykan I, at the end of the Jihad. Today we celebrate a different but equally important victory—peace in the Imperium.

"Even after the fall of the thinking machines, we discovered new enemies in our ranks, those who would pull our civilization in different and dangerous directions. Two extremists tried to tear apart the Imperium from opposite sides." He paused, staring at the ocean of faces, wondering which factions they sided with. *There is only one faction now,* he reminded himself. *My faction.*

"Directeur Josef Venport sought to control us through his monopoly on safe space travel and the distribution of spice. He was a rational but selfish and immoral man, and his unethical stranglehold has now been broken. With the fall of Venport Holdings, our new independent Spacing Guild will guarantee commercial foldspace travel to all worlds in the Imperium."

He let the crowd acknowledge the tremendous opportunity this would create for all of their lives, and then hardened his voice. "On the other hand, Manford Torondo was not at all rational. He was a power-hungry fanatic who manipulated mobs to cause death and destruction, to the detriment of every Imperial citizen. Such extremism has collapsed under its own intolerance."

The crowd response was subdued at first, but gradually it built to louder and more sustained applause as the listeners found the courage to express their real feelings. There would be some among the thousands who still sympathized with the Butlerian cause, but the mounting cheer suggested something else to Roderick—that for all the fury and energy of the fanatics, perhaps the rest of the populace had not approved, but were merely too afraid to voice their real objections. As he listened to the crowd, he detected a ragged edge of relief.

He took Haditha's hand and continued. "Both of those extremists hurt us profoundly. Because of them we lost three members of our family, and our grief is still a painful wound—yet, it is but a microcosm of what others have suffered. The blind ambitions of two men inflicted such a cost on humanity. On each extreme, opposing one another at every turn and harming the Imperium, Torondo and Venport each thought that he alone could drive our future—and both of them failed. We must be vigilant that such devastating ambitions do not tear our society apart ever again.

"As your Emperor I need your help to continue along a new path—one that is much larger than any one person. I seek no glory, for I am but a guide for all of us. Yes, I am just a man." He smiled and looked at Haditha, then raised her hand high. "I have my Empress at my side, and she is ready and willing to anchor me when I need it. She watches over the people, as I do—she has already demonstrated her energy and skill by managing the relief efforts to help the victims of the recent terrible flood."

Haditha spoke, "My husband cares for his subjects, as I do. Whether a tragedy hurts one village or the entire Imperium, the pain is part of all of us." She touched her crown. "The Emperor's heart is with you. I will continue to advise him, support him, and be his sounding board."

"You fully deserve that crown you wear," Roderick said, smiling warmly at her, "but it is a weighty one. I have another token for you, one that is made much lighter by love."

An elderly aide stepped forward from the sidelines to present a flat, ornate box that contained a flower headdress. Surprised, Haditha let out a small gasp as she saw it.

Because of Salvador's chilly, loveless relationship with his wife, he had set an unwise precedent by cutting Empress Tabrina out of his rule. Roderick intended to establish a new precedent, and he meant for all his subjects to see that. The citizens had been inundated with titanic events and an uncertain future, and they needed something to celebrate. They needed to be reminded of what made humanity so special.

He removed the colorful headdress. "Haditha is my partner and my adviser. She rules beside me to temper my decisions and help me fulfill my role. Truly, she is your Empress, as much as I am your Emperor. No Corrino rules alone."

Tears sparkled in Haditha's eyes as he placed the headdress gently around her more traditional crown. Even though Haditha knew full well the significance of the ornamentation, Roderick explained it to the crowd. "This headdress is composed of fifteen flowers from the planet Isla in the Papeete star system. After we were married, Haditha and I honeymooned on Isla. Though these flowers were cut years ago, they will never fade. They will live forever, as will my love for her." He kissed her, then faced the cheering audience. "A fitting addition to my Empress's crown, I think."

Haditha looked perfectly regal and she spoke in a strong voice, tinged with emotion. "I accept this honor with tremendous gratitude and humility. I will seek to do it justice. For the future of the Imperium."

"For the future of the Imperium," Roderick repeated.

He turned as the curved screen behind them withdrew to reveal a large Navigator tank. Attendants wearing uniforms from the new Spacing Guild pushed the tank forward on suspensors. Roderick continued into the voice amplifier, "Norma Cenva, the first and foremost of all Navigators, has her own announcement to make."

He was still upset at how she had tricked him regarding Josef Venport's fate, but he did not believe Norma had done the treacherous Directeur any favors. Venport had been moved into his own tank now, where he continued to undergo his difficult metamorphosis. The mutation and warping of his body had already rendered the ambitious man nearly incapable of speech, or of thinking about anything except the vast universe. Norma seemed to consider it a wondrous thing; Roderick wondered if Venport would agree.

Instead of pursuing further revenge, Roderick would expend his energies on rebuilding the Imperium. The blind desire for revenge, on so many sides, had already caused too much damage.

The strange woman undulated in the tank, her huge eyes shining through the gas. The expectant audience stared at her in fascination; few had ever seen a Navigator before. Norma's words were focused as they came out of the speaker-patch on the tank, as if she had to concentrate heavily in order to achieve precise diction and smooth delivery.

"I am the first Navigator, and the sacred protector of all my kind. The Emperor and I have reached an accord. The Spacing Guild will be the Navigators' strength and shelter, the fabric that binds worlds and star systems together. My Navigators will continue to roam the cosmos. The universe is ours."

When Norma fell silent, she turned to stare straight up through the roof of the tank, although what she could see with her eyes and her mind went far beyond Roderick's capacity to comprehend.

The Emperor knew the audience had not yet grasped the importance of what this agreement would do for humankind. Their collective awe was fitting, though, because this was truly the beginning of a new era.

"You are strong now, Roderick," Haditha whispered to him beside the tank. "Finally, you can become the Emperor we always needed, and we can build the Imperium that the human race deserves, after so many generations of suffering. All obstacles have been overcome."

"All *known* obstacles." Roderick smiled grimly. "I only wish I could see into the future and discover what lies ahead for us."

Beside him, Norma Cenva stirred uneasily in her tank.

The unexpected is not always a surprise.
—Mentat observation

When he arrived on Arrakis as the new Imperial Overseer of Spice Operations, Draigo Roget studied the stark desert landscape. No other planet was as stunning as this one—constantly changing, yet always the same.

He'd served here previously under Directeur Venport, but during that assignment he had considered the arid heat to be oppressive. Now the situation was very different. This time his life depended on his performance.

Draigo should have been executed by Imperial order, but as a Mentat with his wealth of experience, he was an invaluable asset, not to be wasted, and Emperor Roderick had given him a second chance. He prided himself on being a survivor, and during the final negotiations on Denali, he'd salvaged an opportunity, even in Venport's defeat. He had convinced the Emperor that he could be useful to the Imperium. . . .

Now he stood on a promontory above one of his harvester machines and gazed out at the expanse of dunes. It was good to be alive! Among so many complex projections, even a Mentat could experience such joy.

In the harsh atmosphere of this world, he wore one of the native distilling suits, which had been fitted properly by a Freeman expert. Through his sealed goggles, he saw uncountable waves of wind-sculpted dunes extending into the distance like a vast, arid ocean.

A rare bird winged away from the line of rocks—a desert hawk or perhaps a carrion bird. He watched the hypnotic flapping of the great wings until the speck became smaller and smaller. It was so peaceful . . . like standing in the eye of an Imperial storm.

A desert-rigged flyer rested on the rock behind him. He'd flown out here to observe the harvesting operations from a distance, and soon he would take off to visit the crews in their barracks in Arrakis City. In serving the Emperor, Draigo wanted to interview each of the workers, so that he could better assess and manage them. A Mentat was a human being as well as a human computer, and he would glean additional details through personal observations.

One reason he wanted to know the crews: because they would work harder for him if they respected him, and he intended to remake the spice operations, increasing efficiency and safety. He had already delivered Mentat projections to Emperor Roderick, suggesting the best route for success. He was like a Navigator seeking safe passageways for the Emperor to take.

From now on, the production and distribution of melange would be steady, predictable, and profitable. That would pacify the growing number of addicted citizens . . . and would also satisfy Norma Cenva, who needed sufficient quantities to sustain her Navigators. Including Josef Venport.

He wished he could have achieved success for the Directeur, but Roderick Corrino was his master now. Headmaster Albans had taught him that a Mentat was required to provide his master with the best possible answers.

In the distant heat shimmer, he saw one team hustling to fill the harvester with melange before the industrial vibrations attracted a territorial sandworm. From his high vantage, he scanned the sand, but detected no movement that might signal the approach of one of the behemoths. Overhead, a small spotter craft circled, also keeping watch.

He listened to the faint processing sounds of his stillsuit as it collected and recycled perspiration from his body. The desert natives had a saying that a man's moisture belonged to his tribe. Draigo appreciated this philosophy, because it spoke of more than just one man's water on one planet in the Imperium. It was an acknowledgment that no person could function entirely alone, that he required a connection to something larger than himself. So too, any tribe was not entirely alone, but was instead an integral part of the larger organism that comprises the human race, and humanity was ultimately part of—

Draigo paused in his thought process before it could spiral beyond his comprehension. *The Mentat trap.* Instead, he calmed his mind by staring again at the simple purity of the desert. From all his training, he understood the games a mind could play. A Mentat needed to maintain control over his thoughts and not let them drift off course.

In the distance, he thought he saw movement on the sand, but was too far away to be certain. The spotter craft cruised out in a long arc and came back, then circled overhead to double-check before sending urgent messages to the harvester crew. A worm was indeed coming, but the crews were accustomed to this. As Draigo watched, he was impressed by their efficiency. They packed up operations within minutes and prepared to escape.

It was always a tight calculation—the longer the operations continued, the more spice they harvested, but the greater the likelihood that they would lose their equipment. A spice haul was worth far more than the machinery or the people who ran it, however. It was a simple projection.

A large lifter approached from the east, rising over a crest of rocks and racing in for a swift pickup. The lifter hovered over the giant harvester, while half a dozen crewmembers scampered on top of the spice excavator to check the connections. Finished, the brave men dropped through hatches, and the harvester's core and cargo vault was lifted into the sky, leaving only an easily replaceable skeletal framework behind.

Beneath the abandoned factory hull, the great worm surfaced, its eyeless head questing from side to side, as if to chase intruders from its territory. Safe on his outcropping, Draigo watched with analytical fascination as the worm smashed the abandoned equipment and then plunged back into the dune ridge, burrowing deeper until it left only a gully of stirred sand. All marks would be erased as soon as the next windstorm came to sculpt the dunes all over again.

Draigo walked back to his desert-rigged flyer, already planning his analysis of this operation, the cost of the sacrificed equipment, and the most efficient dispersal of scout flyers in future operations. He would make any necessary modifications.

He fired up the engines, and the dusty armored craft lifted up from the rocks and into the rising thermals. When he was airborne, flying out over the dunes, he thought, *I am a Mentat, and I shall continue to adapt myself to this world.*

It was his duty to do this. Headmaster Albans had also taught him ethics and dedication. A graduate of the Mentat School on Lampadas might be assigned to one nobleman or another, but now Draigo—the Imperial Overseer of Spice Operations—was himself a master, and Arrakis was his de facto fief, his planet to rule.

First he needed to know the place, really *know* it, to avoid making mistakes. He looked forward to the learning experience.

Your appointment is a significant success for our family, but you must always be alert or we will lose the ground we have gained, as surely as a stone falls under the pull of gravity.

—Valya's admonition to Danvis
on his arrival at Imperial Court

Vorian Atreides was dead, and thanks to Valya's steady efforts, House Harkonnen was finally on the rise again. She took personal credit for the progress. This paramount goal had always shone like a guiding light in her mind, and—as she had hoped—she could guide both the Sisterhood and House Harkonnen into a bright future. She realized her focus was more intense than anyone else's in the family, more than her siblings or their parents, but she'd stepped into a void. After being downtrodden for more than eight decades, the Harkonnens had grown to accept their situation. They'd become sedentary.

Valya had never done that.

For too long, thanks to Vorian Atreides, the Harkonnen name had been synonymous with cowardice and dishonor. But her nemesis—*their* nemesis—was dead, at last. She'd seen it with her own eyes.

After so much anticipation, Valya would have preferred to kill the man herself and watch the life fade from his eyes . . . but the explosion of his ship in the sky had been satisfying in its own way. She had caused it, and that was enough. Using their own comparisons to genetic records, her commando Sisters had tested blood found on some of the tumbled wreckage and confirmed that it was indeed Vorian's.

When she had seen the DNA results, even though she was already certain Vor had been killed in the explosion, she felt a surge of triumph . . . or at least she wanted to. In her heart, however, the victory felt somehow flat. She didn't know what she had expected to feel—exhilaration, perhaps? Instead, it was a curious sense of finality, reaching the end of a dark goal that had driven her for so much of her life. Was it enough? It had to be enough.

But . . . what now?

She knew the answer to that even as the whispers of Other Memory became louder in the back of her mind. Now, without that life-consuming distraction, she could focus entirely on letting House Harkonnen rise unhindered to the prominence it deserved. And she could build the Sisterhood into an extremely powerful, if quietly invisible, organization. One success would drive the other, and vice versa.

She wanted so much for her family, and most of all perhaps for Danvis, who would carry on the bloodline—as an important Landsraad lord, the planetary ruler of Lankiveil. Valya had to make sure her brother was up to the task. Her brother . . .

Suddenly, Valya's heart felt heavy with a pang of memory. *Griffin* should have been the future patriarch of the family, not Danvis. Griffin, her closest friend, who had shared so much with her, the same goals, the same vision for House Harkonnen.

Until he was killed by Vorian Atreides. She had heard the man deny it, and even though the Truthsayer verified that Vor had not been lying, Valya refused to believe it. Perhaps Vor in his twisted mind had utterly convinced himself of his lack of culpability. Or maybe he had found some other way to engineer Griffin's death without actually soiling his own hands, but Valya would not absolve him of responsibility. It was his fault.

She reminded herself that Vor was dead. She had her revenge. She was triumphant, and she was *satisfied*. But what now?

First, she would help her younger brother in every way possible. Danvis was a Harkonnen too. She knew he would do whatever was necessary. Valya would make sure of that, and he would set a bold new course for House Harkonnen.

Although their father was still the titular Landsraad leader back on Lankiveil, Vergyl was a parochial man whose ambitions did not extend beyond the seasonal whale-fur harvest. She would make Danvis into much more than that.

And as for her own sister . . . Tula had been taken back to Wallach IX, where she was surrounded by Sisters, constantly protected and monitored. She carried an Atreides child in her womb—a disgusting thought, but also a tremendous opportunity, as Valya had finally realized after her revulsion faded. Maybe her revenge wasn't quite over yet, after all.

Tula needed serious reeducation in order to put aside her confusing and contradictory emotions, but Valya was confident that since she had been able to refocus even Dorotea's Orthodox followers, she could certainly reprogram her own sister. . . .

IN THE IMPERIAL Court after Roderick's victory celebration over the Butlerians and Venport Holdings, she felt considerable satisfaction as she accompanied her brother to his first formal reception at the Palace. As a newly arrived
member of the court, he would be presented at a crowded soiree. Danvis had
arrived wearing his finest clothes from Lankiveil, but he still looked out of place
here, his outfit years behind the fashion of the times. A bumpkin.

Valya had immediately intercepted him. Even though all of the Sisters at
court dressed in the distinctive dark robes of their order, she dispatched them to
find new garments for Danvis, swiftly tailoring them to fit her brother's lanky
form. He had looked uncomfortable and out of place, but now he looked dashing and stylish, an impressive young nobleman arriving at the Palace. A *Harkonnen lord*.

Danvis needed to learn so much. . . .

A Chusuk orchestra played on an elevated stage, its members dressed in black
jackets and frilly white shirts. Several noble couples danced on a floor in front
of the musicians, including a wrinkled and ancient Lord and Lady from Zanbar,
who performed complicated, surprisingly energetic steps. The traditional music
was fast-paced and upbeat.

Valya made a note to arrange intensive dance instruction for Danvis. He
had to be better than the other new arrivals, not just in dance but in all things.
He was a Harkonnen, and had to demonstrate his potential.

Now her brother mingled with other new arrivals, young Landsraad sons
and daughters who had come to serve at court. Valya would have preferred to
have Danvis announced with great fanfare, but there had been no time. For the
moment he was just one of many minor nobles, eager to be noticed. Danvis
would have to make his own way, seeking out his own acquaintances and creating his own alliances. Under orders from their Mother Superior, the Sisters at
court would smooth the way for him. No other new arrival had such a powerful
and unexpected resource.

Gaudily dressed men and women chatted about foolish things, holding
wineglasses or long smokettes in their hands. They sampled from melange-laced
hors d'oeuvres that servants carried on silver trays. The sanctioned delivery of
spice had gone a long way toward convincing the people that peace and nor-
malcy was at last restored, thanks to Emperor Roderick.

Young Danvis looked nervous and out of place among the new arrivals, but
she was confident he would discover his internal strength. In the meantime, he
had to learn to hide his weaknesses better.

When she found a chance, she went to him, and walked across the hall at
his side. Many of the guests were part of the Imperial Court not because of their

exemplary talents, but because of important family, business, or political connections. She counted on Danvis to make a name for himself. Perhaps being seen next to the Mother Superior would gain him more prominence. He looked relieved just to have familiar company.

"Be strong," she whispered to her younger brother, and then added with just a hint of Voice, "*You are better than them.*"

Valya led him toward a long refreshment table on one side of the orchestra, where she critically assessed his appearance. His black hair was straight and neatly trimmed, but overall he looked ordinary and colorless, pedestrian in the midst of so many strutting noble peacocks. There would be time to enhance his appearance and his confidence, and House Harkonnen could afford the money. It was a worthwhile investment.

"You will do well here. I have already given you information to turn against your rivals when appropriate, and Sisterhood spies will continue to provide you with valuable intelligence . . . a resource no other noble has." As part of her duty to the Sisterhood, Fielle had reported the trivial secrets and shames of many court members to her, and now Danvis held the information in reserve.

"Why would they do that for me?" he asked, blinking.

"Because I am the Mother Superior, and you are the future of House Harkonnen. If used properly, such knowledge will help you rise quickly." He seemed uncertain, overwhelmed. He would need to be coached further. She nudged him. "Mix with the people. Make certain you talk with the important ones I've identified. Get yourself noticed. Establish connections."

He didn't look at all confident to her. "Penetrating the noble cliques will not be so easy."

"I never said it would be easy. You must have the ambition and perception to impress the right people. Stop at nothing." She pointed to a dignified man who was engaged in energetic conversation with a woman. "That one, for example— he's the head of a mining clan from Hagal, a rival to House Péle, the powerful family of the former Empress Tabrina. He has been struggling for prominence since Tabrina fell into disfavor, so he'll need allies at court. Convince him you can be useful in fulfilling his goals."

Danvis nervously took a glass of Salusan spice-infused wine from the sommelier, and Valya cautioned, "When in public, take small, infrequent sips, only as much as is socially necessary. When you have access to raw spice, use it sparingly. Heighten your alertness, but do not let addiction gain control of you."

"I know all that," he said, in a patient tone.

"I just want to reinforce the importance." She didn't want to imagine her younger brother failing. She could not be with him at court to look over his shoulder, to prevent him from making mistakes. Fortunately, she had other allies here.

She continued to treat him as if she were instructing a fresh-faced Acolyte on Wallach IX. "Never drop your guard—think of the Imperial Court as a battleground. Secure powerful allies, and seek to minimize those who oppose you. You can achieve much of this by discreet action, behind the scenes. Do not be too outspoken, especially in front of those who might wish to do you harm."

"Like the Atreides," he said.

She scowled. "The Atreides are nothing. Vorian is dead, and the feud is over. We're done with it. Now there is nothing to hinder the ascendance of House Harkonnen."

Chin up, he dutifully left her side and disappeared into the throng of people like a hunter on a mission.

Valya made her way to two Sisters who had recently been assigned to the Imperial Court. Sister Sicia was barely past Acolyte stage, a red-haired beauty who could easily seduce any nobleman (and was being trained to do exactly that); her companion, Sister Jean, was more seasoned, dark-skinned and dark-haired, slender in the extreme. The two women greeted her with curt, solicitous bows.

Sicia was breathless. "So far our assignment at court is going well, Mother Superior." She flashed a sparkling smile. "I have already identified three excellent male candidates. All nobles."

Valya's gaze sharpened. "Good. Submit their names so that we can determine the best genetic match before you let yourself conceive a child."

"Yes, Mother Superior."

Sister Jean straightened. "We will continue to submit our reports to Wallach IX. It will be as if you are here yourself."

"I find the Imperial Court impressive, but I am better suited to running the Sisterhood," Valya said. "Meanwhile, watch over my brother. See that he has information he needs, and keep him from making foolish mistakes. He is a blade whose edge needs to be sharp, and continually sharpened."

Sister Jean nodded, not questioning her assignment. Sister Sicia looked at the young man who was striking up conversations at the edge of the reception; she raised her eyebrows, assessing.

"You are not for him," Valya said with a slight scolding tone.

"Yes, Mother Superior." Sicia scanned others in the room instead. Valya realized that she needed to study her brother's genetic profile in the breeding index buried in their computers. Perhaps she did need to secure his bloodline widely, as insurance. She would look into it.

"I have much to monitor back on Wallach IX as the Sisterhood grows," Valya said. "I am pleased to hear that our work here is in good hands."

After the two Sisters melted into the crowd, Valya made her observations, drinking in the patterns and contacts. She saw Danvis dancing with a plain-featured young woman in a low-cut dress and dazzling jewels. Danvis concluded the dance, bowed gratefully to his young partner, and made his way back to Valya.

"Who is she?" Valya asked in a quick interrogation. "Family line? Rank?"

Danvis gave an embarrassed grin. "Second daughter of the planetary leader of Ix. She has direct access to the Empress. They play weekly games together."

"Consider it practice. You can do better. Look for the first daughter of a noble house. Never forget that you are a Harkonnen."

⊸⧢⧢⧢

TWO DAYS LATER, the Mother Superior rode in a private stateroom aboard a spacefolder that was now part of the Spacing Guild. In complete isolation, she blocked out the voices of Other Memory that had been pestering her. She had proved her strength and her vision, and she would make her own choices, in the manner she saw fit.

Valya understood the momentous changes she had wrought—the relief and triumph they had brought her. Vorian Atreides was dead. Her brother was at court. House Harkonnen was on the rise. The Sisterhood grew more powerful day by day.

Everything was as she had hoped. The long struggle was over . . . and it was just beginning.

And yet she felt inexplicably adrift. *Now what?* All alone in a moment of weakness aboard the spacefolder, Valya finally cried softly to herself, not from sadness but from emotional release, for the joy of the victory she had achieved and for the brightening paths of destiny in the future, stretching into infinite possibilities.

Yes, Vorian Atreides was dead. After generations of shame and marginalization, her family would emerge from the shadows. The lie about Abulurd's cowardice, the terrible injustice of it, would finally fade in the light of steady triumphs. Danvis was a key part of it, and his descendants would be as well.

It was one more secret she carried in her mind, in a universe of secrets.

Being a member of the Imperial Court meant much more under Emperor Faykan Corrino or his son Jules than under my brother Salvador's reign, when the nature of the court degenerated. In the early days, it was more a source of pride and responsibility than of pleasure, more focused on the well-being of the citizenry than on the desires of a privileged few. Under my rule, I expect the leadership at court to be relevant, and dedicated to the public good.

—EMPEROR RODERICK CORRINO I, while asking
Haditha to monitor the Imperial Court

After much soul-searching, Willem Atreides knew that his clearest path lay here on Salusa Secundus, building himself up in the Imperium. He had done as Vorian asked, although with a heavy heart. Vor had made his wishes quite explicit.

A generous Korla had delivered the young man to Salusa as promised, in a trading ship filled with treasures salvaged from Corrin. Willem had not known what to expect when he arrived in Zimia and presented his credentials, invoking the Atreides name. But, just as Vor had said, the Palace did have a place for him after all, along with a substantial fund for all of his expenses. He had everything he needed to build a noble family and make his mark on the Landsraad.

He had a chance, a future, whatever he could achieve for himself.

Willem had been a nobody on Caladan, a member of the air-rescue service along with his brother, and now he was a minor nobleman. He had even received a message from Princess Harmona of Chusuk, that she looked forward to finding important Landsraad business that would take her to Salusa Secundus so she could see him again. His heart warmed at the thought, and he could not wait to be with her.

The Landsraad League was still crystallizing, and not every planet had a ruler who was part of the Imperial Parliament. Caladan was considered a distant and insignificant world, but if the young man built his reputation and earned respect, and if the Emperor himself took notice of him, then perhaps Willem could become Caladan's provisional Landsraad representative. Vorian had instilled a steely resolve in him. He was an Atreides, and knew he could do it.

At court, Willem would attempt to advance himself through his dedication and good work, as Vor would have wanted. Objectively, his future looked bright indeed.

But he was his own man, with his own conscience and responsibilities . . . and it was *his* older brother who had been killed so brutally. He expected to learn things here in the court by developing important contacts. And perhaps, through any political influence he gained, he could do something good in Orry's name.

Now, with the violent death of his mentor, the need for Atreides revenge had only increased. Although Vor had insisted that he wanted the blood feud to end, he could not have anticipated his own assassination the way it happened, through Harkonnen treachery. Surely, he would not have wanted Willem to ignore that!

Tula had gotten away with murder, and the fact that she carried Orry's child did not absolve her in the least. He could not forget the pleased expression on Valya Harkonnen's face as she watched Vor's ship explode in the air, and then she and her sister had returned to Wallach IX, where Willem would never be able to reach them.

The Harkonnens had their vengeance, but he didn't have his, nor was he sure he ever would. Yet for honor, Willem could not ignore his own blood responsibility. . . .

Back on Caladan, he had heard stories that the Imperial Court was populated by useless dandies, and in the two weeks he had been here, Willem saw that the assessment was essentially accurate. He took heart, though, to hear that Emperor Roderick had vowed to change the situation, promising to make the courtiers perform useful services to the Imperium. Willem would see if such a thing truly came to pass.

This morning, as he gathered with others on the Palace's upper rooftop landing zone, he knew the new arrivals at court were about to see their circumstances change. Willem was surprised but not shocked by what the Emperor intended to do. He had never been afraid of hard work himself, but many of these others seemed completely unprepared.

Unlike the pampered people around him, Willem wore serviceable clothes without lace or frippery. New and fresh-faced, he'd met only a handful of his comrades here, and had kept a low profile. This day's adventure would be no lighthearted gala or private party at some nobleman's estate, as most of these attendees would prefer. He smiled to himself, thinking of how much good it would do them to help others.

In the river delta remote from the lavish towers of the capital, outlying villages were filled with people who lived without the opulence or conveniences of

Zimia—not because they adhered to strict Butlerian beliefs, but because they had nothing else. Since these people caused no trouble and made no demands, Salvador had paid little attention to their isolated settlements, but the recent flood disaster had changed everything. Haditha had already done great work to rescue and aid as many of the victims as possible, but much more needed to be done.

In celebration of his new Imperium, Roderick made no secret that he intended to create a golden age of human civilization. "And that includes everyone. We will start here at home, with these people who need it the most."

The Emperor had announced he would bring several groups from court out to the disaster site. The sycophants and glory hounds, the opportunists and fops who simply wanted to bask in the halo of the Imperial presence, would now get their hands dirty. Willem was perfectly happy with that—in fact, he was eager to do something worthwhile. Vorian had established him at court, providing whatever the young man needed, but Willem wanted to earn whatever he received. As he had promised Vor, he would do the best he could for himself and for House Atreides.

At the landing zone in the rear of the sprawling Palace, Emperor Roderick had ordered the preparation of transport ships that would be filled with aristocrats, seasoned hangers-on, and young nobles who had come to serve after their families made special arrangements for them.

Before the large groups boarded, the Emperor addressed them all in a somber voice. "As most of you know, a tragic flood struck the river delta last month, ruining villages and displacing thousands of people. Our home guard swept in for the rescue effort and delivered shipments of additional supplies. Empress Haditha has led our efforts to help the needy there, but a tremendous amount remains to be done." He hardened his voice so that the new members of court could understand his meaning. "You are all going to help—it is your duty as nobles in the Imperium."

Roderick frowned at the colorful and inappropriately dressed crowd as they boarded. Some of the courtiers made uneasy sounds, but he continued, "When you all arrived at the Palace, you thought you came for gala banquets, costume balls, and court gossip, but as your Emperor I require more from you. This is how you can best serve the Imperium, how you can best serve me."

Nearly two hundred privileged men and women boarded the three vessels. Some were excited, as if they were about to embark on an outing to see cultural displays in quaint villages. From his experiences in the air-rescue service on Caladan, however, Willem had seen natural disasters up close. He knew that the aftermath of the flood would not be pretty, but he was ready to pitch in and do his best to reduce human suffering and makes lives better. Hopefully he could gain the Emperor's notice on his own merits, rather than relying on Vorian's recommendation.

The line moved forward, and Willem glanced around as the other courtiers filed aboard the aircraft. Out of the corner of his eye he spotted an oddly familiar dark-haired young man who stepped up the ramp onto the second carrier, but the line moved forward before he could get a better glimpse. Willem put it out of his mind, and a few minutes later he boarded the crowded third transport.

After an hour's flight across the continent, the trio of transports arrived in the wide, sloppy mudflat where the delta villages had been. The river waters had receded, but the towns were not yet rebuilt. What had once been a trading outpost town on the river had been erased from its foundations, and although temporary buildings were now erected, the place was still no more than a squalid encampment.

When the transports landed on a flat polymerized area that served as a temporary landing field, many of the courtiers with Willem looked queasy, as if this was not at all what they had expected to see. "Shouldn't this all be cleaned up and reconstructed by now?" asked one young lordling, the third son of House Yardin. "What is taking the home guard so long?"

"I thought Empress Haditha had already managed the disaster," said another with a distasteful frown. "It does not look anywhere near finished."

Willem said to him, "That's why we're here—to do what needs to be done." He was among the first down the ramp, while many of his companions hesitated, obviously not wishing to get mud on their fancy shoes and garments.

Dozens of refugees hurried forward from the temporary camp, looking dirty and hungry. Emperor Roderick had gone ahead in his own faster transport, and now he stood next to a tired-looking Haditha, who wore gloves and sturdy work clothes. As they stood on a rickety reception platform that was only a couple of meters above the mud, the Imperial couple watched the court members step uncomfortably onto walkways that had been laid across the mudflats.

Low-ranking engineers crisply divided the many "volunteers" into teams, so they could receive their work assignments. A number of nobles grumbled and took offense, citing their social status, haughtily mentioning the names of their families or political patrons. Willem went to his assigned team without complaint.

Near him, Empress Haditha addressed the heartbroken villagers rather than the courtiers. "You are all citizens of the Imperium, and we will care for every one of you. See, I have brought more help."

Roderick added, "I present these noble members of my Imperial Court, who also feel for your plight. They will contribute their sweat and hard labor to help you at a time when you most need it. They will work beside you until your town is rebuilt and you have homes again."

Willem realized that the Emperor was testing the dismayed nobles, so he spoke up to set an example. "I will lead a team, Sire—I'm not afraid to work."

Heads turned toward him, eyes glaring, but Willem nodded respectfully to the Emperor and the Empress.

Haditha beamed at him, and Roderick gave him a warm smile. "Very good. Yes, Vorian said I should pay close attention to you."

"I'm willing to pitch in too," said another voice. The familiar-looking young man with dark hair stepped forward. He seemed pale and uncertain, but determined. Willem suddenly felt claws of ice run down his spine.

Obviously pleased, the Emperor raised his voice for all to hear. "Danvis Harkonnen and Willem Atreides, you both provide good examples for these others to follow." He turned his stern gaze toward the uneasy courtiers. "Let these two show you how to do what's best for the Imperium."

Willem trembled, barely able to contain his fury at this unwelcome surprise. As additional nobles stepped forward, accepting their fate, he only heard a roaring noise in his ears.

Danvis looked at him, clearly struggling with his own deep-seated anger. He stood straight and arrogant, gazing sidelong with a ferocious glare.

Willem fashioned a brittle smile in response, but the wheels were turning in his mind as he tried to determine how soon he would be able to kill this Harkonnen for his family's heinous crimes.

He would do it for the honor of the Atreides.